WHITE THAW:
THE HELHEIM CONSPIRACY

WHITE THAW:
THE HELHEIM CONSPIRACY

To Bridget

Best wishes!

Paul Tag

PAUL MARK TAG

iUniverse, Inc.
Bloomington

White Thaw: The Helheim Conspiracy

iUniverse books may be ordered through booksellers or by contacting:

iUniverse
1663 Liberty Drive
Bloomington, IN 47403
www.iuniverse.com
1-800-Authors (1-800-288-4677)

ISBN: 978-1-4759-7825-4 (sc)
ISBN: 978-1-4759-7824-7 (hc)
ISBN: 978-1-4759-7826-1 (e)

Library of Congress Control Number: 2013903318

Printed in the United States of America

iUniverse rev. date: 02/26/2013

To my niece Jennifer Elizabeth Guy,

a woman who embodied the courage, toughness, and intelligence
of my protagonist, Linda Ann Kipling

February 25, 1976-January 27, 2007

PREFACE

White Thaw: The Helheim Conspiracy is a work of fiction. All of the characters, names, incidents, organizations, and dialogue in this novel are the product of the author's imagination or are used fictitiously. That said, I have attempted to create an interesting story set within realistic scientific, theoretical, and geographic boundaries.

I have personally scouted many of the geographic locations for this book and have imagined the action occurring there. I used a Magellan Meridian Platinum handheld GPS receiver to determine the coordinates. The reader can view all locations cited in this book using Google Earth, software that allows one to view Earth locations using satellite imagery. Type in the chapter GPS locations to see where the action in the book occurs. For example, enter the following coordinates from chapter 50: 64 7 54N 21 57 04W. You'll find yourself on the runway in Reykjavik, Iceland, where Kipling's aircraft touches down. As an alternative to this procedure, go to my website, www.paulmarktag.com, where I have posted those photographs for all chapters.

It is important to note the date and time (as well as location) at the beginning of each chapter, particularly early on. That said, except for the prologue, chapters 1 and 2, and the epilogue, all of the action takes place within a two-week period in 2011. All chapters and scenes move forward either simultaneously or sequentially in time.

Finally, please note the cast of major characters and glossary sections at the end of this book. Information there, if needed, will assist the reader as the action unfolds. Information concerning the Naval Research Laboratory organizations and the National Center for Atmospheric Research comes from their Web sites.

Acknowledgments

There are many people who contributed to the research, reading, and proofing that went into the completion of this novel. Foremost among them is my wife, Becky, who offered patience, encouragement, insightful readings, constructive criticism—and the title for this book.

Beyond my wife, my overwhelming thanks go to my primary reader, Robin Brody. Robin helped me develop the plot and faithfully reviewed every chapter as it was being written. His careful analysis and attention to detail kept me focused.

There are several secondary readers who critiqued the entire manuscript after it was completed. In alphabetical order: Leonard Dickstein, Michael Guy, Kris Hoffman, Fran Morris, Roy Rogers, Ann Schrader, Konrad Steffen, and Dennis Van Middlesworth. I also thank the anonymous iUniverse reviewer who made several important suggestions that improved the manuscript and story.

In terms of research, I credit five people. Early on, Robin and I consulted with Kevin Rabe, an oceanographer, who helped us understand northern Atlantic Ocean currents and their physics. Pam Harbor evaluated and corrected my medical references. Leonard Dickstein, in addition to reading the manuscript and offering valuable suggestions, made vital weapons' selection recommendations. Doug Basham reviewed the aviation portions of my manuscript. And finally, I am especially indebted to Professor Konrad Steffen of the University of Colorado, a world-renowned expert on glaciers. He reviewed the entire manuscript but, importantly, gave me critical advice concerning the scientific premise that forms the basis for my story. In addition, he provided important geographic and physical data for Greenland.

One book provided reference material concerning Hitler's final days: Junge, Traudl, *Until the Final Hour: Hitler's Last Secretary.* Arcade Publishing, 2002.

If there are mistakes remaining in the manuscript, they are mine alone; I obviously did not listen carefully enough to the accurate guidance provided by everyone mentioned above.

PROLOGUE

SEEDS

Reichskanzlei-Führerbunker, Berlin, Germany: 52°30'40"N Latitude,
13°22'54"E Longitude
Monday, 10:05 a.m., April 30, 1945

The end was near—even the fanatics knew it. Not only for those in the bunker, but also for the promise of a future dominated by a National Socialist German Workers Party flowing with pure Aryan blood. Their leader would soon face the culmination of a failed war.

Though Reichsführer Friedrich Himmler himself insisted that Hitler leave Berlin, to flee south where an escape route still existed, Hitler refused. His appearance and demeanor made clear to all who knew him that the end was in sight. Rather than risk capture, he said he would kill himself with a gun to the mouth. Eva Braun, Hitler's longtime mistress and recent bride, said that she preferred to take a cyanide capsule. Hitler trusted his personal adjutant, Otto Günsche, to burn their bodies afterward, leaving no trace for the Red Army storming in from the east.

A pallor of hopelessness, frustration, and utter fatigue enveloped everyone as they waited in the subterranean fortress for these final events to unfold. Everyone, that is, except the true believers, those who steadfastly embraced the promise of a Thousand-Year Reich.

If the pressures and errors of the war had forced him to lose hope, Hitler could trust those members of the Third Reich who had the strength of mind to look beyond their mistakes, despite the setback of a war handled so incompetently.

Hans Müller believed in his führer's message. He understood the importance of the *final solution*, to rid the world of the inferiors. He appreciated Hitler's other talents as well, particularly his oratory skills in addressing the masses. Sadly, he also knew that Hitler could have won the war if only he had listened to his generals. The Russian campaign had been a disaster.

Many of Hitler's staunch followers would choose to remain with the führer. However, the future of Nazism required that Müller and his small group move quickly, before the situation became intractable. Vehicles and aircraft standing by to evacuate them wouldn't wait much longer. Available avenues of escape were closing by the minute.

To avoid suspicion, Müller had waited until the end to execute his plot. Now, he and his elite rushed up the steps of the bunker and maneuvered their way through the damaged corridors of the New Reich Chancellery. Müller had been planning this escape for months, once the inevitability of the war's end became clear to anyone other than those who shared Hitler's delusion.

From his position within Deutsche Bank, Müller had begun the transfer of monetary reserves. In those months, when disarray, confusion, and disbelief paralyzed the government, he ordered that gold be crated and moved north, not an easy task during the latter stages of the war. There the gold was loaded onto multiple submarines for transport to foreign ports. A Nazi comeback, whatever form it took, would require resources. Although Müller kept these operations secret, there was no doubt in his mind that the führer would have approved.

Those with whom Müller chose to share his escape plan were few. Near the end, Müller briefly considered including the charismatic and intelligent Joseph Goebbels, the propaganda minister, a devout champion of Hitler's plans. He, of all people, thought Müller, would appreciate the need to carry forth Hitler's vision and would choose to be a part of Müller's movement. But when Goebbels received and refused Hitler's direct order to leave

Berlin, Müller knew that it wasn't to be. Further, rumors that he planned to kill his own six children hardly suggested a man looking to the future. For these and other reasons, Müller concluded that most of Hitler's staff was ill suited to the future of Nazism. Younger, stronger minds and bodies were more suitable for the grand design.

Müller had picked his fellow Nazis carefully, along with an escape route that would take them to Brazil, far from the postwar chaos that would inevitably envelop Germany and the rest of Europe. It would likely take decades to restore order and return Europe to its prewar prosperity. During that time, Müller would fan the fires of the führer's ambitions and make plans for their return to Germany for the final conquest. When that time came, Müller, or his descendants, would return to power. In the interim, if other Nazis of like mind found their way to South America, so much the better.

Müller had requisitioned a two-truck convoy to take them to the airport. Twenty-three full-blooded Aryans whom he had chosen personally occupied the bed of the lead truck; the second vehicle carried only Müller's family. Besides his wife, Helga, there were six others, including his son, Friedrich, and wife, Gertrude, and his daughter, Inge, and her new husband, Winston Kipling. The remaining two were Dieter and Axel, Müller's grandsons by Friedrich and Gertrude, thirteen and two months old, respectively.

About twenty minutes outside Berlin, a terrifying explosion rocked the second vehicle. Müller immediately figured it to be a heavy mortar. Everyone knew that Russian forces were moving westward at a rapid pace. His vehicle shuddered from the impact and, at once, angled sharply downward. The canvassed tarps covering the beds of the trucks did nothing to diminish the horrendous blast that had propagated outward from the explosion. Helga, sitting in the bed with the others, let out a scream.

It was obvious to Müller that the explosion had come from the front of their vehicle. He crawled and slid downward on the flatbed and looked through the shattered glass into the cab. What he saw was unnerving. The windshield was blown out, and Müller saw that both his driver and armed escort were slouched forward. If not dead, they were gravely wounded.

"Everybody, out!" yelled Müller. He climbed up the bed of the truck, jumped to the ground, and ran to the front of the vehicle. There he discovered it resting inside a twenty-foot crater that separated the two trucks. Meanwhile, personnel from the lead truck were hurrying back to help those in the rear.

Realizing that their vehicle was too damaged to proceed, Müller ordered everyone to squeeze together onto the bed of the forward truck. As his family boarded with the other men and women, Müller warily watched Friedrich eyeing his son-in-law. At this late stage, the last thing Müller needed was a scuffle between the two. Inge, aged seventeen and the younger of Müller's two children, had recently married Winston Kipling, a young army lieutenant. Friedrich disliked and did not trust him, partly because Kipling had not been born in Germany.

Over the past month, Friedrich had lobbied his father hard, arguing that it would be preferable for the family to leave Kipling behind to fend for himself. Ultimately, Müller had no choice in the matter. Inge told her father emphatically that if Friedrich had his way, she would not leave the country either. Accordingly, Winston Kipling became the seventh family member accorded the privilege of leaving a ruined Germany.

Their truck arrived at the airport without further incident. Waiting for them were two *Junkers Ju 52* trimotor aircraft, fueled and ready to ferry the group safely out of Germany. The nonfamily members of his group were split between the two eighteen-passenger aircraft, eighteen in the first, and the remainder with Müller and his family in the second.

In a moment of reflection, Hans stared wistfully at his daughter as she climbed into the plane. She was his baby but was a married woman now. Inge was no longer a Müller. She had inherited her husband's name. She had become Inge Kipling.

CHAPTER 1

ACQUISITION

Gremikha Naval Base, near Ostrovnoy, on the Kola Peninsula, Russia: 68°04'29"N Latitude, 39°27'47"E Longitude
Thursday, 10:25 p.m., September 30, 2003

Captain Alexseyev Gudrinko glanced about the bar, waiting for the upcoming meeting when he would sell his soul to the devil. He focused on the yellowing, multiyear calendar on the wall above the hard liquor, confirming that it was the one-month anniversary of the sinking of K-159. With that disaster in mind, he now rationalized that his treachery might actually be warranted.

The navy captain drew his hand across his face and downed a shot of vodka. At least this clear liquid was plentiful and of good quality. You couldn't say that for much else in this godforsaken spot three hundred kilometers east of Murmansk, and home of the Gremikha Naval Base.

Why had the Kremlin chosen a location that had no road or railroad access, where the sea was the only supply route? Worse, once the year 1997 had passed, Russian bureaucracy decided that Gremikha would no longer serve as a submarine base for the Russian Navy. As if Gremikha had not been punished enough, God then gave the devil free rein to choose a demoralizing purpose for this once proud naval base. It would remain as a repository for the dying, decommissioned submarines that had once sailed proudly from these shores.

Gudrinko's job description was hardly an encouraging reference for future employment. With his fifty-five-man crew, his responsibility was to maintain the decaying former stalwarts of the open sea, primarily by pumping air into the rotting hulks so they would not sink while tied up by their moorings. Part of his job was also to prevent theft; formal security was almost nonexistent. Many of the submarines had rusted so much that they couldn't float on their own. To his chagrin, K-159 had once sunk at its mooring. Of course, these weren't just any submarines—they were nuclear powered. Most contained spent uranium fuel, more radioactive and dangerous than the potent uranium-235 isotope from which it had started.

It had happened one month earlier. On August 30, K-159, with its twin reactors and eight hundred kilograms of spent fuel, sank beneath 240 meters of water. If the radioactive fuel had leaked into the surrounding waters, it would have been an environmental disaster. The Norwegians were beside themselves with concern, and for good reason: the Barents Sea was one of the richest fisheries in the world.

Gudrinko checked his watch and looked up, not surprised that Herr Müller had arrived on time. You could count on the Germans for punctuality.

Müller, a tall, good-looking man with sharp features, took a seat. This was to be their third and final meeting.

Gudrinko wanted to appear hospitable. His people were like that—generous, kind individuals, a local population forsaken by the Kremlin. "May I offer you vodka?" he asked in a German dialect he knew to be less sophisticated than his client's native tongue.

"But of course." Müller smiled. "Your vodka is excellent. I should purchase some to take home."

Gudrinko raised his hand, caught the bartender's attention, lifted his glass in that direction, and pointed to his companion.

"I am sorry for your country's loss." Müller appeared sincere. "Have the authorities determined what happened?"

The bartender arrived quickly, snapped a glass onto the old wooden table, and poured. Gudrinko motioned that he should leave the bottle. He raised his glass and waited for his tablemate to do the same. "To your good health. *Vashe zdarovye.*"

"To you, as well."

The details were disgusting. Most of the world already knew what had happened. "You already know it was a November-class submarine, K-159. Twin nuclear reactors. A tug was towing it to the Polyarny shipyard for salvage. What is there to tell? Someone had decided to move it on pontoons. The weather came up, the pontoons came loose, and the ship sank. Nine men dead, only one survivor, and I understand he is a basket case. Who wouldn't be after seeing your friends die and then spending two hours in the freezing water?"

Gudrinko smirked. "I understand that Minister of Defence Ivanov gave him a watch for his courage. The regional governor gave him ten thousand rubles. Do you know how much that is? About three hundred thirty American. I understand that's the same amount they're giving to his dead comrades." He shook his head in disgust. "Assholes. The only reason this happened is because of politics, because the Defence Ministry had to keep its greedy fingers on the money. The Polyarny shipyard is one of the few remaining yards under their control. If the Russian Shipbuilding Agency had gotten the salvage job, this never would have happened." His face flushed. "And if that weren't enough, there was no reason for anyone to have been aboard that submarine. It was a dead ship with no power. It was being towed, for God's sake! Such a foolish loss of life."

Gudrinko purged these thoughts of death from his mind. Müller's arrival here had nothing to do with the past, but with the future. Although there would be hell to pay after it was over, neither he nor the fourteen men with whom he would carry out this treason would be around to accept the blame. Müller had agreed to arrange for their relocation. His cash payment would be enough to fund each of their retirements, if perhaps only modestly by Western standards. And there would be little chance that word of this theft would escape the intense secrecy maintained within Putin's Russia.

Müller got back to the situation at hand. "Can you assure me that they are seaworthy?"

It was a valid question, one that Müller had asked before. "Most of the boats in this port are not. But the two you are getting are the best of what we have. You already know that they will require considerable repair and maintenance, but they will not sink on you. I promise you that the hulls are intact."

Gudrinko pushed his glass to the side. Time to discuss finances. He had already checked with the bank to confirm the initial amount. "And you'll deposit the remainder as soon as delivery is complete?"

Müller finished off his drink. "Two million more, as agreed."

It was time to be a little less serious. "I don't suppose you'd care to tell me what you intend to do with them."

"That's none of your concern. Once this is over, you will forget this entire transaction." Then Müller lightened up. "If it will make you sleep better tonight, I can tell you that your equipment will be used to better the world. What's the saying? We plan to turn swords into plowshares?"

Gudrinko cocked his head at that last comment. *Interesting.* But it was time to return to business. "How soon do you wish to take delivery of your two submarines?"

CHAPTER 2

MINUTIAE

Federal Center for Data Examination, Las Vegas, Nevada, USA:
36°7'51"N Latitude, 115°10'13"W Longitude
Tuesday, 5:55 p.m., November 25, 2003

"Really? And you say you've confirmed this with two sources?" Tom Uphouse wasn't used to analyzing incidents occurring in real time. Most of the data feeds that the FCDE dealt with were hours old at best, and usually days, before their banks of electrified silicon pulled up an inconsistency or abnormality. In this case, the incident had occurred only thirty minutes earlier, according to Stigler.

Navy Lieutenant Commander Jane Stigler, the only military person on Uphouse's staff, was a plank holder, meaning that she had been with the organization since day one. Now serving the second year of a three-year assignment, she had become one of Uphouse's leading knowledge engineers. Her cute, perky demeanor—picture Demi Moore in *A Few Good Men*—belied her considerable intellect. She elaborated on the computer data. "Within three minutes of each other, sir. SOSUS and seismographic records positioned this event at the same geographic location, give or take."

"More than one seismograph?"

"Affirmative, sir. Bermuda, Guantanamo Bay, and Barbados."

"Did they triangulate it?"

"Yes, sir. About one hundred thirty kilometers north of Puerto Rico."

Uphouse continued his barrage. "How strong?"

Stigler was up to the challenge. "Not very, sir. Golden didn't pick up anything."

It took a moment for Uphouse to recall that Golden, Colorado, was the home of the National Earthquake Information Center. He knew Colorado well because it was that state that had the most fourteeners—mountains with peaks of at least fourteen thousand feet—of any state in the union. Uphouse's goal was to climb all fifty-five of them.

"Could the SOSUS people make any sense of what they heard?" Uphouse knew that not much came out of SOSUS these days. SOSUS, the Sound Surveillance System, was a relic of the Cold War. A navy system originally intended to track Soviet submarines as they passed between Greenland, Iceland, and the United Kingdom (the GIUK Gap), SOSUS represented a series of sensitive microphones, called hydrophones, that rested on the ocean floor. They were connected to land stations by underwater cabling. These days, scientists were the primary users of SOSUS, particularly oceanographers who studied whales.

"Same as the seismic signals, what they heard was very weak. But our expert who understands these things says that they did sound like implosions. And catch this! Whatever happened, happened twice."

Uphouse found this statement ridiculous. He stood. "What do you mean, twice?"

"That's what's strange about these data, sir. About two hours apart, the same sequence of signals occurred. Identical, both for SOSUS and the seismographs."

Uphouse blinked. "So let me hear this again. Whatever happened, it happened twice?"

"Affirmative. With almost the same time spacing between the SOSUS and the seismograph readings. The seismic readings occurred after the SOSUS signals."

Uphouse knew that Stigler would relish giving her opinion. "What do you make of this, Commander?"

"The SOSUS signal suggests a submarine in trouble. Assuming that all turned to shit, sir, the seismic sounds could then be the final throes of a submarine hitting the ocean floor."

Uphouse shook his head. "That's what's coming to my mind, too. But twice? What are the chances of two subs having the same problem at the same time and in the same place?"

"Not likely, sir. Unless two collided, of course."

Uphouse glanced at the wall clock and added four hours. "Can you superimpose satellite surveillance?"

"Already on it, sir. In twenty minutes, we'll have a bird within range. Have to use infrared. It's already dark there."

"Okay, here's what we need to do. First thing, call the joint chiefs and see if our navy is having any sub problems. Then follow up to see if anybody else's subs are in the area." The navy tracked those sorts of things. "And I want to hear from you the moment we have satellite recon."

Stigler hurried from his office.

The organization Uphouse headed was used to finding inconsistencies in their data; his team of scientists called them *puzzles*. Solving those riddles was what they were paid to do. Tom Uphouse had been the director of the FCDE since its inception one year earlier, on September 11 of 2002, one year to the day after 9/11.

The Federal Center for Data Examination was established *because* of 9/11. Even the less perceptive members of Congress recognized that this disaster should never have happened. Clues that pointed to the event should have been used to nip the disaster in the bud. Of course, even those who suggested the creation of FCDE understood that most of those clues came from human intelligence, with all its inherent fallibility. Notable among those lapses were reports from Colleen Rowley, an FBI agent from Minneapolis, Minnesota. She testified before Congress regarding information she had forwarded through channels concerning Zacarias Moussaoui, a suspected terrorist. As it turned out, those reports could have led to advance knowledge of the plane hijackings. Because her bosses chose to ignore her—and to make certain that such an oversight didn't happen again—a major reorganization of the FBI took place.

7

At the same time that this weakness in the nation's intelligence came to light, members of the government's in-house scientific pool made an astute point. They stated that, although human-observed intelligence could always be overlooked or ignored, most data in the modern world were sensor detected, not human detected, and available in digital format. Foremost among such records were myriad derived parameters from satellite imagery and sensors. Other more conventional sources of data, such as electromagnetic, seismic, acoustic, financial, and medical, were also available.

It was at this new organization that Tom Uphouse found himself the director. With a yearly budget of $125 million, most of their expenditures went toward the purchase and upkeep of an imposing bank of networked Cray XMT supercomputers and associated storage, all of which would make Silicon Valley proud.

With such mountains of data, Uphouse's staff required sophisticated methods to mine the information. That's where his elite team came in. Computer maintenance personnel, database managers, and computer software designers represented a third of the sixty-plus personnel. The rubber met the road with the remaining two-thirds. They were the knowledge engineers, experts in artificial intelligence who wrote the software designed to glean the precious seeds from their mountain of chaff. On this day, the output from the seismic and SOSUS data represented those seeds.

The only person in the organization with a window to the outside from the thirty-second floor, Uphouse looked back toward the opulence of the Las Vegas Strip. The government, in its infinite wisdom, had chosen the top floor of a major hotel for their organization. As a measure of ingenuity that the federal government rarely displayed, they had acquired this high-rent space for minimal expenditure. Zero, in fact. Government auditors considered the deal a win-win compromise with a hotel owner who hadn't paid his taxes.

Although the FCDE was not a secret organization, per se, Uphouse's bosses in Washington preferred that their new organization remain private, with communication with the outside world on an as-needed basis. *As needed* meant that Uphouse would make contact only when he and his team discovered something of interest. And what better way to keep their organization out of the public's eye than by planting it in the middle of Entertainment Central and tens of thousands of people. Uphouse figured that whoever had made this seemingly illogical decision had been a fan of Edgar Allen Poe's *The Purloined Letter*. In that story, police conducted an elaborate search for a stolen letter using logical methods of investigation; in the end, the letter was discovered out in the open for all to see.

The knock at the door signaled Stigler's return. "None, sir. There are no submarines of ours near the data source."

"What about the infrared?"

"There appears to be one large shipping vessel in the vicinity, but nothing else."

Uphouse contemplated the implications of this statement and waved off Sigler. "Okay, I want you and your team to brainstorm what happened."

"Yes, sir." Stigler practically ran from the office.

Uphouse, still standing, rotated to take in the view outside. The sun had set, and the brilliance of the Strip's lights had taken hold. He knew that although he could order his team to come up with possibilities, that didn't absolve him of his own responsibility. They didn't pay him the big bucks to just sit around and give orders. With PhDs in both mathematics and knowledge engineering, his bosses expected him to use his brain, too.

Another thought came to mind. This would be an excuse to check in with his brother, Rick, also a scientist. Rick worked for another federal agency, one more public and well known: the Naval Research Laboratory in Washington DC. Tom smiled. His older brother never hesitated to remind him that Tom was the dumber of the two sons in the Uphouse family. Tom had graduated second in his class at MIT, whereas Rick, who had sown his oats while spending a few years in the navy before college, completed his undergraduate degree in the same year as Tom. Rick had graduated number one.

Tom checked the time and decided to call his brother in the morning. Rick could provide some insight here. Although Rick now spent his days worrying about the retreat of glaciers around the world, during the time he spent in the navy, he had served two years aboard a submarine.

CHAPTER 3

BAD DECISION

Outside a Secret Location for Operation Helheim in Greenland
Thursday, 7:15 a.m., September 29, 2011

"What's that?" Peter Armstrong, in front and driving the snowmobile, shouted above the engine's roar to his partner, Henry Smithkline. Ahead stood an unusual pattern of ice. As they approached the forward sloping surface, Armstrong slowed their Ski-Doo Skandic Tundra to a halt.

Armstrong and Smithkline, researchers from the Naval Research Laboratory in Washington DC, were at the end of their summer sabbatical. Ten-hour days at the base camp drilling ice cores had produced results exceeding expectations. By week's end, they would fly home. Ignoring the fact that Smithkline was Caucasian, and Armstrong African American, they were affectionately referred to as Laurel and Hardy by their colleagues. Armstrong's stout six-foot-three stature towered over the diminutive five-foot-eight Smithkline.

As compensation for their hard work, and with a few days to spare, the two had decided to reward themselves with an outing. Although the location was too distant to reach by snowmobile, they planned to head southwest in the direction of the spot where, in August of 1981, the Greenland Ice Sheet Project (GISP) was the first to drill an ice core through more than two kilometers of ice, all the way to bedrock. A glance at the snowmobile's GPS indicated that they had traveled twenty-six miles from base camp.

They had left camp at sunrise, which at this time of year was almost five in the morning. In another two weeks, sunrise would advance another hour. It wouldn't be long before the hours of daylight would wither away to nothing. That's how fast the sun gave up its caress as one approached the Arctic Circle.

With the surface too rugged for their snowmobile, Armstrong and Smithkline set off on foot to see what lay on the other side of the mound. After a short hike, they looked down on a surface that was remarkably level.

"That's unusual," said Armstrong. "You could put a soccer field down there, it's so flat. And look over there!" He pointed. "I'd swear that looks like some kind of dome." What they saw was curious but not completely unexpected. On an extensive ice sheet, one could expect unusual variations in a surface responsive to the ebb and flow of mountains and rivers of ice.

"You want to hike down and take a look?"

"Why? I say we continue like we planned. Although we won't actually see it, I want to get as close as possible to where history was made." A coordinated scientific project between Denmark, Switzerland, and the United States, GISP was the first of several follow-up projects. It had taken three years to drill completely through the ice sheet.

"Something's not right here, Peter." Smithkline's immediate curiosity was unusual. Of the two, he was the introvert and rarely made suggestions without deep thought. "Does this look normal to you? And what's that noise? Can you hear it? Sort of a hum."

Armstrong took Smithkline's comments seriously. "You hear it too? I thought the snowmobile's engine was still buzzing in my head."

"Besides, the sides of this little valley here? Does this look like a natural formation to you?"

"Can't say that it does." Armstrong was interested too, but his intuition was telling him to back off. He had learned early in life to trust his gut.

Abruptly, Smithkline pointed across the valley. "Look! There! What is that? Smoke? Steam?"

The two researchers stared at each other in disbelief. "What's going on here, Peter?" Smithkline sputtered.

"This is impossible! There are no secrets up here. If there were another expedition going on, we'd know about it."

"I'm going down to take a look."

"I don't know, Henry. I'm getting bad vibes."

They proceeded down the slope. Across the wide expanse of smooth ice, what looked like a black hole unexpectedly appeared.

"Shit! Somebody's over there."

Armstrong couldn't take it anymore. "Let's get the hell out of here, Henry!"

Smithkline affirmed what Armstrong was thinking. "If we don't know what this is, maybe we're not supposed to know."

Suddenly, what sounded like a burst of automatic gunfire split the silence of the ice. Armstrong couldn't believe it. "What the fuck! Someone's shooting at us?"

With adrenaline surging and his heart beating at near-fibrillation speed, Armstrong led the way back up the slope, not an easy task in bulky clothes and heavy boots. With more shots and accompanying sounds of bullets tearing at the ice, he dived across the top. As he landed on the opposite side, Smithkline's scream shattered the air.

Flattening himself against the ice and turning around, Armstrong pulled his partner over the edge.

Smithkline yelped in pain. "They shot me in the goddamn leg!"

"Do you think you can walk?"

Smithkline put pressure on his bad leg and let out a cry. Tears welled in his eyes. "I think I can."

"Good," Armstrong said. He looked one more time across the expanse and squinted. Two snowmobiles charged in their direction. "They're coming after us. Let's go."

Armstrong jerked Smithkline to his feet, and they walked and shuffled their way down the slope. Whatever the bullet had done to Smithkline's leg, it hadn't broken a bone. Nonetheless, the trail of blood staining the ice meant that his wound was significant.

Armstrong leaned Smithkline against the snowmobile and turned the key to the electric starter. The two-cylinder engine roared to life. He helped Smithkline onto the back of the Ski-Doo and mounted the front. With one look back, he gunned the engine, and they tore away, accelerating the snowmobile to its maximum speed of sixty-plus miles per hour. He looked in his rearview mirror and saw nothing. With luck, their adversaries had only intended to scare them off. Armstrong's teeth chattered, but not from the cold.

Armstrong tried to think rationally. If something happened to them this far from camp, no one would know. He reached down into the forward compartment of the snowmobile and retrieved their satellite phone, their emergency lifeline to the outside world. He handed it back to Smithkline, turned his head, and yelled, "Call Uphouse!"

As he looked into his rearview mirror yet again, Armstrong realized that the prayer that had unconsciously formed on his lips had had no effect; the two snowmobiles were in hot pursuit. And on second glance, their images appeared larger. Whoever was following had more powerful machines that would catch them soon. Would their pursuers interrogate them? Hold them? Would they give Smithkline medical attention? That they had shot first was not a good sign.

Has Henry gotten through to Uphouse? The roar of the wind together with the engine's growl prevented Armstrong from hearing anything behind him. His gaze darted back and forth between the ice ahead and the mirror. Suddenly, it appeared as if the snowmobiles had given up the chase. Armstrong slowed his machine and turned his head to get a better view. Four men were now standing, facing in their direction, with one holding something on his shoulder.

Oh, God! No!

The flash of light didn't last long. In the instant following the explosion and before he lost consciousness, Armstrong looked down from a height of fifteen feet onto the bits and pieces of what had once been his snowmobile. The deep hue of crimson that streaked the ice was the only color that marred the black and white image below.

CHAPTER 4

MEMORIES AND TRUTHS

Pennsylvania Hospital, Philadelphia, Pennsylvania, USA:
39°56'42"N Latitude, 75°09'22"W Longitude
Friday, 3:15 a.m., September 30, 2011

Linda Kipling tried not to think about her father's words from the day before. Instead, she concentrated on memories, so many good ones. Standing by his bedside, she brushed the white hair from his forehead to see if the scar was still visible. Yes, there it was. It had caused him so much embarrassment in the years following her birth.

Kipling watched as a nurse checked the various monitors and tubes attached to her father's body. Several hours earlier, his doctor said that it wouldn't be much longer. She held his hand and willed her love through the frail fingers, straight to the heart of Winston Kipling.

Thoughts of family came to mind, back to her childhood in Colorado during the 1960s, living the untroubled life inherent to the hippy commune that her parents had joined. Despite their carefree approach to living, Winston and Inge valued education and sent their daughter to a Catholic school. She attended there not because her parents were devoutly religious but because that school provided the best education in their community.

That schooling reminded her of Cousin Dieter. She would make a point of calling him after the sun came up. Dieter, twenty-some years senior to Kipling, was one of Uncle Friedrich's two children. She had met Friedrich's other son, Axel, only once, at Kipling's wedding, a union fated to last just a few years. But Dieter had stayed in touch over the years, visiting his Aunt Inge and her family often. Kipling knew little about him, only that he was a successful industrialist in Colombia. He always came laden with gifts. It wasn't until Kipling had gone off to college that her parents admitted that Dieter had paid her high school tuition. Discomfited at not having known this, she wrote and thanked him profusely for his generosity. She always had warm thoughts of him.

Kipling had been a late-in-life gift to her parents. When Linda reached her teenage years, her mother explained that she and her husband both had had reproductive issues that impaired conception. They should forget the idea of a child of their own, their doctor told them. And they did. When Inge's period stopped suddenly at the age of forty-one, she figured that menopause had struck early.

Two months later, when bodily changes made her realize that something was amiss, she hurried to her doctor. Afterward, Inge rushed into the house to give her husband the news that they were going to be parents. He fainted straightaway, banging his head against the coffee table, producing a wound that required six stitches to close. Inge loved to tell that story. And every time, Winston would wince and say, "That's the last time you tell that story, Inge." Of course, it never was.

Kipling blinked. She had expected more drama. The shrill sound of the monitor meant that it was over. She had not seen it coming; it was all so anticlimactic. His chest had simply stopped moving. She bent down with her ear next to her father's open mouth, a tear about to drip from her eye. No sound, no movement of air. She kissed him on the cheek. She then checked her watch, remembering that this waterproof version had been a birthday gift from her father several years back. It read 3:22.

The nurse silenced the equipment and offered a sympathetic glance. For a few moments, Kipling stood silent, alone in her private thoughts. Her father had always said that he hoped his wife would die first. When asked why, he said, "I love Inge, and she

15

loves me. Because I know that for a fact, it would be extremely hard for her if I died first. For that reason, I hope that she is the first to go." Her father had gotten his wish the previous spring. But inherent in that selflessness was the mirrored consequence that the same pain he had spared his wife he had taken on himself. Perhaps that was why he lasted only another six months.

Kipling took one last look, gathered up her father's few belongings, and left the room. The personnel at the nurses' station offered their condolences. Taking the elevator down, she headed toward the exterior doors. She willed her way forward, suddenly realizing how exhausted she was. To the left, she noted the plaque that she had passed for the past five days, boasting that this institution, the Pennsylvania Hospital, had been the first hospital in the United States. It had opened its doors to patients at this very location in 1756.

Kipling exited and collapsed on the bench outside. This was one of those times when an ordinary person would go home and medicate themselves with alcohol to deaden the pain and to drive the imbiber into an unconscious stupor. The trouble with that approach was that Kipling had an unusually high tolerance for chemicals, including alcohol. If the bottle of ibuprofen said to take two pills to alleviate the occasional headache, Kipling took eight. She had identical reactions to barbiturates and other drugs.

With the cool night air enveloping her body, she sobbed softly, the lone descendant of the man on the third floor. Spontaneously, she looked at her watch and took out her cell phone. Rational thought took over, and she abandoned that idea. This delicate situation required more thought. And what would she have said? Further, should she say anything at all?

Kipling rose and plodded toward her rental car. As much as she had been trying not to think about them, her father's final words were too extraordinary to set aside. He said that it had not been an easy decision to make, but he had decided that his daughter needed to know her heritage. What he told her was that Inge's father, Hans Müller, Kipling's grandfather, had been a prominent Nazi during World War II. He had spirited his family, including Inge and her new husband, to Brazil in 1945.

Kipling had known that her descendants hailed from Germany, but she thought they had gone to South America sometime *after* the war. Several years later, Winston and Inge emigrated again, this time to the United States where Winston had family who had come from England in the 1930s. Hans Müller and the rest of his family chose to remain in Brazil, although they later changed their minds about staying there too.

Kipling inserted her key into the door of the rental car and then paused to stare up into the night. Although her father's revelations would take time to accept, she saw no reason to remember her parents any differently. Her father had said that he and his wife were horrified to learn the extent of Hitler's crimes against humanity. As had most of the German population, they had known nothing.

Kipling pulled open the door and shuddered. It wasn't her family's Nazi past that gave her pause. It was the other information her father had revealed, facts that he swore were true, which were far more disturbing.

CHAPTER 5

REINCARNATION

Cartagena, Colombia: 10°23'41"N Latitude, 75°31'19"W Longitude
Saturday, 2:35 p.m., October 1, 2011

"You're sure, are you?" Dieter Müller asked rhetorically of his brother. The news from up north was hardly comforting.

With nervous energy to dissipate, Müller opened the car window and stuck out his arm, letting the gentle rain moisten his hand. The calendar said that it was autumn. But telling one season from another by senses alone proved difficult. Located within ten degrees of the equator, Cartagena, Colombia, had barely noticeable temperature variations over the course of a year. With an average daily high in the upper eighties, the climate took some getting used to. Those who visited from the midlatitudes called it miserable. Most precipitation occurred between May and November.

Müller had inherited the preference for seasonal variations typical of Bavaria, where you could count on snow in the winter and occasional hot temperatures in the summer. Nonetheless, his father, Friedrich, had chosen to move his family and business operations here from Buenos Aires in the early fifties. Too many compatriots had chosen to live in Brazil and Argentina during those early years, making it a wise decision to move, in retrospect. Rabid Nazi hunters had made life uncomfortable.

Müller withdrew his arm but left the window open. He could have it both ways: the natural outdoors together with the air-conditioned artificiality of the limousine that Müller Industries afforded him.

Sixty-seven years old and the elder of two sons—by only eleven months—Dieter was more ambitious than his brother, at least by his own definition. Their parents, Friedrich and Gertrude Müller, were both alive and of sound mind. Friedrich limousined to work daily and kept track of business. Dieter understood that at this point in his father's life, it wasn't because of company business that he made the trek to his office. Father had been looking forward to their new venture for more than fifty years.

Müller Industries, founded by their grandfather after escaping to Brazil, provided everyone in the family with suitable wealth to live as each saw fit. But truth be known, only Dieter cared about the company and did his proper share of work to maintain its success. His brother, Axel, unmarried and childless, still prided himself on being the same playboy he had been decades earlier. Age hadn't marred the chiseled German face of his youth. Frequent trips to the company gym kept his weight under control and his muscles tight.

Sitting adjacent, Axel finished a cell call to one of his current lovers. "Maria sends her regards. You remember her. The redhead, the one you called a hot-blooded floozy."

Although Dieter disapproved of his brother's wanton ways, he tolerated his habits and wasteful spending. Importantly, he knew he could count on him; his loyalty never wavered. And it wouldn't be long now when that support would be crucial. Besides, Axel understood the technical aspects of their venture. Dieter's forte was finance, the money to fund their operation.

"Yeah, I remember." Dieter laughed. "But you know, you might have to put some of your womanizing on hold. Things are moving faster than we anticipated." He reflected. "I wish Grandfather were here to appreciate what we've done. He'd be so proud."

Fifty-eight years! That's how long it had taken to assemble a mechanism, a backdrop, to effect a comeback. The funding necessary to pull it together had been available decades earlier. But they had waited until technology, and a suitable use for that technology, presented itself. Eight years earlier, everything had come together. And all because of the foresight of Hans Müller. If he hadn't taken the initiative to escape Germany in 1945, their lives would have evolved much differently, Dieter knew. But Hans Müller *had* escaped and *had* removed from the German treasury a sizable stash of gold, which today would be the equivalent of fifteen billion American dollars. He had used that money to create Müller Industries and develop the company into an industrial behemoth, with a capitalized value of more than $130 billion.

Müller Industries included three subsidiaries that covered a gamut of technologies, two of which concentrated on energy development and transportation. The third, Müller Pharmaceutical, located in Reykjavik, Iceland, had earned hundreds of millions developing new drugs. Its latest, Aristovar, combined three drugs into one tablet that controlled both blood pressure and cholesterol and, as a bonus, increased bone density. The cholesterol-lowering portion had proven to be even more effective than the powerful statins, the previous gold standard for cholesterol reduction. During early testing of the drug, there had been some negative publicity concerning higher-than-normal death rates. Fortunately, their statisticians showed that this result had been a statistical aberration. Further, during Müller-controlled follow-up testing, they observed no increased death rate.

Although Müller Pharmaceutical produced more than half of the company's yearly profit, it was the energy side that held Dieter's interest and proved to be relevant just now. Müller Drilling supplied nearly a quarter of the equipment and personnel for the world's oil and gas exploration.

In an analogous way, Müller Nuclear did not manufacture nuclear reactors or mine uranium, but instead provided the expertise to run reactors and to transport fissionable material. Their recent overture to the world's industrial nations to store their nuclear waste in underground caves on a geologically stable island off the coast of South America had tongues wagging. Long one of the Achilles' heels of nuclear power, particularly in such ecomaniacal countries as the United States, members of the United States Congress could barely conceal their glee at this obvious solution to a seemingly intractable problem.

"Why hasn't someone thought of this before?" Gordon Skeemer, senior senator from the proud state of Nevada, thundered to an approving audience in Senate chambers. Never missing an opportunity to flaunt his Republican credentials, Skeemer couldn't help but crow that private industry was there to save the day. The administration had had to acknowledge the wisdom of this solution while wincing at the millions spent on developing its own storage facility in Yucca Mountain in Nevada. Dieter smiled to himself. Müller Nuclear would charge an appropriately high tariff for this *obvious* solution to one of the world's vexing problems.

Dieter leaned out the window and looked at the sad gray clouds. He drew back and closed the window. The melancholy of the weather reminded him of the call he had received the previous day. "That was too bad about Uncle Winston. He's been in poor health for some time."

"I really didn't know him like you did," Axel responded, almost in passing.

Dieter frowned. Sadly, what he said was true. There was always someone in a family who paid little attention to the lives of relatives. In their family, that person was Axel. Except for Linda Kipling's wedding some years back, when both brothers flew north to her home state of Colorado, Axel took little note of Aunt Inge and Uncle Winston.

Dieter, on the other hand, valued family, and until Linda had grown up, had made a point of visiting their northern family once a year. In recent years, those visits had trailed off. Only he had returned for Aunt Inge's funeral in the spring. He had made excuses for his brother. In their conversation the previous day, Linda had told him that her father wanted no funeral or service to commemorate his passing. Still, Dieter promised himself that he would visit her soon.

Dieter understood the reason he appreciated his family so much; fate had a way of rolling the dice. It was because of an incident that had occurred when he and Axel had been infants, while the Müller family was escaping Germany in 1945. As the story went, there had been two aircraft waiting to ferry Dieter's grandfather's friends and family safely out of the country. What Dieter and Axel were not told until they were in their twenties was that only one of the two planes arrived at its destination; Allied fighters got the other. What were the odds? Fifty-fifty, of course. It could just as well have been Dieter and his family who did not survive.

Dieter's mind snapped back to the present with the hope that providence might once again favor his family. "You're sure there'll be no repercussions?"

"It's not a problem. They're both dead, and their tracks have been covered. The ice pokers just lost two personnel. That's all."

"Aren't you afraid they'll come looking?"

"You brought this up before. There's nothing left to see, nothing to find."

Dieter grimaced. "People just don't disappear, you know."

"Our people inspected the remains of their equipment. They had one GPS receiver and one satellite phone. We did dodge a bullet with the phone. Most satellite phones these days have GPS capability, but theirs did not. So even if they managed to get a call out, whoever received the call would have had no idea where it came from."

"So we don't know if they made a call or not. Right?"

"You worry too much. It was all over in minutes. It's doubtful they would have had time. They were scared shitless and took off like scared rabbits. Our men had the mess cleaned up within an hour."

"*Um Gottes willen.* I hope to God you're right."

Chapter 6

Goose-Step

Naval Research Laboratory, Monterey, California, USA: 36°35'34"N Latitude, 121°51'17"W Longitude
Monday, 8:05 a.m., October 3, 2011

Kipling leaned the flower vase against her cheek for balance, inserted the key into the door, and welcomed the seclusion of her office. She placed the mixed arrangement on the corner file cabinet and the large bag of letters on the floor. Stress and grief over the past month had taken their toll.

Dr. Linda Ann Kipling, research meteorologist for the Naval Research Laboratory in Monterey, California, looked down at her desk and eyed with reluctance her Work Units. All research carried out at the laboratory was defined and scheduled in these documents.

Although it was an honor to be labeled a principal investigator, a PI, in charge of the research defined in one of these documents, the responsibility was a pain in the ass and something her boss, the eminent Dr. Victor Mark Silverstein, avoided. Like most scientists, Kipling would have preferred to hole up in her office, focusing her scientific training on the problems at hand, without worrying whether other team members were contributing their share. Aside from this obligation to the taxpayer, another problem, a personal one, loomed large since her father's death the previous week.

It wouldn't be long before Silverstein would stick his nose into her office. He'd offer condolences and ask if there was anything he could do. She'd be tempted to unload on him and ask for advice. But was she ethically entitled to reveal sensitive details concerning her family?

First there was this revelation of her Nazi heritage. She certainly hadn't seen that one coming. Back in Pennsylvania, her father admitted that he and Kipling's mother, Inge, had agreed that they would take that ugly secret to their graves. In the end, he decided otherwise.

Kipling flinched from a knock at the door. "Speak of the devil."

Silverstein held out his hands, palms up. "What did I do now?"

"Nothing." Kipling sighed, pointing to her desk. "You wouldn't mind taking over one or two of my work units, would you?"

"Nice try, oh faithful assistant. I've worked too long and hard to get to this stage of my career where I can avoid those damn things."

Kipling shook her head, knowing that Silverstein was stating in modest words the real reason he had few supervisory or management duties. It was partly because of his hard work, but more so because of his reputation and brilliance. He could do anything he wanted because upper management knew they had to keep him happy.

"Thanks for the flowers, Victor." Kipling pointed to the file cabinet in the corner. "They were waiting when I got home Friday. I brought them to work so you could see them. They're beautiful." She looked up with appreciation.

Silverstein took a seat and turned serious, something unusual for him. Normally, he used Kipling as his personal punching bag, someone to bounce ideas off and get angry at when things didn't go his way. "You know that I think the world of you. I'm sorry about your dad. Tell me if there's anything I can do."

Kipling slumped in her chair. "I was at the hospital when he died, Victor. I've regretted not getting back in time for Mom last spring." She paused, making sure she had his attention. "Afterward, I was sitting outside the hospital and almost called you."

"Why didn't you?"

"It was late. Besides, I had to do some more thinking."

"About what?'

"About what Dad told me before he died."

It was hard for Silverstein not to fall back into his usual combative self. "I assume it wasn't some deep, dark family secret."

Kipling grinned. "Actually, it was."

Silverstein cringed and looked up at the ceiling. Kipling felt sorry for him when she noticed his face flush, something most people would never have recognized. She had been around him long enough to recognize the slight crimson blush to his chocolate skin. "I'm sorry. I was trying to make a joke."

"Forget it. Your timing was perfect, actually. That's why I wanted to talk to you."

"Okay. I promise to behave." Silverstein smiled sheepishly.

"I've told you that my relatives came from Germany." Kipling leaned back and gathered her wits.

Without hesitation, Silverstein started spouting. "Yes, as I recall, you told me they emigrated after the war. Your mother's family—Müller, right?—moved to Brazil in 1947, and both your mother and father accompanied them, long before you were born. You were a late surprise as I recall." He smiled. "Your parents moved to Colorado in the early fifties, right before your other relatives moved to Colombia. Your cousin Dieter used to visit you. That's about all I remember."

Kipling marveled. Silverstein was brilliant not only because of his extreme analytic skills that made him an excellent scientist, but also because he remembered *everything*. "Everything you've said and what I've known since before last week is true. Except for one small detail."

Silverstein's eyebrows rose. "Yeah?"

"My information was off by about two years. My grandparents left Germany in 1945."

Silverstein seemed to sense where this was going. "What month?"

"April."

"Beginning or end?"

"End."

Silverstein whistled. "Your parents got out just as the Third Reich was falling apart." He bit his lower lip. "I can see where this is going. Can you cut to the chase?"

The tension of the moment made Kipling want to move around. She stood and faced the window. "Mom and Dad left Berlin with Mom's parents on the very day that Hitler committed suicide. My grandfather, Hans Müller, Mom's dad, had seen the end coming and had planned an escape for our family."

Kipling turned and looked at Silverstein. She knew what he was thinking. "Dad swore to me that he and Mom knew nothing about the darker secrets of the Nazis. Grandfather had used his connections to keep his young daughter's husband off the front lines. Dad worked in the Ministry, shuffling papers and paying bills."

"You do believe him, don't you?"

"Dad said that by the time I came along, he and Mom decided to fudge the dates a little, to avoid any embarrassment that could come of it." Kipling said decisively, "Yes, I do believe him."

Kipling watched as Silverstein closed his eyes. She knew him well enough to know that his quick mind had already formulated the next question. He blinked. "You know what my next question is, and so I'm not even going to ask."

Kipling obliged. "You want to know why after all these years, Dad came clean. That's why I almost called you. The problem is, if I tell you, I'll be betraying my family. Could we talk this over before I spill my guts?"

"From what you've said, any betraying that might be done has already been accomplished by your father. You're off the hook. Over and out. Case closed. *Sayonara*." He placed an imaginary mark on an invisible ledger in the air.

Kipling grinned widely. "Leave it up to Victor Mark Silverstein to find the easiest solution to a problem."

"You know me too well. But don't you agree?"

"Sort of. But I think your argument is bogus. Dad was on his deathbed. Before he faced his creator, he had decided that telling me everything was the moral thing to do."

"I think you've answered your own question. If you respect his judgment, shouldn't you follow through with what he intended? Which might include telling someone else? Otherwise, you could drop dead tomorrow and take his secret with you." Silverstein rubbed his hands together. "So are you going to tell me now?"

"I will, but it's because I need your help. Dad's hit me with something that's more than I can handle." After fidgeting enough in the vertical position, Kipling returned to her chair and looked up hopefully.

"Linda, you've saved my life twice in the past four years. Do you think I'd turn you down for anything?" Silverstein made fists and clenched his teeth. "Besides, I'm hooked." He smiled warmly, eyes wide in anticipation.

Kipling blurted it out. "Dad said that the Nazis are planning to return to power. And he thinks they're going to do it soon." She dithered. "And if that isn't bad enough, those Nazis are my family."

CHAPTER 7

MIA

Naval Research Laboratory, Washington DC, USA: 38°49'18"N Latitude, 77°1'24"W Longitude
Monday, 11:15 a.m., October 3, 2011

Rick Uphouse slammed the phone into its cradle. "Damn it!" He had spent the past fifteen minutes grilling the law enforcement officer on the receiving end of his call. The intensity of his questioning was especially inappropriate, considering that the Greenland police had dispatched a helicopter at his request.

"Was their campsite disturbed? Any sign of violence? Did you find their snowmobile?" After a three-day weather delay, the police had arrived on Monday morning and obliged Uphouse's demand that they telephone him immediately from his men's base camp. Unfortunately, all the answers came back in the negative. Everything had appeared normal. Which, in reality, meant that something was very wrong!

All this uproar had originated from a message on his office voicemail the previous Thursday morning. According to the time stamp, it had been recorded two-and-a-half hours before his eight o'clock arrival. He'd listened to it dozens of times Thursday and Friday. If there was anything of value on the recording, he couldn't make it out. By Friday noon, after he'd contacted Greenland authorities, the name James Bragley came to mind.

Uphouse knew his researchers Peter Armstrong and Henry Smithkline personally. In fact, he was their boss. Using a grant from the National Science Foundation, he had funded their four-month trek in Greenland. They were drilling shallow ice cores to test a new theory for dating ice. They had finished their work and were scheduled to return home Friday.

Once Uphouse understood there'd be a weather delay to the search for his men, he had telephoned Bragley Friday afternoon. Bragley was traveling at the time, and his message said he wouldn't return to NRL until Monday noon. Uphouse had stressed the urgency of the situation and asked him to come by as soon as possible. Bragley was a genius when it came to electronic analysis, and if anyone could help, it was he.

Uphouse heard a knock and looked up. He stood, relieved that the cavalry had arrived. "Thank God it's you, Jim!"

Bragley pulled up a chair. "What's going on?"

Uphouse couldn't stand still and started pacing. "I'll tell you what's wrong. Two of my researchers are missing from their camp in Greenland. It took me four goddamn days to get someone out there to look for them. I just got off the phone."

"Back up! You're going too fast. Who are you talking about?"

"You've met them. Armstrong and Smithkline. Armstrong's the tall, black guy, and Smithkline's the short, skinny, white one. They've been on the ice since June."

"So what? What makes you think they're missing?"

"This." Uphouse called his voicemail and switched the sound to speaker.

Bragley listened to the thirty-five second recording. "There's nothing there, just a bunch of static."

"Listen again." Uphouse replayed the recording.

"Okay, I hear something. You think there's a voice there?" Bragley exhaled. "Let's slow down here. What makes you think this has anything to do with Greenland? You have no idea where that call came from."

Uphouse winced. "You're partially right."

"Talk to me."

29

"First, what it sounds like to me is someone talking into a phone while they're moving. Have you ever tried to talk to someone who's outside, with a cell phone, say, or even a Bluetooth headset, when the wind's blowing? You can't hear shit because of the roar around the microphone. I think that's what this is."

"You're losing me. That still doesn't mean it has anything to do with your men."

"That's what I was hoping too, that it had nothing to do with—" Uphouse cut himself off and shook his head. "I'm sorry. I haven't gotten much sleep, and I'm not making sense. The first thing I did after I heard the message was to call them on their satellite phone." Uphouse hesitated on purpose, to make sure he had Bragley's attention. "They always keep it on for emergencies, not just so they can call out, but in case we need to contact *them*. I called all through Thursday and into Friday morning. That's when I decided to call the authorities. Unfortunately, they've had bad weather, and today was the first they could get a chopper up there. When the Greenland police didn't find any sign of them at the base camp, that's when I knew something was wrong."

"So you want me to do an audio decomposition to see if I can extract the voice from the static?"

Uphouse nodded. "Please. Can you do it?"

"I can try."

"Could you do it right away?" Uphouse wrote down his office phone number and the numerical code for retrieving his mail remotely.

"If there's something there, I'll find it. You'll hear from me by tomorrow afternoon." Bragley headed for the door.

Uphouse slapped his forehead. "Damn! I can't believe this. Talk about bad timing."

Bragley turned. "Now what?"

"I've been so wrapped up in this, I completely forgot that my brother is flying into National tonight. You remember Tom. I think I've mentioned him before."

"Isn't he the brother who works for some hush-hush think tank out west?"

"Yeah. My only brother, in fact. But he quit that job a couple of years ago so he could climb mountains. I think that's all out of his system now, and he's looking for something else to do. I promised to hang out with him tomorrow and give him a tour of DC."

"Not a problem. You have a cell, right?"

"Of course."

"Give me your number, and I'll call you the instant I know something."

"You're a friend." Uphouse pointed to his phone. "It's always attached to my belt." After a moment, he added, "I've got to tell you, I don't have a good feeling about this."

Chapter 8

Reading Assignment

Naval Research Laboratory, Monterey, California, USA: 36°35'34"N Latitude, 121°51'17"W Longitude
Monday, 8:20 a.m., October 3, 2011

"You're joking, right?" Silverstein, eyes wide, cackled.

Kipling showed no emotion. "I wish I were."

The smile drained from Silverstein's face. "So did you ask him why he would suggest something so crazy?" Silverstein's irritation was rising, but he then seemed to realize that it wasn't his place to question his colleague and friend this way.

Kipling accepted Silverstein's bluster. He could be hotheaded. Before he could say something he'd regret, Kipling raised her hand. "I know what you're after. Give me some credit here. You and I think the same way. Dad said that what he was telling me he had pieced together from scraps of information."

"I'm listening. What scraps?" Silverstein's staccato responses punctuated his impatience.

"Let me give you some history." Kipling stood. "When my family left Germany at the end of the war, Dad had been married to Mom for just two months. I was aware of that, although my dates were off by a couple of years. Last week, Dad added some significant details. He said that my grandfather, Hans Müller, had orchestrated the family's escape well before things fell apart in Berlin. With his British ancestry, Dad was the odd man out, the only nonnative in the family, even though he had lived in the country since he was a child.

"Dad said that Mom's brother, Friedrich, disliked him. Even while they were driving to the airport to escape Germany, Uncle Friedrich was arguing that Dad shouldn't come along." Kipling paused. "But as Dad explained it, Grandfather had no choice. If he had refused to take my father, his only daughter, Inge, would have remained behind."

"Sounds to me like that was a good enough reason right there for your parents to hightail it out of Brazil."

Kipling nodded. "I suspect that played a role, although Dad said that it was more because he had relatives here."

"Okay, I'm with you. Keep going." Silverstein leaned backward, hands behind his head.

"While they lived in Brazil, Dad picked up on some of the details of their planned escape. The most significant piece of information was that Grandfather Hans had not only removed his family from Germany, but had also relieved the country of some gold bullion."

Silverstein sat up straight. "How *much* gold?"

"Dad said he never knew. And if Mom knew, she never told him. The impression that he got, though, was that it was *a lot*. That does explain some things. I've looked at the Müller Industries Web page. From the history they provide, the family-run corporation was huge even in the middle 1950s. I figure it would have taken some serious capital to get something like that off the ground."

Silverstein whistled. "I guess you could wonder why, if your parents knew that gold had been stolen from their native country, they didn't tell anyone." He held up his hand. "Sorry! Assuming that your parents didn't profit from that gold, we have to remember that they were family, and you don't squeal on family. It was your grandfather who got them out of Germany, for God's sake."

Kipling let out a snicker. "If you had seen us in Colorado, you'd know that we had no money. Dad did say that he and Mom discussed this. But when you think about it, who would they have told?"

"I assume there's more to your story."

Kipling plopped down in her seat. "As I grew up, I realized that my South American relatives were among the megawealthy. In fact, I learned later that Cousin Dieter had paid for my Catholic school in Colorado."

"Go on."

"Müller Industries makes a lot of its money developing and manufacturing drugs. They have a huge pharmaceutical plant in Iceland, of all places. That's only part of their operation, though. The rest of the company is into oil drilling and nuclear—"

Silverstein cut her off. "Wait, I've heard of this company! These are the same people who plan to store nuclear waste on some island in the southern hemisphere. It sounds to me like Müller Industries is trying to save the world, not destroy it."

"I've forgotten something. It's a minor point, but it will make sense to you later—I promise. My father had always been a weather nut. From stories you've told me, he was a lot like you. As I grew up, he had a weather station outside. He'd take me to the Denver weather office where we'd stare at the weather maps hanging on the wall—as if we knew what they meant. His interest in weather rubbed off on me."

"If that's so, why didn't you major in meteorology for your bachelor's?"

"That's a good question. My adviser suggested biology. I guess that I had too much respect for authority in those days."

"That's sure changed." Silverstein fidgeted. "Again, Linda, this is all very interesting, but you seem to be getting farther away from your relatives and Müller Industries."

"Not as far as you think. During the past decade, after Dad saw Al Gore's movie, his interest in weather transitioned to global warming. He read voraciously and probably knew more about climate change than I did."

Silverstein shook his head. "*An Inconvenient Truth.* Looking back, I can't believe the American public got so sidelined by Bush's policies regarding the environment. We just blew off Kyoto." Silverstein bit his fingernail. "Okay, keep going. I'm still waiting to see how all this ties together."

"Mom corresponded regularly with Uncle Friedrich. Considering the bad blood between Dad and him, Dad never paid any attention. But when Mom died last year, Dad became so depressed that he latched onto anything even remotely linked to her. That's how he ran across the letters. They covered a period of over half a century. Hundreds in all.

"Dad read the letters. He said that ninety-nine percent of what he read was what you'd expect between a brother and sister: family stuff, health issues, et cetera. It was the occasional *oddity*, as Dad put it, that slipped in, something mysterious or out of context."

Silverstein pursed his lips. "You're telling me that your dad read between the lines enough to think that your South American relatives are planning something that would please the führer? I doubt that he was thinking very clearly in his last year."

Kipling's face blazed with anger. She slammed her fist on the desk, making her next point with no ambiguity. "My father was as sharp on the day before he died as I have ever been in my life. If my father says that something is there, it's there!" She snapped to her feet and turned her back.

Although Silverstein often took out his frustrations on Kipling, she knew that he couldn't tolerate her being upset for long. She heard him stand and walk around the desk. He squeezed her shoulders, and his voice quivered. "If you say it is so, Linda, then it is so. You asked me if I would help you, and, of course, I will."

Kipling turned, her face softening. "I do need your help. On purpose, I've not told you everything that Dad told me. I need independent verification." She walked to the corner cabinet, picked up the bag, and handed it to Silverstein. "Between the two of us, you're the genius. Here are the letters."

It was obvious that Kipling had caught Silverstein by surprise. "And by the way, in case you hadn't thought about it, the letters are all in German. If I remember correctly, you studied German in school. I took a language too. Unfortunately, it was Russian."

CHAPTER 9

INSECT IN THE LINIMENT

Müller Family Compound, Cartagena, Colombia: 10°23'36"N Latitude, 75°32'12"W Longitude
Monday, 10:30 a.m., October 3, 2011

Dieter Müller's home office, as opposed to his formal one inside a sterile modern edifice in downtown Cartagena, reflected the trappings of a man of wealth. Situated on a jut of land that protruded into the Cartagena harbor, the Müller estate included the sixteen-thousand-square-foot main house from which his office commanded a picturesque corner. Two swimming pools—one freshwater, one seawater—two tennis courts, a riding stable, as well as various other supporting structures accompanied the colossal mansion. Several of these buildings housed the servants and security personnel required to maintain a residence and gardens of such palatial size. The Müller family owned the entire ten-acre compound accessible by land through only one gated road. In addition to the helicopter pad with resident pilot, a small marina included a thirty-meter yacht that provided the third component of the Müller land/air/sea transportation triumvirate.

Dieter, his wife and two children, his parents, and brother, Axel, all claimed this location as their permanent address. The situation reminded Dieter of Larry Hagman's old television show, *Dallas*, but *Cartagena* instead. To complement these quarters, the family had numerous residences scattered about the globe to which they could be transported quickly by any number of aircraft available twenty-four/seven at the Rafael Núñez International Airport in Cartagena.

While Axel laid claim to being the family playboy, Dieter had remained faithfully married to his wife of thirty-five years, Amelia. Their children, Manfred and Suzanna, had mimicked their Uncle Axel and had not yet chosen spouses, much to their parents' dismay. Dieter knew that his wife yearned for the patter of little feet about the house. Resignedly, they realized that this might never happen.

Watching a Princess Cruise ship pass by through the opulent picture window that framed his antique Indonesian teak desk, Dieter studied the latest data coming in from Operation Helheim. Accelerated operations over the past three years had produced results that were more dramatic than expected. In fact, the worldwide scientific community was taking note.

What his family had begun eight years earlier represented the beginning of the comeback for which his grandfather, Hans, had planned when he escaped Germany. Although the scientific basis for the project had been on the drawing board for a decade prior, October 2003 represented the official beginning.

Axel had worked for two years on a deal with the Soviets, an agreement to purchase two submarines from the collapsing Soviet Navy. Captain Gudrinko, the Soviet officer with whom Axel had negotiated, never suspected that it wasn't the submarines themselves but their four nuclear reactors that were the objects of desire. Their acquisition would allow the Müllers to initiate what would surely be judged by historians as the most clever and devastating human-induced feat of history. Some would call it a crime against humanity, but the Müllers had a different view.

But in addition to the reactors, Operation Helheim needed something more: it needed Gudrinko and the fourteen Soviet men responsible for towing the submarines to the offshore location where the transport ship lay waiting. It was too bad that these men never got the chance to spend their two million dollars, let alone the additional two promised.

Outside the Gremikha Naval Base in Russia, Müller engineers had loaded the spent tools of war aboard one large vessel, in essence a floating dry-dock modified to transport the November-class subs. To make sure that no American or Russian satellite witnessed the submarines' departure from the docks, they conducted their operation during a period when their forecasters predicted overwhelming cloud cover.

On the return to South America, just north of Puerto Rico, once Müller engineers had extracted the reactors from the submarines, they scuttled the remains of the two rusting carcasses. To make sure that the hulks were never to be found again, they dropped both into what oceanographers call the Puerto Rico Trench, specifically the Milwaukee Deep, the deepest spot in the Atlantic Ocean, at more than twenty-eight thousand feet. And since the submarines had given up their dangerous nuclear components, nothing aboard threatened the environment.

Dieter prided himself in his ability to anticipate problems. He was particularly proud of one alteration he had made to the disposal procedure for the submarines. The plan all along had been to scuttle the remains where no one could find them. What concerned him was the potential discovery by the Soviets or the Americans—who had drummed up international cooperation to fund the disposal of these weapons of mass destruction—that two nuclear submarines had gone missing. Their initial concern would have been that they had fallen into the hands of terrorists.

Dieter solved this problem by ordering his technicians to reinstall sections of the hull necessarily removed to extract the reactors. They were welded tight so that, as each submarine descended through the increasing pressures of the ocean, it would eventually implode, simulating the accidental destruction of a submarine at sea. Dieter knew that the Americans had sensitive microphones to detect such underwater noises. And if they knew that two Russian submarines had gone missing, they would conclude that they had met their fate sailing to their next home. Dieter was particularly proud of his ingenuity.

After the transport ship had tied up at the Müller dock facilities in Brazil and the reactors transported to land facilities, refurbishing and refueling of the units began. It took more than a month of continuous work, after which the first of the reactors returned northward on a smaller ship. Several years later, a second reactor augmented the first. Reactors three and four remained in storage. Dieter's life philosophy stressed the need for backups and redundancy.

*　　*　　*

Dieter sensed motion and looked up, surprised to see his brother back home so early in the day. Whereas Dieter preferred to remain in his home office, Axel spent his working days at their downtown headquarters.

Dieter knew from Axel's expression that something was wrong. He stood and walked around the desk. "What's happened?"

"I'm afraid that we do have a slight problem." Axel stuffed his hands into his pockets.

"Those two snowmobilers, right?" Dieter felt his chest tighten. Angry, he assailed his brother. "I thought you said they were dead."

"They were and still are. Everything was destroyed. I told you that."

"Then what?"

"It turns out that they *were* able to get a call out on their phone."

"How do you know that?"

"Remember when I told you we found shreds of a satellite phone? What I told you was correct. Even if they made a call, there was no way for anyone to know exactly where that call originated. But once our men discovered the phone, they did the right thing. They realized that it was possible that a call had been completed." Axel paused. "You may not remember that we are part owner of the satellite phone company that services Greenland."

"Inver Telecom. Of course I know that!"

Axel nodded. "Well, then, you also know that we bought Inver because of Helheim. My point is that, because we record all calls that leave Greenland by satellite, it was only a matter of checking calls made around the time of the incident."

"And?"

"Their call went to the United States. The good news is that the call was apparently made while they were being chased on their snowmobile. There's nothing to hear but static."

39

"What's the bad news?"

"The bad news is that if you do a spectral decomposition of the call, it *is* possible to extract a voice. We're hoping that whoever received this call just dismissed the recording."

Dieter clenched his fists. "What do you mean, *recording*?"

"No one picked up the call; their message went to voicemail." Axel gestured. "Don't worry. It's unlikely that anyone would be clever enough to do an audio analysis to extract the voice."

"And what would you rate the odds of that happening, 99.99 percent? *Gott in himmel!*" The walls reverberated from Dieter's outburst. "You know that we can't take even that tiny a chance. If someone discovers Helheim, it's over."

Axel took a seat and stared at the floor. "Calm down. I'm perfectly aware of the danger."

Dieter returned to his desk. "Do we know where the call went? Specifically, I mean."

"Yes, and we know more than that. The two men on the snowmobile were scientists from a navy facility in Washington DC, called the Naval Research Laboratory. Their camp was twenty-five miles northeast of us. Who knows why they were so far from base. We've identified them as Peter Armstrong and Henry Smithkline. Who they called, we think, was their boss in Washington, a guy named Rick Uphouse. We've been checking him out."

"So you're hoping that Uphouse had no idea what was said on that call."

"That's correct. But even so, there is another problem."

Dieter's eyes rolled upward. "What now?"

"Whether or not Uphouse deciphered the call, he does know that something's wrong because he alerted the authorities in Greenland. Whether that has anything to do with this call, I don't know. Greenland police flew to the men's base camp this morning and initiated a search. It's no secret that the scientists are missing. The question in the authorities' minds is, of course, what happened to them. I'm sure they figure that the two guys had an accident. This is the end of the warm season in Greenland, and it's all too easy for a snowmobile to get eaten up by a crevasse. Their camp was located in an isolated area serviced only by helicopter."

Dieter shook his head. "Unless, of course, whoever received the call has the capability to extract the voice from the recording."

"That's correct. That's why Schnabel is on his way to Washington right now."

After a moment, Dieter realized that he couldn't not know. "I have to ask. What was said on the recording?"

"Are you sure?"

Dieter's grimace and stiffened body posture affirmed to the positive.

"I quote, 'Rick, this is Smithkline. Someone is chasing us on our snowmobile. I've been shot, and we're trying to . . .' Unquote. It stops there."

CHAPTER 10

DOWNER

Federal Center for Data Examination, Las Vegas, Nevada, USA:
36°7'51"N Latitude, 115°10'13"W Longitude
Tuesday, 4:45 p.m., October 4, 2011

As she lowered the telephone, Captain Jane A. Stigler, United States Navy, fought to maintain her composure. She pressed the intercom button. "Call an all-hands meeting."

Following her 2002-2005 stint at FCDE, Stigler never imagined that she would one day occupy the same chair as her former boss, Tom Uphouse. When FCDE became operational in 2002, its top position was treated as a civilian billet. Higher-ups later decided that when Tom Uphouse chose to leave, his position would be filled henceforth by a military officer. Three-year assignments would rotate among the three services. As years passed, many of the staff became military as well. But no one would notice: befitting the quasi-secret nature of their operation, all employees wore civilian clothing. Their cover was an organization called Las Vegas Gaming.

In anticipation of his eventual departure, to provide stability during the military transitions, Uphouse created a more permanent civilian slot that, hierarchically, resided just below his. For that position, Andrew Peters came aboard in December 2009.

Tom Uphouse was the very reason that Stigler became the first military head of FCDE. Following her tour of duty at FCDE in 2005, she had spent another five years at various Pentagon positions, impressing her bosses along the way. When Uphouse decided to call it quits in 2010, he strongly recommended Stigler as his replacement.

Offered the position, especially considering her deep respect for Uphouse, Stigler accepted. The highs that came with the job were lofty ones, including opportunities to make a real difference in the war on terror.

Stigler flinched at the sound of the intercom buzzer. "All personnel are in the conference room, Captain."

Before she left her office, Stigler checked herself in the mirror. Because an impromptu all-hands meeting was rare, particularly so late in the day, she knew that her employees were pondering its significance. The civilians probably worried that their organization had been selected as the latest in a series of government downsizings.

The room was silent. Stigler walked to the podium, straight-backed, head held high, with the bearing expected of a high-ranking military officer. She grasped the sides of the podium and stared out toward her sixty-some employees.

Stigler cleared her throat. "I'm sorry to have to bring you some sad news. I got the word just a half hour ago. Both Tom Uphouse and his brother, Rick, were found murdered in Washington DC this morning."

CHAPTER 11

DECEPTION

Naval Research Laboratory, Monterey, California, USA:
36°35'34"N Latitude, 121°51'17"W Longitude
Tuesday, 5:15 p.m., October 4, 2011

Silverstein covered the short distance from his office to Kipling's. He hadn't come to work until afternoon and hadn't yet seen or talked to her. He composed himself for what he knew would not be a pleasant experience. And on top of his translation of her Uncle Friedrich's letters, the news he had just received from Washington had been equally troubling.

*   *   *

Standing by the filing cabinet, Kipling did a double take. Silverstein plodded in, carrying the same sack in which she had handed over the letters yesterday. He looked out of sorts. "Hi. Are you all right?"

"I just got a phone call with some bad news. You might want to take a seat."

Kipling did so. "What gives?"

"One of our DC colleagues was murdered this morning in Washington. And on top of that, his visiting brother was with him, and they both died." Silverstein pulled up a chair.

"Murdered? That's what you said?"

"Gunshots to the head, within range of tourists, down near the Capitol. Whoever pulled it off was long gone before anyone saw anything."

"Who was it? Who was killed?"

"Someone by the name of Uphouse, Code 6100, Chemistry."

Kipling flinched. "Not Rick Uphouse?"

"You know him?"

"God!" Kipling recalled her earlier work in Colorado, before accepting her current position at NRL. "I worked with him at NCAR, after both of us graduated from Colorado State." She had spent three years working there following graduation with a PhD in 1995. When NRL Monterey made her an offer to move to the West Coast, she welcomed the change, although her stay at the National Center for Atmospheric Research (NCAR), one of the country's foremost meteorological research facilities, had been a fulfilling experience.

"I remember him now. He made a name for himself studying the receding glaciers of the world."

Kipling squeezed her eyes shut, sensing a tear. "I can't believe this. Why would anyone want to kill him? And his brother, too?"

"From what I understand, no one knows much yet. No obvious motive."

Kipling recognized that Silverstein wasn't himself. "What's wrong, Victor?"

Silverstein ignored Kipling's question and pointed to the sack. "The main reason I dropped by was to discuss your Uncle Friedrich's letters. I stayed up all night and came in late."

Kipling folded her hands on the desk. Silverstein's take on the letters to her mother was crucial to accepting her father's provocative statement before he died. "I didn't mean that you had to read them all at once."

"Once I started, I couldn't stop." Silverstein tried to stifle a yawn.

Kipling couldn't wait any longer. "So tell me. Do you think my father made a mountain out of a mole hill?"

"No offense, but that's what I was hoping, that your father had exaggerated what he had read."

"Don't keep me hanging."

Silverstein reached into the bag and withdrew a clipboard. Kipling reached to grab it, but he withdrew. "Before I discuss the parts of the letters that I'm sure your father focused on, let me give you a summary. I bet I know more about your southern relatives than you do."

"No doubt."

Without notes, Silverstein began. "The letters started in 1953, not long after your folks moved here and the Müllers moved from Brazil to Colombia. They continued until a year ago. About three to four per year, on average."

Kipling held up her hand. "Did he say why they moved to Colombia?"

"Oh, yeah. Uncle Friedrich said that things were getting a little too warm for them in Buenos Aires. He didn't have a very high opinion of the Nazi hunters."

"Could you tell whether he knew what Hitler had done to the Jews?" Kipling hated to ask this question. She prayed that none of her family knew anything about Hitler's atrocities.

Silverstein looked closer at his notes. "Can't help you there. The subject never came up in what I read."

Thank God!

"Where do I start?" Silverstein seemed to be gathering his thoughts. "In the fifties, your uncle's letters revolved mostly around his family, in particular his wife and two sons, Dieter and Axel. His wife's name was Gertrude. Did you know her?"

"I've never met Uncle Friedrich or Aunt Gertrude."

"Well, from reading a half century of history, their marriage was a little rocky at times. But they were still together in 2009. I think they're both close to ninety now."

"You see, love prevails in the end."

Silverstein nodded. "If you say so. Anyway, back to the kids. They had their sixteenth birthdays in 1960 and 1961. Both went to college and joined the family business in their early twenties.

Dieter was the older one. That would put them into their mid to late sixties." Silverstein paused. "If I'm telling you stuff you already know, stop me."

"No, please. Listening is like looking through a window into a part of my life that's been hidden from me."

"Dieter was the practical, thoughtful one, Axel the rebellious teenager."

"That makes sense. Dieter always stayed in touch. I only met Axel once."

"Your uncle talked a lot about their company, Müller Industries. It was in 1960 when they began investing in a drug company, Wolfer Pharmaceuticals. They later purchased it and renamed it Müller Pharmaceuticals."

Silverstein looked straight at Kipling. "Do you have any idea what the focus of their letters was in the seventies?"

"Of course not."

"Well, you should. You may recall that *you* came on the scene, unexpectedly I might add, in 1969."

"Oh." Kipling blushed.

"Your mother must have gone on and on about her new child." Silverstein snapped his fingers. "Before I forget, it was in the seventies that your grandparents, Hans and Helga Müller, passed away."

"I never knew them either."

"But it was in the middle nineties that things started to get interesting."

"Nothing 'til then?"

"Nothing more than occasional bluster about how Germany had gone to the dogs after the war. Friedrich's primary rant concerned the Allies, how they had divided Germany, leading to the *rape*—that was his word—of East Germany by the Russians. He was particularly galled when the Soviets built the Wall in 1961."

"He must have been thrilled when it came down in 1989."

"Well, not exactly. It was then that the whole world realized how ruinous the Soviet occupation had been to the economy and infrastructure. He hated the Russians for what they had done. He said that Hitler had done the right thing in attacking Russian soil. The only thing he regretted was his incompetence in conducting the war."

Silverstein looked at his clipboard and pointed. "Okay, here's the first indication of what you've been looking for. In 1994, after one of Friedrich's diatribes against the Russians, he makes the following statement." He read. "'When we return to power, the Russian faggots will be the first to feel our fury.'"

This doesn't sound good. "Keep going."

"Compared to earlier decades, the tone of the letters changed dramatically from the midnineties on, probably as Friedrich became aware of his own mortality and his sense that history had done them wrong. There was less discussion of family, fewer pleasantries. He turned eighty in 2000, by the way.

"Friedrich's words became more and more pointed, about how Germans like him longed for the prestige they had built during the 1930s. He also despised how the Allies had," Silverstein glanced at his notes, "emasculated his country, reducing it to what he considered a third-rate power, even though Germany had immense resources." He looked up. "Incidentally, my guess is that Dieter and Axel never saw any of these letters. If they had, your mother would never have received them." He continued. "It was during this period when Friedrich also began to write more freely about a plan to take back Germany, something he called Operation Helheim. He bragged about the technology and capital that Müller Industries had amassed."

"So you believe my father now, do you?"

"I'm not finished. As I said, Friedrich became looser with his words. He boasted about how his company had invested heavily in the spent nuclear fuel business and that this would," Silverstein stared at his clipboard again, "provide the technology necessary for the German state to be reinvigorated. He was quite proud of some event that occurred in November of 2003. He said he couldn't tell your mother what it was, but did say that it would provide the means for them to, and let me quote, 'bring the European continent to its knees.' Here's another quote of his. 'Sometimes the only way you can build a new society is to start from the ashes up.'"

Silverstein seemed to gauge Kipling's reaction before he continued. "And listen to this sentence. I think he wants to tell your mother something but can't come right out and say it. Here's what he says. 'Remember when we were kids, and we played Vikings, with me Erik the Red, and you his wife, Thjodhilde. Remember where we had to go? I can tell you that we have returned.' Does that mean anything to you, Linda?"

Kipling figured that her face had assumed the color of the ash that Silverstein had quoted. She didn't understand the reference to the Vikings, and it didn't matter. From what Silverstein told her, it was worse than she had imagined. For fear of her voice cracking, she said nothing.

"Except for one more point, what I've summarized is the extent of what I've mined from your mother's letters. Your father was dead right in his analysis."

"You said, *Except for one more point?*" Kipling held her breath because she had purposely withheld one detail her father had revealed on his deathbed.

"I'll quote it directly, Linda. It followed a boastful sequence when Friedrich was fantasizing their return to power. Here it is. 'When we're finished with what we began four years ago, the world will know the true meaning of global climate change.'"

Silverstein paused a moment before he spoke again. "And what's even scarier, Linda? That letter was dated June fourteenth, 2009."

*　　*　　*

Silverstein backed out of Kipling's office. As he left, she sat staring at his notes on the clipboard, incapable of further conversation.

Returning to his office, Silverstein contemplated what would happen next. Through a convoluted pathway, he and Kipling had stumbled upon a monumental secret that demanded action on their part. He recalled his question about why her parents had not turned in their relatives once they realized they had stolen German treasure. He had said that *they were family, and you don't implicate family.* Notwithstanding his advice, Kipling had a big decision to make. And that begged the question of what Silverstein should do if she decided to do nothing.

Further, Silverstein felt awful because he had not told his colleague the entire truth. Knowing her uncanny ability to look beyond people's words, he wondered if she had noticed. He did what she had asked, to determine if her father had exaggerated his claims. Beyond that, Silverstein had held back on one detail.

Back in her office, Kipling had asked whether Friedrich had been aware of Hitler's atrocities toward the Jews. Silverstein told her that the subject never came up. He shuddered as he considered the pain he would have caused had he told her the truth. Friedrich had not only been aware of what Hitler had done, but made it clear that it had been the right thing to do.

Silverstein opened the right-most drawer of his desk and took out the damning letters he had removed from Kipling's sack. He'd take them home tonight so that she would never see them.

CHAPTER 12

GUNTER THE THIRD

Hyatt Regency Washington on Capitol Hill, Washington DC, USA:
38°53'43"N Latitude, 77°00'41"W Longitude
Tuesday, 8:30 p.m., October 4, 2011

Gunter Schnabel III took five Benjamin Franklins from his wallet and paid the prostitute. He could have gotten by with cheaper merchandise but preferred the elite version who guaranteed discretion and anonymity. This one was blacker than sin but much better in terms of technical expression than yesterday's white bitch who had cost him double.

"I'll see you tomorrow?" she asked as he closed the door behind her.

A man of few words, Schnabel said nothing in reply. He plopped himself onto the bed, satiated and sleepy. As he contemplated his next actions, he flexed his left hand to stimulate circulation. Surgery required to repair damage from a knife wound years earlier had left its legacy—stiffness and a sizable scar on the backside.

Nine hours earlier, after listening to the voicemail that had fortuitously arisen from his morning's assignment, Schnabel had begun spitting out orders to personnel back in Cartagena. As he considered the consequences of inaction, he felt a sweat break out on his body. Speed was crucial now. But he could do nothing until his security team performed its magic. They needed to locate one James Bragley. In the meantime, stimulation by a paid whore helped pass the time.

His superiors referred to Schnabel as *der Techniker*, the technician. Beyond his job as head of Müller Security, he solved problems that either required a personal touch or were of such immediacy that they required instant action. Eliminating the threat posed by one government scientist earlier this morning had been the latest complication that required his attention.

Gunter Schnabel III was the grandson of Gunter Schnabel I, former colonel within Hitler's SS. Schnabel's grandfather had met his demise heroically, charging without cover (according to a witness) toward an approaching Russian tank, intent on defending Hitler's compound as the Russians encircled Berlin. Gunter Schnabel II, a lower-ranking SS officer, concluded the war in less dramatic fashion and found his way to Brazil. Following a close encounter with a Nazi-hunter, Schnabel the Second fled yet again and found himself employed by the Müller family in Colombia. There he found a permanent home and a steady career.

Gunter the Third, born in 1965, stepped in to fill his father's shoes after the elder Gunter retired. By the year 2000, Schnabel had advanced well beyond his father's position, to the pinnacle of Müller Industries' Security Division.

The talents Schnabel had inherited through his Nazi bloodline made him a formidable enforcer of the principles defined by his bosses. Dieter and Axel Müller recognized his value and compensated him appropriately. Although he commanded a team of 130 security personnel, when it came to problems his supervisors considered intractable, Schnabel was their go-to man. When such a situation occurred, often as not he preferred to work alone. Ever proud of his name and heritage, Schnabel refused to use an alias, even on difficult assignments. He had convinced himself that he was far too clever to be caught.

Although Schnabel was alone in America's capital city, he had access to an impressive support structure. It was his team in Cartagena that had located one Rick Uphouse, research scientist for the Naval Research Laboratory. They had identified him and provided Schnabel with home and work addresses, together with a photograph. Uphouse's particulars had been waiting for Schnabel when he checked into the Hyatt Regency a day earlier.

Schnabel's trip to Washington had been unexpected. Following the incident with the snowmobilers, he had flown from Cartagena to Greenland straightaway, arriving at the base camp just ahead of an impending storm. There he coordinated the data analysis that led to discovering the satellite phone call from the fleeing trespassers. That phone call prompted his trip to DC on Monday. It had been some time since an operation of such urgency had crossed his desk. With twenty-four/seven access to a Müller corporate jet, Schnabel arrived in Washington within hours.

Privy to all technical details concerning Operation Helheim, Schnabel was not surprised that things had begun to heat up. He had known that once the Müllers decided to go operational some six years earlier, there would be no turning back. At this point in the project's evolution, any threat required immediate action. In his planning, Schnabel had anticipated most contingencies. Unfortunately, there was one variable for which there could be no preparation: the random one. Who could have anticipated that two snowmobilers out for a joyride in the middle of an immense ice sheet would somehow stumble across their operation?

Once Schnabel's staff had determined that Rick Uphouse was the intended recipient of the satellite phone call, they sprang into action. The irony was that if Uphouse had answered the call, nothing more would have come of it because the transmitted static had been unintelligible. Unfortunately, the satellite phone company's data told them that the message had been recorded as a voicemail.

And even more troubling, Schnabel's team concluded, after their electronic analysis of the recording, that it was theoretically possible to decipher the voice behind the static. And the words had not been idle chatter. Everyone understood that if Uphouse cracked the call, the results could prove catastrophic. Authorities would know that something other than an isolated accident had claimed the snowmobilers. Accordingly, Axel dispatched Schnabel to Washington to plug that leak. To make the situation more alarming, Schnabel explained to Axel an even worse scenario, the real possibility that Uphouse had passed the recording to another party for digital analysis. On the phone with Schnabel, Axel became noticeably alarmed.

Elimination of the initial threat had been the place to start. During the hit, the necessity of neutralizing Uphouse's companion proved to be a collateral, albeit unfortunate, occurrence. Remarkably, a fortuitous opportunity presented itself. Schnabel couldn't remember another time in his career when vital information had come to him so easily. Following the deed, he noticed that Uphouse had his cell phone attached to his belt. In the seconds before Schnabel made his getaway, he grabbed it.

Two hours later, when Uphouse's phone rang back at the hotel, Schnabel did not answer it, hoping that whoever called would leave a voicemail. Someone did, and Schnabel left the hotel immediately to retrieve the message. Knowing that it was technically possible to determine the phone's location while he accessed the message, Schnabel walked a distance from the hotel before retrieving the voicemail. He then smashed the phone and threw it into a dumpster.

The information contained in the cell's voicemail proved invaluable. James Bragley had not only identified himself, but also admitted that he had deciphered the words from the recording. Bragley wanted Uphouse to call him immediately.

For this reason, Schnabel needed to stay in Washington awhile longer. It was imperative that he terminate Bragley before he learned of Uphouse's demise. Otherwise, Bragley might share the voicemail recording with the authorities.

Schnabel took a nap as he waited for the specifics he needed to complete his next job.

CHAPTER 13

EIGHTEEN PERMUTATIONS

Federal Center for Data Examination, Las Vegas, Nevada, USA:
36°7'51"N Latitude, 115°10'13"W Longitude
Thursday, 8:30 a.m., October 6, 2011

Every word printed in a newspaper, foreign and domestic, made its way into the FCDE database. Sophisticated computer programs searched for items of interest. Although Internet news summaries provided immediate reporting on headline-type events, personnel at FCDE were often interested in stories having less than front-page status. That said, a significant fraction of FCDE's computer power went toward analyzing blogs and other Internet postings as well.

Captain Jane Stigler rotated away from her desk to face the Las Vegas Strip. What she had just read seemed inconceivable. As if Tuesday's news had not been bad enough, a report from the *Washington Post* compounded Tuesday's tragedy. A second NRL scientist, James Bragley, had been knifed to death in front of his home in Alexandria on Wednesday morning, one day following the demise of NRL's Rick Uphouse and his brother. The mood in the FCDE office had been downbeat ever since the news that their former boss had been one of the slain.

Stigler whipped around and grabbed the phone, pressing the intercom button. "Andrew, could you come in here, please?" Her technical director had one of the best minds at FCDE. Uphouse had stolen him from DTRA, the Defense Threat Reduction Agency, a DOD agency based in Fort Belvoir, Virginia. DTRA's mission was to protect the country from the threat of weapons of mass destruction.

A timid knock preceded Andrew Peters's appearance. With colored pens protected by a clear plastic pocket liner, he came across as the quintessential nerdy geek. Truth was, half of Stigler's staff played that part. Geeks were what it took to do most of the work at FCDE.

The technical director proceeded to stand in front of Stigler's desk, his shoes parallel and touching each other, a personal idiosyncrasy. He rarely sat down when speaking to a colleague.

"Did you catch the news out of DC this morning?" Stigler asked. She noticed that Peters held a manila folder in his left hand.

"You mean about the second NRL scientist that got himself murdered?"

"What do you make of it?"

"Seems to me like someone has it in for government scientists."

"Is that what you really think?" Stigler recalled their former boss's credo. On the wall at the entry to their offices, a plaque remained as the sole physical memory from the years that Tom Uphouse ran the organization. On that plaque was written only one sentence, with Uphouse's signature below: *If you believe in coincidences, you shouldn't be working here.*

"I assume you think the two murders are connected." Peters was good at not answering questions directly. He smiled knowingly and waved the folder in the air. "When I caught the preliminary report at home this morning, I came in early." Both Stigler and Peters had secure connections to FCDE computers from their homes.

"You're good to have around, Andrew. Speak to me."

Peters remained planted in the same spot (Stigler had once timed him at more than forty-five minutes). "My thoughts probably parallel yours. Were the murders connected? Was this part of a larger government conspiracy? Was it an inside job?"

"Conspiracy? Inside job? What the hell are you talking about?"

"Don't you remember Joe Turner in *Three Days of the Condor*? Robert Redford, 1975. CIA employee Turner goes out to get lunch and comes back to find everybody in his office dead. He spends the rest of the movie trying not to get killed himself, only to discover that the CIA was doing in their own people. Since Rick Uphouse and this Bragley guy were both NRL employees, it could be an inside job."

Stigler finally understood. She shook her head and smiled. Peters, an avowed movie nut, was always quoting from movies to make points, sometimes ridiculous ones. "Do you mind not pushing the envelope too far here? Let's just deal with what we know."

"Okay, for openers, I think it's important to find out if Uphouse and this new murder victim knew each other. I've already checked this out. They worked in different parts of NRL. Uphouse was a scientist in Chemistry, and James Bragley—that's the guy's name—worked in Acoustics. If we can find a relationship between them, that might give us a leg up on why they were killed."

"And how could we do that?" Stigler leaned her head back severely. "Communications. That's a possibility." While the laws governing Homeland Security prevented them from listening to live calls, their charter did allow them to trace the routes of calls. They also had access to anything recorded. For both landline and cell calls, that meant that they could determine if individual phone numbers ever crossed paths.

"Bingo. I wrote the code this morning."

Stigler was impressed but didn't want to swell Peters's head by complimenting him further. "And?"

"You called just as I was printing the results. I haven't looked yet."

"I think it's time."

Peters opened the folder and removed a single sheet of paper. After a moment, he looked up. "Houston, we have liftoff."

"What's it say?"

Peters laid the sheet sideways on the desk for both to see. "Rick Uphouse and James Bragley each had three phone numbers." He took a yellow pen and highlighted each of them. "A home number, one NRL work number, and one private cell number. I cross correlated all six numbers. That gives eighteen permutations if you count calls in both directions. You can see here where there were a few calls between their work numbers back in the spring. And then nothing all summer until," Peters pointed at the sheet, "last Friday, the thirtieth of September. That call went from Uphouse's work phone to Bragley's work phone."

"I think you're onto something, Andrew."

"It gets better." Peters took a breath. "Look here. On Tuesday, the very day when both Tom and his brother were killed, Bragley called Rick Uphouse's cell."

Stigler grabbed the sheet and stared at the numbers and times. "What's this mean? There's an M next to each of those calls."

"That's the best part. That means that neither of those calls resulted in a live connection. And both times, the caller left a voicemail. That means we'll be able to hear what's on those recordings." Peters sprinted to Stigler's side of the desk. "Can I use your computer?"

Stigler stepped aside and watched as Peters did his magic. Although she understood the technology at FCDE, she didn't have the training to make requests through the system herself.

After minutes of typing, Peters spoke. "Okay, I've locked into the Washington DC phone system. First I accessed Friday's call from Uphouse to Bragley. That was a landline call."

"Couldn't he have deleted it once he listened to it?"

"Doesn't matter. Messages don't get erased right away." Peters poised his finger in dramatic fashion. "What we'll hear is the actual message. Here goes."

They listened to the voice of their former director's brother. "Jim, this is Rick Uphouse. I know that you have audio tools that can decipher sound waves, and I need your help with a recording I have. Jim, this is very important. Please call or come by as soon as you get this message."

A moment passed before either spoke. Stigler was the first. "Interesting, huh?"

Peters seemed to be in deep thought. "Okay, give me a minute, and I'll access the call from Bragley's NRL number to Uphouse's cell. It's on a different database."

Audio tools to decipher sound. Very important. Call me soon. Stigler thought about what she had heard.

Peters finished. "Here we go."

The second recording was clear, this time from a new voice. "Rick, this is Jim. I told you I'd call as soon as I had something. And you for sure want to hear this. You were right to be concerned about Armstrong and Smithkline. Call as soon as you can. Better yet, come to my office. Hurry!"

Peters spoke first this time. "Did you notice Bragley's voice?"

"He was excited. And who are Armstrong and Smithkline?" Stigler looked again at the sheet of paper. "Andrew, what does this letter A mean next to each message?"

"I didn't see that!" Peters grabbed for the sheet. "It means that someone retrieved both voicemails. The A stands for answered."

"Andrew, your sheet has only the day of the month. Can you retrieve the exact time for the second message we just heard, as well as the time for the retrieval?"

"Sure." Peters entered a few more keystrokes. "Bragley left the message on Uphouse's voicemail at eleven thirty-one on Tuesday morning. Uphouse retrieved it at eleven thirty-seven, six minutes later." He swiveled on his chair back toward Stigler. "But that makes no sense."

"Understood. From what we know, Tom was murdered between nine and ten in the morning."

Peters relinquished Stigler's chair and resumed his standing position. "What do you think we should do now?"

Stigler reclaimed her seat. "Andrew, our former director and my friend was murdered on Tuesday. I want to find the son of a bitch who did this. You remember how tenacious Tom was. If the situation were reversed, you know that he would have done the same for us."

"I agree. And Bragley may have lost his life because of information he had."

Stigler sighed and pursed her lips. "I know."

CHAPTER 14

THE LETTER

Naval Research Laboratory, Monterey, California, USA: 36°35'34"N Latitude, 121°51'17"W Longitude Thursday, 8:45 a.m., October 6, 2011

Silverstein noted the time. Kipling usually arrived at work by seven thirty or eight. He dialed her office again. For good measure, he walked down the hall to see if her door was open. If he didn't hear from her soon, he'd call her at home.

On top of learning this morning of yet another assassination of an NRL scientist, Silverstein needed to talk to Kipling for another reason. From her reaction Tuesday afternoon, he was concerned about her mental well-being. He stared out at the morning fog just beginning to break.

Dr. Victor Silverstein played a unique role at NRL, laying legitimate claim to being one of the navy's preeminent scientists. Fifty-two years old, he had worked for the navy his entire career, some twenty-nine years.

Silverstein had been a student prodigy who attended Pennsylvania State University. In 1975, he had enrolled there in the field of meteorology at the age of sixteen. Three and a half years later, he received his BS diploma, in another year his MS, and two and a half years later his PhD. He shared departmental distinction by being one of only two meteorology students who had *never* received a grade lower than an A on *any* course, either inside or outside the department.

As word of Silverstein's brilliance spread beyond Happy Valley (colloquial name for the Penn State surrounds), numerous commercial and government laboratories competed for his talents. Silverstein ended up choosing a small research facility in Monterey, California, far removed from Pennsylvania and his native Atlanta, Georgia.

The Monterey division lay organizationally within the larger Naval Research Laboratory in Washington DC. The division title, Marine Meteorology, belittled the scope of work conducted at this organization. Research ranged from developing sophisticated computer models that predicted weather on both regional and global scales, to producing scores of satellite-derived weather products, to applying Artificial Intelligence techniques to weather problems, with a variety of projects in between, some classified.

A ringing phone broke the silence, and Silverstein checked the caller ID. It was Ringwald. Silverstein had left a message when he first arrived this morning, asking the DC scientist to call.

"Hello, Mike. Thanks for calling back."

"No problem. What can I do for you?"

"I'm sorry to bother you, what with all that's going on back there. I learned just this morning about the guy from Acoustics." Mike Ringwald was the only one Silverstein knew personally from the Chemistry Division at NRL, where Rick Uphouse had worked. Silverstein had befriended Ringwald a few years back when both scientists were making proposals for project money.

"You can imagine the reaction here. Three scientists gone. And now James Bragley from Acoustics. And that doesn't even count Uphouse's brother."

"Whoa, Mike! You're saying five? I know about Uphouse, Bragley, and the brother. Who else?"

"You wouldn't know this. Before Rick was murdered on Tuesday, he lost touch with two of his scientists in Greenland."

"What do you mean, lost touch?"

"Peter Armstrong and Henry Smithkline were finishing their summer's sabbatical on the ice, planning to return home this week.

Last Thursday, Rick lost contact with them; he couldn't raise them on their satellite phone. He called the authorities in Greenland, and they sent a chopper to take a look. No signs of anything suspicious at their camp. Their snowmobile was gone, though. The thinking is that they accidentally drove into an ice crevasse. They say that after the summer melt, it can be very hazardous there. There's not much else that could make them just up and disappear. Rick was beside himself with worry."

Silverstein leaned back. "I didn't know that, Mike. I'm sorry." He paused. "What about this guy James Bragley? Did you know him?"

"Nope."

"Did Rick know him?"

"I have no idea. He's over in Acoustics, you know."

Silverstein wanted to know more. "What's the scuttlebutt? All I know is what I've read over the Internet."

"Victor, it's a puzzle. Apparently, Rick's brother, Tom, was visiting for the day, and Rick had taken off from work to act as tour guide. Not far from the Capitol, they were killed in broad daylight, gunshots to the head. Then Bragley was knifed in front of his own house. You can imagine that a lot of people here are on edge."

"I *can* imagine. Do the police have anything?"

"If they do, they're not talking to us. Everybody wonders whether the murders are related."

"Well, listen, if there's anything we can do for you, don't hesitate to call."

"I appreciate that. Good-bye."

The sequence, all within a week: Greenland scientists disappear; their boss is murdered; another NRL scientist is killed. Suddenly, Silverstein's mind clicked. NRL's top scientist possessed multiple talents that made him the exceptional researcher he had become. Beyond his analytic ability lay his gift to recall not only everything he had ever read, but voices, faces, and conversations as well. Sometimes he wished he had been spared this faculty. Inconsistencies would bug him until he figured them out. In this case, the information that he recalled hadn't occurred that long ago. It was the day before yesterday.

Silverstein opened his drawer and removed a copy of the summary sheet he had given to Kipling. He ran his finger along the appropriate sentences: *Remember when we were kids and we played Vikings, with me Erik the Red, and you his wife, Thjodhilde. Remember where we had to go? I can tell you that we have returned.*

Bringing up Google on his computer, Silverstein typed *Erik the Red* and *Thjodhilde.* Before long, he was reading the history of the famous Norseman, including his family's flight from Norway to Iceland and his subsequent expulsion from Iceland where he was accused of murder. And where did Erik and Thjodhilde go? Greenland, an island popular history credits Erik as discovering. *Greenland!* Silverstein reread Uncle Friedrich's words: *I can tell you that we have returned.*

Silverstein rested his face in his hands and breathed in the warm air. Was Greenland where Kipling's uncle suggested that they had returned? But what could be so important there? Hardly an obvious staging area for a Nazi resurgence. But still, that out-of-the-way island had now shown up twice. A coincidence? He remembered the final point he had made to Kipling, her uncle's boast: *When we're finished with what we began last month, the world will know the true meaning of global climate change.* Silverstein's eyes grew wide.

His heart hammering, Silverstein phoned Kipling's office again. No answer. *Where is she?* He dialed her home number. Nothing. He leaped to his feet, intending to check her office once more, this time entering with his master key. Immediately upon rising from his chair, he heard a knock. He jerked open the door, ready to interrogate his colleague as to her whereabouts. Instead, he startled Sally, the command secretary from across the street.

Silverstein backed off. "Sorry, Sally, I didn't mean to scare you. What's up?"

Sally caught her breath, apparently relieved that Silverstein hadn't run her over. She handed him an envelope. "Linda came to me yesterday afternoon and asked that I give you this. She said to wait until nine this morning."

"She asked you to wait?"

"Yes, sir."

Silverstein thanked Sally and returned to his desk. He ripped open the envelope and spread out the two-page, handwritten letter. Kipling's neat cursive hand made for easy reading:

Dear Victor,

I'm sorry to be so mysterious, but I felt I had no choice. You would have talked me out of going. By the time you read this letter, I should have arrived in Cartagena, Colombia.

As you no doubt suspected from my reaction to the letters on Tuesday, I have been torn to pieces by all of this. To think that my own relatives are behind something even remotely connected with World War II and the Nazis has devastated me.

I didn't get any sleep Tuesday night. I really wanted to talk to you, but also knew there was no point: I knew what I had to do. My first thought was to call my cousin Dieter and ask him about the letters. But the more I thought about it, the more I realized that wasn't good enough. I had to ask him in person, and I had to act alone. As you said, you don't snitch on your family.

I am optimistic enough to hope that there is a logical explanation for all of this.

Still, I am not naïve. If you have not heard from me within twenty-four hours, you can assume the worst. If that occurs, you have my blessing to do whatever you think is necessary to get to the bottom of the threats from Uncle Friedrich's letters. I know that you have the connections to make that happen. Until then, I ask that you stand pat and don't come after me. I know you all too well!

On a personal note, I have to tell you that it has been my honor and pleasure to work with you these past years. More than you'll ever know.

Your faithful colleague, Linda

Silverstein felt as if he had been punched in the stomach. His friend and colleague had chosen to place herself in the line of fire. From personal experience, he knew that she didn't lack for bravery to carry it out.

She wants me to just wait around for a day, twiddling my thumbs? I don't think so!

The first thing to do was obvious. He opened his cell phone and dialed Kipling's. As expected, the call went directly to voicemail.

He tried to keep his voice steady. "Linda, this is Victor. I just read your letter, and what you are doing is not a good idea. I just got off the phone with Washington. What you don't know is that a second NRL scientist was murdered yesterday. And that's not the worst of it. Last week, two scientists that work for Uphouse went missing in Greenland. The more I look at the clues, Linda, the more I'm concerned that what's happening is connected to what's described in your uncle's letters. Linda, please don't go to your cousin's house, at least not until you talk to me. Please call me. For God's sakes, Linda, please call!"

Silverstein knew that this was the perfect time to make one final point. "And remember, Linda. If you ever need me. Anytime, anywhere."

Silverstein folded his cell and stared toward the door, seeing nothing.

More than you'll ever know. That was what she had written. He was surprised to feel a rush of warm blood course through his body.

CHAPTER 15

VISUAL POLYGRAPH

Müller Family Compound, Cartagena, Colombia: 10°23'36"N Latitude, 75°32'12"W Longitude
Thursday, 1:15 p.m., October 6, 2011

Sitting at his desk, Dieter Müller fidgeted and pushed away his lunch. Normally, he ate his noonday meal on the veranda overlooking the harbor. After decades of enduring the stifling temperatures of Cartagena, he actually preferred the heat and humidity. But considering all that had transpired over the past few days, eating outside seemed to be an inappropriate luxury.

It was a little after one in the afternoon. Axel had said that he would return from his downtown office after lunch. Only a day had passed since Schnabel had eliminated a second party who knew about the voicemail from Greenland.

Dieter looked up and saw Axel strutting toward him, a smile on his face. He took a seat. "I think our leak has been plugged."

"If we're lucky, Uphouse and Bragley are the ends to this fiasco. But that still leaves the mess in Greenland."

"That's why I'm smiling. The police have concluded that the two researchers had an accident on their snowmobile."

"They've called off their investigation?"

"That's what the Greenland newspapers say. So I think you can rest a little easier."

The phone rang. "Yes," Dieter answered. "Send him in." He caught Axel's attention. "Gunter's back."

Schnabel appeared shortly. Dieter took in the image of a man who, as far back as he could recall, had never shown remorse for anything. Further, he was 100 percent dependable. A near-perfect employee, Schnabel was an imposing specimen of the male gender. With a square jaw, short-cropped, blondish-brown hair and a well-proportioned torso, he could easily have taken the place of a Hollywood action figure, *à la* Arnold Schwarzenegger. At six foot two and a muscular 195 pounds, he had the physical attributes and intellect necessary to accomplish whatever sensitive tasks the Müller family might dictate. In fact, he was the very model of the superior Aryan.

"Come in, Gunter. Take a seat."

Dieter wanted to hear Gunter's rendition of his trip directly. Everything he had heard so far had been by way of Axel. "Are you sure we're in the clear?"

Schnabel sat straight, at attention. "From Bragley's voicemail to Uphouse, I think he was doing him a favor, deciphering the recording. There's no reason to believe he would have confided in anyone else. By the next morning, he was dead. I'd say we're in the clear."

Axel spoke. "You've done a superb job. I doubt that we have anything left to worry about." He stared across at Dieter. "Don't you agree?"

Dieter wasn't sure if he agreed or not, but before he could respond, the in-house phone rang again. He held up his finger to the others and took the call. "Yes." He listened and stared out into space, his mind struggling to make sense of what the gate guard was telling him. "You say that a cousin of mine is here, at the gate?" He listened further, still not comprehending the significance of what he was hearing. "Bring her to the house, to my office."

Dieter addressed the two men in the room but mainly his brother. "Our cousin, Linda Kipling, Aunt Inge's daughter, is here."

"Linda, from California?" Axel's mouth dropped open. His voice trailed off as he too pondered this odd event. "Were you expecting her?"

Dieter shook his head. "I talked to her last week when she called about her father's passing. No! I wasn't expecting her."

*   *   *

The noonday sun beat down mercilessly as Kipling waited by the guardhouse, fanning her face with a map of Cartagena. The stifling humidity made her want to take a shower. It had been cool when she departed Monterey on Wednesday evening. Black slacks and blouse, appropriate for the cool central California coast, made little sense here, only ten degrees from the equator.

Upon arrival in Cartagena, she had taken the hotel shuttle to the airport Hyatt where she left her suitcase. She then shuttled back to the airport, rented a car, drove it to within several blocks of her cousins' address, parked it on a side street, hailed a taxi back to the airport, and then shuttled once again to the hotel. There she took a second taxicab to her cousins' residence.

"Mr. Müller asks that I bring you to him." One of the two gate guards pointed toward an electric cart.

As they made their way on multicolored concrete paths that wound along the grounds, Kipling realized that what she had read about the Müller family's wealth was not an exaggeration. Her mouth agape, she stared at perfectly manicured gardens, sculpted trees, swimming pools, meandering walkways, statues, and inlaid-stone driveways that intermixed perfectly with various structures, a few of which appeared to be living quarters, presumably for the servants. She had never seen such a gorgeous estate.

The path took a turn through an enclosed arbor, with vegetation so dense that it blocked the sun. Accelerating on a straightaway in the vegetative tunnel to a speed approaching that of a runner, the moving air felt almost pleasant. Kipling could see the end of the tunnel ahead. Halfway through, the driver slowed to a stop at an intersection, a crossroads covered in vegetation. The driver looked left and right and then accelerated quickly. They soon burst into the open air. The main house dominated the scene ahead.

Kipling had seen beautiful homes before. The Monterey Peninsula where she lived had its wealthy residents, and Pebble

Beach and Carmel had their share of mansions. But if there were any estates as impressive as this one, she hadn't seen them. The three-story building ahead stood resplendent in white, with massive overhangs and decks on all sides. It wasn't hard to imagine that the structure itself covered a third of an acre. Manicured grass, exotic flowers of types she had never seen, and several gazebos cocooned this beautiful residence. Had she not known that her cousins lived here, she would have thought the structure to be part of a luxury resort. And everywhere, from the moment they had left the guardhouse, workers were busy trimming and cutting, painting and cleaning, performing all the tasks necessary to keep the estate in pristine condition. On the opposite side, Kipling caught a glimpse of the ocean.

The cart ride brought them to a covered side entry. Kipling's chauffeur disembarked and gestured toward a female attendant who opened the door.

"My name is Marta. Follow me, please." The uniformed woman's face transformed from a brief smile into a no-nonsense expression that Kipling imagined appropriate for a formal servant.

Momentarily dazzled by the trappings of wealth, Kipling regained her focus. She hadn't spent an ungodly sum of cash on a last-minute airline ticket and flown more than 3,500 miles to be distracted by her cousins' prosperity. She was here because letters from her Uncle Friedrich had troubling implications. What else could she have done? She could have telephoned her cousin. That would have been the safe thing to do.

But safe wasn't what this was about. Finding out the truth from relatives who might be about to unleash some unknown havoc on the world was what it concerned.

After several turns through hallways in the huge house, Kipling could hear voices ahead. Her attendant stopped short of a room that looked like an office, knocked on the open door, and motioned Kipling inside.

A man seated at a large desk rose when he saw Kipling. Two others, in chairs facing him, also stood. Kipling recognized her cousin, Dieter, as the one at the desk.

Dieter's greeting was warm. While the others stood in place, he walked quickly toward Kipling and gave her a hug. "We had no idea you were in Colombia," he stated before turning to face his guests. With his arm on Kipling's shoulder, he introduced the two men. "Linda, you remember Axel, my brother."

Axel took a step forward. "It's a pleasure to see you again."

Kipling remembered Axel from her wedding. She responded politely. "Thank you."

Dieter directed Kipling's attention to the second man. "Linda, I'd like you to meet Gunter Schnabel, one of our employees. Gunter's father retired from our company some time ago, and Gunter has been filling in ever since." He gestured toward Schnabel. "Gunter. Linda is our cousin from America. She lives in California."

Schnabel snapped his heels together and stepped forward. He reached for Kipling's hand and kissed it. Before he retreated, she noticed an S-shaped scar on the back of his left hand. "A pleasure," he stated. His demeanor gave Kipling the creeps.

Dieter addressed Schnabel. "We'll talk later."

Schnabel marched from the room.

"Please, sit down." Dieter gestured toward Schnabel's chair. "Would you like something to drink?" He pointed toward Kipling's clothing. "Once you're here for a while, you'll learn that black is the last color we wear in this climate." He smiled.

Kipling removed her backpack and sat down. She was thirsty and accepted Dieter's offer.

Dieter lifted a phone but then covered the mouthpiece with his hand. "Have you had lunch? I can order something to eat as well."

"No, thank you."

Now that the pleasantries had run their course, it was clear to Kipling that Dieter and his brother weren't sure what to say. Axel went first, stating the obvious. "We were sorry to hear the news about Uncle Winston."

Dieter returned to his seat behind the desk. After Axel's lead, he continued the conversation. "And only months after Aunt Inge. You have our sincere sympathy."

"Thank you," Kipling replied. Their responses seemed genuine, but she remembered that only Dieter had stayed in touch over the years.

Awkward silence ensued. It was obvious that Kipling's cousins were waiting for her to explain her sudden appearance at their residence, so far from home. A knock at the door broke the tension. A young woman, in a uniform identical to that of Kipling's earlier escort, carried a tray with glasses, ice, and assorted beverages. She placed the tray on the desk and left the room quickly.

Kipling leaned across, chose a bottle of sparkling water without a glass, and took a large, satisfying drink.

"Linda, if someone had asked me this morning to make a list of the least expected things to happen to me today, I'd say that your arrival at our doorstep wouldn't even have made the cut." A quizzical expression appeared on Dieter's face. "Are you in trouble? Do you need help?"

Do I need help? Yes, but not in any way you can imagine.

Even in the face of this confrontation, Kipling remained calm. Since childhood, she had recognized her unusual ability and had joked to herself that she would make a good spy. During a stint as a game warden in Colorado before returning to graduate school, Kipling received documented confirmation of what she was capable of. After learning that the National Park Service's office in Denver had a polygraph, she bragged to her coworkers that she could fool the device. Goaded by her challenge, her colleagues arranged for a demonstration. The expert in charge said that her claim was ridiculous, that in his twenty years of professional experience, not one person had fooled him. She asked how he could possibly know that, and that pissed him off. In front of her amazed coworkers, his smugness evaporated when she lied to him repeatedly while wired to his electronics. He admitted that there hadn't been one blip on his recording to indicate an untruth.

But despite her ability to remain calm under difficult circumstances, Kipling wondered whether she could cope with the likely outcome from this meeting, the alienation of her only remaining family.

On her flight to Colombia, Kipling had weighed various approaches to determining the truth from her Müller relatives. She decided to be direct. Her ace in the hole was her boss, who by now had read her letter. She knew that if he hadn't heard from her within the twenty-four hours she had requested, he would send in the cavalry. With his connections to the CIA, Silverstein would ferret out the veiled implications buried within her Uncle

Friedrich's letters. She had made a point of leaving copies on her desk in open view.

Kipling also knew that Silverstein would be furious and beside himself with concern over her safety. Their escapades over the years had brought them close. They had risked death together on several occasions. Because she knew that he would immediately try to reach her on her cell, she retrieved his voicemail upon arriving in Cartagena. The new information that he provided was noteworthy. She would make use of it in her opening statement to her cousins.

Kipling returned her empty bottle to the tray and steeled herself. She looked first at Dieter and then Axel, ready to assess their reactions. "Dieter, Axel, I apologize for being so blunt. I need to know if you had anything to do with the two scientists who went missing in Greenland last week. Or the two NRL employees who were murdered in Washington DC."

Kipling would have needed to observe only one face. Only an eye-blink's worth of time passed before she knew that she was in serious trouble.

CHAPTER 16

ORANGE DOT

Federal Center for Data Examination, Las Vegas, Nevada, USA:
36°7'51"N Latitude, 115°10'13"W Longitude
Thursday, 11:30 a.m., October 6, 2011

An assassin was on the loose, and they needed to act fast.

Before Peters had walked out the door an hour earlier, they had uncovered one relevant piece of information. *You were right to be concerned about Armstrong and Smithkline.* That's what Bragley had said to Uphouse in his voicemail.

It didn't take long to determine that men with those names worked in the same NRL branch as did Rick Uphouse. Armstrong and Smithkline, in Greenland on a summer sabbatical, had disappeared the previous week. That detail, together with the voicemails of Uphouse and Bragley, painted a composite image that tied together disparate pieces of their puzzle: Rick Uphouse had asked James Bragley to decipher an audio message that involved Armstrong and Smithkline. Bragley had completed the task and asked Uphouse to come by for a report. *You were right to be concerned about Armstrong and Smithkline.* Twenty-four hours following the murders of Rick and Tom Uphouse, Bragley was dead too.

A knock at the door. "Come in!" Stigler yelled, on edge. She had already bit her fingernails down to the quick on one hand and was moving to the other.

Peters apologized. "Sorry, it took me longer than I thought. I don't have the answer yet, but I have the software in place." He pointed to Stigler's computer and sped around the desk.

"Tell me this is going to work."

"Oh, it'll work, all right." Peters started typing. "Whether the results will be useful is another question."

Stigler took the guest seat opposite Peters, nervously tapping her foot on the floor. What Peters had suggested earlier was that they should be able to determine the physical location of whoever had retrieved Uphouse's voicemail. They already knew that Rick Uphouse himself could not have listened to it. He had been dead for more than an hour by the time the message was left.

Although most civilians didn't know it by its name, Enhanced 911, they knew its impact as a complement to basic 911 landline technology. First demonstrated in Chicago in the mid-1970s, this improvement allowed emergency personnel to determine the address of the caller automatically. The invention was a godsend for law enforcement and fire personnel who, previously, sat by frustrated when a caller had no idea where he or she was.

For cell phones, since a call could originate anywhere within range of a cell tower, determining the location proved more challenging. At first, software operated by local 911 personnel could triangulate a position to within a mile or so. Those were the limits of the first phase of Enhanced 911 for cell phones.

The second phase was far better, using what was called the Assisted Global Positioning System (AGPS). Using GPS technology, this advanced system could narrow down a phone's location further, to within hundreds of feet, assuming that the user's phone included a GPS capability; most phones these days did. What most civilians didn't know was that the same technology that made Enhanced 911 feasible for cell phones applied to all cell calls, not just the 911 variety. And what even fewer citizens knew was that the data necessary to make this happen were available long after the call terminated.

"Okay, here it is." Peters looked over his shoulder. "I've located the call that retrieved the voicemail from Rick Uphouse's phone. Thirty-seven minutes after eleven, six minutes after it was recorded."

"The location, what form does it take? Lat, long?"

"Yes." The computer beeped, and Peters pointed to the screen with one of his multicolored pens, a blue one, from his shirt pocket. "Okay, here we go: thirty-eight degrees, fifty-three minutes, thirty-nine point three three seconds north latitude; seventy-seven degrees, zero minutes, thirty-nine point three seven seconds west longitude. I'll use Google Earth to see where this is."

A computerized software system that allowed users to view high-resolution satellite images from around the globe, Google Earth was an invaluable tool used frequently at this facility. Stigler watched as Peters typed in the numbers. The initial global view zoomed down to the eastern part of the country and then to the Washington DC area.

"Whoever it was, was right here when he retrieved the message." Peters pointed to the middle of the screen.

Stigler walked around to Peters's back. "Back out the image a bit, so we can get some perspective." She watched as the location became more identifiable. "There's the Capitol. That's just blocks north of where the murders took place!"

Peters swiveled toward Stigler. "You want to hear what I think happened?"

"Go ahead." Stigler sat on the corner of the desk.

"Let's assume that a professional hit man did both the Uphouse and Bragley killings."

"Okay. But it could be a hit woman."

Peters sneered. "Okay, I'll *try* to be politically correct. Let's say a hit person. Follow me, here. Let's say that when he murdered Tom and Rick, he saw Rick's cell phone. He grabbed it. Later, the phone rang, but he didn't answer. By chance, Bragley leaves a voicemail that the hit man gets later, giving him the very information he needs concerning Bragley. And, get this. If the guy understands cell phones, he knows that his location can be traced when he retrieves the message. So to protect himself, he drives or walks somewhere away from where he's staying. That explains the six-minute delay. Let's see if there's a hotel nearby."

Wait a second! Stigler held up her hand. "There's a big problem here! How could it be that the murderer just happened to stay at a hotel within blocks of the crime itself? More likely than not, he would have had to tail Tom and Rick from somewhere, probably Rick's house. He wouldn't have known where they were going."

"I see what you're saying." Peters nodded. "If the murderer tailed them in his car, he would have parked when they parked and followed them on foot. To my way of thinking, it could have been just dumb luck that the hit took place near where he was staying. I know you think that's a big coincidence, but why else wouldn't he have been long gone from the scene of the crime when he retrieved the voicemail?"

Stigler had to acknowledge that his last point was a good one.

Peters rotated back to the screen. He drew an imaginary circle around the location with his finger and moved closer to the screen. "Take a look."

"What is it you want me to see?"

"My circle is a block or two in diameter from the caller's location. See the blue and orange dots on the map? They're places of interest."

"I know." She looked closer. "I see only one dot within your circle. It's an orange one."

Peters slid the cursor to overlay the dot, and a pop-up window appeared.

Stigler leaned in closer. "Well, I'll be. It's the Hyatt Regency." Only a moment passed before she formulated her strategy. "Okay, we're definitely out on a limb here, but for Tom's sake, we need to do *something*."

Peters headed for the door. "I'm on it."

Stigler yelled out. "You don't know what I want."

"Yes, I do. You want me to find out the names and addresses of everyone who stayed at the Hyatt around those dates."

"Close. I'm sure there are hundreds of people who stayed there. You need a search strategy. First, I want you to search all records from Sunday night through yesterday, Wednesday. Look for anyone who stayed there Sunday, Monday, Tuesday nights, or just Monday and Tuesday."

"Hold on." Peters removed a pen from his pocket, this time a red one, and began scribbling. "You're thinking that our guy left town on Wednesday."

"That's right. A professional wouldn't hang around any longer than necessary."

"Okay."

Stigler grimaced. "Let's hope that the lists are short. Next, segregate each list by home address. For openers, I want just two divisions. Those who live in the United States and those who live outside. Crosscheck the names against all airline manifests since last Saturday. I want to know where those people came from."

"Anything else?"

"Yes. First make some discreet inquiries through our contacts in Washington. I want to know if the police there know anything more than we've learned from the media."

"Okay. What else?"

"Assuming that Washington's finest can't help us, I want all of this information on my desk by four this afternoon."

CHAPTER 17

SAMUEL BRODY'S BABY

Müller Family Compound, Cartagena, Colombia: 10°23'36"N Latitude, 75°32'12"W Longitude
Thursday, 1:50 p.m., October 6, 2011

Dieter Müller did his best not to react to his cousin's dramatic statements. He noted that Axel hadn't done as good a job at concealing his shock. "Linda, what are you talking about? Washington DC? Greenland? You're talking nonsense."

Kipling continued, appearing embarrassed. "I'm sorry to have shocked you like that. You know that I work for the Naval Research Laboratory, and it's not every day that two of our scientists get themselves murdered. One was an old colleague of mine. On top of that, we're missing two others in Greenland on a summer research project. You have no interests there?"

How could she possibly have tied us to the two missing men on the ice? Or Washington DC? "Of course not. Why would you suggest something so preposterous?"

"You don't know anything about something called Operation Helheim?"

Helheim? Dieter willed himself to hold his emotions in check. "You're upsetting me, Linda. You've barged into our house without warning and made accusations. How would you feel if I had flown to Monterey, walked into your house, and brought up similar foolishness? If I said we suspected you of murder?"

Dieter shifted his hands from the desktop to his lap, for two reasons. First, to make sure that any trembling of his extremities was hidden from sight. Second, to trigger the switch on the bottom of the drawer, an emergency button linked directly to security, installed years earlier but never used until now.

Although her accusations couldn't have been more provocative, Dieter was impressed with Kipling's tenacity. She continued. "So you're telling me you've never heard of Operation Helheim?"

Dieter couldn't help himself. He rocketed to his feet, emotions unleashed. *"Gott in Himmel!"* He had to phrase his next question carefully. They needed to know how she had obtained this information. And importantly, whether she had shared it with anyone else. "Linda! Has someone put you up to this, or did you make it up on your own?"

Kipling bent over to retrieve her backpack. She unzipped the top compartment and removed what looked like bound packets of papers. She placed them on the desk. "Your father and my mother corresponded for more than fifty years. When Dad died, I took possession of his things. What you see are Uncle Friedrich's letters from 1990 on. Your dad is the one who mentioned Operation Helheim."

Dieter pulled the packets toward him. He recognized his father's writing on the envelopes and then burst out laughing. "My dear cousin. You've scared me nearly to death. Are you telling me that you have deduced all of this from the writings of a senile old man?" He looked directly at his brother, hoping that Axel would share in the pretense.

Axel made up for lost time. "You had me going too, Linda. I can tell you exactly what Operation Helheim is because I was involved in that."

Dieter played out his response seriously. "You know about this Helheim, Axel? It's news to me."

Axel stood and faced Kipling. "Linda, you must be aware that our company does a lot of work with spent nuclear fuel. In fact, I'm rather proud of what we're doing, making our own contribution to going green, as you Americans call it. Our company is building the world's safest repository for spent nuclear fuel. We've found a geologically stable island in the southern Atlantic, with underground caves that haven't moved in a thousand years. But before we found *this* location, we had another spot that didn't work out so well. That was Helheim."

Axel turned toward Dieter. "Dieter, you've forgotten." He laughed. "And I understand why." He sat down and faced Kipling. "We spent millions on this other location—"

Dieter cut him off. *Axel always was a quick thinker.* What he was explaining was true, although it hadn't been called Helheim. *Time to board the train.* "Sorry to interrupt, Axel, but you're making me look like a fool." He faced Kipling. "I damn well know about this project. It cost us dearly. I'd completely pushed it out of my mind." Dieter did his best to appear upset and sat down.

Axel continued. "You'll forgive my brother. He worries about the books. I'm the one who works in the field, who gets the real work done." He smiled in Dieter's direction. "Anyway, to continue my story. After two years of development, we discovered an underground river that made the location unsuitable for storage of much of anything. A huge disappointment. Fortunately, we located the new site." He pointed toward Kipling. "If you haven't kept up with what we've been doing, please go to our website. I think you'll be pleased."

While Axel continued his explanation, Dieter removed the rubber band from one of the packets, pulled off the top letter, and read. *What else has our father foolishly let slip in his correspondence with Aunt Inge?*

Dieter finished reading and looked up. It was imperative that they quantify any further slips their father had made in these letters. "Linda, I'm surprised that your German is good enough to have translated these letters. Did you do it yourself?"

"Of course!"

"Well then, you've made a mountain out of a molehill, all from the ramblings of an old man."

Dieter caught movement out of the corner of his eye. Schnabel stood in the doorway.

"Linda, I'm sure you're tired. And after this, you must be emotionally drained as well, considering that you flew all the way here to discuss something so silly as my father's letters. I insist that you stay the night, as long as you want. It's the least we can do for you." He pointed to the door. "Gunter will show you to one of our bungalows.

"Gunter, our cousin will be staying over. You will see to it she has a comfortable room."

Dieter raised his hand toward Kipling. "Please join us for dinner. We'll have a laugh over all of this. And please, take advantage of our estate. I think you'll find it quite lovely. If you need anything, just ask." He pointed to Schnabel. "And tell Gunter where you left your luggage. He will retrieve it for you."

Dieter made eye contact with Schnabel, establishing an understanding that this last statement held additional meaning.

Kipling replied politely, "Thank you. I will." Dieter couldn't gauge Kipling's reaction. There was nothing to read in her face but quiet resignation, showing neither disappointment nor acceptance of their explanation of Helheim. *What more did Father write in his letters?*

"Well then. Seven o'clock for dinner?"

Dieter followed Kipling to the door and watched her disappear down the hallway. When she was safely out of sight, he closed the door and exploded. "What was Dad thinking, to mention such things to Aunt Inge? He could have jeopardized our whole operation!"

Axel showed strain as well, but his words took on a more constructive tone. "Let's split up the letters and see what else Father said. We have a couple of hours to invent more lies."

Thursday, 3:05 p.m., October 6, 2011

Realizing that the threat from his cousin was more serious than any they had faced since Helheim was conceived, Dieter performed several actions before reading the letters. Because there was a certain risk in leaving Kipling to her own devices, Dieter had called Schnabel, delivering only two coded orders, *Hotel* and *Silence*. Hotel meant that their guest was not to leave the compound; she could roam the grounds but was to be kept under surveillance. Silence signified that the estate was to be rendered electronically

81

secure, meaning that no wireless communications entered or escaped. To accomplish this, the estate's communications center would blanket the area with electronic noise, preventing any wireless phone from obtaining a signal.

At Axel's suggestion, Dieter performed a third action. He scribbled a short note, called in Marta, and asked that she deliver it to Kipling, along with some refreshments.

For the next hour and a half, Dieter and Axel skimmed their father's letters. They divided the stacks and agreed to highlight any that appeared incriminating.

Axel finished looking at the highlighted sections from Dieter's pile. "Well, it's not good, but it's not hopeless." He hesitated. "Still, I'm amazed! How Linda could tie together what's in these letters to what happened in Washington and Greenland is astonishing to me. She must be a genius."

"I've always known that she's a smart girl."

"And in case it didn't occur to you, we can't let Father or Mother eat with us tonight. Father's hardly the senile old man you described. We should send them downtown for a couple of days."

"I know," Dieter agreed. But there was something of more concern. "What worries me, from what I know of her language skills, I doubt that Linda translated these by herself, particularly with Father's poor handwriting."

Axel stood. "If that's the case, we need to stop this hemorrhage before it spreads."

Dieter looked up from his stack. "Call Gunter in. If Linda's working with someone else, we need to know who it is—and fast. You can be sure that whoever that is knows she's here."

Thursday, 3:20 p.m., October 6, 2011

Kipling glanced about her bungalow suite, marveling at the luxury. Schnabel had accompanied her and departed. They had retraced most of her earlier electric cart ride, this time on foot, leaving the immediate mansion grounds by way of the vegetative tunnel through which she had ridden earlier. This time, she could see that both ends of the intersection where they had stopped previously spilled out into gardens on either side.

There had been no idle conversation on the walk over. Schnabel barely spoke, consistent with Kipling's unpleasant impression of him earlier. Not long after he departed, Marta came by with a tray of beverages, cheese, and crackers, accompanied by a poorly written note in German signed by Dieter. Kipling recognized only a word or two and set it aside.

Kipling looked for a phone. She found one, but it had no buttons, obviously connected to someone within the compound. The first thing she had checked when the door closed earlier was her cell phone. There had been no signal. She found this surprising, considering that when she exited the taxicab earlier, her phone had had four bars.

One wall of the guesthouse featured two square picture windows that faced back toward the main house. She peered out at the beautiful gardens. Well, she thought, she had done it. She could imagine her cousins now frantically reading Uncle Friedrich's letters, wondering what else he might have said that had prompted her to fly to Colombia. Still, she had to give them credit for their creativity, suggesting that Operation Helheim involved spent uranium. Regardless, when she had made her provocative initial statement, their eyes had given them away. They had lied.

Kipling suddenly felt a spasm of concern. She hadn't figured on Dieter's assessment that she may have had help translating the letters. The last thing she wanted was to involve Silverstein. Thankfully, he was safe back in Monterey.

So what to do now? They had invited her to dinner. Dieter and Axel were no doubt planning to explain away any further provocative statements they discovered in the letters. She smiled to herself: What were the odds that she would finally meet Uncle Friedrich and Aunt Gertrude? *Zero!*

A knock at the door drew her attention. She opened the door, and Schnabel walked in with her suitcase from the hotel. "Your luggage, madam."

"Thank you." Kipling watched as Schnabel departed.

Kipling checked her wristwatch and added two hours to what was still Monterey time. That made it 3:35 in Cartagena. She drew the curtain, locked the door, and removed the German-English dictionary she had brought in the backpack. She'd need it to translate the two-sentence note that had accompanied the tray. It didn't take a rocket scientist to realize that Dieter was testing her.

Before tackling that task, one other concern remained. Kipling carried her suitcase to a stand by the bathroom, opened it, and stared at the contents. Having a background in law enforcement from her days as a forest ranger, Kipling knew the tricks of the trade and had set in motion what was commonly called a *Brody Trap*, named after FBI agent Samuel Brody, the person credited with its invention in the early 1950s. Anyone who had watched *Dr. No*, the first James Bond movie from 1962, knew of this technique, if not its name. When Bond pasted a hair from his scalp across the closet doors, its later absence told him that someone had opened them. One of his adversaries had fallen for the Brody Trap.

Before leaving the hotel in Cartagena, Kipling had confirmed that her version, only marginally more sophisticated than Bond's, had survived the rigors of airline transport. Although a professional who opened someone's suitcase surreptitiously would memorize the placement of the contents so that the owner would never suspect that their bag had been searched, a Brody trap, by definition, was irreversible.

In Kipling's suitcase, this minor feat of legerdemain consisted of two separate strands of thread, so fine that they would break with even the slightest tug. She had sown them onto a blouse, one connected to the neck, and the other to the shirttail. The other ends she had attached to opposite sides of the suitcase's cloth lining. Even with rough handling, it was unlikely that both threads would break simultaneously. Neither thread had broken during the flights from Monterey to Cartagena.

Gently, Kipling lifted the contents along the sides where she knew the threads were attached. *Both* had snapped! That meant that Dieter's henchman, Schnabel, had searched her bag. Just one more nail in the coffin of Kipling's all but certain indictment of her Müller cousins' veracity.

Schnabel had probably already reported that he had found nothing of consequence in her bag. Of course, she had planned it that way. One versatile tool that Schnabel would certainly have considered suspicious, and which the airlines would likewise have questioned had they found it during the security search, Kipling had transferred from her suitcase back at the hotel.

Everything that Kipling needed for her planned escape this night lay tucked inside her backpack.

CHAPTER 18

DRILLING DOWN

Federal Center for Data Examination, Las Vegas, Nevada, USA:
36°7'51"N Latitude, 115°10'13"W Longitude
Thursday, 3:58 p.m., October 6, 2011

Stigler knew that she had put a lot of pressure on Peters, expecting him to respond to her demands so quickly. But as anyone in law enforcement knew, the trail from a crime could cool fast. For Tom Uphouse and the legacy of the organization he founded, Stigler intended to track down any clues while they still possessed a workable body temperature. At one minute before four o'clock, she was pleasantly surprised to hear the knock.

Peters walked in holding a sandwich and a Pepsi in one hand, and sheets of papers in the other. "Don't be mad, okay? This is the first chance I've had to grab a bite since breakfast."

"Why would I be mad?"

Rather than taking his usual standing position, Peters grabbed a chair. He seemed exhausted. Between bites, he made his first point. "Before I show you what I've put together, you need to know that the Washington police have nothing."

"I was afraid of that. Tell me what you've got."

"First of all, it's a credit to our organization that we have what's on these sheets." Peters waved them in the air. "There is no omnibus database of hotel records. The good news is that most large hotel chains, like the Hyatt, do have their own database. I asked Hank if he could hack in without being detected. It didn't take him long."

Stigler rolled her eyes but understood that was the very reason that Tom Uphouse had hired Hank Wainright. Having infiltrated—just for the fun of it, he'd said—some of the most secure electronic databases in the Western world, this Ivy League student from Massachusetts had been sentenced to a prison term of five to ten until Tom Uphouse made a deal with the Justice Department to allow him to serve out his time working for the FCDE. That had happened back in 2006. Wainright found his niche working for an organization whose bread and butter resided in developing complex search codes. Neither he nor the Justice Department ever looked back.

Peters continued. "For Sunday, Monday, Tuesday, there were twenty-five people who stayed all three nights at the Hyatt. For Monday and Tuesday only, there were a total of seventy-six." He handed across two sheets of paper.

"That means we have one hundred and one suspects." Stigler scanned the names. "You've included women."

"Of course. You'd have my ass if I didn't."

"Can I borrow your black felt tip?"

Peters obliged, and Stigler crossed out those with obvious female given names. Although there weren't as many as the men, in the process she narrowed the list by fifteen. "Okay, we're down to eighty-six."

Peters swallowed the last of his sandwich, took a sip of soda, and slid two new sheets of paper toward Stigler. "This summary *begins* with the eighty-six men left after you remove the women."

Stigler winced and playfully tossed back his pen.

Peters grinned in reprisal. "What you asked for next was to divide these into two groups, those with a US address and those with a foreign one. But before I did that, I did something obvious. At least I think it's obvious."

"What's that?"

"Although all listings have one person as principal, some have two or more names. What I did was take out both couples and families. It's doubtful an assassin would bring along his wife and kids."

"Good thinking." *Peters is worth every penny he's paid.*

"If you do that, you cut the list by another twenty-five, getting us down now to sixty-one. Next, I did what you said. Separated the domestics from the foreigners. Take a look."

Stigler scanned the two lists on the page. "Only three came from outside the country, with the rest from the States. Where'd you go next?"

Peters finished his soda and slouched in his chair. "You asked that I check airline records. But before I did that, I looked at the complete data files that Hank found for us. I wanted to see if there was anything else that could be of use. When you check into most any hotel, they usually ask what company you're with. Those who are there on business usually put it down. I've got to tell you, this was a big break for us. When I scanned the employers, there seemed to be a pattern. Guess what? There's a three-day electronics conference at the hotel this week."

"Good catch! So you removed people who work for companies dealing with electronics."

"Yes. Forty-two of those from the US work for IBM, Cisco, and so on, names appropriate for someone attending such a conference. It's unlikely our assassin would be clever enough to notice the conference going on and write down a false employer."

"What about the foreigners?"

"Good news there, too. Two of the three came from Siemens in Germany. That brings us down to sixteen US and one foreign."

"That's a more manageable number."

"Then, while I was at it, I used our own databases to identify government employees."

"With just a name?"

"I used the name but cross correlated it with the home address listed at the hotel. Eight of the seventeen work for various government agencies. Again, it seems a stretch to think our executioner is a federal or state employee." He handed across another list with the names and employers of the seventeen.

Stigler scanned the tally. "Of course. The Hyatt is located just up the street from the nation's Capitol. Now we're down to eight US and one foreign."

"Next, I tackled the airline cross comparisons you wanted. But to help narrow the search, I used one other piece of information that they usually ask for at the hotel desk."

"Don't tell me. Name, address, employer . . ." Stigler thought. "Credit card number."

"Good guess! Unfortunately, Hank tells me that data is encrypted. He said that he could crack the code, but it would take a lot more time."

"If it's not that, then what?"

"If you're keeping your car at the hotel, they usually want to know the make, model, and license number." He handed across one final sheet of paper.

"Exactly." Stigler snapped her fingers.

"If you look to the right of each remaining name, you'll see either a blank space or a license number."

Stigler counted. "One, two, three, four, five. Five of the nine have cars. The one foreigner and four of the domestics." She looked up. "That's impressive, Andrew, but so what? Assuming that our assassin flew into Washington, he could just as easily have taxied or used the hotel limousine."

"That's correct, but it does give us one more scrap of information. Because we can access rental car records, we'll know at least which airport the car came from. That limits the flights that we have to check. As it turns out, all the cars were rentals."

"I see."

"I then cross-checked the people who had rentals against airline records for anyone flying on Sunday or Monday and leaving the area on Wednesday. Rentals came from all three airports that serve the Washington area: Reagan National, Washington Dulles, and Baltimore."

"Any luck?"

"For four of the five, the address listed at the hotel agreed more or less with both the location of the originating flight and the culminating flight afterward. No surprises."

"What about the fifth?"

Peters sat up straight. "Our final list of suspects consists of eight domestics and one foreigner. But I found it interesting that of the five people who had rented a car, it was the foreigner who didn't come or leave on an airline. That oddity made me take a closer look."

"Let me get this straight. You said that one of the car renters—" Peters interrupted. "He rented the car at Dulles, by the way."

"You're saying that he rented the car there but didn't fly in or out from that airport? How can that be?"

"My question, exactly. So I got to thinking. Not everyone who flies into an airport flies there commercially."

"Some have their own planes!"

"So I did some snooping. The question was, how could I tie . . ." Peters looked at his sheet. ". . . this guy, Gunter Schnabel, to a particular aircraft that had flown in or out of the airport."

"Schnabel. That sounds German. So how did you do it?"

"Schnabel gave his home address as Cartagena, Colombia, and he works for a company called Müller Industries. Once I knew that, I went into our master database of private aircraft around the world. His company has six aircraft, two props and four jets." Peters smiled. "And guess what?"

Stigler nodded. "One of those planes flew into Dulles?"

"Yup! One of the jets. Came in on Monday and left Wednesday."

"That's great work, Andrew, but it looks to me like we still have nine suspects and no way to narrow them down."

"It's too early to throw in the towel. There's one critical detail concerning Schnabel's aircraft that's significant."

"What do you mean?"

"Remember when I told you that the other people with car rentals flew both from and to the locations identified by the addresses given at the hotel?"

"Yeah. That's what you'd expect. Are you saying that Schnabel didn't fly back to Colombia?"

"Oh, he flew back to Colombia all right."

"Well then, what's the problem?"

"On Monday, he didn't arrive into Washington from there."

"Andrew, get to the point. So he came from somewhere else. The guy has a private jet, for goodness sakes. He can fly anywhere he wants."

"But what if I told you that Gunter Schnabel had flown in from Greenland?"

Stigler blinked. "Armstrong and Smithkline went missing in . . ."

Peters nodded. "Do you think Tom Uphouse would consider that a coincidence?"

CHAPTER 19

ONE IF BY LAND, TWO IF BY SEA

Müller Family Compound, Cartagena, Colombia: 10°23'36"N Latitude, 75°32'12"W Longitude
Thursday, 6:30 p.m., October 6, 2011

Gunter Schnabel continued his report to Dieter and Axel Müller. "She's just returned from a walk. We've been following her movements for the past hour and a half."

"Has she acted suspiciously?" Dieter worried about her motives.

"Not at all. In fact, she seems to be enjoying herself."

Dieter wanted nothing left to chance. "You said she came by taxi. She implied she came directly from the airport, or the hotel rather. Did you check? The last thing we need is to find out that she has an accomplice sitting outside the gate."

Schnabel gave the appearance of a man in control. "Yes, sir. We printed a photo of her from the gate surveillance camera and checked with cabbies who had picked up fares from the Hyatt. One of them said that he remembered her. He said she was alone, and all she had with her was the backpack."

Axel stated the obvious. "And you've beefed up security at the gate?"

"Yes, sir. She'll not get past the gate."

Thursday, 6:40 p.m., October 6, 2011

Linda Kipling had returned to her cabin some ten minutes earlier, having managed her way back in the dwindling twilight from the southern beach. It was there that she had set the stage for her escape.

On that beach, Kipling had languished while watching the sun dip below the horizon. Before leaving the bungalow, she had successfully deciphered Dieter's note telling her that dinner had been postponed until eight o'clock. In fact, the one-hour delay fit better into her plans. She had already decided that she would not be eating with her cousins.

It was at four o'clock in the afternoon when Kipling had decided that she needed to determine whether her escape plan was feasible. She feared the worst, that her cousins had no intention of allowing her to leave. With backpack in hand, she had strolled out the door. Starting at the northern beach, she walked counterclockwise around the perimeter of the estate. In the process, she discovered the marina and the helicopter pad, more examples of her cousins' expensive indulgences. Her tour had culminated at the southern beach. No one had stopped or questioned her.

Kipling confirmed what she had learned from Google Earth satellite images back home, that the Müller estate was a peninsula. Positioned northwest to southeast, and bearing a striking resemblance to a certain erect male body part, the only way onto the compound by land lay at the neck of the peninsula, attached to the mainland. That was where the guardhouse stood, where she had entered earlier in the afternoon.

A seven-foot-high chain-link fence separated the Müller estate from the modest residential area outside. Hidden by dense foliage both inside and outside the compound, the fence meandered its way to the beaches on both sides of the guardhouse. It then continued into the water a distance. Escaping by swimming along the shore beyond the fence appeared to be a reasonable option.

Although Kipling had been free to roam the grounds, she sensed eyes following her. Before long, she spotted cameras, some obvious on stands, and others cleverly hidden among vegetation.

As numerous as they were, she felt confident that sections of the beach were free from surveillance.

A lot of thought had obviously gone into the layout of the compound, very practical from a maintenance standpoint. All locations on the estate were serviced by paths, some hard-paved and some gravel. Considering the army of gardeners and maintenance personnel that it took to maintain this Garden of Eden, whoever designed the layout had given considerable thought to its upkeep. Within eyesight of most locations on the compound sat a maintenance shack. She kept an eye on one positioned close to the northern beach. She watched as personnel retrieved and returned various trimmers and other garden tools. Complete with a bathroom and an outside drinking fountain, each enclosure had a different design, with decorative windows, and was made to look like a natural part of the landscape.

On her way to the northern beach, she had intentionally walked past the guardhouse. There was a noteworthy change. Compared to the two guards in tropical attire she had seen earlier, four uniformed men now staffed the entrance, two with German shepherd dogs. And whereas Kipling had seen no weapons earlier, each of the guards now carried a machine gun, further indication that the game had changed.

Thursday, 7:15 p.m., October 6, 2011

Five minutes earlier, one of Schnabel's security personnel from their downtown office had brought the recording to Dieter's office. Dieter and Axel Müller, staring at the electronic device, listened a second time.

> *Linda, this is Victor. I just read your letter, and what you are doing is not a good idea. I just got off the phone with Washington. What you don't know is that a second NRL scientist was murdered yesterday. And that's not the worst of it. Last week, two scientists that work for Uphouse went missing in Greenland. The more I look at the clues, Linda, the more I'm convinced that these murders and disappearances are connected to what's*

94

described in your uncle's letters. Linda, please don't go to your cousin's house, at least not until you talk to me. Please call me. For God's sakes, Linda, please call. And remember, Linda. If you ever need me. Anytime, anywhere.

The compound communications center, designed and installed under the direction of Gunter Schnabel, had intercepted Kipling's attempted cell call. While blocking it, they had decoded her telephone number. It was then a simple matter of penetrating her cell phone database to retrieve her messages. For the second time in as many days, a chance voicemail had proved invaluable.

After listening to the recording, Schnabel's downtown office acted quickly. They hacked into the NRL intranet and found only one person named Victor who worked at the Monterey office of the Naval Research Laboratory. His complete name was Victor Mark Silverstein, one of the facility's scientists. A search on the Internet revealed that he and Kipling had worked together on various projects, proof that Schnabel's team had found the right man.

Dieter glanced at his watch: 7:20 p.m., forty minutes before dinner. Kipling apparently knew enough German to have deciphered Dieter's scribbling, not embarrassing herself by arriving early.

"What do you think, Axel? We need to decide about dinner. Do we continue playing the game?"

Axel replied stoically. "I don't think there's any point in making up more stories. And from this recording, we know there's someone else out there who could be a problem. Whether either realizes what's going on in Greenland, it doesn't matter. They know too much."

"Let's think this through, Axel. If we continue with dinner, maybe we can stall her."

Axel shook his head. "Stall her for what, Dieter? For another couple of hours? Keep her here for another day or two? What does that buy us?"

Dieter turned his back on Axel and stared out at the evening skies. The gardens were barely visible; the sun had set more than an hour earlier. What Axel was telling him was obvious. The shock of the thought made him catch himself as he inadvertently backed into his chair. He had known Linda since she was a baby, and now they were . . .

Axel placed his hand on his brother's shoulder. "What else can we do, Dieter? Whether or not she's figured out Helheim, she's found us out."

"I can't believe it's come to this, Axel. Someone from our family. Aunt Inge's daughter! We can't just kill her."

"Then you tell me what we should do. Do we hide her away somewhere and wait for Helheim to finish? We could do that. Would that make you feel better?"

Dieter hung his head. He didn't know what to think. Memories of his yearly trips to Colorado flooded his mind, as well as the stark reminder that it could have been his family who died escaping Germany. Linda was family, and family needed to be treasured. "Let's at least have one last dinner with her."

Thursday, 7:45 p.m., October 6, 2011

It was time to head to the main house for dinner. Kipling took a last look at her suite. She had transferred all items she needed into her backpack, including a change of clothes. With everything inside, the bag had more heft than usual. It was too bad she would lose her suitcase and everything in it. As she was about to open the door, a thought occurred. She grabbed a cracker and a piece of cheese from the tray Marta had brought earlier. One more time, she checked her pants pockets, two of which were zippered. Important documents, including her passport and credit card, were there, protected inside plastic bags.

Kipling opened the door slowly, strolled casually outside into the humid evening air, and looked around. Nothing to incite alarm. Decorative lights on poles illuminated the compound well enough that larger features were discernible. The guards at the gate ambled about and seemed bored. They probably knew that Dieter had invited her for dinner. She walked the pathway until it came to the trellised tunnel. Inside, miniature electric bulbs cast a dull light on the secluded vegetation. Her organic enclosure smelled wonderful. She arrived at the intersection where the electric cart had stopped earlier and looked back to confirm that she was no longer visible from the guardhouse. Straight ahead would take her to her cousins. A left turn would take her to the southern beach. To the right was the northern beach.

It was time. Kipling turned left. She broke off a few morsels from the cracker and cheese and tossed them in the center of the pathway.

With that accomplished, Kipling reversed her direction and took off running.

Thursday, 8:05 p.m., October 6, 2011

"She's late," Dieter said as he and Axel waited outside the door.

Axel walked into the open and gazed at the stars. "Americans are never on time."

Dieter stepped back into the hallway and walked briskly toward the dining room where Marta was making last-minute preparations. "Marta, would you please call Linda's room? She knows we're expecting her for dinner."

He watched as Marta dialed and listened. "There's no answer, sir."

Dieter hurried back to the front porch. "Any sign of her, Axel?" Upset, he yanked at the collar of his shirt. Something was amiss. "I'm calling Gunter." He removed his cell phone and pressed the button for Schnabel's speed dial. Schnabel had his own quarters on the estate.

"Gunter! We were expecting our cousin for an eight o'clock dinner. Check her room. See what's keeping her."

Dieter started pacing, and Axel responded. "Calm down, Dieter. You know there's no way she can leave the compound. She probably fell asleep."

Moments elapsed, and Dieter's phone chirped. "Where is she?" He didn't like what he was hearing. "I'll meet you there."

Dieter took off jogging, with Axel close behind. As he approached the guesthouse, Dieter saw that Schnabel had brought in reinforcements from the gate, three men and two dogs. Instead of their German shepherds, they had brought two bloodhounds from the estate kennel. The dogs howled as they approached.

Dieter recognized Kimmel, Stultzman, and Bauer. Each guard had two flashlights and was scanning the surrounding gardens. Dieter pushed past Schnabel and entered the guesthouse to check for himself. "Her suitcase is still here."

He returned outside to address Schnabel. "Are you sure the gate's protected?"

"Wiener's there. You know that no one gets past Wiener."

Dieter knew what Schnabel was implying because Kurt Wiener was one of the toughest men on Schnabel's team and had a temper when things didn't go his way. On two occasions, the Müllers had had to intercede with local police after Wiener had taken his responsibilities more seriously than his bosses had intended. To further complicate his resume, he had a reputation with women. His wife had divorced him, ostensibly for beating her; rumors abounded that he hated women. If Schnabel told Wiener that no one was to pass through the gate, then it would be so.

Dieter took command. "Okay! She's here somewhere. Let's start look—"

Manfred Kimmel, the only person on the Müller staff who could be considered overweight, interrupted. "Sir, I saw her when she left her cabin."

"When, Kimmel?"

"I'd say about five or ten minutes before eight. She headed toward the house. I watched her enter the tunnel myself. She didn't come back out. I'm sure of it."

Dieter and Schnabel led the way back to the tunnel. Inside, they came to the intersection, stopped, and scanned both directions. No point in looking straight ahead because they would have seen her as they waited on the porch.

"Give me one of your lights." Dieter motioned toward Kimmel.

"Over here!" Schnabel pointed to the ground in front of him. He bent down and picked up pieces of something, spreading them out on his hand. "I think your cousin was hungry."

Dieter walked closer and shone his own light on Schnabel's palm. "Okay, everybody. Let's head off in this direction. Start in the southeast corner, blanket the area, and move clockwise. She's here somewhere."

While the others proceeded, Dieter hesitated. "Kimmel."

Kimmel stopped and walked back. "Yes, sir."

"Why don't you check out the other end?" Dieter pointed in the opposite direction.

The remaining group of five men and two dogs made their way through the southern branch of the tunnel and headed toward the chain-link fence that divided the estate from the residential areas outside. The dogs knew that something was up, and they bayed intermittently.

Dieter, Axel, and Schnabel walked directly toward the chain-link fence where it intersected the water. It didn't stop at the water's edge but continued out another seventy-five feet, extending from the bottom to a minimum of four feet above the water. Beyond that distance, another twenty-five feet of it rested just near the water's surface, depending upon the tides. Anyone attempting to leave the compound by water had to swim at least one hundred feet beyond the shoreline.

It wasn't long before Stultzman yelled out. Rather than proceed to the fence, he had headed straight to the water's edge. The others hurried over.

On the sandy beach, about fifteen feet from the water, under a low-hanging tree, lay Kipling's black clothing. Footsteps, now mostly eroded by the lapping water, disappeared into the dark water. Dieter trained his flashlight on the water at the end of the fence. He saw nothing.

There was a moment of silence as they realized the implications of what they saw: that Kipling had escaped the compound by swimming around the protective fence. Fortunately, only a short time had passed. She couldn't have gotten far. Dieter briefly considered ordering a boat to patrol the waters but decided otherwise. There wasn't time.

Axel issued the order this time. "Gunter, Stultzman, head outside the compound. You know where to look. She'll return to shore at the first opportunity." He pointed to the remaining guard, Leon Bauer, the dogs' handler. "You stay here."

Schnabel and Stultzman took off running toward the front gate. Dieter yelled after them. "Radio back immediately!" Schnabel waved his hand in the air.

Axel picked up Kipling's black clothing and gave it to Bauer. The two bloodhounds had been a fixture on the compound for years. Particularly for this situation, Bauer kept them on a leash. They had a reputation for heading off on a hunt for no good reason.

Dieter understood Axel's thinking. Bloodhounds were one of the best breeds for tracking. He watched as Bauer rubbed Kipling's clothing around the dogs' noses. Dogs of this breed could lock onto a scent in seconds.

As they watched the process, Dieter and Axel realized that something was wrong. The dogs seemed confused.

*   *   *

Kipling had a clear view of her guesthouse from her vantage point, the maintenance building closest to the north beach. Once she had exited the tunnel to the north, too far distant from the guardhouse to be seen, she had run there for cover. Inside, crouching beneath one of the windows, she watched as the action unfolded in front of her.

First, someone, presumably Schnabel, had met up with three of the gate guards and entered her suite. Minutes later, two men appeared from the opposite direction, probably Dieter and Axel. Aside from the barking of the dogs, the building's walls muted their voices.

Once the group entered the tunnel, Kipling had to make a decision. The danger of leaving too soon was that she did not know which way the men would turn at the intersection inside the tunnel. Her pursuers may not have seen the crumbs of food she had left behind to trick them. If they exited the tunnel on her side, they could easily spot her in the open. She cracked the door and listened.

To Kipling's relief, the dogs gave them away. Their sound was certainly too distant to have come from the tunnel exit nearest her. They had headed in the opposite direction.

Kipling opened the door enough to slide out, listened, and closed the door behind her. She crouched down and crept back toward the rear of the shed. There, opposite the tunnel and facing the beach, she pushed herself flat against the wall. *What was that?*

Kipling heard a sound to her left. Milliseconds later, she noticed a light. *Shit!* A single guard was walking some fifteen feet to Kipling's left, his flashlight scanning the darkness on either side of him. His right hand rested on his holstered gun. Kipling looked left and to his rear. He was alone.

This was serious trouble. Not only did he block her path to the beach, but if he saw her, he would yell out and alert the others.

Kipling reacted immediately. She had no choice. If she waited, he would have moved too far away. And if he turned around, he would see her immediately.

With the guard walking slowly toward the beach some twenty feet distant, Kipling took off running toward him at full speed. In her mind flashed another occasion when she had reacted the same way, four years earlier, in Fort Collins, Colorado, when she had had to disarm the terrorist, Ghali. Although she had practically destroyed her shoulder in the process, she had achieved her goal. This time, it wasn't clear that the result would be as satisfactory.

Kipling had traveled half the distance to the man before he heard her movement. In contrast to her Colorado experience, where Ghali hadn't turned in time, the guard was quick enough to rotate completely to face Kipling. As she sped toward him, she dropped her backpack. Instinctively, she transformed her forward momentum into a formidable weapon. At once, Kipling's body extended horizontally with the ground, her legs folded, knees almost to her chin, and feet aimed like a compressed battering ram at the guard's torso. In the split second before impact, Kipling thrust her legs forward. The rush of air escaping the man's mouth was palpable.

Kipling fell to the soft earth uninjured. She quickly leaped over to the overweight guard, grabbing a nearby stone but not sure of what her next action would be. Should she knock him out? There'd be a real danger she'd kill him in the process.

God smiled on Kipling. As she straddled him, rock poised, a wheezing sound revealed the obvious: she had knocked the wind out of his lungs. From a similar experience during high school soccer, she knew that he was temporarily harmless.

Kipling crouched and looked around. No other threats. She noted the guard's handgun. Tempted to take it along, she decided not to. *No matter what happens, I'm not going to shoot anyone, particularly my cousins.* Instead, she removed it from the holster and threw it out of reach. She then grabbed her backpack and took off running up the beach toward the northern fence. Her dark-colored backpack, together with black slacks and blouse, did a good job of obscuring her in the dark shadows.

As she ran, she complimented herself on altering her original strategy. At the beach during the afternoon, she had intended to change into identical, clean, dark clothing from her backpack and leave her dirty clothes on the beach as a diversion, suggesting that she had swum away. Once she realized that the security staff had dogs, she decided instead to leave behind her clean, unscented clothing. The downside was that the dogs' handler would realize that she had tricked them. But, she thought, that was better than being chased by dogs.

Kipling jogged close to the water's edge. Moonlight accented the shoreline. Another seventy-five feet ahead, she could see the fence where it entered the water.

Suddenly the sound of the baying dogs became louder. No doubt, they had discovered her ruse.

*   *   *

Dieter had examined the clothes himself and realized that Kipling had duped them; he had seen her sweating in his office earlier. These clothes were clean. He immediately recalled Schnabel and Stultzman and told them to rendezvous at the front gate. Dieter was positive that Kipling had not swum off from the southern beach.

Dieter, Axel, and Bauer arrived at the gate moments before Schnabel and Stultzman. Wiener marched back and forth, taking his duty very seriously. Before Dieter had an opportunity to explain what had happened, Schnabel's walkie-talkie crackled. Since all the guards stood in front of him, Dieter assumed that it was Kimmel, who had gone off separately in the tunnel.

Schnabel answered. "Go ahead, Kimmel."

There was silence. Again, static and crackling but with no other sound.

Dieter had given the order to Kimmel. "When we all turned left to go to the southern beach, I sent Kimmel north, through the tunnel."

As a group, Dieter, Axel, Schnabel, the two guards, and the two dogs took off in that direction.

*　　*　　*

Seeing the fence ahead, Kipling stepped into the water to hide her tracks and slogged through the remaining distance to the chain-link fence. She looked briefly to her left, out into the water, and considered the option of escaping in that direction, that prospect prompted by a childhood memory.

As a youngster, Kipling had been called cantankerous. She had had a temper too, a quality that had ameliorated over the years. Recalling one particular manifestation of that anger still made her cringe.

For many years, she and her parents had vacationed in a lakeside cabin during the summer. For some long-forgotten reason, the eight-year-old had taken offense to something her mother had said to her, probably a well-deserved reprimand. With temper in tow, she decided to punish her parents and formulated a fiendish retribution.

After lunch, Kipling headed toward the lake, making sure her tracks were visible before entering the water. Because swimming had come naturally to the precocious child, she swam off but didn't go far. Once away from the shore, she made a right-angled turn and swam toward the shoreline. Instead of returning to land, she hid in the water among bushes near the shore.

When Kipling's parents came to look for her and saw tracks that disappeared into the water, they became hysterical, yelling her name repeatedly across the water. Soon, neighbors got involved, followed by a flotilla of rowboats plying the waters. When they came near the bushes, Kipling ducked underwater and breathed through a large drinking straw she had taken from the kitchen. After an hour or so of more commotion, even this rambunctious child realized she had punished them enough.

To her discredit, Kipling decided that it wasn't to her advantage to come clean. So, swimming underwater through the bushes, she escaped into the woods. Doubling back behind their cabin, she approached her parents from the rear.

"What's going on?" Kipling yelled innocently as she approached. Her mother and father, by then paralyzed with fear that their only child had drowned, showered her with hugs and kisses, so happy to see their darling Linda again.

Kipling chose never to tell her parents what had really happened. Years later, she still recoiled at the cruelty she had inflicted on well-meaning people.

Pushing aside that memory, Kipling decided that hiding in an ocean or swimming away was not an optimal solution for this situation, particularly since she had made plans for another way to escape. She turned right instead, edging her way back onto land and through the dense vegetation that completely smothered the fence on either side. Once inside the thicket, Kipling crawled on her stomach for another fifteen feet. Whatever shrubbery this was, not only was it dense, which left her in complete blackness, but it also had thorns that poked through her pants and blouse. Kipling stopped, reached back, and removed her backpack. By touch, she found her LED flashlight. What it revealed was unbelievably dense brush. Particularly with the thorns, she couldn't go much farther.

Kipling heard the dogs yelping as they moved up the beach. It wouldn't be long before they came to the spot where she had entered the water. She crawled another five feet and couldn't go any farther. She had almost screamed out when a thorn penetrated her thigh. This location would have to do.

Painfully repositioning herself into a crouch, Kipling at once felt another thorn pierce her shoulder. She had been dragging her backpack by her side. She opened the large compartment on the top and reached to the bottom, where she felt the reassuring mass, all twelve ounces of it, of the single item that she had transferred from her suitcase back at the hotel.

Kipling trained her light on the fence. Standard issue chain-link. It wouldn't be a problem. A marvel of compactness and mechanical gearing, the Coblank L5000X, a mechanical bolt cutter only seven inches long, would easily create an escape hole through the stiff wire. With carbide cutting tips and triple-reduction gearing, the L5000X could cut through wire or cabling as thick as three-eighths of an inch, and all with the power of only one nine-volt battery.

Kipling completed the last of a dozen or so cuts to create a hole big enough to crawl through. As she finished, she heard voices clearly. German words barked out staccato from more than one person. She recognized Dieter's voice. Before turning her body around to face in their direction, she extinguished her light. She then backed through the hole in the fence, butt first. As she drew the last of her body through the opening, the dogs' howls intensified. They had sensed her presence and were located just on the other side of the hedge! She could see flashlight beams trying to penetrate the six feet of dense vegetation. She recognized Schnabel's voice, yelling.

Reaching through the opening, Kipling retrieved her backpack. Not knowing whether there might be parallel fences, she made a conscious decision to hang on to the L5000X in her right hand.

From only a few feet away, the voices sounded as agitated as the dogs. There wasn't much time. She had to exit the hedge on the outside and hit the ground running. Facing away from the fence, she again hit the switch to her light, looking for an easy way through the thicket. There wasn't one. Instead, she grabbed the back of the backpack with both hands and set off on hands and knees, perpendicular to the fence, using the suede covering as a shield as she crawled forward through the blackness. It was all she could do to keep from yelling out in pain as the thorns penetrated her legs and arms. Fortunately, the backpack protected her face and eyes. In what seemed a much longer time than it actually was, Kipling burst through to the other side.

*   *   *

Dieter was beside himself with anger. Kipling had now tricked them twice. Earlier, they had found Kimmel after his encounter with Kipling. He pointed in the direction of the northern beach. Except for him, everyone took off running. It was easy to follow Kipling's feet in the sand. When the tracks entered the water, they again thought that she had decided to swim for it. Schnabel ordered

Stultzman to walk along the water's edge to the fence. There he discovered Kipling's tracks again, leading to the conclusion that she was hiding inside the hedge.

The hedge was nearly impenetrable. Their head gardener had recommended the Pyracantha bush specifically because of its unforgiving nature, its terrible thorns. A few years back, a local teenager, intent on bragging to his friends that he had climbed the fence into the Müller estate, had made it as far as the fence. There he waited, until his screams brought help from the guardhouse. No one since had made that mistake.

Dieter stood and imagined what was going on inside the hedge. The dogs continued howling, and the guards tried in vain to see anything inside.

Axel suggested that they just wait her out. Dieter, ever mindful of Murphy's Law—if anything can go wrong, it will—issued one more order to Schnabel. "Just to be safe, send Wiener to the other side."

*   *   *

Now outside the perimeter that enclosed the compound, Kipling emerged from the thicket much the worse for wear. Thorns had penetrated her clothing many times as she inched her way through four feet of needled hell. Seeing nothing but open space in front of her, she raised herself to her haunches, excited at the prospect of finally making her escape in her car. Unfortunately, in her peripheral vision, Kipling picked up the sight of a man running full tilt toward her.

She considered her options. As he raced toward her, Kipling questioned her earlier decision not to take the other guard's gun. Still, there was only one of him. And with arms pumping, he hadn't drawn his weapon. If she tried to outrun him, he might decide otherwise. Kipling concluded that her only option was to take him on. Waiting for the inevitable, she stood tall and dropped her backpack, comforted somewhat by the weight of the L5000X gripped tightly in her right hand.

As her assailant came running toward her, his bearing became more menacing. She could tell that he had no intention of stopping until he had bowled her over. Kipling stood her ground and waited.

The bull male charging her had the momentum to do some serious damage, but he obviously had no idea what to do with his mass. As his hands reached for Kipling's torso, she sidestepped his advance. Still, he managed to grab some of her clothing. As his body passed in front of hers, Kipling had the advantage and took it. Gripping the L5000X as tightly as possible, she swung her right arm in a large loop, catching the back of her assailant's head.

The guard released his grip, and Kipling remained standing. He landed hard, letting out a mighty bellow. To Kipling's surprise, he rebounded quickly and lunged toward her. Kipling was unprepared for such a quick recovery. He slammed into her. The impact jarred her bones and forced the wind from her lungs. She felt sick, gasping for air. He didn't stop. His momentum pushed her back until she lost footing. The world suddenly spun, and she knew that she was going down; his considerable bulk was coming down on top of her. Ignoring the nausea that roiled in her stomach, she concentrated on tightening her chest muscles. The last thing she wanted was to suffer the same fate as the guard she had encountered by the maintenance shack.

The look visible in the man's eyes was terrifying. Whatever his job at the estate, he obviously had issues. Kipling's heart raced. Outweighing her by perhaps sixty pounds, his mass on her body kept her rigid. His next action was to slap Kipling's face hard with his left hand. She saw stars as the man's hands found their way to her neck, thumbs pressing down mercilessly.

Unless something dramatic happened, Kipling knew that she was done for. Involuntarily, her chest quivered as she tried first to inhale and then to exhale, with neither action succeeding.

Just when Kipling thought she would pass out, the pressure on her windpipe relaxed for an instant. She managed a partial breath, enough to restore some mental clarity and lower the degree of absolute panic permeating her being. To protect herself, she remained motionless. She soon understood what was happening. The man on top of her had become aroused and was nuzzling her left breast. This guy was getting it on with a woman he was simultaneously strangling!

Should she try to scream? Kipling knew that would alert the posse on the other side of the fence. In a moment of clarity, Kipling gathered her wits and realized that both her arms were free. Better, she had maintained her grip on the object she held in her right hand. Although her adversary had eased his grasp briefly, both of his hands were still tight against her neck, his wrists pressed against the sides of her chest.

Kipling maneuvered her thumb to the topside of the L5000X, to the button that would activate the carbon-tipped blades. Although the device was designed to cut through only small diameter objects, the blades at the end spread to more than an inch apart.

Kipling knew that this device was her only hope. With what little oxygen remained in her extremities, she brought both hands inward toward her body, pressing the open mouth of the L5000X hard against the man's left wrist. Simultaneously, her left hand secured this arm several inches down from the wrist. When both hands made contact, she pressed the button. Not that much power would be necessary: flesh, blood, and bone would be like butter to this apparatus. Worried that she may have disabled the device when she had used it as a club a moment earlier, Kipling had never felt so happy as when she heard the whir of the electric motor. Both hands pressed hard to feed the man's wrist into the hungry mouth of her cable-cutting savior.

It took more than a second for the man on top of her to realize what was happening and then to respond to the excruciating pain as his left wrist was nearly severed. From the crunching sound that the blades made as they closed shut, Kipling knew that she had struck bone.

His scream splintered the quiet of the night. Both hands simultaneously released their grip on Kipling's body. She rolled to the right to dump the man's now limp body to the side. She watched as his right hand, perhaps involuntarily, went to the aid of the other one dangling from the end of his left arm.

Still gasping for air from her ordeal, Kipling trained her eyes in the direction of the guardhouse. It was still clear. She stood, fell immediately back to the ground, and tried again, this time successfully. She grabbed her backpack and was about to give the L5000X a mighty heave into the water about twenty feet away. At that instant, she recalled her father's admonition: *never burn a bridge just because it makes you feel good.* Standing behind her attacker so that he couldn't see, she tossed the device into the adjacent hedge.

With her heart racing and her lungs retching for air, Kipling doubled over. She raised her head, looked right, left, and straight ahead. Her car had to be somewhere to the left. She started slowly, wobbling back and forth as blood and oxygen returned to her extremities. Knowing that reinforcements would be arriving soon, it wasn't long before Kipling hit full stride. Still terrified, she looked behind her but saw nothing.

On the morning's trip from Miami to Cartagena, Kipling had memorized the schedule for this evening's returning flights. As she saw her rental car ahead, she prayed she'd make it in time to board the one departing at 10:10.

*   *   *

Still thinking that Kipling might be hiding in the brush on their side of the fence, Dieter and company stood guard. Faintly, however, they heard what sounded like a scuffle on the side opposite. It must be Wiener, thought Dieter.

Frozen in anticipation of Wiener's verbal announcement of what was happening, the Müller contingent waited.

The shriek that pierced the evening air made each of them involuntarily step backward. Their mouths dropped open as they tried to imagine what could cause the sickening human moans that followed. To make matters more confusing, they couldn't tell from the pitch of the sounds whether they came from a man or a woman.

CHAPTER 20

EMERGENCY EXIT

Rafael Nunez International Airport, Cartagena, Colombia: 10°26'46"N Latitude, 75°30'58"W Longitude
Thursday, 9:35 p.m., October 6, 2011

"Now boarding Zone 1." *Thank God!* Kipling had upgraded her coach ticket to first class to allow her to be one of the first to board the aircraft. It was hardly out of the question that her cousins had sent their goons to the airport in search of her.

The drive back to the airport had been uneventful enough—uneventful only if she could ignore the pain coming from one part of her body or another. She had no idea how badly she was bleeding until she crawled out of her rental car. Fortunately, the car seats were faced with leather, and she had time to wipe the surfaces.

Inside the airport, Kipling rushed to the first bathroom she could find. It would be less than optimum for someone to notice blood on her clothing and hands, some of it from her assailant's wrist. Fortunately, her black pants and blouse did a good job of hiding stains. Inside a large bathroom stall intended for the handicapped, she stripped and assessed the damage from the thorns she had crawled through: more than a dozen punctures deep enough to be oozing blood.

Before entering the bathroom stall, she had grabbed paper towels, soaking half in water. Kipling then employed the time-honored method used by men to stop bleeding from shaving cuts. After washing and drying the wounds, she added layers of toilet tissue to clot the blood. For the most severe gashes, it took four layers. For those on her back that she could not reach, there was nothing more she could do. Her final change of clothing from her backpack was identical to what she had on. One remaining accessory, a black baseball cap, would partially hide her face.

At the gate, Kipling checked the time: twenty-five minutes until departure. Her heart hammered as she waited for the first-class passengers in front of her to board. *Surely, they won't try to grab me in public.* Still, knowing the clout the Müllers no doubt possessed here in Colombia, nothing seemed out of the question. *Finally!* The agent scanned her boarding pass. Head down, she kept moving, arms cradling her backpack as she entered the Jetway.

* * *

Gunter Schnabel snapped shut his cell phone, having received Dieter's blessing. He watched as Kipling walked out of sight. She was wearing the same dark clothing—now with a hat—he had observed at the estate. He had made it to the gate only moments earlier, having sprinted from the Delta counter. Following her arrival in the afternoon, his men had determined Kipling's airline. He had taken a chance, and it had paid off. When he got to the airport, he purchased a ticket for the only remaining Delta flight leaving for the United States this evening, to Miami.

Schnabel's bosses would not be getting much sleep tonight. Back at the estate, once everyone realized that Kipling had bested his security personnel, Dieter Müller was furious. Schnabel had never seen him so angry. Schnabel had calmed him down with common sense, explaining that, until she left the country, they had an excellent chance of nabbing her.

Kipling had boarded the plane in Zone 1, likely flying first class in the forward part of the aircraft. At the Delta counter, Schnabel had purposely asked for a window seat toward the rear of the plane where he could remain unnoticed. To facilitate a brisk walk down the aisle to avoid being seen, he waited until everyone had boarded. His task would prove far easier if she thought that she had eluded her pursuers.

*   *   *

Kipling claimed her seat in the first row, 1D, the leftmost of four first-class seats, next to the window. She stowed her backpack in the overhead and waited. Until this aircraft left Colombia's terra firma, she knew that she wasn't safe. She had seen too many movies where local officials had boarded planes right before takeoff, in time to remove a fleeing, cornered passenger. Opening a hatch, jumping to the ground, and escaping across numerous runways did not seem like a realistic option.

Now that she was aboard, she intended to scrutinize each passenger to make sure that she didn't recognize anyone from the estate. She grabbed a magazine, held it up to hide her face, angled her head to the left, and inspected each person as he or she moved down the aisle.

Dozens of passengers passed by. The steady stream dwindled to a trickle.

*   *   *

Gunter Schnabel checked his watch. They'd be closing the door soon. He handed the agent his boarding pass and proceeded down the Jetway. He thought through his strategy, contingent upon his spotting Kipling before she saw him. Once he identified her, he would face quickly in the opposite direction so that she could not see his face. He had one advantage: no one else who had boarded the plane was dressed completely in black.

As Schnabel entered the first-class cabin, he couldn't believe his good fortune. Directly to his left in the front row sat Kipling, holding a magazine to cover her face. Black clothing, bottom and top. He immediately turned to face right and accelerated down the aisle.

Schnabel smiled to himself, realizing that his ingenuity had once again paid dividends. *Linda Kipling, you've met your match.*

Whether on this aircraft or in Miami, you're a dead woman. Now that he thought about it, though, why be in a rush? To take drastic action aboard the aircraft could prove risky. His quarry wasn't going anywhere. Near the end of the flight, he'd offer someone in the first row of the main cabin a monetary incentive to switch seats with him. He'd be right behind her as she exited the plane. Until then, he'd sit back and enjoy the flight.

As he made his way to row thirty-six, he turned and looked back but couldn't see much in the first-class section. No matter. He opened his cell phone to make the call. Dieter Müller would be pleased to know that the head of their security detail had this situation well in hand. The Müller family could sleep well tonight after all. Following that call, he'd make one more, to order up his own aircraft to meet him in Miami. After Kipling was dealt with, he'd chart a westward course—to Monterey, California.

* * *

Kipling was about ready to lower her magazine when one more pair of male legs revealed itself at the lower limits of her view. A flight attendant had just announced that all was in order and that the door would be closing.

As the man passed to her left, she turned in his direction. Unfortunately, he was looking to his right as he moved, now more quickly. *Strange.* In contrast to most passengers, he carried nothing: no bag, briefcase, or jacket. Kipling lifted herself from her seat to get a closer look. She accepted the risk that he might turn and spot her.

It was in the fraction of a second before he entered the main cabin that Kipling saw it. If he had held his left hand only slightly differently, she would never have caught it. The S-shaped scar was unmistakable. *Think! Was the scar on his left hand or on his right hand? He kissed my right hand while holding it with his right. The scar was on the opposite hand!* She hastily assessed the man's build. No doubt. This was Dieter's employee, the man she had met in the house when she arrived in Dieter's office this afternoon. *Gunter Schnabel.*

Kipling dropped back into her seat, shaking with fright. The man sitting next to her asked if something was wrong. *This can't be!* In the sixty-five minutes that had elapsed since she had gone running from the hedge at the estate, her cousins had sent Schnabel scurrying to the airport. He had determined what flight she was on, bought a ticket, and made it to the gate in time to board the plane.

With only an instant to decide, Kipling pondered her choices. She could stay on the aircraft and hope to elude Schnabel once they arrived in Miami. *No, that was no good!* He was probably already on the telephone arranging for someone to snatch her when she exited the plane.

Ignoring the confused look on the face of her seatmate, Kipling jerked herself out of the seat. She opened the overhead bin, flipped out her backpack, and lunged forward. "I'm getting off the plane," she announced to the flight attendant. As the confused woman stood back and watched, Linda Kipling jumped the gap and sprinted up the Jetway.

CHAPTER 21

INCIDENTS PAST

Federal Center for Data Examination, Las Vegas, Nevada, USA:
36°7'51"N Latitude, 115°10'13"W Longitude
Thursday, 7:45 p.m., October 6, 2011

Stigler's stomach growled as she scanned her notes dating from eight years earlier. Following his brilliant breakdown of the data from the Hyatt, Andrew Peters had begged off further discussion, saying that he had to pick up his daughter from school and that he would return after dinner. This interruption came at an opportune moment. The company name, Müller Industries, brought back a memory from her previous stint at FCDE. She chased down the folder, located in one of ten file cabinets Tom Uphouse had bequeathed her when she took over his job.

Except for a few lingering employees and the guards staffing the entry to FCDE, everyone had gone home for the night, and Stigler's office door stood open. She heard noises, looked up, and saw Peters carrying a Styrofoam container.

Peters smiled smugly. "I was right! I knew you wouldn't have the sense to eat. If you like meatloaf, mashed potatoes, and green beans, you're in luck."

"Bless you!" Realizing how famished she was, Stigler grabbed the box, opened it, and made a show of smelling the aromas from the home-cooked meal. She opened her desk drawer and removed the emergency utensils she kept there.

Peters was about to sit down. "You need something to drink."

With her mouth stuffed, Stigler nodded and pointed with her fork. "Diet Coke, please."

While Peters retrieved a can from their common refrigerator, Stigler wolfed down the food. He returned, pulled the metal tab on the can, and set it before her. As she continued eating, she pushed a manila folder across the desk.

Peters seemed pleased that he had done something good for his boss. "What's this?"

"Take a look."

While Peters perused the contents of the inch-thick file, Stigler finished her dinner. "What does this have to do with anything?" He glanced at the folder tab. "This is from 2003. Something about some strange noises picked up by the SOSUS grid."

Stigler made her way to her private, in-office bathroom, one of the benefits of being the director, and washed her utensils. On the return, she elaborated. "This was back when I was the military deputy under Tom. You know how, every once in a while, we hear or see things that we never figure out. You're looking at one of them. I puzzled over this one for months."

"What happened?"

"I was a junior knowledge engineer back then. Considered myself hot stuff, by the way." Stigler laughed. "I've been reviewing my notes ever since you left."

"And you think this has something to do with our murders in Washington?"

"I'll get to that." Stigler paused to stow her flatware. "You know what SOSUS is, right?"

"Of course. Sound Surveillance System. Relic of the Cold War, when our biggest worry was a Russian sub sneaking through the GIUK gap and blowing us to kingdom come. The good old days, actually. Underwater microphones, very sensitive, can pick up a whale fart."

Suddenly noticing that it was getting dark outside, Stigler stood and opened the drapes that she often kept closed during the daytime. The lights from the Strip splayed out in front of her.

"Correct. On the twenty-fifth of November in 2003, SOSUS picked up an underwater signal that, according to the experts who interpret these things, sounded like a submarine imploding. As if one had sunk. And what's more, there were two of them."

"Two implosions?"

"Correct."

"I assume these were in the Atlantic somewhere."

"Just north of Puerto Rico. And following the SOSUS implosions, there were corresponding thumps recorded on seismographs in Bermuda, Guantanamo Bay, and Barbados. We triangulated the seismic signals to the same location as the SOSUS."

Stigler knew it couldn't last. Peters returned to his usual standing position. "So you're saying that two submarines bit the dust, at the same time, and at the same place."

"Within about fifteen minutes of each other."

Peters nodded, digesting what he was hearing. "The obvious explanation is that two submarines collided, and both dropped to the ocean floor. How likely is that, though, that they'd both sink—" He stopped in midsentence.

"What?" Stigler noticed Peters's eyes fixate at the same time he stopped talking.

Peters cupped his mouth in his left hand and squeezed, his face suggesting confusion. "It's probably nothing." His earlier demeanor returned. "As I was saying, how likely would it be for two submarines to sink at the same time?"

What was that all about? "I agree. Of course, the first thing we did was to check with the navy, and they reported nothing out of the ordinary. For months afterward, we kept our ear to the ground, wondering if anyone had lost a submarine or two in the Atlantic. After months of disappointment, we, or rather I, gave up. I doubt anyone has looked at this file since."

For someone in their business, Peters asked the obvious. "Nothing from satellite imagery?"

"It took us about an hour to get a bird in place. Since it was dark, we had only infrared."

"And?"

"One large shipping vessel in the vicinity, steaming south."

"Oil slick? Debris?"

"We looked the next day but found nothing. Because I had no other leads, I made a point of following that ship. And once I had visible imagery, I got a better look. This was a *large* ship. I trailed it to Brazil. I watched it for a couple of days, the longest I could justify use of our high-res. Other than the offloading of several large containers, I didn't see anything else unusual. After that, I gave up, and here you see the file."

"That's an interesting tale, Captain, but you have yet to answer my question. What the hell does this have to do with the price of salami?"

Stigler closed the draperies. It was time to go home. "What this has to do with what's happened in Washington may be nothing at all. But if you don't believe in coincidences, then it may be related." She gathered her jacket, continued to the door, and held it open, suggesting that Peters go home too.

Peters held his ground. "You know, don't you, that you have a dramatic streak in you? I'm not leaving until you bring the hammer down."

"My parents used to tell me the same thing. Okay, here goes. The ship that I followed to Brazil, as well as the port where it docked, was owned by Müller Industries. I'm sure you remember from this afternoon that Gunter Schnabel works for that company." A pause later, Stigler added, "Is that significant? I don't know, but I think it merits further investigation."

Peters nodded, his puzzled look returning. "You don't mind, do you, if I borrow your file to look at in the morning?"

CHAPTER 22

INTENDED RENDEZVOUS

Müller Family Compound, Cartagena, Colombia: 10°23'36"N Latitude, 75°32'12"W Longitude
Friday, 6:20 a.m., October 7, 2011

Dieter Müller couldn't decide if he should have fired Schnabel or given him a bonus for quick thinking. After deciding to do neither, he slammed down the bedroom phone. He buzzed Marta and asked that she wake Axel. They'd meet in Dieter's office.

Kipling's previous night's shenanigans had fostered a series of late-night emotions: disappointment that Kipling had escaped, followed by relief that Schnabel had cornered her on an airplane flying to Miami. And now, repeated disappointment.

Thinking back on the events from the previous evening, Dieter couldn't fathom that his cousin, Linda Kipling, a simple government scientist from California, had outfoxed not only him and his brother, but a crack security team as well. *Crack? In fact, they looked more like bumbling idiots!* Even after she had snaked her way through the fence and the Pyracantha, Wiener had represented the final obstacle that should have prevented her from going farther.

When they had caught up to Wiener on the opposite side of the fence, no one could believe what they saw. He lay on the ground, gushing blood from a hand severed at the wrist. How Kipling had overcome a guy as tough as Wiener was mindboggling. Even using a knife to accomplish such an act seemed impossible. Dieter couldn't wait for his explanation.

Kimmel, the first of the guards to have had a run-in with Kipling, saved Wiener's life by applying his belt as a tourniquet to Wiener's upper arm. Kimmel and Bauer then took him to the hospital. At 1:45 in the morning, word came down that surgeons had reattached the partially amputated hand. How successful the surgery would be remained to be seen.

Following Wiener's departure to the hospital, Schnabel had made the logical suggestion that he rush to the airport to ensure that Kipling did not leave the country.

Dieter entered his office and headed straight to the window. He opened the curtains, the morning sun offering its kiss to the tropical horizon. Before long, Axel charged through the doorway. "What's happened?"

His mind fuzzy after only a few hours sleep, Dieter limited himself to just three words. "Schnabel lost Kipling."

Axel plopped himself into his usual chair. "You told me they were on the same plane to Miami. How could he lose her on an airplane?"

Dieter backed away from the curtains and leaned forward on his knuckles on the desk. "Gunter says that when he got on the plane, Kipling was sitting in first class. He was one hundred percent certain. The only thing that could have happened, he said, was that she got off the plane after he had taken his seat. From where he sat, he admitted that he wouldn't have seen that."

"Well then, it's obvious that she recognized him when he boarded and jumped ship." Axel stood, hands in his pockets. "And Gunter didn't know this until they landed in Miami?"

"Essentially. About ten minutes before landing, he noticed that she wasn't in her seat. By then, more than two hours had passed, about twelve thirty our time. On the ground, Gunter called his people to run down the manifests for all flights leaving Cartagena. There was an eleven o'clock flight to Panama City, and Linda *was* on that one. In fact, she arrived there about the same time as Schnabel landed in Miami." Dieter backed away from the desk.

"But here's the good news. When she scheduled the Panama City flight, she also booked her complete return: Houston, Dallas, San Francisco, and then Monterey."

"If I know Gunter, he's pissed as hell and will fly to Panama City to track her down. I doubt there were any flights out of there until morning." He checked his watch. "Besides, it'd be easier there."

Dieter understood Axel's thinking. Maneuvering in a Spanish-speaking country, particularly one where bribes carried some weight, would prove easier. "That was Gunter's first thought. Before he left here, he'd had the sense to order his own plane to Miami."

"So why are we talking here? It's only a couple of hours from Miami to Panama City. Gunter should have arrived there before Linda left."

Dieter kept his emotions in check to cover his annoyance that Axel always expected things to play out with perfect German precision. "Gunter's no fool. He did the math. As I said, when Linda bought her Panama City flight, she also booked the rest of her trip, the first being an early morning flight to Houston. Six o'clock. Gunter said the flight time from Miami to Panama City is almost three hours. Remember that Gunter's plane didn't arrive in Miami until one thirty or so. Assume another hour to refuel. So that's two thirty. Even under the best of conditions, he'd have arrived in Panama City only minutes before Linda flew out."

Axel frowned. "Okay. So the backup is to intercept her in Houston?"

"That's the plan. Gunter says it'll take more than four hours for Kipling to fly from Panama to Houston. She'll get there about ten thirty. Since it's only a two-and-a-half-hour flight from Miami, Gunter decided to give his crew some shuteye. When he called a half hour ago, they had just left Miami. They'll arrive in Houston in plenty of time to intercept her at the gate."

"That won't be that easy in the States. How will Gunter even get through to the gate?"

Dieter nodded. "I asked him the same question. He said he has Transportation Security Administration credentials that will work at any airport."

"So all we have to do now is wait. What time did you say? Ten thirty?"

"Yeah. And that's ten thirty Houston time, same as us." Dieter didn't have to remind Axel that Colombia didn't use daylight saving time.

"This time we'll get her."

After what had happened last night, Dieter felt less than certain. In an unusual display of bravado, he voiced hope. "I think Linda has finally outfoxed herself. She has no idea whom she's up against." What they had going for them was Schnabel. He didn't take failure well.

Physically exhausted, Dieter wanted to conclude the conversation.

Axel maintained his gaze. "You haven't changed your mind, have you?"

Dieter knew what he meant and felt sick about it. "Nothing's changed. Gunter's orders are to make sure Linda doesn't leave the airport alive."

CHAPTER 23

WAKE-UP CALL

Halcyon Heights home subdivision, Monterey, California:
36°33'30"N Latitude, 121°46'28"W Longitude
Friday, 4:25 a.m., October 7, 2011

Fully clothed, dozing on his living room recliner, Silverstein awoke with a snort. Another cup of coffee was in order.

Following delivery of Kipling's letter the previous morning at NRL, Silverstein had spent the day fretting. He had responded impulsively after reading her letter, vowing to the office walls that he wouldn't just sit back and do nothing, that he would charge off like the white knight he imagined himself to be. But reality soon set in. Mostly because he had no idea of what he could do to help her, but also because she'd be furious if he didn't abide by her request, he acceded to Kipling's plea to wait.

At work, Silverstein recognized that he had turned into a worthless government asset. He signed out for leave and headed home, intending to spend the day surfing the Net, scrutinizing bits of a puzzle that had fascinating implications. He and Kipling were in possession of secrets that had global ramifications.

Armed with a fresh cup from the kitchen, Silverstein returned to his recliner. He stared at his clipboard, where he had written the salient points:

> *Two NRL scientists missing in Greenland*
> *Several days later, their boss, Rick Uphouse, is murdered in Washington DC*
> *A day later, a second NRL scientist, James Bragley, is killed*
> *From Uncle Friedrich's letters: "Sometimes the only way you can build a new society is to start from the ashes up."*
> *From Uncle Friedrich's letters: "Remember when we were kids, and we played Vikings, with me Erik the Red, and you his wife, Thjodhilde. Remember where we had to go? I can tell you that we have returned."*
> *From Uncle Friedrich's letters: "When we're finished with what we began last month, the world will know the true meaning of global climate change." Dated June 14, 2009, only a little more than two years ago.*

At the office, before Sally had surprised him with Kipling's letter, he had made the connection that made his mind spin: the reference to Erik the Red. In the latter half of the tenth century, after some family troubles, Red's parents had fled from Norway to Iceland. Then, after being accused of several murders himself, the authorities banished Red to Greenland. *I can tell you that we have returned.* Was Kipling's uncle boasting that the Müller family had returned to Greenland? Did he mean it literally or figuratively? And was it a coincidence that two of Silverstein's Washington colleagues had gone missing on that same island?

With thoughts of Greenland, the missing NRL scientists, and global climate change crisscrossing his mind, Silverstein's eyelids grew heavy. It wasn't long before he heard an alarm. Alone on the Greenland ice, he responded to the threat by running away. The agitation inside his head was enough to waken him. When he opened his eyes and saw light beaming from the windows, he checked his wristwatch. It was after seven!

Silverstein faced right, collecting his bearings. The deafening sound had not come from his dream. It was the telephone next to his chair.

"Hello."

"It's me."

"Where the hell are you? Are you still in Colombia?"

"I'm on a plane, on my way to Atlanta. This one still has the back-of-the-seat telephones."

Silverstein pushed himself up from the recliner, mostly to restore blood flow in his still-fuzzy cerebral cortex. "Atlanta? I saw the itinerary on your desk. I thought you were flying through Miami."

"Yeah. Well, it's a long story. Listen . . ."

Something's wrong! Silverstein stood stiffly, phone pressed hard against his ear, staring at the ceiling. Kipling sounded exhausted and wasn't making much sense. "Talk to me, Linda!"

After a very un-Kipling-like pause, she spoke deliberately. "I can't go home to Monterey, Victor. From Atlanta, I'm flying direct to San Francisco. Could you meet me there?"

Kipling was asking for help. "I've told you before, Linda, that all you have to do is ask. I'll pick you up at the airport."

Her response was unexpected. "No! I'd prefer you not do that. Just give me the name of a hotel, and I'll meet you."

A thought came to mind. "I have a better idea. I have a friend who has a condo in the City. He's told me it's mine anytime I want. I'll set that up, call work, and hit the road. How does that sound?"

"Thank you, Victor."

Silverstein had stayed at his friend's place once before and remembered the address. He gave it to Kipling. "Give me a time window, would you, so I know when to expect you?"

"My plane leaves Atlanta at one thirty. That's ten thirty your time. Hold on a second."

Silverstein could hear a flight attendant making an announcement in the background.

"Okay. I'm supposed to land in San Francisco at three thirty. So expect me sometime around five."

Silverstein was already planning his day. "Got it. I have plenty of time. I'll drop by work instead of calling in. Anything you need?"

"Thanks for asking. Since you're stopping by work, in my left desk drawer is my apartment key. Go there and bring me a change of clothes, a pair or two of pants and some tops. Some underwear too. Maybe some toiletry items. You'll find them."

She didn't take any luggage to Colombia? "Anything else?"

"Yeah, if you don't mind. Do you have a first-aid kit?"

What? "Listen, Linda. You're scaring me. Are you okay?"

"I've got to go, Victor. I'll see you this afternoon." The line went dead.

It was 7:14. Plenty of time to clean up, make arrangements with his friend, wrap up at work, drop by Kipling's apartment, and make the two-hour drive to San Francisco.

Silverstein hurried to the hall closet where he kept his earthquake supplies. California residents needed to be ready for the big one. He retrieved his humongous first-aid kit, complete enough to service his own field hospital, and then stopped to think. *Why doesn't Linda want to come back to Monterey? Is someone following her?* With that thought, his next stop was his bedroom safe.

Sixty miles south of Cuba, Delta flight, Panama City, Panama, to Atlanta, Georgia, USA
Friday, 10:14 a.m., EDT, October 7, 2011

Linda Kipling hadn't wanted to talk anymore. She snapped the phone back into its slot and pushed her seat into the full reclining mode. The passenger load on this flight was low; no one sat nearby.

Kipling couldn't get the previous night's events out of her mind. Because she had to be sure that Schnabel had not seen her exit the aircraft in Cartagena, she had hid near the gate to confirm that the aircraft departed with her pursuer aboard. Once Kipling knew that was so, she had run frantically back to the airline counters, to find *any* flight leaving Colombia at that late hour.

Fortune had smiled. There was an eleven o'clock turboprop to Panama City, Panama, a short flight to a neighboring country that would put some distance between her and her cousins. The helpful agent arranged her entire itinerary back to Monterey, albeit with a convoluted route through Houston. Kipling didn't care. Getting home alive was what was important.

The flight to Panama had landed after midnight, leaving Kipling alone in the terminal to await the six o'clock to Houston. The five-and-a half-hour wait hardly justified finding a hotel. Instead, she curled up in a secluded corner and tried to sleep.

Kipling had nearly dozed off when she sat bolt upright. *How had her cousins' henchman, Gunter Schnabel, known that she would be on that very flight to Miami?* She hadn't even known it herself until she arrived at the Cartagena airport. And in time for him to drive to the airport, purchase a ticket, and make it to the gate? She considered the possibilities. The only explanation was that Schnabel knew that she had flown to Colombia on Delta Airlines. Figuring that she would try to leave on the same airline, he must have gone immediately to that counter.

Think, Linda, think! How could Schnabel have known which airline she had arrived on? Kipling recalled that she had made a point of removing her luggage tag back at the hotel. There was nothing inside the suitcase to suggest Delta as her carrier. Further, she hadn't mentioned to her cousins that she had flown from Miami, a possible giveaway. And for her entire stay at the compound, Kipling had kept her return ticket inside her pocket. All of this suggested that Schnabel had ascertained that information on his own.

From a sitting position on the carpet, Kipling buried her face in her hands. If Schnabel had the capability to search airline databases to find her initial ticket, it wasn't too much of a stretch to think he would repeat the process and determine her new route through Panama City.

I have to assume the worst! The flight to Miami has arrived by now, and Schnabel knows that I've flown the coop.

Kipling ran the numbers in her head. Assuming that Schnabel had access to a private jet, would he have enough time to fly from Miami and arrive in Panama before six? Kipling breathed easier when she realized that was a stretch. Her next reaction frightened her more: they had more than enough time to catch up with her in Houston!

Sleeping fitfully until five, Kipling then dragged herself around the terminal. The airline television monitors suggested another option, an American flight to Atlanta that departed at 7:30. When the agent arrived at his station at six, Kipling was the first in line.

Apart from the irritation of spending money on yet another fare, the American itinerary had one fewer connection and arrived in San Francisco about the same time as her previous itinerary. If Schnabel intended to catch her in Houston, he'd be disappointed.

Safely winging her way toward Atlanta, the hypnotic hum of the aircraft brought Kipling's thoughts back to the present. Still paranoid, she released her seatbelt and half stood, peering about the aircraft. She flinched as one of her shoulder injuries made itself known. She sat down, adjusted her clothing to remove pressure from the wound, and fell asleep instantly.

CHAPTER 24

CLASSIFIED INFORMATION

Federal Center for Data Examination, Las Vegas, Nevada, USA: 36°7'51"N Latitude, 115°10'13"W Longitude Friday, 8:05 a.m., October 7, 2011

Jane Stigler made her way through the casino that comprised the bottom floor of the flamboyant hotel in which the FCDE made its home. Except for a single locked stairwell, a private elevator provided the only access to the top floor of the building. Many of her employees routinely took the stairs as a way of staying in shape. It never ceased to amaze her that, no matter the time of day, folks waited in line to give away their hard-earned money to the gambling establishment. It didn't take the considerable computing power of the FCDE to tell her that the odds favored the house.

After exiting the elevator, Stigler walked the hallway leading to the entrance to their facility, entered the nondescript suite that fronted the FCDE, and greeted the two guards who staffed the formal entrance. The steady hum of air conditioning and computer equipment partly muffled their responses.

Instead of heading to her office, Stigler took a detour. Most employees were on the job, their office doors open. Several offered greetings. Peters's door was closed, but she could see light under the door. She knocked, waited, and was about to leave when Peters appeared at the end of a stretched phone cord. "I'm sorry, Andrew. Didn't know you were on the phone."

Peters cupped the phone's microphone. "Give me a few minutes. I'll be right down."

Stigler mouthed *sorry* and walked off.

As she entered her office, Stigler recalled Peters's reaction during their conversation the previous evening. What amplified that memory just now was that Peters was speaking on a STU-III phone. That meant that he was engaged in a classified discussion. STU-III telephones had become operational in 1987 when the National Security Agency introduced them to government facilities. That technology allowed two parties, assuming they each had their own STU-III, to converse through an encrypted medium that prevented eavesdropping.

Stigler barely had time to sit down before Peters knocked on her open door. She asked him point blank. "What was it last night that you reacted to?"

"Can I close the door?"

Stigler waved her hand. Something was up.

Peters stepped to his usual spot. "What I'm going to tell you is classified. I've just received clearance to tell you." He nodded toward the window.

Stigler knew the drill. She rose and closed the drapes. Both knew that it was electronically feasible to eavesdrop on conversations through window glass. She also understood that Peters's nod meant that he was about to give her privileged information. Many civilians would assume that Stigler's Top Secret clearance gave her license to know all government secrets. But all government employees understood that any classified information he or she possessed was on a *need to know* basis only. Stigler returned to her seat and waited.

"You know that I worked for DTRA."

Stigler was well aware of Peters's history. "Of course. The Defense Threat Reduction Agency. We stole you! I think they still hate us for that."

"After the Cold War, one of our jobs was to implement several treaties. Those treaties concerned weapons of mass destruction that existed in various Eastern Bloc countries. The idea was to round them up and destroy them following the breakup of the Soviet Union."

"That's the way I understood it."

Peters seemed to reminisce as he spoke. "It was common knowledge that the Soviet maritime fleet had fallen into severe decay in the 1990s. In particular, the Soviets mothballed numerous nuclear submarines that had reached the end of their operational life. The international community understood this and contributed money to dismantle them. It was expensive. Six to ten million dollars apiece."

"I'm with you."

"My job was to keep track of those subs, especially the nuclear ones. I spent most of my days looking at spy satellite images. The big worry at the time, other than ridding the subs of their nuclear fuel, was that some might end up in the wrong hands."

Where's he going with all this?

Peters continued. "I don't know if you know it, but looking at spy satellite imagery is no fun. The media make a point of saying that you can read numbers on a license plate. If you have a stationary target, that's fine because you can return over and over again to look at the same spot. But if you're trying to find something that can be moved around, it's nearly impossible." He stopped talking for a moment, seemingly to make sure he had Stigler's attention. "What happened was, in November 2003, I lost two of my submarines, similar to K-159, November-class. One day they were sitting at the dock in Gremikha, and a couple of days later, they were gone."

"How could you lose them? I thought that orbiting satellites image the same spot on the earth twice a day."

"That's right." Peters smiled.

"Well, then."

"Clouds."

Stigler slapped her forehead.

Peters spoke conciliatorily. "People often forget that."

"Well then, somebody obviously moved them."

Peters nodded. "Yes, but where? I spent days looking for them at the Polyarny shipyard, which is where they would have gone next. They weren't there."

"So what happened?"

"We asked the Soviets where they were."

"And?"

"They said that we must have been mistaken, that all of their submarines were accounted for."

Now I understand! "So you think that what SOSUS heard were those two submarines?"

"Yes."

"Could they have left Russia under their own power?"

"Maybe. Some of the subs were obviously in better shape than others."

"Then one possibility is that someone took them and scuttled them."

"To me, that's more likely. What are the chances that two subs would both have a catastrophic accident at the same time and in the same place? By the way, in terms of timelines, everything clicks. One of the reasons I called DTRA this morning was to get the exact date when my subs went missing. The incident in your file occurred three weeks later."

"That ship that we saw leave the area, was it big enough to hold two submarines?"

"That was part of what I did this morning, running down that ship. It's essentially a floating dry-dock. No question about it, it's big enough."

Stigler laid her hands flat on the desk. "That has to mean that those submarines were taken for their nuclear reactors, and that's what was offloaded in those boxes in Brazil."

"Four VMA-type reactors, each having a thermal capacity of seventy megawatts. The crates you saw in Brazil were large enough."

The room was silent while Stigler digested this new information. "I'm with you, but there's something here that doesn't make sense."

"Go ahead."

"To remove the reactors, they would have had to cut open the sides of the submarines. That's the only way to do it." Stigler motioned with her hands. "If that's the case, we wouldn't have heard any implosions on the SOSUS grid. If they scuttled them, they would have filled with water right away."

"My thoughts exactly."

"Well then, we have a problem."

"Not necessarily. What did the SOSUS experts tell you happened?"

"I've already told you that. They said it sounded like two submarines had imploded and crashed to the bottom. The fact that the seismographic traces followed the SOSUS noises confirmed that thinking. We assumed there had been an accident."

"Eureka! I think that whoever brainstormed this operation got a little too smart for his own good." Peters shook his head. "And if I had received the same SOSUS and seismographic data that you had, I would have concluded exactly what you did. But what they didn't anticipate was that someone like you would have imaged the area and have seen that ship steaming away."

Stigler thought this through. "You think they sealed the submarines?"

"Yes. I think they welded the openings back shut, enough to make them watertight. Somewhere on the way down, they'd have gone kaboom. They *wanted* us to think two submarines had met with an unfortunate accident. *Voilà!* The only submarines known to be missing were those from the Gremikha Naval Base."

"If that's so, we have a problem that's a whole lot bigger than the fate of four government scientists. And, I'm sorry to say, Tom's murder."

Peters finally relaxed and took a seat. "That's true, but I'm willing to bet you a week's pay that everything we're looking at is connected."

CHAPTER 25

STYMIED

Müller Family Compound, Cartagena, Colombia: 10°23'36"N Latitude, 75°32'12"W Longitude
Friday, 10:55 a.m., October 7, 2011

The night had been a long one. Following his sunup meeting with Axel, Dieter Müller had taken to the sofa in his office. He had slept fitfully, a disquieting dream taking hold. He had found himself standing in the front yard of his estate when he looked down and saw water lapping over his feet. The sensation of water soaking through his shoes jerked him awake. No better than the dream, the world to which he returned included the disquieting realization that Kipling's escape had far-reaching implications—with the dreaded result foretold by his dream occurring even sooner than planned.

Dieter checked his watch: 10:55. Three and a half hours had passed. He rolled himself upright, hunched over, and rubbed his eyes. Kipling's schedule, as relayed earlier by Schnabel, should have put her into Houston some twenty-five minutes earlier. Schnabel would call soon. Dieter heard a noise and glanced to the side.

Axel marched in, his greeting consisting of one word. "Well?"

His vision still fuzzy, Dieter focused on his brother. "If you're wondering if Gunter has completed his assignment, I don't know. I'm sure he'll call soon."

"Linda was supposed to arrive in Houston after ten, right?"

The desk phone rang. Dieter jumped to his feet, one leg still asleep. The caller ID indicated that it was Schnabel.

Dieter was afraid of what he'd hear. "Yes."

While Axel hovered on the opposite side of the desk, Dieter listened to Schnabel's summary. "Call me when you know," ordered Dieter.

Axel stared, waiting for the update. Dieter hesitated, afraid that if he said it aloud, he might jinx them even more. "Linda didn't show up in Houston. She didn't take that flight."

"I thought you said Gunter had her itinerary, that she was flying through Houston."

"That's correct."

"If not Houston, then where did she go?"

Dieter explained. "Gunter doesn't know. He's been on the phone, and they're checking that out right now."

"For Christ's sake, why didn't Gunter know that before he spent hours flying there? Linda's making us look like fools."

The pitch of Dieter's voice rose. "I know that! But you can't blame Gunter. Once Linda bought a new ticket out of Cartagena, who would have thought that she'd change it after she arrived in Panama?"

Again, the phone. "Atlanta?" Dieter remained silent while Schnabel made a suggestion. "Makes sense. Get back to us after you arrive."

Dieter elaborated to Axel. "Instead of flying to Houston, Linda bought a second ticket home, this time through Atlanta. Atlanta, San Francisco, and then Monterey."

Axel gestured. "At every step of the way, Linda has outwitted us."

"I'm as frustrated as you. But you know, this might actually work to our advantage. Gunter says she'll arrive in Monterey after six tonight, eight our time. That gives him plenty of time to get there before she lands."

Axel grabbed three fingers. "We've already lost her three times. And now we're chasing her all the way to California?"

"That's precisely my point. She's going home. Think about it. And to tell you the truth, I was worried about Houston. Sometimes Gunter is too fearless. But once she arrives in Monterey, she has to leave the terminal, and it'll be considerably less risky for us."

"What if he misses her again, in Monterey?"

"That's where she lives!" Dieter yelled, but then backed off. "But you're right. Gunter is aware of this and said that he will check her progress. This time, he'll at least know if she's on the Atlanta-San Francisco flight." He stared at Axel. "And he said not to give up. If all else fails, he said, he has one more ace to play."

"What's that?"

"He didn't elaborate but said that our connections through Inver Telecom might prove useful in locating our cousin." Dieter remembered one other point he had intended to make. "In terms of Monterey, you do remember that there's someone else we need to worry about. This is another advantage of her returning home."

"Silverstein?"

"Yes, Silverstein. And from that message on Linda's cell, I'll bet you he's the one who picks her up at the airport." Dieter was feeling better. "Two birds with one stone."

Axel took a seat, seemingly less agitated as well. The brothers stared at each other. Dieter broke the gaze and rotated in his chair to face the full light of the day. The sky had a brilliant hue of blue, the grass outside a rich deep green, as perfect as the world could be. Yet, a simple visit from an American relative had tarnished the colors in their pristine world.

"If Linda gets away, we have a decision to make. And if we assume that she knows everything, what will she do with that information?" Axel was facing the reality that Dieter was trying to ignore.

The worst-case scenario was too much for Dieter to face. "How much *could* she know? She has letters from a senile old man."

"Senile old man? You've read those letters."

"They're generalities. Nothing specific. Certainly nothing to tie us to Greenland."

Axel pressed on. "She told us right here that she knows about the missing scientists."

"Of course she does. They work for the same organization she does."

"Okay, let's assume I buy into your denial. Let's assume she knows only what's in the letters and about the missing men in Greenland." Axel paused. "And the two men in Washington, by the way. I'm sure you'd say that there's no possible connection between all of that and Helheim. If that's so, please tell me why our cousin, who isn't a wealthy person, bought an expensive ticket to fly here to bring all of this up in person. She could have called."

Dieter had always understood that their carefully crafted return to power might begin sooner than planned. Operation Helheim had been operational for six years, incorporating a steady-as-she-goes strategy, moving so slowly that the world's scientific community had interpreted Greenland's environmental changes to be part of the natural progression scientists attributed to global warming. The Müllers had fooled them all. *Wouldn't it be the ultimate irony if a family member brought it all crashing down?*

"I don't want to think about it." Dieter shifted in his seat, avoided Axel's gaze, and continued his rationalization. "You're right. She *did* come here. Doesn't that tell you that she *doesn't* know everything? And she doesn't know any more now than before she arrived. *We* didn't tell her anything."

"I hope you're right. But we'll have to do what we have to do if Linda has connected the dots, *and* we can't stop her. We have too much invested."

Plan B, a doomsday scenario, would accelerate Operation Helheim to the limit. As unpleasant as the consequences would be, the Müller family had decided early on that if their plot escaped their bubble of secrecy, they would resort to a much quicker means to their end. It would be an event that all nations on earth would consider a terrorist deed of global proportions. Compared to the acts perpetrated on the United States on September 11, 2001, their final act of defiance would affect the entire planet. Even their in-house scientists disagreed on the outcome, the final condition that would befall Planet Earth. Would the world end? No, but the results would certainly be catastrophic. In terms of their objective, to set up world conditions under which the Nazi movement could again gain a foothold, it would provide the same opportunity as their original, slower strategy.

Dieter stood and stuck his hands in his pockets. "Let's hope that Gunter can stop this before it goes any further. Otherwise, God help us."

CHAPTER 26

CRY BASTION

Federal Center for Data Examination, Las Vegas, Nevada, USA:
36°7'51"N Latitude, 115°10'13"W Longitude
Friday, 11:15 a.m., October 7, 2011

It was almost lunchtime. Nearly three hours had elapsed since Stigler and Peters had parted company, with the understanding that their investigation had reached a stalemate. What had initially seemed like a straightforward, forensic analysis of a crime committed against their former boss had developed into a complex series of events having international implications.

The knock at the door was strong. Andrew Peters marched in, making a beeline to his usual spot. "We need to do something. And I think I know what to do."

"You do, do you? Let me fill you in on some realities. Everything we've concluded regarding Gunter Schnabel has been circumstantial. Unless the DC police have some physical evidence tying him to the crimes, we have nothing. And how are we going to—"

Peters held up his hand. "I'm not talking about finding Tom's killer."

"Then what *are* you talking about?"

"I'm talking about the missing submarines and their four nuclear reactors." Peters became animated. "Not that finding Tom's killer isn't important. But what we've discovered this morning scares the hell out of me, Captain."

"You're forgetting that 2003 was eight years ago! Don't you think that if someone stole those reactors to do something evil that we'd have heard about it by now?"

This comment caught Peters off guard, and he responded a little less confidently. "Not necessarily," he said. "What if they were taken for some long-term goal? Remember . . ." Peters counted on his fingers, "the first World Trade Center bombing occurred eight years prior to the 2001 bombing. These people have patience."

Stigler didn't like the analogy. "The 1993 bombing had nothing to do with *al-Qaeda.*"

Peters's lips curled at the corners. "So they say. But you're not seeing what I'm saying. Not all people intent on doing bad things are impatient."

The points Peters was making were valid, and Stigler didn't like it. "Okay, okay! Point taken. But what are you suggesting we do with information that's some eight years old? Our charter has us contacting our sponsors only when we have something substantial to act on. You know we'd lose our credibility if we made calls every time some little thing bothered us."

Peters was becoming irritated, a trait Stigler wasn't accustomed to seeing in him. He lowered his voice. "This isn't some little thing, Captain. Besides, I'm not suggesting that we call Washington. I'm saying that there's more that we can do at our end."

Stigler put her hand behind her head and massaged her neck. The tension of the past two days had settled into her upper back. "And that is?"

"Cry Bastion."

"I beg your pardon."

"*Cry Bastion.* Don't you remember the 1971 movie, *Play Misty for Me?*"

Peters was doing it *again.* Stigler did recall this movie and decided to humor him. "Yeah. One of Clint Eastwood's early films, his directorial debut, as I recall. Pretty intense."

"Do you remember the scene at the Sardine Factory restaurant when Clint's character, Dave Garver, meets Jessica Walter's schizoid Evelyn Draper?"

Stigler shook her head in mockery. "It's coming back to me. Go on, make your point."

"Garver goes into the restaurant, sits down at the bar, and starts talking to his bartender friend, asking about the cute Draper sitting at the opposite end. When the bartender tells him that Draper has rebuffed all advances that night, Garver suggests that he and the bartender play a game of *Cry Bastion*. Cry Bastion is a nonsensical board game, but with increasingly wild exclamations on both sides, designed to ensnare anyone within earshot. Before long, Draper edges over to see what all the excitement is about. They stop the game. Garver admits that the only purpose of the game was to attract her attention." Peters seemed pleased with himself.

Stigler shook her head. "I assume that from all of this you're going to make some point."

"You don't see it." Peters seemed puzzled.

"See what?"

"The analogy I'm making."

Stigler turned her hands face up. "Andrew, in case you haven't noticed sometime during your lifetime, your mind works a little differently from most of us. No, I don't see it."

Peters didn't seem to take offense. "Clint's character's goal was to attract Draper's attention because he found her attractive. I say that we need to attract the attention of Müller Industries."

"How would that contribute to getting us any closer to implicating them in anything?"

"It might not, but I bet we can make them sweat. And if they sweat, they're going to react and maybe do something dumb."

"So what do you propose?"

Peters unfolded a piece of paper from his shirt pocket. "I'm suggesting that we send them an anonymous e-mail. It would go something like this." He read. "We know that Gunter Schnabel murdered three men in Washington DC. We also know that you are responsible for two men missing in Greenland. What is more important is that we know what you are doing with the nuclear reactors that you took from two Soviet submarines in 2003. If you care that this information remains confidential, you will respond to us.

"Within forty-eight hours of the transmission of this e-mail, you will reply, signaling that you agree to our demand. Once we have received your reply, we will provide a numbered Swiss bank account into which you will deposit ten million US dollars. Once you make payment, you can be assured that this matter is settled, and there will be no further monetary demands on our part."

Stigler's eyes widened. She stared at Peters, shocked at his proposal but amazed at the beauty of the logic. "I like it. But in fact, we're bluffing because we have no idea what the nuclear reactors are being used for."

Peters shook his head hard. "Doesn't matter. All we have to do is convince them that we do know. And if we're on to something, I guarantee that we'll get a response. When Dave Garver played Cry Bastion, he wasn't sure either whether it would work out in his favor or not. But he got the girl."

"Yeah, but you're forgetting something. I do remember that movie, and I'm not sure who got whom. In the end, Garver wished he had never met Draper. She nearly killed him."

"Are you afraid that we're pushing the envelope here?" Peters knew how to press Stigler's buttons.

"Hell, no!"

"Well, then?"

Peters was correct. Because the FCDE had nothing more to go on, they needed to force Müller Industries out from under their shell. "Okay, let's do it. Work on the words some more and get back to me. But before you go, three questions come to mind. First, can you be certain that the e-mail can't be traced back to us?"

"No problem. Either for transmission or their reply. There are ways of handling it through multiple servers that make it failsafe."

"My second question is a practical one. To whom would you send the e-mail? Obviously, it's got to go to the top."

"I've done the research. Two brothers, Dieter and Axel Müller, run the company. We know their e-mail addresses and have ways to bypass any SPAM filters. For good measure, I suggest we e-mail both of them."

Stigler agreed. "One more thing. How do we set up a Swiss bank account? If they decide to pay us off, I want the money. That would go a long way toward upgrading our computers." As fast as Silicon Valley kept designing more powerful computer chips, FCDE personnel never seemed to have enough computer power.

"I have no idea. Don't you have somebody *you* can call?"

"That's fair."

Peters raised his hand. "When do you think we should send these e-mails?"

Stigler started to answer but then realized that it was Friday. She didn't mind coming in over the weekend but knew that it was unfair to ask the same for Peters. "You know that tomorrow is Saturday."

Peters's answer surprised her. "Remember that this was my idea, and it's got me hyped. I'll be here all weekend if necessary. What about you?"

"Not to worry. But do you think the Müllers work on Saturday?"

"I doubt that executives like them ever stop working."

The excitement was taking hold of Stigler. "Okay. We'll send them out tomorrow morning at eight, ten their time."

Peters headed for the door but stopped short. "Oh, there's one more thing. Remember yesterday when we traced Gunter Schnabel to that private jet?"

"The one that came from Greenland, right? And then you said it returned to Cartagena on Wednesday."

"That's correct. Well, just for the heck of it, I put a tracer on it. That's easy to do these days. Since Schnabel's our number-one suspect, I figured that this might be his personal jet, and it wouldn't hurt to know where he is."

"Good thinking, Andrew."

"Well, last night, the plane took off for Miami. At eleven p.m. Who takes off in the middle of the night?"

"People often fly at night."

"Okay, if that doesn't impress you, this should. The plane arrived in Miami, and two hours later, it was on its way to Houston, Texas. Why didn't they fly straight to Houston?"

"Maybe they had to pick somebody up."

Peters rolled his eyes. "Well, here's the *coup de grâce*. Just minutes ago, it took off again, this time with a flight plan to—get this—Monterey, California. Tom's murderer will be flying practically right over us."

The mention of Monterey brought back fond memories. "I guess you know that's where the Naval Postgraduate School is. I've been there several times for courses and conferences."

It was clear from Peters's expression that he wasn't interested in Stigler's musings. Her voice took on a more serious tone. "Do you want me to call Nellis and have 'em shot down?"

Nellis Air Force Base, located outside Las Vegas, was home to the US Air Force Warfare Center. They prided themselves in providing air combat training for every type of aircraft in the Air Force inventory. Nellis was also the location for FCDE's private aircraft, a corporate-sized jet available twenty-four/seven.

For the first time since he entered the room, Peters surrendered his game face and laughed hard. "That's a good one, Captain."

CHAPTER 27

BREAKDOWN

240 Lombard Street, San Francisco, California, USA: 37°48'15"N
Latitude, 122°24'19"W Longitude
Friday, 5:10 p.m., October 7, 2011

Silverstein busied himself about the condo, preparing for Kipling's arrival. She had called his cell some fifty minutes prior. Her plane had landed a little late, but she was on her way. Concerned about her physical condition, he suggested that she splurge and take a taxi, rather than schlep her way to the airport subway station.

As exhausted and discouraged as Kipling sounded, Silverstein decided that she wouldn't have the energy to eat out. Instead, he had meandered about the neighborhood until he found a serviceable grocery store. He purchased a head of romaine lettuce, a few tomatoes and mushrooms to go with it, fresh asparagus, and a loaf of San Francisco sourdough bread. To highlight the dinner, he bought a pound and a half of wild Alaskan salmon. Salmon was one of Kipling's favorites.

Antonio Vargas, the friend who had offered up his digs, had informed Silverstein that the unit had a fair number of staples, including a fully stocked, refrigerated wine cabinet. He should take advantage of whatever he could find, Vargas had told him.

Silverstein's relationship with Vargas had a most unusual beginning. Silverstein returned a bag containing some thirty thousand dollars cash that Vargas had inadvertently dropped while responding to an emergency call from his wife. Vargas, a young construction contractor at the time, said that the cash represented nearly his entire life savings. He had been on his way to the bank, the money a deposit toward one of his first construction contracts. If Silverstein had not been so honest, he said, the loss would have ruined him. Silverstein had refused any reward. In the twenty-some years that had since passed, Vargas never failed to look for ways to repay Silverstein.

Still, that Vargas had offered his San Francisco condo was generous. Silverstein knew Vargas to be even more anal-retentive than himself. The unit was exquisitely furnished, with not only expensive furniture, but delicate glassware and antiques. His welcome would be short-lived if anything happened to Vargas's prized possessions.

Silverstein prepared the salmon for broiling, using his personal favorite, an olive oil, black pepper, garlic rub. Abruptly, he experienced a spasm of concern. Not only because Kipling needed physical care—why else would she have asked him to bring along a first-aid kit?—but because of the conditions under which they would be meeting. The beautiful condo, with its spectacular view, was certainly a romantic getaway. But in all the years they had worked together, he and Kipling had never become involved in that way. Not that he hadn't considered it! He had always had a physical attraction to her.

In terms of physical attributes, there was nothing not to like about this forty-two-year-old female: five foot ten with long, lean legs, blonde hair, and a fetching figure. That she was white and he black made no difference to Silverstein. Adopted as a baby by white Jewish parents and raised in racially mixed Atlanta, he saw the world less in black and white than did the average citizen. Shades of gray were far more interesting to him.

But knowing that a romance that turned sour could damage a professional relationship that had reaped benefits for them both, Silverstein had steadfastly avoided even a hint of impropriety.

But how long could he hold out? On more than one occasion, Kipling had stormed through his nocturnal dreams, and not in situations where they found themselves discussing the vagaries of the weather. Other than sleeping in adjoining hotel rooms while on business, the last time they had slept under one roof (in separate beds) was in 2009.

Silverstein winced at that last thought. That was when Caliph Ishmael, the brother of the Ishmael twins who had inadvertently met their demise in a high-speed chase near Silverstein's house, had come gunning for revenge. In the ensuing fight inside Silverstein's home, Silverstein had made a heroic stand but, in the end, had been beaten to within an inch of his life. In dramatic fashion, Kipling arrived and killed the intruder. In fact, that was the second time in as many years that she had saved his life.

So they'd be alone together. Fortunately, the unit had two bedrooms. The master bedroom, which he'd give to Kipling, was decorated beautifully. A massage table, covered with a soft, luxurious towel, stood in front of a picture window that took advantage of a stunning view of the water.

Silverstein looked about the kitchen. The salmon lay warming to room temperature, ready for broiling, the salad made, the asparagus sitting in water ready for steaming, and the loaf of bread awaiting the knife. They could eat now or wait, whichever Kipling wanted. As the wine cork popped from its bottle, following his persistent tug, he heard a knock at the door.

* * *

Kipling stood and waited.

The flight into Atlanta and the connection through to San Francisco had passed uneventfully. Although she had developed a crick in her neck from looking behind her, there had been no further sightings of Schnabel. Whether or not he had had the foresight to chase her to Houston, Kipling decided that she had made the correct decision in changing her return route.

At the San Francisco airport, Kipling had tried to improve her appearance but with little success. As she stood ready to meet her colleague, she pulled the collar of her blouse high around the

147

neck. Her matted hair, wrinkled clothes spotted with blood, and the condition of her face would certainly produce a reaction from Silverstein. She hurt, and not just from physical wounds. More than anytime she could remember, she needed the comfort of an embrace.

*   *   *

Silverstein walked quickly to the door, prepared to lash out at Kipling's stupidity, to think that she could take on her cousins singlehandedly. She could be so impulsive.

Upon opening the door, his first reaction caught him flatfooted. His eyes widened, and his lower jaw dropped involuntarily. Moisture formed around his eyes. He couldn't hide his reaction. "Linda . . ."

Silverstein looked her over. In front of him stood a woman whom he could have passed on the street without recognizing. Starting at the bottom were black sneakers, followed by black pants and a black blouse. Scattered about the cloth were dark splotches, mostly on the legs, but also on the shoulders and arms. *Is that blood?*

But it was what he saw from the neck up that had startled Silverstein. The left side of her face was black and blue. Something or someone had struck that side of her head.

Silverstein responded instinctively, holding out his arms. The space between them shrank to nothing. His arms enveloped Kipling's body, fingers pulling her gently to him. With her face buried in Silverstein's chest, she began to sob. In all the years he had known her, he had never witnessed emotion of this sort from this Amazon of a woman. Between them, Kipling was by far the stronger, with considerable reserves of stamina, courage, and resilience. But at this moment, she was in emotional shambles.

Silverstein tried to back off, but she held on. He edged their bodies into the room and pushed the door closed with his foot. He knew what he had to do.

When he felt the slightest release of Kipling's grip, Silverstein pulled himself free and hoisted her off her feet. The massage table in the master bedroom would do nicely. He maneuvered his way into the bedroom and lowered her onto the table. Once horizontal, she lifted her head inquisitively. He leaned over. "Close your eyes. I'm going to take care of you."

Silverstein now understood why Kipling had asked him to bring a first-aid kit. He retrieved it from the living room. As he headed back, he located the wall thermostat and clicked on the heat. San Francisco was known for its cool temperatures.

Upon his return, he was pleased to see that Kipling hadn't moved. His eyes took in the battered body in front of him. He knew that the first thing he needed to do was take off her clothing. He started with the shoes. Next came the black socks that matched her colorless outfit. He inspected her feet, pleased to see that they appeared unharmed. It was on her lower extremities where Silverstein knew there was a problem. At the waist, he undid the button at the top of Kipling's pants and slid down the zipper.

As Kipling raised her hips to allow her slacks to pass downward over her black panties, he sensed no resistance. Once the pants slid past her feet, Silverstein saw the extent of the damage: more than a dozen bloody spots on the front of her legs. He looked at one closely. It was blood-red and covered by multiple layers of tissue paper, obviously put there to stop the bleeding. Her remedy had been mostly successful, with only a few of the wounds still seeping blood. The tissue glued together by dried blood would prove a challenge.

What's happened to her? If Kipling had been shot with buckshot, there was more to do here than just cleaning up wounds. She'd need surgery, and he didn't have that sort of expertise. "I have to ask, Linda. Were you shot?"

Kipling replied in a whisper. "Thorns."

Thorns? He grabbed her ankle and gave it a tender shake. "I'm going to clean these up."

Silverstein opened his kit and removed a bottle of alcohol and a packet of absorbent pads. He spotted one scratch that extended for more than an inch but had the least amount of dried blood. He started there. "I'm going to use alcohol to break down the paper tissue. Once I think it's clean, I'll cover each wound with a bandage. It'll sting now and then, but I'll take it slow."

The first one went easy, but it got harder. Most of the wounds necessitated repeated dabs to break down the paper tissue. Silverstein worked slowly. He used tweezers to pull away tissue when it loosened from the flesh. More often than not, the tissue removal caused blood to ooze again. He applied repeated pressure until the blood clotted.

By the time Silverstein bandaged the last of the leg wounds, natural light from the window was waning. He checked the digital clock by the bed. It was 6:20. An hour had passed.

"I need to check the rest of you." Silverstein moved up to Kipling's chest and, starting from the top, unbuttoned her long-sleeved blouse. He was staring at her face when she opened her eyes. Only a heartbeat passed before she closed them again. Silverstein hoped that she had not seen the wetness that had repeatedly replenished itself around his eyes since he had first seen her in the doorway.

With Kipling's help, Silverstein removed her blouse. He expected to see more of the same because blood had stained the sleeves, mostly on her upper arms. He needed to keep moving but stopped.

Silverstein couldn't help himself. He stared, his gaze beginning at the top of her chest, lingering over her protruding breasts, descending past her abdomen and hips, down her legs, and ending at her toes. This was the first time he had seen her body this close to naked. The black bra matched the panties and contrasted starkly with the tan white of her skin. She was gorgeous. He sensed saliva ready to drip from his lip and refocused his efforts.

Moved by the sight of her beautiful, undressed body, Silverstein's vision returned to Kipling's face. The sun had just about given up its daily allotment of shine. In this dim light, the damage to her face that he had noticed in the doorway earlier hadn't stood out, particularly with the collar of her blouse pulled high. He reached across and switched on a corner lamp. His gaze was drawn immediately to additional bruising: dark, circular marks around the sides and front of her neck. *Someone tried to strangle her?* Silverstein's heart thrashed from the emotion this sight created. He drew deliberate breaths to compose himself.

Anxious to determine if he had identified all of Kipling's injuries, he slid his left hand under her back and placed his right hand on her hip. "Turn on your side. I want to take a look at your back." She obliged, and Silverstein was relieved to see that her back was mostly clean. Whatever trouble Kipling had faced, it had come head on.

Silverstein then rolled her flat on her stomach. He took stock. The scratches and gashes on her upper shoulders and arms were similar to those on her legs, although fewer. Where she could reach, she had again applied tissue paper to stop the bleeding. He continued the process he had perfected on her legs. Thirty-five minutes later, he finished bandaging the last of her wounds.

Silverstein examined the marks on her neck and face and remembered the old rule of thumb: apply ice initially and heat later on. Since these injuries had obviously occurred some time ago, there was no point in applying ice. And looking more closely, he was pleased to see only dark areas, with no redness to indicate infection. He realized that there was one more thing he could do. "I'll be right back."

On his return from the kitchen, Silverstein stopped by the bathroom for a bar of soap, two washcloths, and several towels. He plunged the first cloth into the pot of hot water he had retrieved from the kitchen tap, made lather with soap, and proceeded to wash the exposed portions of Kipling's body. He worked lovingly on one small section at a time, first applying the soapy cloth, then rinsing with a second one, followed finally by the towel. As he finished each area, he left a second towel behind to keep her warm. He worked slowly around the face and neck, waiting for the heat from the cloth to be absorbed into the bruised tissue. He repeated the process for her backside.

Silverstein, finished, took a moment to look out the window. He had been so intent on his task, the sun had set without his noticing. The corner lamp provided the only illumination to the room. He maneuvered to the head of the table and gazed down, pleased with himself. He had done the best he could.

Having lain quietly for nearly two hours, Kipling opened her eyes. Silverstein smiled affectionately. "In my distinguished, professional opinion, I think you're going to be just fine."

Silverstein was worried: Kipling did not return his smile. His heart ached. Had he done something wrong? Instead, after several seconds, her face took on an expression more tender than any he had seen in their years together. She whispered, "Victor."

"Yes, Linda."

"Make love to me."

CHAPTER 28

REMEMBERING FITZBY

240 Lombard Street, San Francisco, California, USA: 37°48'15"N
Latitude, 122°24'19"W Longitude
Friday, 8:45 p.m., October 7, 2011

Linda Kipling savored her last bite of salmon. Silverstein had
broiled the wild fish to perfection, the black pepper and garlic
providing a complementary taste sensation. The wine, a 2001 Pinot
Noir from the condo's wine cellar, tasted elegant.

Kipling's gaze alternated between her partner across the table
and the beautiful evening view of the Embarcadero, the eastern
waterfront roadway of the Port of San Francisco. She recalled
that its history dated back to the Civil War. There hadn't been
much talk during dinner. Having been colleagues for some twelve
years, the idea that they had suddenly become lovers was not
something either took lightly. Subconsciously, she had wanted it
to happen for some time. The confluence of events—her weakened
emotional condition, the romantic location, the erotic sensation of
Silverstein's strong hands caressing her injured body—they had all
conspired to make it happen. She had no regrets and hoped that her
partner had none either.

As she turned away from the view, Kipling decided to break the
ice. Her words beginning with "Victor—" were met simultaneously

by Silverstein's "Linda—." That broke the tension, and they laughed. "You go first," she said.

Silverstein's laugh transitioned into a smile and, further, into a soft expression uncommon for him. "Before I get very angry at you for doing something stupid and putting your life in danger, I want to say that I won't forget the last three hours. I've never had such an erotic experience in my life." He wiped at his eyes. "There, I've said it."

Kipling returned his gaze in kind, marveling that such a declaration had come from the same man that she and her NRL colleagues knew all too well: overly confident and self-assured, arrogant, having little tolerance for fools.

"Ditto, Victor. Ditto." Kipling's hand caught up with Silverstein's as his inched forward.

Uh-oh! Kipling sensed that the party was over. Silverstein withdrew his hand and began his assault, his face changing from tenderness to irritation. "What the hell were you thinking, Linda?"

Kipling stopped short of laughing. "Put yourself in my position, Victor. Wasn't it you who told me that you should never rat out your family?"

"Yeah, I said it, but I wasn't suggesting you should put your life in danger to prove a point."

"Okay. You tell me what *you* would have done. Before you'd make that final decision to sell out your kin, how would you have determined that what you were accusing them of was true? Confronting them face to face wouldn't have occurred to you?"

Her research colleague conceded his position far sooner than Kipling expected. "Maybe you're right. Besides, I don't want to fight. I was so worried, felt so helpless, when I received your letter." He winked. "Very clever, by the way, and dramatic. Having Sally deliver it to me just as you arrived in Cartagena. I was impressed."

Kipling grinned ear to ear. "I knew you'd appreciate that."

"Okay, give me the whole story. I want to hear it all."

Over the next twenty minutes, Kipling provided relevant details. She finished her story. "And so, there I was in Panama, wondering how Schnabel had been clever enough to get on the same plane with me in Cartagena. I decided not to take any chances. I bought another ticket and came home through Atlanta. I'd bet you that he was waiting for me in Houston." Kipling paused. "And by the way, for the same reasons, I didn't want to return to Monterey either."

"Aren't you getting a little paranoid here?"

Kipling reacted instantly to this patronizing comment. "Paranoid? Paranoid? Five minutes ago, wasn't it you who was afraid that I had placed myself in danger? And weren't you listening?" *Didn't I make the description of my escape graphic enough?* "I came this close," Kipling allowed a quarter of an inch to show between her thumb and forefinger, "to being strangled. Do you think something's changed in the last twenty-four hours? Victor, my cousins want me dead! And they have resources to burn." His comment really pissed her off.

Silverstein backed off immediately. "I apologize. I was going to say that we head back to Monterey tomorrow, but now I'm not so sure."

Kipling calmed down and changed tack. "Tell me more about what you said in your message yesterday, about the men missing in Greenland."

Silverstein explained everything he had learned from Mike Ringwald at NRL, including that Rick Uphouse died only days after he lost touch with his scientists in Greenland. Also, the belief that the latter had somehow met their demise on their snowmobile.

"Give me a break." Kipling shook her head. "Uphouse gets himself murdered just after he discovers they're missing. What do you think the chances are that his guys had an accident?"

"Close to zero. Too much of a coincidence."

"And this guy, Bragley. Did he know Uphouse?"

Silverstein pushed back from the table and folded his hands on his lap. "I asked Ringwald that. He had no idea."

"That would be useful to know. Maybe Uphouse had figured something out, about what happened in Greenland. Maybe Bragley was privy to that same information."

"Tell me again how your cousins reacted when you mentioned Greenland."

"I laid it on the line. When I got your message after I got off the plane, I practiced what I was going to say. Here are my words, word for word: *I need to know if you had anything to do with the*

155

two scientists who went missing in Greenland last week. Or the two NRL employees murdered in Washington DC over the past two days. I mentioned Helheim too."

"You didn't mince words."

"I didn't fly three thousand miles not to get a reaction. I watched their eyes."

"And did you? Get a reaction?"

"You know the expression, *like a deer caught in the headlights.* I've got to hand it to them, though. They came up with some feasible answers to my allegations."

"Such as?"

"First, they denied everything, suggesting that I had a lot of nerve to come into their house and accuse them of murder."

"That's an understatement. You did have a lot of nerve." Silverstein chuckled.

"By the way, I didn't tell you that I took some of the letters with me and handed them over. They brushed those aside, saying that I couldn't trust the writings of a senile old man."

"Yeah, well, from my reading, I didn't sense any senility."

"Then, Axel went off on a detailed explanation of Operation Helheim. He said that it had to do with their spent uranium project. Before they found their current location on that island in the South Atlantic, they had another site where they had invested a lot of money, only to find out that it wasn't geologically stable. They were quick on their feet, I'll say that."

Silverstein continued his questioning. "You didn't believe them?"

"Not for a second. But let's get back to our brainstorming. What could they be doing in Greenland that would be so important that it required murder?"

"You know what's going on there, don't you?"

Kipling knew where he was going with this. "Of course. Greenland is melting. Glaciers that have been stable almost forever are retreating. Global warming and all that."

"That's what I keep coming back to, too."

"So what? Global warming is, by definition, global. Humankind is adding greenhouse gases that are trapping heat. *Voilà.* Global warming."

Silverstein stood and walked into the living room. When he returned, Kipling recognized the copies of her uncle's letters she had left back at the office. He leafed through the stack. "I've been thinking about these. Take this one." He began reading. "*Remember when we were kids, and we played Vikings, with me Erik the Red, and you his wife, Thjodhilde. Remember where we had to go? I can tell you that we have returned.*"

"What do you think that means?"

"I did some research. Erik the Red's family had a history of getting into trouble. That's why they left their native Norway and settled in Iceland. Then Erik got himself accused of some murders there and was banished from Iceland. And where do you suppose he was banished to?"

"Greenland?"

"Yes. And then history ended up giving him credit for founding the place." Silverstein returned to the letters and flipped a few more pages. "And I'm sure you remember this one. *When we're finished with what we began last month, the world will know the true meaning of global climate change.*"

Damn! Kipling wished that she had pressed that point, as well as her Uncle Friedrich's boasting that they would soon return to power in Germany. For the latter, though, she knew that her cousins would have said that those were merely the fantasies of an old Nazi. "You're not suggesting that my relatives are somehow melting the Greenland ice?"

"I don't know."

That's impossible! "Okay. Even if there were some way to do that, which I'm sure there's not, how could that in any way facilitate a Nazi return to Germany?"

Silverstein grinned widely and leaned back in the chair, not answering.

What's he up to now? "What?"

"God, I'm glad you're back, Linda. There's no one else in the world I'd rather trade barbs with."

If Kipling had been the blushing type, she would have. But she wasn't. "I'll take that as a compliment. Now answer my question. How would melting Greenland help the Nazis return to power?"

Silverstein turned serious. "Have you kept up with any of the climate change theories?"

"Not really."

"Me neither. So while you were gone yesterday, I spent some time surfing the Web. You know about the Gulf Stream. Right?"

Kipling had taken several courses in oceanography. "Of course. It's part of the ocean's heat conveyor belt, transporting warm water from the tropics to the North Atlantic. That's why Western Europe has relatively mild weather. You realize how much effect the Gulf Stream has when you look at a globe. Much of Europe and Scandinavia are at the same latitudes as Alaska."

"That's right. If Greenland's ice were to melt—how much it would take I don't know—that by itself might stop the Gulf Stream."

"Really? Why?"

"What happens now is that the warm surface water travels north and rids itself of its heat, eventually cooling to the point where its higher salt content makes it denser than the water beneath. Then it sinks."

Kipling's mind floated off into a childhood memory. "I'll never forget a vacation we took when I was ten years old. My parents took me to the Great Salt Lake in Utah. I was a good swimmer, but it was really hard because you were buoyed up so high in the water." She looked up. "Sorry, go on. You were saying."

"After the cooler, saltier water sinks, it flows back to the tropics in the deep layers of the ocean." Silverstein paused to make a point. "And what do you suspect happens if you mix in fresh water from the glaciers?"

It was basic physics. Kipling knew the answer. "Because the fresh water is less dense, it'll stay on top. Are you saying that's enough to squash the Gulf Stream?"

"That's what experts think. And here's the scary part. We've known for a long time there have been ice ages. The prevailing thinking has been that the transition from a non-ice age to an ice age has been slow. But in the last thirty years, after scientists studied ice cores all the way down to bedrock, they've determined that some transitions have been shockingly rapid, over a period of only several years." Silverstein shook his head. "Can you believe that? They think there's a delicate balance that can change in a flash. If another ice age comes down on us, parts of the northern hemisphere could well become uninhabitable. Whether shutting down the Gulf Stream would bring on an ice age is anybody's guess."

Kipling appreciated the concept. "But for sure, if you shut down the Gulf Stream, it would make the climate in Western Europe worse, not better. That would lead to an economic down . . ." She stopped to give that some thought.

"Exactly. Western Europe would be hurting. Temperatures would drop, and precipitation would decline. That would wreak havoc, leading to political unrest. You'd have conditions similar to those under which the Nazis gained a foothold in the 1920s."

"This is too much to fathom, Victor. You don't spite your face by cutting off your nose."

"Unless you're desperate. Or you're planning for the long term. Remember that by the end of the war, Hitler would have sacrificed anything and anyone to remain in power, including the German people. In fact, he blamed *them* for losing the war."

Kipling didn't like the sound of this. She stood and stared out the window, arms folded. She noted the lights of a ship transiting in the distance. Until now, the threat from her cousins had been muted in generalities spawned by vague references in letters that were years, and even decades, old. Maybe she shouldn't have taken her father's deathbed statement so seriously. Maybe she shouldn't have asked Silverstein to read the letters. Maybe she shouldn't have made the trek to South America. Maybe, maybe, maybe. But she had, and she did.

Kipling turned back, frustrated. "We should never have gone down this road. Unless they somehow got hold of Fitzby's laser, it's preposterous to think that there's a way to artificially melt the Greenland ice."

She shuddered at that last thought. Four years earlier, she and Silverstein had played a key role in defusing a planned terrorist event. A brilliant but vengeful American scientist, Cameron Fitzby, had teamed up with a moneyed Middle Eastern group to hoist a powerful laser into satellite orbit. In college, Fitzby had developed a theoretical method to intensify and steer hurricanes by heating

159

the water around them. And with that instrument, he had proved the technique. Unbeknownst to everyone except Kipling and Silverstein, he had targeted a Category 5 hurricane on Washington DC, an event that, had it occurred, would have produced a disaster comparable to that of September 11, 2001.

Silverstein replied. "I thought of that, too. But according to my sources, that laser is history. Its power degraded fast. So I think we can discount that possibility."

"Okay, then. It's ridiculous to think that my cousins could somehow melt the Greenland ice." Kipling stared at Silverstein, hoping for a measure of agreement from one of the great scientific minds in the field of meteorology.

Her hopes deflated when Silverstein's response didn't match her expectations. Drumming his fingers on the table, he responded, "I hope you're right."

Exhaustion having progressed into a shroud of stupor, Kipling was having trouble thinking. She squeezed at the corners of her eyes and tried to formulate a response, but a sound from the living room interrupted. *Oh!* "That's my cell phone." She hadn't bothered to turn it off after calling from the airport.

Kipling passed Silverstein as she headed toward her backpack, still lying by the doorway. He looked up as she passed. She removed the phone and glanced at the originating number. The caller ID registered *unknown*. "Hello. Hello." She listened and thought she heard an open line, but there was no response. She disconnected the call, turned off the power, and headed back to the table. "Must have been a wrong number."

A wave of fatigue overwhelmed Kipling, and she felt unsteady on her feet. She put her hand on Silverstein's shoulder. "Victor, I'd like to talk more, but it'll have to wait. I'm dead. Could we go to bed, please?"

Silverstein took her hand, led the short distance to the bed, and pulled back the covers. He removed her robe, tucked her in, and gave her a kiss. "You go to sleep. I'm going to stay up a little while yet."

The cliché was true. No sooner had Kipling's head touched the pillow than her consciousness wafted away into a sea of nothingness.

CHAPTER 29

TWO BIRDS, ONE STONE

Monterey Jet Center, Monterey Peninsula Airport, Monterey, California, USA: 36°35'21"N latitude, 121°51'31"W longitude Friday, 9:25 p.m., October 7, 2011

The temperature on the digital display on the outside wall read fifty-two degrees Fahrenheit. Gunter Schnabel made the conversion to Celsius: seventeen degrees colder than what he was accustomed to in Cartagena. He shivered in his short-sleeved shirt outside the Monterey Jet Center, a facility known as a Fixed Based Operator (FBO). Having the use of his own corporate jet, Schnabel used FBOs frequently. They provided parking, refueling, and other services for the noncommercial pilot. This one was located adjacent to the commercial terminal at the Monterey Peninsula Airport.

"Hello. Hello." Schnabel covered the mouthpiece of his cell phone as he listened. He waited for Kipling to hang up. There was no need to worry about keeping her on the line.

Compared to the technology described in old movies, telephone traces these days were nearly instantaneous, and Inver Telecom had prepared for this call. Schnabel's team had acquired Kipling's cell number when she tried to call from the Müller compound in Cartagena. By completing a connection with her telephone, existing technology ensured that her location could be determined. Only the accuracy of that position was in question.

Schnabel, two pilots, and his team of five security personnel had arrived from Houston by late afternoon. The 1,600-mile trip had taken less than four hours.

In Cartagena, Schnabel's team had confirmed that Kipling had boarded the Atlanta to San Francisco flight. From there, her itinerary had her flying to Monterey, departing at 5:25, with a 6:10 arrival. Aware of her shenanigans in Panama, his orders were to call him after the airline system confirmed that she had boarded the San Francisco to Monterey leg. When no record of such boarding came, rather than trust his source, Schnabel chose to wait inside the terminal, his men randomly dispersed about the arrival area. But true to his information, Kipling did not show. Figuring that she might still arrive on the 8:45 flight, Schnabel returned later, to be disappointed yet again.

As well as having met Kipling, Schnabel knew what to look for in her friend Silverstein. The Cartagena office had located an online photograph of her research associate, a nigger. Aboard his jet, Schnabel downloaded two .jpg files and printed them for his men to memorize.

At 8:55, Schnabel decided there was no point in waiting any longer. Kipling either had decided to stay the night in San Francisco or had rented a car to make the two-plus-hour drive to Monterey. If the latter, she should have arrived home already. Either way, it was time to play his ace in the hole, calling her on her cell phone.

Outside the terminal, Schnabel stood stoically, eyes ahead, arms folded to stay warm. He was waiting for a response from his man, Bernard Kerr, talking with personnel at Inver Telecom. Schnabel wanted to know whether Inver had successfully locked onto some form of address for Kipling's cell.

The accuracy of that location would be a function of the type of cellular telephone Kipling used. A newer phone would provide accurate Global Positioning Position (GPS) coordinates. From an older version, Inver Telecom could still obtain her position, but the result would be less precise. Anything would prove useful since they had no idea whether Kipling had remained in San Francisco.

The signal that Schnabel was waiting for came not from Kerr's face, but from his hand, when he began writing on a notepad. He tore off the paper and handed it over.

Finally! It read: "From GPS, 240 Lombard Street, San Francisco." Kerr expanded on the address. "The images from Google Earth suggest that it's an apartment building, sir."

Schnabel looked across, caught the attention of his man standing guard at the stairway to his jet, and traced circles through the air with his index finger.

Your luck has finally run out! Kipling was probably already asleep in that building. They had no idea which apartment she was in, but it didn't matter. When she left in the morning, they would be there to greet her. If Silverstein happened to be her escort, they'd have a bonus.

Schnabel ran to the plane, its engines already turning. The Müllers' cousin from America had made him look the fool more than once over the past twenty-four plus hours. It wouldn't happen again. It was time to complete this mission and head back to civilized temperatures.

CHAPTER 30

BLACKMAIL

Müller Family Compound, Cartagena, Colombia: 10°23'36"N Latitude, 75°32'12"W Longitude Saturday, 10:15 a.m., October 8, 2011

The e-mail arrived on Dieter Müller's laptop a little after ten in the morning. He was working in his office after having had a reasonably good night's sleep, albeit augmented by a sleeping pill. He called his brother on the intercom. "We have a problem. Get down here."

He reread the message. *Is this a joke from one of my staff?* Hadn't it been enough that someone from his own family was threatening the future of their project? Now an anonymous stranger on the Internet was blackmailing them for ten million American dollars?

Axel rushed in. "I assume you've heard from Gunter, and our problems are over."

"I'm afraid not." The printer spewed out a copy of the e-mail, and Dieter handed it over. "Someone claims to know what we're doing in Greenland and wants ten million dollars in hush money. They specifically mention the Soviet submarines and the reactors."

Axel's complexion lightened considerably. "We need to get Gunter in on this fast. See if he can trace the source."

"You think it could be one of our own?"

Axel leaned over Dieter's desk, pressed the intercom button, and ordered coffee. "Impossible. Everyone who's part of Helheim has been vetted at length. You know how thorough Gunter is. Between the two of us, we've probably met everybody at one time or another."

What Axel said was spot on, thought Dieter. Schnabel had personally interviewed every Helheim employee, and that included more than 150 men. No women worked on this project. When opposite sexes interacted, there was always the potential for a romantic relationship. And if that happened, too much could go wrong if a relationship soured. For a venture of this magnitude, the brothers Müller had no tolerance for error.

Dieter grudgingly agreed. Going after an in-house problem would have proven far easier to address. "I suppose you're right. Besides, if it were someone inside, why would they have waited so long? We've had the reactors for eight years, and they've been running for six."

There was a knock at the door. Coffee had arrived. Axel accepted the tray and pushed the door closed with his foot. He poured himself a cup and offered one to his brother, who declined. "Do you think it's a coincidence that this is happening just two days after our cousin comes barging into our house?"

This comment caught Dieter off guard. "You're thinking Linda could be behind this? Even if she wanted to, that would be impossible."

"Why?"

Dieter reached for his copy of the e-mail and snapped it with his middle finger. "Because whoever sent this knows about the submarines and the reactors. I've read Dad's letters, and there's nothing about them in there. How else would she have determined that? And eight years after we ditched the subs? Think about it."

"I've read those letters too, Dieter, and I agree there's nothing there, although there is a reference to 2003. Dad did let that one slip. But you're assuming that Linda gave you *all* the letters. I've read them again. There were sequences when it seemed to me that some were missing. I don't think it's a certainty that Linda has nothing to do with this."

Dieter leaned back, blowing air upward through his hair, a headache taking hold. "I can't fathom Linda doing something like this to us, to me. I paid for her schooling, for Christ's sake. Until Thursday, she's never been anything but respectful to us." He stopped to think. "And here's something. Don't you think that if she knew about the submarines, she would have asked us about them? No, I don't buy it."

"Maybe this Silverstein fellow has her coerced. Maybe she's in love with him. She could have shown him the letters. Maybe he's a greedy son of a bitch, and he saw some easy money."

US government scientists blackmail Müller Enterprises for $10 million? Ironically, that would be the preferred outcome. Since Thursday, this was the second of two threats to Operation Helheim. If they had come from the same source, that would certainly simplify things. But how could they determine that? The e-mail stated that they had forty-eight hours to respond. That gave them until ten o'clock, Monday morning.

Abruptly, Dieter leaped to his feet. *"Schiss!"*

Axel flinched at Dieter's outburst and spilled coffee on his pants. *"Was?"*

"If Gunter takes out Kipling, we'll never know if there's someone else behind this."

Axel's eyes widened. "When did you last talk to him?"

Terrified that Gunter had already completed his mission, Dieter tried to remember. "When . . . when . . . when I got up, two hours ago. He and his men had the apartment building surrounded and were waiting. I told him to do what he had to do."

Dieter dived for the phone. "I hope to God we're not too late!" A few seconds later, he slammed the phone down in its cradle. "Damn it to hell!" Immediately, he took out his cell and tried again. "Cell is out too." He looked across at Axel, who didn't have to ask what the problem was. Both knew that the Colombian phone system could be problematic at times.

Axel sighed. "Just put it on automatic redial. It's normally not out for very long."

CHAPTER 31

INTERSECTION IN TIME

*240 Lombard Street, San Francisco, California, USA: 37°48'15"N
Latitude, 122°24'19"W Longitude*
Saturday, 8:20 a.m., October 8, 2011

Kipling helped Silverstein tidy up as they prepared to leave. They
had slept until 6:30, had a leisurely breakfast, showered, and
rounded up their possessions. Except for her backpack, Kipling had
nothing to pack. She had purposely avoided discussing her South
American relatives. The ambience, beautiful view, and pleasant
memories from the previous evening made her want to make the
most of the morning before confronting the unknown outside.
Although it embodied some risk, they had decided to return to
Monterey.

Standing by the door, Kipling watched as Silverstein dashed
about the unit. He said that it was important that nothing be left out
of place. While she waited, she powered up her cell phone. On the
way out of town, she'd check her voicemails at home and work.
Perhaps her cousins had left a message explaining how everything
that had occurred over the past several days had been one colossal
misunderstanding. *Wishful thinking, indeed!*

Kipling led the way out the door, and Silverstein closed and
locked it.

Federal Center for Data Examination, Las Vegas, Nevada, USA: 36°7'51"N Latitude, 115°10'13"W Longitude
Saturday, 8:21 a.m., October 8, 2011

Some twenty minutes earlier, Jane Stigler had watched Peters press the *send* button in Microsoft Outlook. The previous afternoon, they had finalized the Müller e-mail, which turned out to be nearly the same as Peters's initial version.

She stared at the alphanumeric sequence on the sheet in front of her, thirty-four characters in length. With the help of suspicious personnel at the Central Intelligence Agency, Captain Jane A. Stigler, United States Navy, now had her own personal Swiss bank account. She imagined long in the future telling her grandkids about her escapades in the navy. "And you had your own numbered Swiss bank account, Grandma?" he or she would ask. Grandma Stigler would reply, "Why, yes, yes I did."

Stigler looked up to see Peters returning, paper in hand. It hadn't been obvious to her yesterday, but she realized that they now had nothing more to do. "You know, Andrew, it's not like we need to sit here all weekend waiting for a reply. We can do that at home."

Peters nodded. "Yeah, but I have new information. The plane that we think might be Schnabel's left Monterey last night and is sitting at the San Francisco airport." Peters had fixated on Schnabel's travels.

"You don't say?" She knew that her demeanor suggested that Peters's obsession with Schnabel's travels was a waste of time.

"You do recall their itinerary. Cartagena, Miami, Houston, Monterey, and now San Francisco."

"I did offer to shoot him down for you." Stigler grinned, making further light of Peters's fascination with these details.

"Yes, and I appreciate that." Peters smiled as well, but then shook his head. "Can't you get excited that the man we think murdered Tom is sitting in the next state over?"

"You don't know that for a fact. That he's on that plane."

"The whole point of my bringing it up again, though you *clearly* aren't as interested as I am, is that I can prove it's Schnabel.

I could kick myself for having missed this before." Peters bit his lip. "Do you remember when we tracked Schnabel in DC?"

"Yeah! That was like the day before yesterday. I think I praised your ingenuity appropriately."

"Yes, you did. What I've ignored, though, is one other key piece of information on Schnabel's rental record. It wouldn't have shown up on the hotel registration."

"What's that?"

"What's the one thing they always ask you for when you rent a car?"

Stigler thought for a moment. "Your phone number so that they can reach you when you forget to return the car."

"Precisely." Peters held up his paper. "Here's Schnabel's phone number. I've checked it out, and it's a cell."

"Probably one peculiar to Colombia."

"Doesn't matter. All cell phone companies have roaming agreements with local carriers in foreign countries. My wife and I took a riverboat cruise last year, starting in Budapest, Hungary, and ending in Nuremberg, Germany. Our cell worked all the way through. Even in Prague, where we stayed afterward."

"So you're saying that if he used his phone here, we can trace it."

"Yes. And if his cell is GPS-equipped, which is likely, we'll pinpoint his location accurately."

"But that's what you've surmised all along, that he's on that plane. So what?" Stigler still had no idea where this was going.

Peters's exasperation came through in his tone of voice. "I don't know *so what*. But don't you agree this is worth investigating?"

"Maybe. Prove it to me." Stigler stood and beckoned Peters to her computer.

"It'll be easy this time." Peters began hammering on the keyboard. "All I have to do is search for any incoming and outgoing phone calls to this number." He pointed to his sheet.

After several minutes of quiet, Peters broke the silence. "Houston, we have liftoff. Here are the calls that were made to and from Schnabel's cell. We have the length of the call, whether it was incoming or outgoing, and the general location of where he was at the time."

Peters studied the data for a moment. "Son of a bitch! Look at this, Captain. I was right! This telephone was used in Miami, Houston, and Monterey. Likely as not, the other calls were made inside the plane along the route."

Stigler knew to give credit where credit was due. "Very impressive, Andrew. Unless his wife uses his cell phone, you've proven that Gunter Schnabel is now in San Francisco." She bent down to take a closer look. "Now that you've gone this far, could you get the exact location for each stop? It would be interesting to see if Schnabel left the airport proper."

"Good thinking. I'll retrieve the lat/longs for each call."

A few minutes later, Peters motioned to the screen again. "Okay. Here they are, together with the earlier info. I'll print it."

"Could you make me a copy, please?"

"No problem." Peters clicked the print button again. "What I need to do now is plug these into Google Earth. I'll do the first one for Miami." It wasn't long before the runways and terminals of the Miami airport appeared on the screen. "At least at the time of this call, he was right at the airport."

Stigler watched as Peters ran each of the coordinate sets through the same sequence. For Houston, calls were made from two locations, the tarmac *and* the terminal. At the Monterey airport, all calls were made from the same spot. True to form, the last call came from the San Francisco airport.

Stigler studied her sheet. "Tell me if I'm interpreting this correctly. It looks to me like all calls were made to and from one number."

"That's correct. Give me a second." Peters typed some more. "To and from Cartagena, Colombia." He raised his finger in the air. "But that number isn't a cell. It's a landline."

"Probably his boss."

"I wouldn't doubt it."

"What's this?" Stigler noticed one call that didn't fit the pattern. "Last night, from Monterey, he called somebody else. But the call lasted only a few seconds."

Peters looked closer. "You're right. It's an 831 area code. Let me check where that's located." A moment later, he read from the screen. "California's area code 831 is a North American area code which covers Salinas, Hollister, Monterey, Santa Cruz, and the northern Central Coast."

"Schnabel was in Monterey, making a local call."

"Yeah, but let me check to see if it's a landline or a cell." A few keystrokes later, Peters had the answer. "Interesting, Captain. It's a cell."

"Can you determine its location like you did for Schnabel?"

"Shouldn't be a problem."

Stigler had to admit to herself that this was getting exciting.

"Okay, here are the coordinates." He followed his earlier procedure, and the Google Earth map appeared on the screen. "The phone that Schnabel called was located in San Francisco. Somewhere in the vicinity of 240 Lombard Street."

"Okay. You've got me hooked. Schnabel makes a call to that phone and then flies to San Francisco." Stigler looked closely at the lines of information on her sheet. "According to this, the call was made at nine twenty-five in the evening. From your records of Schnabel's plane, can you tell me when he flew out of Monterey?"

"I have it here. He was in the air by nine fifty-five."

Stigler touched her forehead. "You almost have to conclude that Schnabel flew to San Francisco as the result of that phone call." She checked her sheet again. "But that call lasted only seconds. That wouldn't have been enough time for the callee to tell Schnabel where he was."

"Unless Schnabel has access to the same advanced technology we have." Peters turned back to the computer.

"You're scaring me, Andrew. Is there any way we can find out whose number that is?"

"I'm already on it, Captain. That's an easy one. We have master databases of every phone number in the country, whether it's listed or not."

Stigler felt a chill. Knowing that death and destruction followed Gunter Schnabel's earlier travels in Washington, their fortuitous discovery of his erratic flights about the country could have an ominous meaning.

"I've got it. The number belongs to a female, a Linda Ann Kipling."

"Do you have her address?"

"Yes. She lives in Pacific Grove, on Lighthouse Avenue."

"That's on the Monterey Peninsula. Okay, follow me here. Let's say that Schnabel is looking for her. She lives in Monterey, and so that's where he flew."

Stigler listened as Peters continued her logic. "And then, from his phone call, he discovers she's not home. For a fact, we've just confirmed that she's in San Francisco. Let's suppose he's been chasing her across the country, and he expected her to fly to Monterey last night. When she didn't arrive, he called her cell to determine her physical location. When he learned she was in San Francisco, he flew there straightaway."

Facts were compounding rapidly. "Linda Kipling. Who are you? Andrew, search our databases for any Linda Kiplings. We need to know something more about this woman. Where she works would be a good place to start."

"Okay. We have federal, state, and private databases."

"Start with federal. There are a lot of military folk in Monterey and civilians who support them. Besides the Naval Postgraduate School, Monterey is home to the Defense Language Institute."

"Okay, that will make the search a little more tractable. I'll start with DEERS."

DEERS, the Defense Eligibility Enrollment Reporting System, contained information for all military and civilian employees of the Department of Defense.

Peters typed furiously. "Okay, here goes." He dramatically hit the return key.

The tension was getting to Stigler. She began pacing, eyeing Peters to the side. Suddenly, he took off his glasses and pressed his face close to the screen. She ran over and leaned over his shoulder. "Andrew, what is it?"

Two words came from his mouth. "Holy shit!"

"What, Andrew? What?"

Peters rotated slowly in his chair, his gaze unfocussed in the distance before his eyes met Stigler's. His face was ghost white. "Captain!" His words came out in spurts. "Linda Kipling . . . is a PhD scientist. She works for a division . . . of the Naval Research Laboratory."

Peters's words hit Stigler with the impact of an electrical shock. *Two of the three men murdered in Washington DC worked for the Naval Research Laboratory.* Rather than wasting time responding to Peters's outburst, she dove for the phone, simultaneously scanning her sheet for the cell number. She needed to reach this Kipling woman before it was too late.

CHAPTER 32

CORNERED

240 Lombard Street, San Francisco, California, USA: 37°48'15"N
Latitude, 122°24'19"W Longitude
Saturday, 8:33 a.m., October 8, 2011

Schnabel and his men had been in position around the apartment
complex since before midnight.

A less disciplined operative might have figured that Kipling
would not leave until morning. He'd have gotten some shuteye
at a nearby hotel. But Gunter Schnabel did not take chances, and
his team knew better than to gripe. Luckily, their aircraft came
equipped with a stash of additional clothing, including jackets, to
stave off the cool San Francisco night air.

The apartment complex was larger than Schnabel had expected.
It took him and his entire five-man team to cover all exits. He had
walked the grounds and had selected for himself a location where
he could watch what he considered the most likely exit point for the
building, the underground parking garage. Schnabel communicated
with his men by two-way radio, with each man reporting on a
fifteen-minute basis.

If Kipling was inside, and Schnabel had no doubt that she
was, when she exited the building accompanied, preferably, by an
African American named Victor Mark Silverstein, each man had

orders to finish off the two swiftly. There would be no subtlety in the killings. Each man carried a silencer-equipped handgun. Two shots to the head were the accepted execution style. Each team member had orders not to allow either one to escape by foot or by automobile. Schnabel's men were well paid and expected to perform under dire conditions, whether those involved the threat of physical harm or capture by authorities. Each man was protected in two ways: by body armor and a five-million-dollar insurance policy (funded by Müller Enterprises), the latter paid to the family if the breadwinner died or became incarcerated.

"Stay alert," he said to his men. "It'll be over soon."

Over the past hour, a few people had left the building, significantly less than on a workday, this being a Saturday.

*   *   *

Silverstein and Kipling made their way down the hall from their condo.

"My car's in the parking garage. It's seven flights, but if we take the steps down, we'll come out right by my car." Silverstein opened the door to the stairs and pointed downward, intending that Kipling precede him. The door had almost closed. "Damn!"

Kipling blinked. "What?"

"I forgot to leave a thank-you note. That's an obsession I can thank my mother for." He tossed her his keys and smiled. "Last night must have rattled my brain. You know my Porsche. Spot 729. I'll meet you out front. It won't take but a minute. Sorry."

Kipling continued down the steps. She flinched when the door slammed above her. Seven floors later, she turned left into the cavernous space that housed the cars. Sure enough, Silverstein's prized silver Porsche sat just feet away. To make sure she had the correct vehicle, she pressed the button on the key fob and heard the distinct sound of the car's security system. She opened the driver's side door and tossed her backpack into the backseat. Kipling was not unfamiliar with Silverstein's car. They had once exchanged vehicles for a weekend, Kipling's powerful BMW R 1200 GS motorcycle in exchange for Silverstein's 911 Turbo.

Kipling inserted the key into the ignition and turned it clockwise. The throaty sound of the 415-horsepower twin-turbocharged engine spooled to life. She had enjoyed that weekend with Silverstein's car and had never told him of her spirited jaunts up Laureles Grade near Carmel Valley, a favorite trek for sports car enthusiasts on the Monterey Peninsula. She reversed the car out of the parking space and had just shifted into first gear when she heard the faint sound of the Hallelujah Chorus coming from her cell phone.

Shifting into neutral, and with her foot on the brake, Kipling reached into the backseat for her backpack. She removed the cell and checked the caller ID. It was an unfamiliar number.

"Hello."

"Is this Linda Kipling?"

"Yes, who is this?"

"What are you doing right now?"

"I beg your pardon." *A crank call?*

"Whatever you're doing at this instant, I ask that you stop. If you're behind locked doors, stay put."

"Who the hell is this?"

"My name is Jane Stigler. I'm a captain in the US Navy, and I work for the Federal Center for Data Examination in Las Vegas, Nevada. I have reason to believe that your life is in danger at this very instant. Does the name Gunter Schnabel mean anything to you?"

*　　*　　*

Schnabel's position on the ramp at the entrance to the parking garage afforded him a view of most of the single-level underground parking, including two stairways that connected the subterranean space with the floors above. A small pair of binoculars provided visual details that he couldn't otherwise make out in the dim light. Although disappointed that a tall black man hadn't accompanied her, Schnabel knew that he had, at last, caught up with the troublesome California cousin who had disrupted his bosses' lives over the past two days.

176

Schnabel had watched Kipling back out of the parking space and proceed forward, surprised that this simple government worker drove as exotic a car as a Porsche. Unexpectedly, her vehicle stopped. He focused on the windshield. She appeared to be talking on her cell.

He scanned the garage. No one else was in sight. This was his opportunity. He would move. Quickly, he radioed for reinforcements, ordering his men to cover the exit to the parking garage. Even if he didn't get off a shot, they would finish the job.

Schnabel estimated the distance between them to be forty meters. Unfortunately, he didn't have the advantage of being anonymous. Kipling had met him in Cartagena. The trick would be to approach the vehicle from as hidden a position as possible. He ran to the side, low and behind vehicles. Luckily, Kipling appeared to be absorbed in her telephone call.

*   *   *

Kipling's mind labored frantically to process the information she had just received from a total stranger. This call was no prank or mistake. This Stigler woman knew not only Kipling's name, but also that of the person she had been avoiding for the past day and a half. And she sounded not only sincere, but terrified. *Whatever you're doing at this instant, I ask that you stop. If you're behind locked doors, stay put.*

Her survival instincts taking hold, Kipling's adrenaline kicked into gear. *What was that?* Had she seen motion out of the corner of her eye? There was no point in continuing the discussion. The message had been delivered. She threw the phone onto the passenger seat. She faced left where she had sensed motion. It took only a microsecond to see the male form, some fifty feet away. *Schnabel!*

Kipling's hand leaped to the gearshift and rammed the car into gear. Simultaneously, she floored the gas pedal and released the clutch. Four patches of rubber remained on the painted floor as she flew down the aisle between the cars. In the rearview mirror, she saw what she feared: Schnabel standing in place, his weapon leveled at her car. Instinctively, she ducked her head below the dashboard,

177

not a split second too soon. Immediately, a barrage of bullets tore through the Porsche's metal skin and fabric top. The ones hitting metal were the loudest, but the one that pierced the back window and then shattered the front windshield was the scariest.

Lifting her head in time to slam on the brakes, Kipling barely avoided a head-on collision with cars parked along the opposite wall.

* * *

Schnabel had emptied one clip from his semiautomatic and was loading a second when a unique pattern of beeps inside his earpiece indicated an incoming call from his bosses, either Dieter or Axel Müller. Their call couldn't have come at a more inopportune moment. He had to decide: choose between finishing his assignment or answering the telephone within two rings as mandated by his contract. Because he knew that his men were advancing from the entrance, and there would be no escape for Kipling's Porsche, he chose the latter.

"Schnabel here. I've got her in sight. Mission will soon be over."

Schnabel recognized Dieter Müller's voice. "Abort, abort! Do not, I repeat, do not, kill Kipling or Silverstein. Bring them back to Colombia."

Schnabel watched as his men, guns leveled, advanced down the ramp toward Kipling's vehicle. Switching to his two-way radio, he ordered, "Cease fire! Cease fire! I have received orders to take Kipling alive. All of you respond that you have received this order!"

Five acknowledgments came in sequence.

* * *

Kipling saw the men closing on her down the ramp, guns leveled in front of them. She briefly considered turning toward them and running them over like bowling pins. Unfortunately, she also knew that with multiple men firing simultaneously, the chances of her emerging alive from that confrontation were not good. She looked in the opposite direction, to her right.

Whipping the steering wheel in that direction, Kipling again floored the accelerator, her head bobbing back and forth to see through the shattered glass covering most of her viewing area. A hundred feet or so ahead of her, an electrically lit sign marked another exit from the parking garage, probably another stairway to the living units above. She screeched to a halt, flung open the car door, leaped out of the vehicle, took a quick look to her rear, saw five men running toward her, and took off toward the steps. She figured there was a fifty-fifty chance she would arrive at the doorway alive. It came as some surprise to her, then, that she passed through the doorway without hearing any shots fired. What also didn't make any sense when she had looked back was that each man had his gun arm hanging to his side.

Federal Center for Data Examination, Las Vegas, Nevada, USA: 36°7'51"N Latitude, 115°10'13"W Longitude

Seconds earlier, Captain Jane Stigler had transferred the call to her speakerphone and had turned the volume to maximum. The first sound they heard was the unmistakable resonance of tires squealing, followed seconds later by more squealing. Kipling was obviously inside a vehicle. It was what they heard in between that brought chills. Pinging sounds and, at once, a crashing noise. Following this sequence came two more distinct sets of screaming tires. Then came some seconds of silence, followed by voices in the background, followed by more quiet.

Stigler issued an order. "Andrew! Call San Francisco PD."

240 Lombard Street, San Francisco, California, USA: 37°48'15"N Latitude, 122°24'19"W Longitude

Silverstein had found some paper in the desk drawer in the living room. He sat at the kitchen table and reread his note:

Dear Antonio,
Thank you for the use of your beautiful apartment. My friend Linda and I had a wonderful stay. I cooked dinner, and we had a lovely evening, enjoying the view

*and drinking your wine. Your place is beautiful. Knowing
how particular you are about your things, I feel blessed
that you trusted me with its care.*

*Please let me know if there is anything I can do in
return for your hospitality.*

Sincerely, Victor

Silverstein had no sooner signed the letter than a panicked
female voice disrupted the silence. "Victor! Victor! Open the door!
Open the door!"

CHAPTER 33

SPEEDY RETREAT

240 Lombard Street, San Francisco, California, USA: 37°48'15"N Latitude, 122°24'19"W Longitude
Saturday, 8:48 a.m., October 8, 2011

Kipling had made a last-second decision she hoped she wouldn't regret. As she ran up the steps to the seventh floor, she had to decide whether to involve her colleague. The smarter tack might have been to elude Schnabel by leading him away from the condo.

Silverstein jerked open the door. "What's wrong?"

Out of breath, Kipling pushed past him and slammed the door shut. "The guy who's been chasing me since I left Colombia was waiting down in the garage. Gunter Schnabel's his name."

Silverstein appeared incredulous. "You're joking!" His disposition changed instantly. "Damn! It was that phone call to your cell last night. That was how he found you. I was so stupid not to suspect something. Where is he now?"

"He chased me in the garage. I escaped up another set of steps and ran here." Kipling slowed her words. "Unfortunately, it's not *he*, it's *they*. There were five or six of them."

At once, Silverstein ran over to his bag.

"What are you doing?"

The reason became obvious. "I brought this along just in case."

* * *

From his earlier position on the exit ramp to the parking lot, Schnabel knew the layout of the garage. As he arrived at the spot where Kipling's vehicle had screeched to a halt the first time, he watched his men chasing after her prior to her escape up a second set of stairs. Knowing that they finally had her cornered, he called out on his two-way, ordering three of them to back off, go outside, and cover likely exits.

When he caught up, Schnabel motioned to the remaining two to accompany him inside. The last thing that Schnabel did after firing his weapon at the receding car had been to note the unit number of the parking spot from which Kipling had driven. She might be returning to her apartment. The only complication was that his earlier, straightforward orders to eliminate Kipling had been superseded. He'd need all of his persuasive powers to convince her to return to Colombia—not an easy task considering her fresh memory of the hail of bullets that had riddled her car. Further, he'd have to do it quickly.

In response to Schnabel's order, his two men holstered their weapons.

* * *

Kipling mentally kicked herself in the shin; she had made the wrong decision. *Silverstein's parking spot.* "Damn!"

"What?"

"I was so stupid. The spot where your car was parked had the unit number on it."

"Are you sure he saw the car?"

Kipling frowned. *How am I going to tell him what happened to his Porsche?* "Oh, I think he saw the car, all right."

Silverstein's confused look evaporated when a tapping sound came from the door. Instinctively, they froze. Schnabel couldn't know for sure whether she had returned to the condo, Kipling figured. They should bluff him out.

"Dr. Kipling, this is Gunter Schnabel. I had the pleasure of meeting you in Cartagena. I need to talk to you." Kipling recognized Schnabel's voice.

Kipling raised her finger to her lips. Another thought came to mind. She could save her colleague. She whispered, "Victor, go hide in the bedroom."

Silverstein's facial response made clear that was not going to happen.

The voice at the door turned forceful. "Linda! I think you're behind this door. I know that you're scared because you think I'm going to kill you. You may not believe this, but after I shot at you, Dieter called. Something's changed, and he doesn't want you harmed. We need to talk, and I don't have much time. Either you open the door, or I break it down."

What Schnabel said was consistent with what Kipling had observed. The men chasing her in the garage had lowered their weapons. Earlier, their guns were pointed toward her.

Kipling faced Silverstein and issued a nonnegotiable order. "Go into the bedroom and wait. It'll be obvious whether I need you or not."

Tiptoeing to the door, Kipling glanced back to make sure her partner had left the room. She spoke aloud. "If my cousins told you to leave me alone, why do we have to talk?"

"I'll explain that to you. Either open the door, or I open it for you." A pause. "Please."

What are the odds? Kipling wondered. From this seventh-floor unit, there was no other exit. If Schnabel broke down the door, the racket might be enough for the neighbors to call the cops. Then again, by the time authorities arrived, whatever was going to happen would be over.

Kipling made an intuitive decision. She undid the lock and stepped back into the middle of the room. "The door's open."

Her heart hammered as Kipling watched the doorknob turn. The door opened, and Schnabel walked in. In a gesture of conciliation, he raised his hands. "I assure you that I will not harm you. Everything's changed." He then turned to the rear and nodded. Two other men followed him into the room, also with hands in the air. The last to enter closed the door.

Trying to breathe calmly, Kipling kept her voice steady. "What do you want to talk about?"

"What I told you was true. Dieter called me right after I shot at you. That is the reason my men did not fire as you ran toward the steps."

Then why are they still here? "It seems to me, then, that you should go home. You've wasted a long flight from Colombia."

"I will do that, Dr. Kipling. But I have new orders. The Müllers want you to come back with us to Cartagena."

"I think I'd rather die here in my own country, Mr. Schnabel."

"I've worked for the Müllers a long time, Dr. Kipling. If they wanted you dead, they would want it done as far away as possible. Still, I understand your concern." Schnabel motioned that he wanted to retrieve something from his jacket. "I'm going to remove my cell phone." He did so, pressed a single button, and held the device to his ear.

Before Schnabel could say anything, Silverstein's voice punctuated the air. "I don't think Linda wants to return with you to Colombia." Kipling backed up to stand alongside Silverstein, who had his firearm trained on the intruders.

Tension in the room ratcheted up several notches. Schnabel's goons, perhaps instinctively, reached for their holsters. He hurriedly motioned that they stand down.

From Kipling's viewpoint, more than surprise had registered on Schnabel's face. An awkward smile. "It's a pleasure to come face to face with you, Dr. Silverstein. In fact, we were hoping to make your acquaintance. You are invited to Colombia as well."

Silverstein's head snapped in Kipling's direction. *How did they know about Victor? I never mentioned his name.* She shook her head to signal that she was equally perplexed.

Schnabel raised his finger again while simultaneously putting the phone to his ear. "This is Schnabel. Mr. Müller, I am here with your cousin who tells me that if she is to die, she would rather do so in her own country. Would you care to talk to her?" He handed across the phone. "It's Dieter."

Kipling took the phone, unclear in her mind what to do. The past two days had been a whir of activity that had left her unsure of anything. Her visit to Colombia had obviously struck a nerve. Why else would they have chased her thousands of miles? *No!* It was time that *she* control the situation.

Schnabel's phone was the flip type that gave her plenty of leverage. She took one half in her left hand and the other in her right. Surprisingly, it took more force than she expected to snap the two halves apart. She threw the mauled pieces onto the floor in Schnabel's direction. "I think I'll stay here, Gunter. May I call you Gunter?"

If the situation hadn't been more serious, Kipling would have laughed aloud. Apparently, the last thing Schnabel had expected was to see his phone destroyed by a pissed-off female. His face turned a reddish hue. "Why did you do that, Dr. Kipling?"

"You're a smart man. Isn't it obvious?" Kipling cocked her head in mocking response. "We're the ones holding the gun."

Schnabel took a step forward; Kipling and Silverstein retreated in unison. "Please reconsider. Mr. Müller wants you to come back with us, and it is my job to make that happen."

*　　*　　*

Silverstein was scared, and his hand holding the gun began to shake. He didn't like the looks of the situation: three aggressive-looking men who gave little indication of backing down.

He understood that his weapon gave him considerable advantage, as well as an ethical responsibility. How far should he take it? From Kipling's description of her escape, she had gone through hell. Further, from what he had just heard, Schnabel had apparently shot at her in the garage. But he also said that his bosses had changed their minds. Was that a ploy? To think that orders had suddenly changed strained credulity. If Kipling's cousins needed to talk, there was the phone. No trip to Colombia was necessary.

Silverstein figured that it was his turn to say something. "I think it's time for you to leave. You should know that while I waited in the bedroom, I called the cops." In fact, not only had he not called anyone, he hadn't even thought of it.

Schnabel looked at his two men and nodded. He moved to his left by several feet, upsetting a coffee table in the process;

glassware shattered on the floor. The three men now stood adjacent to each other, maybe six feet away from Silverstein and Kipling. In response, Kipling moved to her right, reaching down, perhaps instinctively, to pick up a large glass vase that she had admired the previous evening.

What happened next was not what an outsider witnessing the situation would have expected. Incredibly, the second man to Schnabel's right began to advance toward the outstretched gun. Silverstein stood transfixed, unbelieving. The threat of death should have been enough to cause anyone to back off. Could Silverstein kill another human being? He had done so in the past, but only after a fair fight where both sides had had their opportunities. This was different.

Silverstein retreated to the entrance to the master bedroom. "Don't come any farther. I'll shoot."

The man to Silverstein's left kept moving, and then the other one started to advance as well. Schnabel was staying put, letting his men face the danger. What should he do? He considered shooting his attackers in the legs. A police friend had told him that, when such situations presented themselves, they were taught to respond with deadly force. If that was what the police did, then he would do so as well.

* * *

Kipling crouched in position, arm raised with the heavy vase.

Multiple actions transpired in seconds. Two explosions came in succession from Kipling's left. Silverstein had had no choice. Both of Schnabel's goons had advanced on him. Kipling saw both men hit, but then, unbelievably, each one continued advancing. A third blast followed. *Bulletproof vests?* Out of the corner of her eye, she saw both men jump Silverstein, hurling him backward against the wall, shattering the front to a glass curio cabinet. Simultaneously, Schnabel dived across the room toward Kipling, who stood ready for combat, vase held high. She was ready, but Schnabel came in low and impacted Kipling's legs. By doing so, he had protected his head. The best that Kipling could do was to bring the vase down hard on Schnabel's back, shattering it to pieces in the process. In response, Schnabel flipped her completely over his head and onto the carpet. Before she knew it, Schnabel had her pinned, and she found herself helpless.

To her left, Silverstein was fighting furiously, with bodies crashing about the room, causing further damage to their host's delicate treasures. But his struggle was short-lived. He was disarmed, and it wasn't long before the two professionals had him subdued.

The room turned suddenly quiet. Schnabel maneuvered himself so that he was sitting up, astride of Kipling. He was breathing hard and didn't seem happy. But neither was Kipling, and she couldn't help but rub it in. "I still think you should leave. How soon do you think the cops will come?"

Schnabel ignored Kipling's remarks, instead turning toward his partners. "Felix, lend me your phone." He tossed it over.

Schnabel dialed and waited. "Schnabel here. If you want your cousin to return with us, you have only a minute to convince her. Police are on their way. But you'll be pleased to know that Dr. Silverstein has joined us." He handed down the phone.

Kipling chose not to repeat her earlier dramatics. Instead, she steered clear of any pleasantries. "Your man Schnabel nearly killed me just minutes ago. And if you need to talk, I'm right here, Dieter."

Dieter's voice was appeasing. "You've every right to be angry with me, but I must say that some of the blame rests with you. You stood us up. Axel and I were looking forward to a pleasant dinner together."

The nerve of Dieter to suggest that this trouble rests on my shoulders! "That doesn't change the fact that, had one of Schnabel's bullets been a little more accurate, I'd be a ghost right now hounding you from the other side."

"*Touché*, Linda. *Touché*." A moment passed. "I am a practical man, Linda, much more so than my brother, Axel. I have decided to tell you everything you want to know. That is what you want. Is it not?"

Nothing made sense here. "And why would you do that?"

"Because something has happened since you left here, something that threatens many years of work. I need to look into your eyes and determine whether you are involved. The irony is that I hope that you *are* the one responsible. And if so, you can have the ten million."

"Dieter, I have no idea what you're talking about."

Her cousin's tone of voice came across as much as a plea as it was an order. "Then come to Cartagena and tell me that face to face. Your friend, Dr. Silverstein, has an invite as well. I think you have enough time to arrive here by dinner. Once we talk, you and your friend will be free to leave. All I ask is that you hear us out."

"Dieter, if you were in my shoes, would you believe you?"

"I've never lied to you, Linda." Kipling could hear a snicker in the background. "Oh, I guess there was that one little one. That bit about Operation Helheim. That wasn't quite correct. But tonight, I promise, I'll tell you the truth. And you might even come around to our way of thinking. In any event, you'll be free to leave. You have my word."

Kipling had a decision to make. Schnabel could easily kill them now if that was what her cousins wanted. Something had obviously transpired to make them change their minds. She saw two choices. One was to delay a little longer. Cops would come, and their captors would certainly flee. If cornered, however, Schnabel might choose to finish them off as a consolation prize.

But there was a serious downside to that way of thinking. Even with the best of outcomes—if they survived and Schnabel was captured—she would still know nothing about the mysterious threats uncovered in Uncle Friedrich's letters. The Müller family was trying to protect a secret serious enough that a half-dozen men had chased her across the North American continent. This would have occurred only if Dieter and Axel assumed she knew of their plans. Which she didn't! And wouldn't, unless she returned to Cartagena where, implausibly, she'd be told the truth. And this: *The irony is that I hope that you are the one responsible. And if so, you can have the ten million.* What the hell was that all about?

Kipling made her decision. In the grand scheme of things, her life meant little. If she died following through on her father's deathbed revelation, so be it. There was much more at stake here than the life of a government scientist.

Still, there was one person in this room who deserved none of that risk.

Kipling handed back the phone. "I'll go back with you on one condition. You need to release my friend, Victor." She nodded in his direction.

Before Schnabel could reply, Silverstein's explosive response caught everyone off guard. "No!" He paused a beat. "That won't be necessary. I'm going with you."

Schnabel seemed pleased with Silverstein's response and rose to his feet, freeing Kipling. He gestured to his men to do the same for Silverstein. Silverstein got up and did not appear to be hurt.

From the floor, Kipling lifted herself to her elbows and made a recommendation. "Well, then, I suggest that we get the hell out of here."

CHAPTER 34

KIDNAP?

Federal Center for Data Examination, Las Vegas, Nevada, USA:
36°7'51"N Latitude, 115°10'13"W Longitude
Saturday, 2:15 p.m., October 8, 2011

Captain Stigler listened intently to the police version of what had transpired at the 240 Lombard Street condominium complex in San Francisco, California. After asking several questions of the police chief and requesting that he call back immediately if he learned anything further, she pressed the disconnect button and buzzed Peters.

Following their eavesdropping on what had sounded like a violent sequence of events in the vicinity of Kipling's cell phone, all had turned silent. In fact, their phones remained connected for more than an hour, until one of San Francisco's finest noted the phone sitting on the seat and said hello.

Peters entered the room with a laptop under his arm. "Schnabel's on his way home." Ever vigilant in tracking Schnabel's airplane, Peters had determined hours earlier that Schnabel's jet had departed San Francisco at 10:35, less than two hours following Stigler's call to Kipling. "Anything new?"

Stigler responded. "I just got off the phone with their chief of police. He's supposed to call me back if he learns anything else that seems relevant."

"And?"

"It's been quite a day in San Francisco. While gunshots aren't unusual in his city, this one took the cake, he said. Not only was there what we heard over the phone, gunfire was also reported on the seventh floor of the building."

"Let's cut to the chase." Peters looked grim, obviously assuming the worst. "Is Dr. Kipling dead?"

"Not that they can tell."

Peters blinked. "What do you mean, *not that they can tell?*"

"There was no body and no sign of blood."

"You said there were other shots too."

Stigler amplified on her comment. "Correct. But by the time police got there, everyone was gone. A neighbor identified the unit where he heard gunfire. Building management opened the door. The place was a mess. There apparently had been quite a fight. But no body and no blood."

"And the car?"

"Shot to hell. What used to be a nice Porsche now needs serious bodywork. But again, no sign of blood."

Peters took a seat. "The only thing that makes sense now is that Schnabel kidnapped Kipling. But why would he settle for that when he seemed to be trying to kill her?"

The phone rang. "Captain Stigler here." She listened for a while before responding. "Let me write that down." She repeated the statement, as much for herself as for Peters. "DMV says the Porsche belongs to a Victor Silverstein who lives in Monterey." She tore off the sheet, handed it to Peters, stood away from her desk, and pointed to her computer.

The phone conversation continued. "Let me make sure I heard you right. Not long after a resident called the police, someone reported a woman leaving the building in the company of four men, one an African American." She listened further, bored by irrelevant information, and thanked the police captain for his quick response.

It wasn't long before the FCDE databases coughed up what Peters was looking for. "Victor Silverstein is Dr. Victor Mark

Silverstein, and he also works at the Naval Research Laboratory in Monterey." He craned his neck toward Stigler. "And if I heard you correctly, you said that Kipling left the building with a black man? Silverstein is African American."

Stigler reclaimed her seat.

"Did the witness think Kipling was taken by force?" asked Peters.

Stigler replayed the phone conversation in her mind. "No! She was a resident, and she passed them outside the main entrance. She remembered what she saw because it was odd, five people walking together, with serious expressions and no conversation. No one was touching anyone, she said, nor did anything appear out of the ordinary. The black man, Silverstein presumably, was carrying a bag."

"The woman just didn't see it. They *were* taken by force. Why else would Kipling walk away with someone who had just tried to kill her?"

"You're probably right, but tell me then: why is she still alive? We know for a fact that Schnabel leaves dead people in his wake and that someone was shooting at her car." Stigler shot to her feet. "Goddamn it! I don't understand *any* of this."

Peters stared at the floor. "This Silverstein fellow must be an innocent bystander. Probably Kipling's friend, or even a lover, since they were likely staying together in that apartment."

"At the least, we know that he's her colleague, since they work at the same place."

Peters opened his laptop, did some typing, and looked up. "Kipling and Silverstein have written technical articles together, going back some eight, nine years."

Stigler plopped down in her chair and cupped her face in her hands. "Schnabel flies all the way from Colombia to track down Kipling. Why? We have no idea. But you can be sure it's no coincidence that she happens to be an NRL employee. Except for Tom, Schnabel seems to be targeting only researchers from that organization. First Greenland, then Washington, and now California."

Stigler stared at Peters, hoping that he was making more sense out of this than she was. "What are you thinking?"

"Is that everything the police told you?" Peters had thrown the ball back into her court.

"Everything of consequence. The chief did say that they called the guy who owns the condo. Silverstein had apparently asked him if he could use his place for the weekend, saying that he was meeting a friend there."

Peters's head snapped upward. "He met Kipling there? They didn't drive to San Francisco together?"

"So what? She probably drove up separately." Stigler saw no significance to that fact.

"If that's so, why was she driving Silverstein's car?"

"Maybe she flew in."

With that last statement, Peters jumped to his feet. Stigler knew to get out of the way as he slid into her seat. It was clear where he was going with this. But so what? Kipling was probably returning from a business trip, having planned to meet Silverstein in San Francisco on the return home. "You're wasting your time. Where she flew in from is irrelevant."

NCDE's databases were comprehensive. It was a simple task, now that they knew Kipling's full name, to search airline records for any recent flights. It wasn't long before Peters had something and was scanning the screen. He swiveled to face Stigler head-on. "Do you want to take back what you just said?"

"Is that a trick question?" Stigler cocked her head to the side.

Peters made his point. "Linda Kipling arrived in San Francisco yesterday afternoon. She had been flying since Thursday night."

"So?"

"Guess where her first flight originated."

"How would I know?"

"Cartagena, Colombia." Peters pretended to fire a weapon with his fingers. "Does that sound familiar?"

CHAPTER 35

TROUBLE AHEAD

Dassault Falcon 900DX, 890 miles northwest of Cartagena, Colombia, over the Caribbean Sea
Saturday, 5:05 p.m. (Cartagena standard time), October 8, 2011

Forehead pressed against the window, Silverstein peered out toward the horizon visible from the port side of the airplane. Based upon the time of day, together with their stated destination, he surmised that they had just passed the Yucatan Peninsula and were flying over the Caribbean Sea. Earlier, over the Gulf of Mexico, he recalled the catastrophic oil well spill that had occurred there the previous year.

The flight had been smooth. Except for Schnabel's muffled voice to the rear (he had been speaking on the telephone almost continuously since they had taken off), the hypnotic drone of the three Honeywell turbofans would normally have been enough to lull Silverstein into a relaxing, deep sleep. The operative word was *normally*. He and Kipling sat next to each other at the front of the cabin, no doubt put there so they could be watched. Not long after they boarded, the pilot informed them that the return trip to Cartagena would take about six hours.

Silverstein had ridden on business jets before. Two memorable occasions from 2007 and 2009 came to mind. Compared to the accommodations from his earlier jaunts, this trip had upper class written all over it. That became obvious as they approached Schnabel's aircraft, parked at the San Francisco airport. Even someone unskilled in telling one business jet from another would have noticed the difference. This baby had three engines. Silverstein knew that the only aircraft besides larger airline types to have more than two was the Falcon line built by the French company Dassault. This one was an object of beauty. It seated twelve and oozed extravagance, complete with a galley and luxurious bathroom.

This day had had its share of surreal moments. The first occurred after Silverstein fired his handgun at Kipling's attackers back at the condo. He had soon realized that they had all worn bulletproof vests. That his shots had no effect proved, in retrospect, to be a blessing, considering that everyone involved in the altercation was alive and unharmed. Had he actually killed someone, the day would have turned out much differently.

The second of those moments came as the lot of them, Schnabel, two of his five henchmen, and Silverstein and Kipling, walked casually from the mayhem they had created. Even as they fled the building where they had wreaked havoc, police cars were rolling up on surrounding streets, sirens blaring. Based upon the meager evidence left in Silverstein's car and the condo, authorities would have been hard pressed to decipher what had happened.

Silverstein stole another glance to the rear of the plane and then engaged Kipling, seated to his right. Her head rested against the headrest, eyes open. "What do you suppose's going on with Schnabel?"

"You're the one who speaks German. Can't you make anything out?"

"I only catch a word now and then. It's hard to believe he's been on the phone all this time because of us."

"He seems to be pissed about something."

"I've caught that too." Silverstein squeezed Kipling's arm. "You okay?"

Kipling faced slowly in his direction. "Yeah. But I'm sorry that you've been sucked into this. It's not your problem."

"I beg to differ. Besides, knowing what we already know, together with your cousin's promise to tell us *everything* at dinner tonight, you couldn't have dragged me away."

With that thought, Silverstein's mind wandered into the past. There was another reason, buried in his youth, that mandated his decision to accompany Kipling. Because of inaction on his part, someone very special in his life had died. The memories were still painful.

*   *   *

The year had been 1982, summer, July. Victor Mark Silverstein had just completed his PhD in meteorology at Pennsylvania State University and was headed to his first job in Monterey, California. That position marked the beginning of a career that continued to this day. On his drive from Pennsylvania, he decided to stop in Pittsburgh, to visit the parents of a former girlfriend, Sylvia Brown, an undergraduate he had dated the previous year. She had unexpectedly dumped him, and he wanted to follow up, to see how she was doing. He didn't consider it inappropriate to visit because he had always gotten along well with her parents. He had never understood why Sylvia had left not only him, but Penn State as well.

What he learned from the Browns poisoned his life for the next twenty-five years. They told him why she had left the university: Silverstein's roommate, Cameron Fitzby, also a meteorologist, had raped her, resulting in a pregnancy. And horror of horrors, not long afterward, she committed suicide, unable to face the shame that bore down on her deeply religious family. Silverstein knew that he would forever blame himself for her death. If only he hadn't naively accepted Sylvia's vague reason for leaving, that she saw no future to their relationship, he could have stopped the unfolding disaster.

For the next quarter century, Silverstein bore a debilitating hatred for his old roommate, avoiding Fitzby for fear that he would kill him if given the opportunity. But in 2007, fate brought them together in an international escapade that culminated in Fitzby's death at the hands of a Middle Eastern terrorist—although, in

Silverstein's eyes, that man, named Ghali, had ethics far higher than those of Fitzby. Fitzby's death provided closure to the crime, but it failed to remove the guilt that weighed on Silverstein.

With that memory stenciled onto the fabric of his mind, Silverstein's behavior back at the condominium in San Francisco had been preordained. God had provided someone new in his life, and he would follow her to the ends of the earth to protect her.

*   *   *

Silverstein turned around and caught Schnabel's eye. He didn't seem very happy. His men were either sleeping or reading. Whatever the problem that had Schnabel in a dither apparently was of no concern to them.

Silverstein had been dumbstruck at the professionalism of Schnabel and his crew following the knockdown drag-out brawl back at the condo. Whatever Kipling's cousin Dieter had told Schnabel prior to arriving at the condo (Kipling had filled in the details of what had transpired in the garage) had changed Schnabel's mission, and he apparently wasn't one to dwell on past unpleasantries. Following their casual stroll from the building, the final group of seven men and one woman traveled to the airport in two vehicles. There they made their way across the tarmac to Schnabel's aircraft. The Dassault Falcon took to the air within minutes. Once aloft, they were offered lunch and told to make themselves comfortable. No constraints, no threats.

A hand found its way onto Silverstein's leg. Kipling squeezed and followed it with a nuzzle to the ear. "Are *you* okay?" she whispered.

"I'm fine. Really! This will all work out," he lied. From all that had happened to Kipling, together with their reading of Uncle Friedrich's letters, Silverstein couldn't imagine this turning out well. Still, he wasn't about to share his concern. "Maybe there's some innocent explanation to all this. Why else would your cousin promise that we could just walk away afterward?" *On the other hand, maybe Dieter is one lying son of a bitch.* He hoped that Kipling couldn't sense the apprehension that lay behind his smile.

Responding to a patch of rough air, Kipling steadied the leftover Coke on her tray. Unexpectedly, she flinched, and Silverstein noticed. "What's wrong?"

Kipling looked behind her. "I forgot to tell you something."

"What?"

"Remember when I told you that I peeled out in your car, and Schnabel came running after me, shooting?"

"I remember." Silverstein already suspected that the resale value of his Porsche wasn't what it used to be. Kipling had expected him to be upset. He could afford to repair the damage.

"That's correct. But you don't know why I took off in your car. I would probably be dead right now if I hadn't gotten a phone call."

Silverstein caught his breath. "What are you talking about?"

"You gave me the keys, and I got into your car. I backed up and was ready to go forward. At that very instant, my cell phone rang. I had turned it back on when we left the condo. You're not going to believe who it was." Kipling seemed to be gathering her thoughts. "A Captain Jane Stigler. Said she was from the Federal Center for Data Examination in Las Vegas."

Silverstein had read about the agency, commissioned after 9/11. "Go on."

Kipling turned to face Silverstein squarely. "Catch this. She said she was calling to warn me. Told me to be careful, not to go anywhere. At first, I thought it was a crank call, but what she said next changed my mind. She asked if the name Gunter Schnabel meant anything to me. You talk about timing. As soon as she mentioned his name, I looked out, and there he was! Then everything happened the way I told you."

Silverstein processed what he was hearing. Obviously, the feds were tailing Schnabel and somehow concluded that he was after Kipling. *And they were right!* If there hadn't been enough data previously to suggest that two civil servants from Monterey had stumbled across an international intrigue of some significance, having another government agency trailing Schnabel made that unambiguous. "At least this means we're not in this alone."

"Yeah, that's just wonderful," Kipling responded sarcastically. "If the feds are involved, that's further confirmation that we're in a shitload of trouble."

"Maybe Schnabel knows that too." Silverstein cocked his head back in his direction. "That would be worth getting upset over."

CHAPTER 36

PLAN C

Müller Family Compound, Cartagena, Colombia: 10°23'36"N Latitude, 75°32'12"W Longitude
Saturday, 6:05 p.m., October 8, 2011

Dieter and Axel stared at the speakerphone linked to their security chief flying off the coast of Colombia, soon to land. Throughout the afternoon, information, suggestions, and occasionally heated words had passed between them.

"Okay, Gunter," Dieter said, "keep on it. For now, deliver Linda and Silverstein to the compound. Tell them dinner's at nine."

Axel stood and arched his back in a stretching motion. "What'll we do, Dieter? We have only until Monday morning, right? Are we going to pay or call their bluff?"

Dieter had no idea what to make of the blackmail message. If there were absolute assurance that $10 million would be the end of it, the price was acceptable. But that wasn't usually the case when blackmail was involved.

They had spent most of the afternoon listening in as Schnabel barked orders to his security team in Cartagena, attempting to sleuth where the e-mail had originated. Even with, arguably, the best IT team south of the equator, nothing had come of their investigation. "We can't trace the e-mail. That means our best hope is with Linda."

Axel's tone oozed sarcasm. "I know that's why you asked her to come back. But you don't really believe it's her, do you?"

"No, I don't." Dieter shook his head. "I can't believe I'm actually *hoping* that one of our flesh and blood is blackmailing us."

"On the other hand, it may not be so farfetched for this Silverstein fellow." Axel began wandering about the room. "He's a nigger, you know. And a Jew, to boot, if you can believe that. No doubt a lowlife looking for a quick score. She's probably in love with him."

Dieter grimaced. Schnabel had told them he suspected that the two had stayed the night together in San Francisco. To think that Linda could be sleeping with a black man or, even more disgusting, a Jew-nigger, was abhorrent. Such a thought reminded him that what they were planning couldn't come soon enough. Sadly, the world was filling with mongrels. Schnabel's staff was working hard to determine everything they could about Kipling's colleague. "We'll know more soon."

Dieter would normally have scheduled dinner at an earlier hour. But with the dossier on Silverstein promised by eight o'clock, they needed time to study it before dinner.

"You and I need to talk." Axel had settled down and took a seat. "We need a plan for tonight. I heard you on the phone." He paused and then raised his voice. "Are you out of your mind? You don't really intend to tell them *everything*?"

"Of course not. Just the basics."

"Well then, after we find out what we need to know, they'll need to go."

They'll need to go. The euphemism was obvious. But Dieter had promised to release both Kipling and Silverstein. "We can't kill her. What I say still counts for something, Axel."

"That doesn't hold for the nigger."

"I gave my word for him, too."

"Your word, your word! You and I are worried about the future of our race, and you're concerned about your word. How are you going to convince our cousin not to go home and call a press conference?"

Dieter enjoyed playing games with his brother. "Do you not believe in what we're doing?"

Axel scowled. "Of course, I do. Why would you ask?"

"Then, if that's so, why shouldn't we be able to convince someone else, particularly family, that what we're doing is important for the future of our children?"

Axel nodded. "You certainly have confidence in your persuasive powers. But if that doesn't work, you need a backup plan. And don't you think they would agree with us just to save their hides?"

Dieter was not unaware of that possibility. Schnabel had suggested that he monitor the dinner tonight, looking for facial clues to indicate whether Kipling and Silverstein were telling the truth. Lenses embedded in the wall would provide video to Schnabel and a trained psychologist (available on call from a local university). "First, I'll convince her that what we're doing will lead to eventual good for the—"

Axel cut him off. "You're repeating yourself." He laughed. "On the other hand, even if you can't convince Linda, you could probably persuade the nigger. Ironically, he'd probably agree with us."

Dieter allowed the hint of a smile to escape the corner of his mouth. "If Plan A doesn't work, there's Plan B. Linda is an environmental scientist and will appreciate what we've put together. Even if she disagrees with our motives, she could hardly not be impressed. Hell, Axel, we've fooled the world. If there were a Nobel Prize in our category, we would be the hands-down winner. We could make her part of it. She'd take part of the credit. What scientist wouldn't jump at the chance?"

From the expression on Axel's face, Dieter knew that he wasn't buying it. Axel splayed his hands in front of himself. "I assume there's a Plan C."

"You know as well as I that we have a persuasive argument that Linda won't be able to ignore." Dieter's lips tightened. "Knowledge of a doomsday scenario has a certain impact on people. She'll have no choice but to keep quiet."

Axel grinned. "That's cruel, Dieter, but it'll be effective. She can make the decision. We'll respond accordingly."

Dieter turned off his computer and started for the door. Less than three hours to get ready. His arguments would need shaping, although the most important one would require little eloquence. He turned back to Axel. "For us, it's a win-win. Unfortunately, she's not going to see it that way. She'll be pissed as hell."

"Not much of a loss." They continued down the hallway. "You know me. If push comes to shove, I'd much prefer to speed up the process."

Whether their operation continued at its current slow, evolving pace, or accelerated because of Kipling's unplanned meddling, it would produce the same result, the opportunity for German power to resurrect itself and reclaim a world denied them more than half a century ago.

CHAPTER 37

UNEXPECTED

Müller Family Compound, Cartagena, Colombia: 10°23'36"N Latitude, 75°32'12"W Longitude
Saturday, 7:35 p.m., October 8, 2011

The sun had set on the Müller compound. Dinner would be served at nine, Schnabel had emphasized after dropping them off at the same bungalow Kipling had inhabited some forty-eight hours earlier. She was surprised to see her suitcase in the same spot as when she had departed Thursday night. Apparently, there'd been no other guests in the interim.

Silverstein walked to the picture window, taking in the evening view. Kipling noted the time. An hour and a half until dinner.

Kipling wanted to talk but figured that the room was bugged. "Why don't we go for a walk? The grounds are gorgeous."

Her colleague—and now recent lover—hadn't said much since they landed, although his demeanor seemed positive. "Sounds good to me. My legs are still cramped." He faced Kipling and grinned. "How far do you think we'll get before we run into Herr Schnabel?"

"I'm taking Dieter at his word. He told me we're free to leave when we're ready." Kipling held out her hand. "Come over here."

Kipling met Silverstein halfway. They fell into each other's arms and stood for a moment, enjoying an embrace before heading for the door.

Outside, Silverstein reacted the same way Kipling had when she first arrived. "Boy, it would take me awhile to get used to this. I've been in Monterey too long." The year-round moderate temperatures of the central Californian coast had spoiled them both.

Kipling glanced about, deciding which way to go. She chose to head toward the southern beach where she had initially thrown off her pursuers. That area was the most remote, with little opportunity for Schnabel to eavesdrop, she figured. "Let's go this way."

They walked a little before Silverstein started the conversation. "I've lived a privileged upbringing, never wanting for anything. But I've always wondered what it would be like to live among the mega wealthy." His hand made an arch through the air. "I think your cousins are among that elite group. Even hired hands like Schnabel have an aircraft fit for a head of state."

"I think we knew that about my cousins."

"Yeah, but to witness it firsthand makes it much more impressive." Silverstein lowered his voice. "Everything's probably bugged."

The volume of Kipling's voice matched Silverstein's. "I agree."

They arrived at the beach. Kipling remembered where she had left her clothing. The moonlight, together with the artificial lighting about the compound, allowed adequate visibility. Her black outfit was gone.

Knowing that white noise created by the splashing waves would confuse any remote listening device, Kipling suggested that they walk near the water. She pointed to the underwater fence that protected this flank of the compound. "At first I considered swimming out of here, but as you can see, that's not easy."

"So how did you get out?"

In the quasi-darkness, Kipling couldn't read Silverstein's face. Back in San Francisco, she had appreciated that he hadn't grilled her on the gory details of her escape. Her bruised body was evidence enough that it hadn't gone well. "I'll tell you all about it some time. Right now, I think we need to formulate a strategy for tonight."

Silverstein cleared his throat. "It's pretty obvious, isn't it? They talk. We listen. Beyond that, I wouldn't mention your conversation with Stigler. We have no idea how she or the FCDE fits into the picture."

"I agree. But shouldn't we decide on some signals between us? Just in case."

"Good point. If I cough or clear my throat, that means I sense something is up and that we need to be careful. You do the same. Okay?"

"And in response?"

"The receiving party acknowledges the signal by taking a sip from a glass. Do you think we'll have wine?"

"My family's German. There'll either be wine or beer."

"Okay then. To acknowledge my concern, take a sip of water."

"And what does it mean if I choose wine instead?"

"It means you disagree or have no idea what the hell I'm signaling about."

"So what do we do then?"

Silverstein chuckled. "I have no clue. There's only so much we can do with hand signals."

*   *   *

After their walk to the beach, Kipling and Silverstein showered and dressed. They both had fresh clothing to change into: she from her suitcase, and he from the bag he'd brought from San Francisco.

Kipling understood the German penchant for punctuality. This time she arrived at the front door of the mansion precisely at nine. Her cousins stood waiting. The pathway through the vegetated tunnel had impressed Silverstein.

Dieter nodded toward Kipling. "I apologize that we got off to such a rocky start on Thursday. I hope that we can make it up to you tonight."

Axel extended his hand. "It's good to see you again."

All eyes settled on Silverstein, and Kipling began the introductions. "Dieter, Axel, I'd like you to meet my colleague,

Victor Silverstein. Victor has worked for our facility his entire career. I only came on the scene in the late 1990s." She smiled. "He had pity on a new researcher and took me under his wing. We've worked together ever since."

Dieter stepped forward, extended his hand, his heels clicking in time. "Dieter Müller at your service. Call me Dieter. But I understand that it's *Dr.* Silverstein."

"It's Victor, please. In our business, most of us have some form of advanced degree. We are simple government scientists." He pointed to Kipling. "Linda finished her PhD just before she came to us in Monterey. She's done quite well for herself. You should be very proud."

Dieter motioned them inside and closed the door. "In fact, we know that. I've made a point of following Linda's career. My dad and her mother, siblings you know, remained close over the years." He continued the introductions. "Victor, this is my brother, Axel. I don't know how it is in your family, Victor, but in ours, I've always been the stable, level-headed one. Axel's the rebel."

Axel offered his hand and smiled. "A pleasure. But don't believe what you hear."

Silverstein nodded toward Dieter, his response obviously intended for him. "Thank you for inviting me along. But I must say that you shouldn't complain."

"What do you mean?" Dieter seemed surprised by Silverstein's comment.

"About your family, I mean. As you no doubt have noticed, I have a Jewish name, but it didn't start out that way. My father died before I was born, and then my birth mother died in a traffic accident when I was six. I was left an orphan with no brothers or sisters. My adoptive Jewish parents who took me in had no other children. And their siblings had all died in the Holocaust. Once Mom and Dad passed away, I had no family left. You can understand why I'm envious of someone having a family like you."

Kipling caught herself before her gasp became obvious. Her surprise came for two reasons. Silverstein was treading on thin ice. In their earlier discussion regarding a strategy for the evening, she hadn't even considered that Silverstein might choose to play mind games with their hosts. He was an expert at that. Afraid that the evening had started out on the wrong foot, she eyed Dieter and Axel, waiting for their reaction. Except for a beat of awkwardness, Dieter responded in stride. "I agree with you. Family is very important." He pointed down the hallway. "Shall we?"

As they entered the dining room, Kipling compared its look to what she remembered from her stroll through the Müller residence the previous Thursday. The large table had been plain then, glistening dark wood with only an arrangement of flowers to give it note. Now its appearance was far different: a white linen tablecloth accented by napkins, candelabra, and candles, all in a deep maroon color. Even the flowers, which she recognized as tropical varieties, featured deep shades of red. Each place setting continued the theme set by the tablecloth, plain white china with a single silver ring around the edge for accent and an ornate M in the center. Crystal, one for water and the other for wine, framed the plates to the rear. Consistent with the European custom of not drinking water from the tap, a bottle of water sat next to each water glass. To the sides, multiple spoons, forks, and knives, obviously sterling, completed the ensemble.

Kipling had experienced magnificent table settings before, usually at a conference center related to a scientific meeting; one a few years back in France came to mind. But never in a private home. Two male table attendants stood in place. The maroon accents to their uniforms matched those of the table.

Only four place settings graced the table. Obviously, Uncle Friedrich, the single human being ultimately responsible for their being there, wouldn't be playing a part in this intimate dinner. Kipling had hoped to meet her aunt and uncle.

"Would you care to sit here, Linda?" Dieter pointed to the left-most chair across the table. "Victor, you can sit next to Linda." His words were followed quickly by the nearest attendant moving forward and readying the chair for her. The Müllers sat opposite. The beautiful flower arrangement sat to the side so that vision among the foursome remained unimpeded.

The hosts opened their napkins to signal the start of the meal. At that cue, the attendants approached the table and poured wine for the first person on his side of the table. They then switched sides and completed the pour for the person opposite. Kipling could have sworn that the liquid from both bottles began to flow into its respective glass at the same precise time, not only for glasses one and two but also for three and four. An impressive display of German precision.

Dieter raised his glass in a toast. "I hope you enjoy Riesling. As you know, Germany makes the best in the world." He suddenly turned serious. "I know that you agreed to come here because you have questions you want answered. In fact, we have a few of our own. But first, why don't we enjoy a relaxing meal together?" Again, he raised his glass to his guests. *"Prost!"*

Thus far, the evening had evolved as Kipling had expected. However, one earlier statement had caught her completely off guard. There had been a second reason for Kipling's reaction to Silverstein's response back at the door. Over the decade she had known and worked with Silverstein—and considering that she thought she knew everything about his unusual upbringing—he had kept an awful secret to himself. Not once had he mentioned that anyone from his parents' family had died in the Holocaust.

CHAPTER 38

MORTON'S FORK

Müller Family Compound, Cartagena, Colombia: 10°23'36"N Latitude, 75°32'12"W Longitude
Saturday, 10:25 p.m., October 8, 2011

Kipling thought to herself that an outsider listening to the dinner's progression wouldn't have suspected anything out of the ordinary. Initially, conversation revolved around the history of the Kipling family after they moved to the States. Kipling filled in details of her upbringing, and her cousins provided interesting facts about their postwar years in South America. After those topics had run their course, Dieter changed the conversation. "Tell me exactly what it is you do."

Silverstein obliged, summarizing research they had accomplished over the past decade.

The meal had progressed through multiple courses. Except for the soup, all had been very German. Kipling enjoyed the appetizer but noticed that it may not have been to Silverstein's liking: herring served with beetroot, the latter being another name for a red beet. *Vichyssoise*, a French soup, followed. Considering the hot climate, this cold soup of pureed leaks, onions, and potatoes seemed appropriate and refreshing.

Having experienced her share of German cooking as a child, Kipling knew that it tended to be heavy. The main course substantiated that view. Dieter made a point of describing the dish, called *Schweinsbraten*, a pork roast, a specialty he said came from Munich. Alongside on the plate were large, round potato dumplings with a side of red cabbage.

Silverstein did not appear to be enjoying the meal; except for the *Vichyssoise*, California cuisine was nothing like this. Kipling remembered that he had followed a kosher regimen as a teenager and wondered whether Dieter had served pork on purpose, an insult to Silverstein. His demeanor perked up a little with the dessert, Black Forest cake, accompanied by coffee and a dessert German *Eiswein*.

Two hours later, the meal was over. Except for the cups and glasses, the attendants cleared the table. They then left the room. It was time for the main event. The clock down the hallway signaled an hour before midnight.

Dieter folded his hands on the table. He looked at Axel and made his first statement. "The reason we invited you back here is to ask you a very important question."

Kipling had no idea where this was going. In her mind, her cousins had secrets to share, not the other way round.

"I will get right to the point. Axel and I want to know if you two are blackmailing us."

If her cousin had suggested that Kipling had returned to Colombia to murder the entire Müller family, she couldn't have been more surprised. Her shock was evident. She turned toward Silverstein, who stared back, turning his palms face up.

Dieter unfolded his hands and gripped the edge of the table, pushing himself backward. "I want to know if you're blackmailing us for ten million dollars." He made a point of directing this question toward Silverstein.

"I have no idea what you're talking about. And if Linda's behind this, she's certainly kept it a secret from me."

Kipling made the point more forcefully. "Whoever's doing this to you, it's not us! First of all, I wouldn't do such a thing, and neither would Victor. Second, I have no idea *why* I would be blackmailing you." *But I'm sure you're soon going to tell us.* "I think it's time you tell *us* what's going on. As you promised."

"In a moment." To Kipling's eye, Dieter seemed disappointed.

Axel leaned over and whispered into Dieter's ear. Dieter nodded and continued. "Two days ago, you were the accuser, charging into our home out of the blue. Tell us what *you* know."

That I can do. "Everything I learned came from the letters your father sent to Mother. It's clear that something's going on, but we," Kipling nodded in Silverstein's direction, "have no idea what." She waited for an appropriate beat of silence. "I can promise you that neither Victor nor I have had anything to do with any blackmailing."

"Give me a moment, please." Dieter excused himself and left the room.

Awkward silence hung over the table, with no eye contact from Axel. Silverstein took Kipling's hand. Soon, Dieter returned. Before sitting down, he whispered something to Axel.

Dieter looked Kipling in the eye. "I believe you, Linda. Ironically, we had hoped that you and Victor were, in fact, behind the e-mail."

"What e-mail? What secret are you keeping that could be worth that ungodly amount of money?"

Axel nodded toward Dieter, as if giving his blessing. Dieter took a deep breath. "You've heard about the Greenland ice cap, how the movement of glaciers has accelerated over recent years?"

"Of course! Who hasn't? We aren't climatologists, but we do understand the concern over what the melting ice means."

"Everything that's happening there isn't a natural phenomenon." Dieter sat up straight. "Axel and I are responsible for some of it, I'm proud to say."

Kipling and Silverstein stared at each other. *Axel and I are responsible for some of it, I'm proud to say.* But how could they accomplish such a thing? Moreover, why?

Silverstein had a stronger personality than Kipling, and except for his mentioning the Holocaust earlier, she had been impressed by his restraint. With Dieter's provocative announcement, his forceful nature took hold. "You're joking, of course!"

Dieter chuckled, obviously pleased that he had made an impact on two individuals he likely perceived as highfalutin PhDs. "No, I'm not." He gestured toward Kipling. "In fact, the project name is Helheim, which you surmised."

Kipling chose to keep quiet. She'd let Silverstein ask the obvious question. "How?"

Axel this time. "We've placed two nuclear reactors on the ice. It was not an easy task, I can tell you. It took four years to become operational; that was back in 2007. Ever since, we've been pumping steam down to bedrock. We chose a glacier that has already shown signs of accelerated movement."

"You'll cause an environmental catastrophe." Silverstein's voice remained remarkably calm. "I assume you know what scientists think, that the fresh water from the glaciers could change weather patterns across Europe. And that's in addition to the devastation caused by increasing ocean levels."

It was Dieter who replied to this comment. "We're fully aware of what we're doing, Victor. It will take a little while longer before we reap the benefits of what we're doing."

Silverstein appeared incredulous, as was Kipling. *Benefits? How do you perceive that creating an ecological disaster qualifies as a benefit?*

*   *   *

For another hour, Kipling listened to her cousins expound on their achievement. Dieter came across not as a maniacal fanatic, the kind one might associate with a James Bond movie. His logic was precise and understandable, if you could accept what would be termed by any rational individual a terrorist act of historic proportions. He made the case that the world had fallen into such disrepair, as evidenced by the worldwide recession that began in 2008, that it needed drastic attention. But to effect change, it was necessary to first make things worse. He likened the process to chemotherapy where some sickness preceded curing the disease.

Incredibly, near the end of his presentation, Dieter suggested that they join their team. He promised Kipling that she could play a role in the operation. He told her that, as a scientist, she'd never again have such an opportunity.

The visitors listened intently, at once fascinated by the technical wherewithal to produce such an act and, simultaneously, by its utter lunacy.

Silverstein was in his element. Instead of getting upset, as Kipling was doing, he seemed to enjoy the give and take. He laughed, something that hardly seemed appropriate—or smart—considering the delicacy of their situation. "So let me get this straight. You think that once you destroy Europe by turning it into an ice box, you and your fellow Germans will ride in on your white stallions and save the day?"

Dieter brought his hand to his forehead. "I would put it in other words."

"If what you've described is correct, I'll give you points for what you've accomplished. But I can save you further time and money by telling you that it won't work. For two reasons."

Dieter's head snapped backward. He was clearly taken aback that anyone would question his logic. "And, pray tell, what are those reasons, Dr. Silverstein?" Dieter had retreated from a first-name basis. It was hard not to interpret Silverstein's comments as talking down to Kipling's cousins.

"First of all, you're about to be found out! Your secret will soon be common knowledge. And when that happens, I don't think I'd want to be in your shoes."

Shit! They had agreed that there would be no mention of the call from Captain Stigler. It was time to use their signals. She coughed hard into her hand.

Silverstein looked over. "Are you okay, Linda?"

To emphasize her point further, she continued hacking but then stopped, figuring she had made her point. "I'm okay, Victor."

In response, Silverstein took a sip of wine.

What? He doesn't understand that what he's doing is dangerous? He wants to continue playing his mind games? As angry as she was with Silverstein for wanting to reveal her recent interaction with the FCDE, she also knew that his mind operated faster than her own did. If he was playing a game, he already knew where he was going with the conversation. Few people could outthink him.

Although Dieter did a good job of controlling his emotions, his eyes gave him away. "Go on, Dr. Silverstein."

"As I've already said, you'll be found out! Or, do you have another secret worth ten million dollars? You told us yourself: you're being blackmailed. Your e-mailer obviously has enough information to convince you he's a threat."

Interesting! Silverstein hasn't given away Stigler. He's throwing back into their faces information he just learned from them.

Dieter took a slow sip from his *Eiswein*. "For the sake of argument, Dr. Silverstein, let's say you are correct. Who do you think would be behind such a thing?"

Uh-oh! Be careful, Victor.

"How would *I* know?"

"Before you arrived, our man Schnabel did a little research on you. A very capable man, Herr Schnabel." Dieter proceeded to remove a sheet of paper from his pocket and gave it a quick scan. "And from what he learned, I must say that you were a bit modest in your assessment of yourself. I am impressed by your credentials. You have the highest security clearance of anyone at your facility, with special compartmentalized access to highly classified projects."

How the hell did they find that out? I didn't even know that Victor had compartmentalized access.

Silverstein nodded. "I'm impressed by your research. But do you really think that if someone in our government knew about your operations, they would resort to blackmail? They'd be more likely to send in the Marines."

"Perhaps. But the lure of big money makes people do crazy things, Dr. Silverstein. I'd wager that these e-mails came from someone in your government."

"Well I can tell you that I knew nothing about all of this until Linda showed me your father's letters." Silverstein shook his head. "But I'm not stupid. A few details that we *are* aware of are falling into place. I assume it was you who killed our men in Greenland, since that is where you say you positioned the reactors. What happened? Did they stumble upon your operation?"

"That was unfortunate. We abhor the senseless loss of life. But I think you can understand that we had no choice in that situation."

Kipling felt blood drain from her face. Her cousins just admitted that they had murdered two men.

Silverstein continued. "And it wouldn't be too much of a stretch to conclude that you were also responsible for the three other people who died in Washington. Two of them were our NRL colleagues."

"Again, most regrettable. There were loose ends that needed tying."

Regrettable? My cousins are cold-blooded killers.

"I am amazed that you are so forthcoming with this information. I can only assume that you intend to kill us as well. You've learned the unfortunate fact that neither Linda nor I had anything to do with your e-mails. What were you going to do? Buy us off?"

Dieter waved his hand in a matter-of-fact manner. "We would have tried that, of course. But I'm sure you recall that I promised Linda that you would be free to leave after our dinner together." He nodded toward Axel. "We haven't changed our minds. But the more we've talked this evening," Dieter glanced at his watch, seemingly surprised at the late hour, "the more I realize that someone in your position might be able to determine who is blackmailing us. Until then, we'll probably have to pay them off. Unfortunately, they'll want more. But paying the ransom will buy some time. Until *you* can find them."

Only the faint ticking of the clock down the hallway broke the stillness. Kipling's cousins wanted them to become part of their conspiracy. *But why would they think we'd go along?*

"I give up." Silverstein shook his head. "You know something else that we don't. Why would you think that we would help you?"

Axel jumped into the conversation. "Before we answer that question, could we back up a little? You said there were two reasons why our plan wouldn't work. Do you mind telling us what the second is?"

"I'd be happy to. I presume that the model for your comeback is the postwar situation that existed in Germany after World War I. The Allies had laid down such stringent conditions that the populace was beaten down and frustrated. Inflation was rampant and the country's spirit gone.

"Hitler took advantage of that situation. It was like a perfect storm, an ideal situation for a charismatic, skilled orator to whip the population into a frenzy. For you to think that you could reproduce such a situation and introduce someone with the charisma of an Adolf Hitler is pure fantasy. You couldn't expect the German people to react in the same way. Human predictability is less certain than even the weather. You must know that." Silverstein closed his eyes and shook his head. "I'm missing something here."

Dieter smiled knowingly. "You are quite intuitive, Dr. Silverstein. I'll give you that. I can understand why you have done so well in your field. Why would you think we would limit ourselves to . . ." His voice trailed off. "I think I should stop there. It's not wise to tell you *all* of our secrets." He motioned toward Kipling. "Sorry."

"But back to my question, please." Silverstein gestured. "Why do you think we'd help you?"

Kipling watched as Dieter and Axel faced each other and smiled. *Here it comes!*

"We think you will help us because you know that what we're planning will lead to a better world. In fact, Linda, I am still hoping that you will take us up on our offer." Dieter pointed to Silverstein. "You and Linda could be a team."

Dieter folded his hands on his chest. "But beyond that, it is true that we have some additional leverage. Our strategy all along has been to melt the ice cap slowly, over several years. However, we do have a backup plan that will do the job much faster. And from Axel's point of view, he prefers this course of action." He grinned. "I warned you that he's a rebel."

Dieter unfolded his hands and leaned forward on the table. "Our men in Greenland are very dedicated. If we issue the order . . . or the operation becomes compromised, they have precise instructions about what to do. You are smart people. I think you can figure it out."

Abruptly, Kipling understood and knew that Silverstein had figured it out as well.

Dieter couldn't help but have the last word. "I assume you know what it means for a nuclear reactor to go supercritical." He paused to let the words sink in. "Our scientists calculate that our two reactors would melt their way down to bedrock in less than two hours. I would think that such a possibility would be a sufficient inducement for you to make sure that never happens. But if it does, the two of you can take credit."

With tension in the room having built to a crescendo, Dieter seemed to all but lick his lips as he prepared for his next statement. "With that in mind, might we count on your help to find out who's blackmailing us?"

CHAPTER 39

COMPLICIT

Federal Center for Data Examination, Las Vegas, Nevada, USA: 36°7'51"N Latitude, 115°10'13"W Longitude
Saturday, 8:35 p.m., October 8, 2011

"You can have the last piece." Stigler had her eyes on it but chose to be polite. The salty pepperoni was hard to resist.

"Are you sure?" Peters asked.

"Please, go ahead." Stigler folded the pizza cardboard into quarters and stuck it in the trash. "I think it's time we called it a night. We've batted this around long enough." Stigler yawned, hiding her mouth with the back of her hand. "If we're on to something, we'll find out by Monday morning."

Peters downed the last of his bottled water and tossed the container. "I'm not so sure. It was my idea, but the fact is that our little blackmail was built on a house of cards. If we've gotten even one detail wrong, the Müllers will know it's a hoax." He grimaced. "And either way this works out, we have trouble. If they ignore us, we're back to where we started and—"

Stigler stepped on his words. "And if they pay us . . . what do we do then?"

"I don't know. But we'll know for a fact that we're onto something really serious."

"What I wouldn't give to be a fly on the wall in Cartagena." They knew that Schnabel's plane had landed in Colombia some hours earlier.

Peters leaned back, hands clasped behind his head. "You know, we've been concentrating on our little blackmail, but we can't ignore the fact that we now know that two American citizens are being held by foreign nationals."

"What do you want me to do? Call Washington and ask that they mount a rescue mission? And," She angled her finger down toward Peters's chest, "you've been assuming all along that Kipling's an innocent bystander in this whole mess."

Peters uncoupled his fingers and jerked forward. "We've watched a trail of NRL blood stretch from Greenland to Washington. You think she's involved in that? From everything we know now, Kipling should have been dead in San Francisco this morning."

Stigler was ready. Peters had just made his first error in logic. "That's my point! She's *not* dead! And she and this guy, Silverstein, walk out of the building alongside the bad guys as if nothing has happened. Plus, you've forgotten—thanks to you, I might add—that we also know that she was in Cartagena just a couple of days ago. She flew there and back commercially, on her own. You tell me! Is it too farfetched to consider that she's in on this?"

"I don't buy it." Peters rubbed his nose against the back of his hand.

It was time to go home. Stigler's brain was fried. "I don't disagree. I'm playing devil's advocate here. Nothing makes sense. Which is precisely why we need to keep an open mind. I don't have to remind you that this all started with what we're pretty certain of, some stolen nuclear reactors." She paused for effect. "We can't disregard the possibility that Kipling is one of the enemy. Don't you agree?"

"So what are you saying?" Peters wasn't giving in.

"What I'm saying is that, if and when Kipling returns to California, we'll be waiting. She owes us an explanation."

"And until then?"

"For openers, I think I'll come in tomorrow and make some phone calls. It wouldn't hurt to know a bit more about our two Monterey scientists."

CHAPTER 40

GOOD-BYE

Müller Family Compound, Cartagena, Colombia: 10°23'36"N Latitude, 75°32'12"W Longitude
Sunday, 6:05 a.m., October 9, 2011

How she found herself back inside the mansion at this late hour was a mystery. Linda Kipling could see every detail and even pick out the scent from the flowers—as well as hear the voices down the hall. If her senses weren't so keen, she could have sworn that this was all a dream. She stood just outside the dining room. The table had been cleared, with the vase of flowers returned to adorn the glistening surface. She proceeded down the hallway, past the ticking grandfather clock.

As she tiptoed farther, the voices grew louder. They were coming from the office she had visited some three days earlier. The door was closed, but as she drew closer, she recognized the voice of Dieter Müller.

". . . maybe you're right."

"Of course, I'm right." Axel's more guttural intonations were unmistakable. "What good does it do to keep them alive? Be realistic, Dieter. Why take any chances?"

"But what about our blackmailer? Silverstein has connections. He might be able to locate the source."

Axel's voice grew quieter. Kipling pressed her ear against the door. "We've dealt with this sort of thing before, Dieter. Gunter won't sleep until this is solved. We'll pay them off for openers. And we'll always have our fallback solution if things go to hell, with or without our cousin and her companion."

"You make a good point. I suppose I've let feelings get in the way of sound judgment."

"We're agreed then?"

Kipling couldn't believe what she was hearing. Two more names would soon be added to the list of the fallen at NRL.

There was a break in the conversation, and she reacted too slowly. The door opened, and Kipling found herself face to face with Axel. Unconsciously, she tried to scream, but fear intervened. She couldn't breathe, let along form words. Soon, lack of air turned into hyperventilation. The air seemed thin, certainly not dense enough to form a word. She needed to call Victor to come save her. "Vi . . . Vi . . ."

It was too late. Axel grabbed her from the rear and put his hand over her mouth and nose. She could no longer breathe at all.

*   *   *

"Linda! Wake up! Wake up!"

Kipling heard the words; it was a familiar voice. With her head held tightly, she whipped her body back and forth, trying to escape Axel's grip. She forced air through her mouth, but no sound would come, only sickening whispers.

"It's all right. It's Victor. You're safe." Kipling felt a warm, encompassing body come down on top of her. The weight was pleasurable and had a familiar scent.

She opened her eyes, her mind clawing its way out of the Müller hallway and back into the bedroom where she and Victor had gone to bed some four hours earlier.

Gradually, Kipling's breathing quieted, and her heart rate slowed. One of the most terrifying moments of her life, whether real or imagined, had ended.

*   *   *

Kipling languished in the shower, relishing the hot water cascading over her body.

It had taken a good ten minutes of Silverstein's comforting embrace for Kipling to shed the terror that had so dominated her nightmare. It was only a dream, he told her. Besides, he said, they would know soon enough if a roadside ditch would be their new home. "Gallows humor," he said as he offered up a big smile.

She couldn't decide which had given her the greater shock: her nightmare or the previous night's dinner when her cousins had stated that they had not only murdered people, but had put in place a plan to wreak the single most devastating act of terrorism imaginable.

To top it off, Kipling's cousins chose to blackmail *her*. In exchange for their silence, Dieter offered not to activate their doomsday scenario: Chernobyl many times over, two radiating balls of uncontrolled nuclear fission melting through centuries of built-up ice—and releasing God knows how much deadly radiation into the atmosphere.

A voice interrupted her thoughts. "Linda. We need to get going. We have a breakfast invitation."

Kipling opened the shower door. Silverstein was waiting, holding a large towel, beckoning her forward. She buried herself in the fuzzy wrap. "Victor. I've never been so scared in my life. My family is crazy."

Looking into Silverstein's eyes, Kipling saw the strength and genius that she had known for the past decade. If there was a solution to be had, they would find it together. His words were calming. "God knows we've been in dire situations before, you and I. We made it through, didn't we? We'll do it again."

With those words, her confidence returned. Dr. Linda Ann Kipling would do what she had to do to stop her cousins.

*   *   *

Three hours later, Kipling and Silverstein boarded a taxicab outside the gate of the Müller compound. Dieter had offered transportation to the airport. Mindful of her dream, she opted for a taxi and asked to make the call herself. Dieter found this request amusing. At breakfast, he had offered Schnabel's jet for their return trip. Ironically mindful of their carbon footprint, Kipling opted instead for a commercial airline, and Dieter arranged for two first-class tickets to Monterey.

The midmorning meal in the garden had provided no new information. Dieter again suggested that they join the team. But mostly, this final meeting reiterated his threat of what would happen if they told anyone about Operation Helheim. But beyond this personal situation, over which they had control, there loomed the blackmailer. In words reeking of understatement, Dieter suggested that any information they could find to alleviate this threat would be *most appreciated.* He handed them both a card. "Anytime, day or night," he said.

As the taxi drove away, Kipling thought about the woman who had identified herself as Captain Stigler. She had known that Schnabel was on Kipling's tail, threatening harm. Which meant that she may have connected him to the NRL murders. Could she have sent the blackmail e-mails? If so, was there a selfish interest behind it? Or was it part of a larger, tactical plan of action?

*   *   *

At the airport, Kipling and Silverstein stood by the security check-in. Their afternoon flight to Miami would be boarding soon. Dieter had arranged for them to spend the night there, with a morning departure to San Francisco scheduled for the next day.

The last few minutes had been quiet between them. "Are you sure?" Silverstein was making one last pitch.

Kipling memorized Silverstein's face. Tears formed. "They're my family. I have no choice."

"It'll be dangerous."

"We've discussed all this. If there's another option, you should tell me now."

There was the real possibility that they might never see each other again. They hugged one last time.

Silverstein entered the line for security, his head turned, gazing back. Kipling took one final look, turned around, and walked in the opposite direction.

CHAPTER 41

CAT AND MOUSE, ONE

Naval Research Laboratory, Monterey, California, USA:
36°35'34"N Latitude, 121°51'17"W Longitude
Monday, 7:25 a.m., October 10, 2011

In terms of seniority and pay grade, only one person at NRL Monterey outranked Dr. Victor Mark Silverstein: Dr. Harry Kitchen, the superintendent of the Marine Meteorology Division. He wrote Silverstein's performance standards and was his boss. Silverstein was good at what he did and was left alone to do it. As a rule, both men steered clear of each other. It had been months since they talked.

It was somewhat surprising to Silverstein then when he found Kitchen waiting at his door. Silverstein glanced at his watch. He rarely came in to work at such an early hour and knew that Kitchen preferred a later arrival as well. Something was up.

"Harry! Why are you here so early?" Silverstein gave him a quick look as he jammed his card key into the electronic lock. Kitchen didn't seem particularly happy.

Without a word, Kitchen followed Silverstein into the office. Silverstein took his seat behind the desk. "What can I do for you?" He motioned his boss to the guest chair.

Kitchen continued standing and came to the point quickly. "Does the name Jane Stigler mean anything to you?"

Silverstein suspected immediately what had happened. "Stigler. Yes, I remember the name. She's the navy captain in charge of the Federal Center for Data Examination in Las Vegas. Why do you ask, sir?"

"She called me at home, yesterday, Sunday. She seems to think you and Kipling are involved in some kind of *intrigue*. That's the word she used."

"Intrigue, sir? Did she tell you what she meant by that?"

"I asked but was told that the situation was too sensitive to discuss."

"What did she want?"

Kitchen relaxed a little, his demeanor softening. "She asked a lot of questions about you and Linda: your background, how long you've worked here, what I thought of you, and so on." He stared down inquisitively, apparently hoping that Silverstein would offer up some details.

Silverstein didn't break, his facial expression refusing any conciliation. "That's very interesting, sir."

"Is there something I should know, Victor?"

There was no need to lie. "I can assure you, sir, that except for me and Linda, this in no way involves NRL Monterey. And I have to agree with Captain Stigler. The situation is a sensitive one."

Silverstein had numerous connections within the federal government and the military and held a Top Secret clearance that gave him access to many classified projects. Kitchen knew all of this but also knew better than to ask specifics. Still, Silverstein understood it was highly unusual for anyone to question Kitchen regarding two of his personnel, and on a Sunday, to boot.

"Captain Stigler asked that you call her as soon as possible." Kitchen handed over a scrap of paper, turned to go, and then hesitated. "You should know that Stigler asked even more questions about Linda than you. Do you think I should talk to her?"

Silverstein again responded honestly. "I'm afraid she couldn't tell you any more than I have. As a matter of fact, Linda won't be in today. She said to let everyone know that she might be out for a week or so."

With that remark, Kitchen's eyebrows rose. "If you need anything, you'll let me know, won't you?"

"Yes, sir, I will. Thank you." Silverstein appreciated his superintendent's offer of help.

Silverstein's mind was in a fog, and he needed coffee. Rather than stay the night in Miami, the plan before Kipling had chosen to remain behind in Cartagena, Silverstein had boarded a 7:25 nonstop to San Francisco, arriving an hour before midnight. A two-hour rental car ride had him home by two o'clock and in bed shortly after. Awake not even four hours later, he chose to go to work. He couldn't help his colleague by sleeping.

Back at the airport in Cartagena, Kipling had made her decision, and Silverstein couldn't refute her reasoning. The Müllers had put her in an untenable position for which there was no satisfactory solution from outside her cousins' sphere of control.

The two NRL employees had discussed what they could do. To neutralize the threat in Greenland, they needed several crucial pieces of information. How quickly could the personnel in Greenland activate their doomsday plan? Would onsite staff make such a momentous decision themselves? Finally, if the Greenland operation were overrun with overwhelming force, would it be possible to reverse any sabotage of the reactors?

Their discussion had centered on the practicality of a surprise attack on Greenland. She emphasized that there was only one way to obtain the necessary intelligence. She would go undercover and work for the Müllers. After all, they had offered her a position within their organization.

Kipling would tell her cousins that she wanted to be part of such an impressive project. She would also inform them that Silverstein was aboard as well but needed to return to work. He would use his sources to try to locate the source of the blackmail. In reality, he would be working with Kipling from the outside. When she uncovered the chink in the Müller armor, Silverstein would be ready to call in the cavalry.

At the airport, once Kipling had informed Silverstein that she would be staying behind, he purchased two electronic devices he thought would prove useful to her, one of them a temporary-use cell phone for unbugged communication. He emphasized that, to be safe, she should only use it away from the Müller Cartagena compound.

Silverstein grabbed his coffee cup, hopeful that someone had brewed the morning's first pot. Afterward, he'd come back and get down to research. He needed to better understand the operation of nuclear reactors. Rather than spend time surfing the Web, he had a better source. One of his roommates at Penn State, Richard Marshall, had majored in nuclear engineering. Marshall had remained at the university and had advanced to a professorship within the Department of Mechanical and Nuclear Engineering. Silverstein glanced at his watch; it was late morning in Pennsylvania.

As Silverstein got up to leave the room, his phone rang. He compared the number from the caller ID to the one Kitchen had given him. They were the same.

This circumstance presented a dilemma. What advantage would there be in talking to Stigler? She'd ask him questions that he wouldn't, couldn't answer. Alternatively, he'd like to ask her if she had anything to do with the blackmail e-mail. But if he did that, she'd ask how he had known such a thing.

There was no advantage in talking to Stigler. For the moment, Silverstein couldn't be bothered.

CHAPTER 42

CAT AND MOUSE, TWO

Müller Family Compound, Cartagena, Colombia: 10°23'36"N Latitude, 75°32'12"W Longitude
Monday, 9:45 a.m., October 10, 2011

"You don't say?" Gunter Schnabel replied to the phone. He had just excused himself to take a call from downtown.

Dieter and Axel Müller had been discussing their options at Schnabel's command center onsite. It was a convenient location for Schnabel to communicate with his downtown security personnel. This three-room outpost teemed with computers and communication gear, most of which maintained the security of the compound itself.

Ever since Schnabel's return to Cartagena late Saturday, he and his team had been working doggedly on discovering anything they could concerning the e-mailed blackmail threat. Schnabel affirmed to Dieter and Axel that there was no way they could trace the origin of the electronic transmission. That didn't mean that they were without options, he told them. How they replied to the blackmailer—who had asked for a response in a little more than an hour—could well determine how this played out.

Dieter's flip response to his guests at Saturday night's dinner, when he said that they would simply pay off the blackmailer and move on, was boastful—and naïve, as he well knew. That wasn't the way it was done. The Müllers had previous experience.

The first step would be to delay the payment, telling the blackmailer that it would take time to come up with such a large amount. In fact, that wasn't the case; Müller Enterprises' pockets were deep. Second, they would negotiate for a smaller sum. During this back and forth, the idea was to ferret out the identity and location of the bastard. This desired endpoint often transpired in step three, when the handover of the ransom occurred. In all previous instances, the blackmailing parties made errors that led to their demise. Not once had anyone obtained monetary compensation.

But before they even considered those steps, it was imperative to determine the veracity of the threat. Dieter read the threatening e-mail yet again:

> *Dear Dieter and Axel Müller:*
>
> *We know that an employee of yours, a man by the name of Gunter Schnabel, murdered three men in Washington DC. We also know that you are responsible for two other men missing in Greenland. What is more important is that we know what you are doing with the nuclear reactors that you took from two Soviet submarines in 2003. If you care that this information remains confidential, you will respond to this e-mail. Otherwise, everything that we know will be passed on to the Central Intelligence Agency of the United States government.*
>
> *Our request is simple. By Monday, eleven o'clock a.m. your time, you will respond, telling us that you agree to our demand. Once we have received your reply, we will provide a numbered Swiss bank account into which you will deposit ten million US dollars. Once you make payment, you can be assured that this matter is settled, and there will be no further monetary demands on our part.*

Everyone involved had studied the details of this threat. Everything said was true. But as Axel pointed out, it was not what was said that stood out, but what was not mentioned. *What is more important is that we know what you are doing with the nuclear reactors that you extracted from two Soviet submarines in 2003.*

Could the blackmailer be bluffing? Why hadn't the letter included further specifics? Was it possible that the writer knew nothing about the Greenland operation? That was Axel's point and what, he said, should form the basis of their reply.

Schnabel completed his telephone call and looked over. "We may have caught a break."

Dieter blinked. Axel edged forward in his chair.

Schnabel held both hands in the air. "I should have thought of this earlier. Let me take you back to what happened in San Francisco, just prior to your phone call. What you don't know is that I was the one who saw Kipling first. I was the one monitoring the underground parking when I identified her walking toward her car. I then positioned myself to take her out as she drove by. But when she got into her car, I saw through my binoculars that she had picked up her cell phone. Figuring that her conversation might give me enough time, I decided to go to her instead. I ran out of sight, along a parallel wall. When I arrived, I knew that I had a clear shot. But *precisely* at that instant, she turned her head toward me and floored the accelerator. By the time I reacted, it was too late. It was then that you reached me and told me to call off the hit."

"What's your point, Gunter?" It wasn't obvious to Dieter where this revelation was headed.

"While I stood perpendicular to her car, she was still on the phone. When she turned toward me, it wasn't like a casual glance in my direction. Remember, she was talking on the phone. It was a quick turn of the head. And here's what's important. She looked scared. She had that look immediately, before she could have recognized me as a threat."

"And so, you're thinking that she received a warning."

"Yes, sir, I do."

Dieter thought about this for a moment. "Go on."

"It wasn't until this morning that I realized that we might be able to determine who it was she was talking to. Had it been

Silverstein? The key was that I knew Kipling's cell number. You'll remember that my call to her in San Francisco was how I located her in the first place. So it was a simple matter for Inver to go back into her records database and see who made that call to her. Maxwell from downtown just gave me that information."

"And?"

"That call came from the Federal Center for Data Examination in the United States. They're in Las Vegas, Nevada."

Dieter had a question and started to speak, but Schnabel held up his hand. "The only thing we know about this organization is that it was formed after 9/11 to fight terrorism. I wouldn't rule out the possibility that our blackmail threat came from there."

Axel, who had contributed little to the conversation, came to life. "This is significant, Gunter. You mentioned earlier that you thought the blackmailer might be bluffing. Two can play that game. It seems to me that we can now do a little bluffing of our own."

"I agree. Our reply can be short and to the point. I'll work on a draft." Schnabel returned to the chair behind his desk.

Dieter recognized a second opportunity. "I congratulate you and your team on this discovery. But I think there is a second windfall we can reap from this information."

The past twenty-four hours had provided more than one surprise. The last thing Dieter had expected after saying good-bye to Kipling and Silverstein Sunday afternoon was her return five hours later. She had come straight to the house and announced that she wanted to take them up on their offer. She said that although she considered what they were planning to be extreme, as a scientist she couldn't pass up such an opportunity. Dieter remembered her words because he couldn't have agreed more: *to measure and document the greatest weather modification project ever considered by mankind.* Silverstein, she emphasized, saw it her way as well but would observe from afar. And to make sure that Dieter's threat never proved necessary, she said that he would do what he could to determine the source of the blackmail. She admitted that his chances were slim. The US government was a huge organization.

Dieter made his point. "Linda tells us that she wants to be part of our team. We're probably all skeptical of her motives. And from what you've just told me, two questions come to mind. One, why didn't she tell us about that phone call Saturday night at dinner? It seems to me that it would have been relevant."

Schnabel and Axel nodded in agreement.

"And two, if she had a reasonable explanation for hiding this information, do you think she'll tell us now? She says she's on our side."

Two more nods came back in reply.

It was important to move on this quickly. "Gunter. Let's write our response and get it out. As soon as that's done, find Linda. Tell her we'd like to talk to her." Dieter looked at his watch. "Tell her to meet us in my office at eleven thirty." Almost as an afterthought, he added, "And if you don't mind, let me do the talking. If she's going to lie, I want the satisfaction of looking her in the eye when I nail her to the wall."

CHAPTER 43

TICKET TO RIDE

Federal Center for Data Examination, Las Vegas, Nevada, USA:
36°7'51"N Latitude, 115°10'13"W Longitude
Monday, 8:47 a.m., October 10, 2011

This is impossible! Stigler blinked at what she saw, followed by an unconsciously delivered expletive. She immediately raised Peters on the intercom. "Get the hell down here. Now!" She read the short e-mail again.

A hurried knock came soon. Stigler ran across the room and whipped open the door. Peters stood there, having never seen his commanding officer in such an excited state. "What is it, Captain?"

Stigler motioned him inside and closed the door. Leaving him to stare at her back, she returned more slowly to her desk, realizing that she needed to curb her emotions. She replied in a measured tone. "If I remember correctly, you assured me there was no way the Müllers could determine the origin of the e-mail we sent."

"I did. Tracey explained it to me in detail. Our e-mail went through a minimum of seven servers. It's impossible."

Backing away from her desk, Stigler motioned Peters around the side and pointed to her monitor. "Then tell me how this could have happened."

As she looked over his shoulder, Peters took off his glasses and read the incriminating words:

> *To whom it may concern,*
>
> *Whoever it is who is threatening us with blackmail obviously has confused us with someone else. We know of no murders in Washington or of any missing personnel in Greenland. As far as us having some sinister plans using a nuclear reactor, we are at a loss to know what you are talking about. Please tell us exactly what you think we are doing and where, and we will investigate from our end. Ours is a large company. If there is something going on at Müller Enterprises that we should know about, you can be sure we will get to the bottom of it.*
>
> *By the way, please tell us why someone from the US Federal Center for Data Examination would be sending us such a ridiculous note. If this continues, we will have no choice but to notify your commanding officer, Captain Jane Stigler.*
>
> *We expect not to be bothered by you again.*
>
> > *Yours sincerely,*
> > *Dieter and Axel Müller*

A devilish grin lit Peters's face. "Unbelievable."

"Why are you smiling?" Stigler couldn't understand why he wasn't as alarmed as she was.

"Those clever bastards!" Peters looked up. "They're doing to us exactly what we did to them. We bluffed them, saying that we knew what they were doing with the reactors. They're so confident of their secrecy that they're bluffing back. In other words, they're saying, if you've got something, tell us what it is. Otherwise, buzz off, turkeys."

Stigler rolled her eyes. "I realize *that!*" Peters was missing the point. "Did you read the second paragraph. They've found us out."

"Not really."

"What do you mean, *not really?*" Peters, despite his brilliance, could be downright naive at times.

"Their letter consists of two bluffs. Mentioning us is the second. There's no way they know where this e-mail came from. You can take that to the bank."

"Did you read the same words I did?" Stigler recognized that her voice was rising. "They mention my name specifically. A blind squirrel just doesn't find a buried acorn, you know."

"Now that's another issue that we need to discuss, an important one, but I can assure you that they had no way of tracing this back to us."

Stigler motioned Peters out of her chair. As emotional as she was, she did believe him. Suddenly, it came to her. "Son of a bitch!"

"What?"

"Who's the one person connecting us to the Müllers?"

Peters took a seat. "You're not suggesting that Kipling told them who it was that saved her life back in San Francisco?"

"Why do you keep defending her?" To Stigler, Peters was avoiding the obvious. "More and more, the evidence says she's in cahoots."

Peters looked to the ceiling and clenched his fists. "Think about what you just said, Captain. It makes no sense. Gunter Schnabel works for the Müllers, and we know that he tried to kill Kipling. Why would she tell them who called and probably saved her life?"

Several minutes passed as Peters paced back and forth. He snapped his fingers. "I've got it. These guys are as clever as we are."

"What? How?"

"How did we find Kipling?"

Stigler fumbled through her memory. "We knew Schnabel's cell number, and we checked the calls that he made. The last one was to Kipling in San Francisco."

"That's correct. And what does that mean?"

"Andrew, my mind's frazzled. Don't keep me in suspense here."

"Schnabel had Kipling's number; that's how he called her. In the same way that we found *her* by tracing who Schnabel called, the Müllers looked at Kipling's phone records and traced the call we made to her."

"Shit!" Stigler had returned to her seat. "And now they've tossed the ball back into our court. The problem is we have nothing to throw back."

"That's true, but we do have Silverstein. He could be our ace in the hole."

Peters was making a good point. The first information that he provided to Stigler when she arrived earlier was the flight itinerary of Victor Mark Silverstein. Interestingly, flight reservations out of Cartagena had both Kipling and Silverstein scheduled to fly to Miami on Sunday night, and then on to Monterey the next day. Why had Kipling not returned home as well? Only Silverstein took the Miami flight, and rather than stay the night, he took an evening flight to San Francisco. Rental car records confirmed that he then rented a car to Monterey. Stigler had been trying to reach him at work and at home all morning.

Stigler was getting impatient. She dialed and asked for the superintendant. "Dr. Kitchen. This is Captain Stigler again. Sorry to bother you, but can you tell me if Dr. Silverstein has come in today?" She listened to his reply. "Thank you so much. Good-bye." She looked up at Peters. "Silverstein's at work. In fact, Kitchen—that's the name of Silverstein's boss—says he already talked to him this morning and gave him our number. I'll try his office again."

For the fifth time, Stigler dialed Silverstein's office, but the call rang through to voicemail. She had already left two messages. "He's ignoring us, Andrew."

"It certainly seems that way. But I still say they're not involved in whatever the Müllers are doing."

Stigler conceded the point. "Okay, I respect your opinion. I agree there's evidence to make a case on both sides of the argument. The question we have to ask ourselves now is: where do we go from here? We can't flush them out with another e-mail," Stigler pointed to her monitor, "until we have something more. We have no clue what they're doing with the reactors. They're bluffing us back, and goddamn it, it's working. Unless Silverstein talks, I'm afraid we've reached the end of the line." She stared at Peters hopefully.

"Let's back up some." Peters shook his head in frustration. "Since this all seemed to start in Greenland, maybe that's where the action is."

"Nuclear reactors in Greenland? What would be the point?"

"I don't know. Trying to stay warm?" Peters laughed halfheartedly, but Stigler didn't appreciate the humor. He continued. "But the two men there for sure went missing before the murders in DC."

"The epicenter may be well upwind of Greenland. God knows where."

"But why would there be a stop-off in Greenland, an out-of-the-way place like that? It seems to me there's a good chance *that* is ground zero."

Stigler thought of something. "You know, maybe there's a clue with those scientists. What were they doing?"

"I looked into that. They were drilling ice cores for their research. Apparently, that's what scientists do in Greenland; they drill ice cores. There's little reason to believe there's foul play among the scientists. Several countries have cooperative efforts. Besides, it was just the two of them at their base camp. They had been dropped off by helicopter months earlier."

"Is that where they went missing?"

Peters looked up and pursed his lips. "No. Their snowmobile was gone, and so were they. Wherever they ended up disappearing to, it was somewhere away from the camp. The authorities think they might have had an accident, driving into a ravine or something like that."

"What if they saw something they shouldn't have?"

As part of the FCDE's charter, as when they had trained DOD satellites on the Atlantic and, later, Brazil, they could do it again. Although a request to look at miles and miles of ice might raise eyebrows, their organization had congressional authority to do so.

Peters was already on his feet. "It might take a day or two to realign the birds."

Stigler felt some relief, sensing that their investigation had regained traction. "Okay, do it. Calculate the effective range of their snowmobile and divide by two. Start looking in concentric circles from their base camp." She pointed toward the ceiling.

"One more thing. When you make your request, make sure we have access to both high-resolution visible *and* infrared."

Stigler jammed her fist into her hand, pleased with herself. If the Müllers had something to hide within range of the NRL base camp, they would find it. Then again, if FCDE stumbled across the snowmobile and the bodies of the missing men, they would be providing the relatives with closure. But beyond this, Stigler knew there was something else that couldn't wait.

"Andrew?"

"Yes, ma'am."

"Not fifteen minutes ago, I talked to Kitchen at NRL. Silverstein's at work right now, and he obviously doesn't want to talk to us. Call Nellis. I want you and me to be in the air to Monterey as soon as possible."

CHAPTER 44

CHEMICAL COERCION

Müller Family Compound, Cartagena, Colombia: 10°23'36"N
Latitude, 75°32'12"W Longitude
Monday, 11:15 a.m., October 10, 2011

Kipling busied herself about the bungalow, organizing her few possessions. It had been less than eighteen hours since she returned to the Müller compound and completed an acting job worthy of an Oscar. In her mind, she mocked her brilliantly thought-out prose. *Oh, how I've seen the light, Cousin Dieter. What you explained to us Saturday night made so much sense, Cousin Dieter. I said to Victor at the airport, "How could I walk away from the opportunity of a lifetime?" I'm here to take you up on your generous offer, Cousins Dieter and Axel. I'm here at your beck and call. I want to help.*

Yeah, right! Kipling had made the decision to help—but to help destroy the maniacal fantasy of two men intent on continuing the deranged vision of a lunatic from 1940s Germany.

At the airport Sunday afternoon, she and Silverstein had been paranoid, expecting to stumble upon Schnabel around every corner. Their only option to stop the Müllers, she told Silverstein, was to determine their Achilles' heel.

To accomplish that, Kipling needed to convince her cousins that she could be trusted. That thought was brought to the fore an hour earlier when Schnabel had called, asking her to meet him and the Müllers in Dieter's office. She doubted that Dieter had even considered that she'd take him up on his offer to join their team. Now that she had called their bluff, they would try to trip her up, to uncover any inconsistency in her story. For that reason, Kipling made an important decision. She would give away some key information.

*   *   *

Kipling retraced her steps from the previous Thursday and entered Dieter's office. Dieter Müller, Axel Müller, and Gunter Schnabel all stood to greet her. Only Dieter offered a warm response. He pointed to a tray of beverages. "Would you care for anything, Linda?"

"I'm fine, thank you."

"Please take a seat." He gestured toward a free chair. Axel and Schnabel took their places, and Dieter returned to his desk.

Only four days had passed since their initial confrontation in this same room where she had accused her cousins of killing her colleagues and planning something nefarious. Astoundingly, they had since admitted to both.

Dieter initiated the conversation. "I'll get right to the point. When you—"

It was time to go on the offensive. Kipling raised her hand.

Dieter cocked his head. "What is it, Linda?"

"Before you start, may I say something?"

"Of course."

"Since we're all on the same side here, I want to contribute as much as I can. I'm not going to hold back anything." Kipling steeled herself.

"Go on," said Dieter.

"You already know most of what I know. I came here based on your father's letters."

Dieter interjected. "Regarding those, I'm curious. Did you really translate them yourself?"

Kipling blushed, allowing her body language to suggest a shy and nonthreatening personality. "You got me there. No, my German isn't that good. Victor did that for me."

241

Dieter nodded. "I suspected as much. Continue, please."

"There is one thing that I do know and that you don't. It may be important." Kipling faced Schnabel. "This is a little embarrassing, speaking to someone who tried to finish me off back in San Francisco." Considering the delicacy of the moment, the expression, *finish me off,* sounded less harsh than *murder.*

Schnabel replied. "You'll forgive me. There was nothing personal. And now that I understand that we are partners, I hope that you will forget that unfortunate episode."

Kipling maintained eye contact with Schnabel. "Do you remember right before I took off in the Porsche—"

Schnabel cut her off. "Was that your car, by the way?"

Stay focused, Kipling. "Heavens, no. I own a Toyota Prius. You already know that I had flown into San Francisco. Victor drove up to meet me. It was his car."

Schnabel seemed satisfied.

"Anyway, here's the important thing I want to tell you." *Here goes!* "I had just gotten a telephone call."

As Kipling finished this statement, she observed reactions from all three men. "If it hadn't been for that phone call, I might not be here today. The person calling warned me that I was in danger. That was the reason I turned my head and saw you, Gunter. The reason this is important is that, it seems to me, there may be a relation to your blackmail. Maybe, and maybe not. But you need to know this. The person who called identified herself as Captain Jane Stigler from the Federal Center for Data Examination. This organization was formed after 9/11 to combat terrorism. They're in Las Vegas."

Kipling paused to let her testimonial settle in. It was apparent that her hosts had not expected such honesty.

Schnabel took up the questioning. "Did this Captain Stigler say anything else?"

"The call didn't last long." Kipling decided to leave nothing out. "The purpose of her call, she said, was to warn me that I was in danger. Here were her exact words: 'Does the name Gunter Schnabel mean anything to you?'"

Dieter chimed in, anxious. "What do you make of all this?"

"I don't know. But whether or not they know anything that could compromise your operation, they've obviously had reason to follow

Gunter. And how all this came down to phoning me, I have no clue. I've never met or heard of this Stigler woman. Neither has Victor."

"Why didn't you tell us this Saturday night?" Dieter was leaving no stone unturned.

There was a rational answer to offer. "On Saturday night, I had just gotten here. You forget that only hours earlier you tried to have me killed. Would you have spouted out this information then? But now I am, and I've told you. Back home, Victor's looking into this. Obviously, even though we know where this Stigler is, it's not exactly to our advantage to make contact, even if Victor knew her, which he doesn't. Yesterday, at the airport, we talked about this all afternoon."

Dieter raised his finger. "One more thing, your friend Silverstein. How sure are you that you can trust him? He seems quite astute."

"Victor?" Kipling chuckled. "He's the least of your problems. He'll do anything I say." She imagined Silverstein's howling reaction to these statements. "I didn't mean to monopolize our discussion. What is it you wanted to see me about?"

It seemed to take Dieter a moment to gather his thoughts. "I, we," he gestured toward Axel, "need to know what role it is you want to play in Helheim. Have you given this any thought?"

"I have. What you've put together here is incredible." *Lay it on thick, Linda.* "I want to understand every aspect of this operation. In particular, I want to go to Greenland. Although I've been trained as a scientist, I'm an engineer at heart. Is there any way you can get me up there?"

"It's possible. You wouldn't know that our operation there exists entirely below the surface. It's almost like living in a submarine, although we have a few more creature comforts. Experience has taught us that assignments much longer than a month start fraying people's nerves. For that reason, we rotate staff in and out every twenty-five days. Your timing couldn't be better. The next group leaves here tomorrow morning."

So far, so good! Now to add some practicality to my request. If I suggest that I'm planning my life after my return, it'll ease suspicion. "That's perfect. But you know that I do have a job back in Monterey. I told Victor to put me in for a couple weeks of leave. The sooner I return, the less suspicion I'll raise."

243

The one person who hadn't yet said anything was Axel. With her last statement, his face flushed, and he stood. "How are we to know that you're not here to sabotage us? Last week you accused us of this and that, and now you want us to believe that is all behind us? I don't buy it." As an exclamation mark to punctuate his statement, he folded his arms.

Dieter amplified Axel's concern. "Axel makes a good point, Linda."

Having anticipated that it might come down to this, Kipling had her response ready. "I'm not sure what I can say to convince you. Telling you about Captain Stigler's call is probably enough to land me in jail back home. As far as my going to Greenland, you surely don't think I'll cause you any problems there. You've made very clear that you hold all the cards. But once I thought it over, I decided I'd rather be on your side."

Kipling stared at the floor. After an appropriate beat of time, she raised her head and stared Axel in the eye. "I tell you what. Surely," she gestured toward Schnabel, "with all of the security you maintain in your company, you must have ways of telling if someone's lying. A lie detector machine, perhaps?" She waved her hands. "I only know what I've seen on TV. Before we leave for Greenland, why don't you hook me up and test me."

Probably because they didn't know what to say, there was no response.

Kipling put the cherry on top. "But you won't find anything. I can tell you that."

*   *   *

Dieter Müller walked Kipling to the door. "We'll talk this over and let you know." The door closed behind her.

"I don't care what you say. I don't trust her." Axel jumped to his feet.

"What do you think, Gunter?" Dieter wanted to hear the response of a professional.

"I certainly didn't expect her to tell us about that phone call."

Walking aimlessly about the room, Axel stopped abruptly. "Don't you think it was a little strange that she offered up this information straightaway?"

"You've always been one suspicious son of a bitch." Dieter was the only one in his family who could speak to Axel like that.

Axel returned to his seat, leaned forward, and stared at the floor. "Somebody around here needs to be."

Schnabel continued calmly. "I found it interesting that she offered herself up to our testing to convince us she's telling the truth."

Dieter agreed. "What are the chances she could fool a lie detector?"

"It's unlikely, but I've heard stories."

"Again, you're not seeing it! We're playing right into her hands." Axel wouldn't give up. "She wouldn't have brought this up if she didn't know that she could beat the machine."

Dieter admitted to himself that Axel had a point. "She did control the conversation, from the phone call from Stigler to the lie detector bit."

Schnabel looked up. "She can't control everything. Remember her words: *with all of the security in your company, you must have ways of telling if someone's lying.* You know that we have other ways to make people talk."

"I don't want her hurt." Dieter knew where Schnabel was going with this.

Axel nodded. "That's not a bad idea, Gunter. Which drug would you use?"

CHAPTER 45

HEART ATTACK CITY

*Naval Research Laboratory, Monterey, California, USA:
36°35'34"N Latitude, 121°51'17"W Longitude
Monday, 11:20 a.m., October 10, 2011*

The phone rang, and Silverstein checked the caller ID, relieved that it wasn't yet another call from Las Vegas. It was Richard Marshall from Penn State. "This *is* a call I'll take," he said aloud.

"Hello."

"Richard here. How the hell are you, Victor?"

Silverstein leaned back. "I'm fine. How's Mary? How's Cynthia?" The last that Silverstein had seen Marshall was when he attended his wedding years earlier. Less than the customary nine months later, he had received the announcement for the birth of their baby girl.

"They're both good, Victor. Life's good. What can I do for you?

"I need to pick your brain. You're still a nuclear guru, right?"

"I'm at your disposal. Shoot."

Silverstein had improvised a reason for his questions. "Richard, I'm involved in some what-if scenarios that involve nuclear reactors. Terrorism-type situations."

"No problem. If I don't know the answers, I'll know who to hook you up with."

"Thanks, Richard. Let's start at the bottom. What are the power ranges of nuclear reactors these days?"

"Okay, the first thing you need to know is how reactors are rated. There are two measures of reactor output: megawatts thermal and megawatts electrical. All reactors produce heat, so the usual output quoted is megawatts thermal. The people on the commercial side of things like to quote megawatts electrical. In general, electrical output is only a third to a fourth of the thermal output."

"I understand." *Megawatts thermal seems fitting, given what Kipling's relatives are up to.*

"Okay. At the upper end, figure upwards of a thousand megawatts, although that's megawatts electrical. Those are the commercial reactors that light up houses. Figure three to four times that in heat."

"What about the lower end? How small can you get?"

"What comes to mind when you ask that question is the PM-3A. That was the one built by the Martin Company for researchers at the Antarctic, on the McMurdo Sound. That was in 1962. They wanted it to power the station down there. That baby put out about ten megawatts thermal, more than enough for what they needed."

"Physically, how big was it?"

"I've never seen it, but it was designed to fit inside a C-130. In the end, that didn't matter because they took it down there on a boat."

"So if they're small in size, does that mean that their output is also small?"

"Hell no. The United States Navy set the standards, and the best examples are the reactors they use, like on nuclear submarines. You know the history, right?"

"Educate me."

"All modern reactor know-how came from the 1940s and 1950s when Admiral Hyman Rickover oversaw the development of the reactor for the first nuclear submarine, the *Nautilus*. Even the development of commercial reactors started with that work. Anyone paying attention at the time would remember the date of August 1958. That's when the *Nautilus* went underneath the ice on the north pole. That was a big deal. Anyway, to answer your question, they're small but powerful. Those reactors put out, say, fifty to maybe two hundred megawatts thermal. Even fifty megawatts is a lot of power. For comparison purposes, a diesel-electric locomotive puts out about three or so megawatts electrical. If we multiply by four, say, that would be equivalent to twelve thermal."

Silverstein did the math. "So a nuclear submarine reactor can put out something like four to fifteen times what a locomotive does?"

"Yes. But don't forget, all modern submarines have two reactors. The *Nautilus* had only one."

Now to get to a more sensitive question. "Okay, second question. How hard is it to trigger a meltdown in a reactor?"

"Whoa! That's something that can ruin your day. Realistically, for modern reactors, it's practically impossible. They're controlled by software systems that are double, triple, quadruple redundant. You'd have to break into the system and rewrite the code. And besides that, modern reactor designs also make it hard to do something stupid like that."

"And so . . . if I wanted to trigger a meltdown, what would be the easiest approach?"

"What you'd want is an older reactor, one that doesn't have all the redundancy and fail-safe systems designed into modern versions. The older ones were very user-controlled, meaning that they were susceptible to human error. Think Chernobyl. So to answer your question, if your goal is to trigger a meltdown, I would get hold of an older Soviet design, say one built before the late sixties."

"And assuming that I wanted to trigger this meltdown, what would I do?"

"I think you know the answer. You know that there are fuel rods and control rods in a reactor. All you do is yank out the control rods, and there you go, uncontrolled nuclear fission."

"And if I yanked out the control rods, like you say, how much time would I have to reverse that process if I realized I had made a mistake?"

"What do you mean how much time?"

"I mean, how much time to turn things around, to get the nuclear fission under control before it was too late?"

"Victor, you wouldn't have *any* time. With the control rods removed, there's nothing to stop the uncontrolled fission. We're talking an exponential increase in neutrons flying about."

"Give me a number, Richard."

"Okay, you want a number? It's only an estimate because we don't exactly *do* these kinds of experiments. I'd say you'd have five seconds before the reactor mass melted its way through its pressurized container."

"And so, if we reinserted the control rods within that time, we could stop it?"

Marshall's voice radiated exasperation. "You're not appreciating how fast things happen here, Victor! I'd say that once your clock ticks beyond the one-second mark, you've already bought the farm."

Monday, 1:40 p.m., October 10, 2011

The remaining conversation with Marshall had been short. In terms of technical details, Silverstein had heard enough. To plan an attack on the Greenland site, their only hope was for Kipling to gain control of the reactor facility and hold everyone off until the assault force arrived. Timing would be crucial, and the margin for error zero.

Silverstein listened to the gurgle of his stomach. He had skipped lunch, contemplating the implications of the Marshall phone call.

The phone rang again, and Silverstein checked the caller ID. *Out of area.* At least it *wasn't* Las Vegas. "Silverstein here."

The voice on the other end made his heart skip a beat. "Victor, it's me."

"Linda, how are you?"

"Victor, you're on speaker phone here. I'm in the room with my cousins and Gunter."

Kipling had indeed made progress if she was already on a first-name basis with Schnabel.

"Just a second, Linda. I need to close the door." The door was already closed, but those few seconds gave Silverstein a moment to collect his thoughts. He hadn't expected to hear from Kipling so soon, and certainly not in a conference call with her relatives. "Okay, go ahead. How are things going?"

Kipling sounded upbeat. "Since you've left, I've had more time to think about our decision to cooperate, and I'm positive we made the right decision." Silverstein knew that these words weren't intended for his benefit. At the airport, they had discussed how they would handle communications. Except for the throwaway cell phone he had bought for her, they had to assume that all calls would be monitored.

"I agree, Linda. I couldn't have imagined that it would turn out this way, but now that it has, you need to make the most of this opportunity." Silverstein knew how to play the game. "I'll support you any way I can."

"That's why we've called. But hold on a second. I'll let Dieter do the talking."

Silverstein gripped the phone tighter, his hands moist with perspiration.

"Victor, it's me, Dieter. Linda has told us about the phone call she received from a Captain Stigler back in San Francisco." *Interesting. Linda either offered this information in a defensive move or found herself in a position that forced her hand.*

"Your timing is coincidental, sir. As soon as I got to work this morning, the phone started ringing." *No point in mentioning that this Stigler woman also called my boss.* "She has left messages, saying that she needs to talk to me, probably because she can't reach Linda. I've been avoiding her calls. I figured that's what you'd want me to do."

Dieter, again. "I think we have to bite the bullet, Victor. We need to know if she's the one behind this blackmail."

I was afraid it would come to this! "I'll do what you say, but it could get dicey. I wouldn't be surprised if this Stigler knows everything that happened in San Francisco."

Kipling came back on the line. "Victor, you and I both know that you're one clever boy. If anyone can come up with an explanation, it's you. Talking to her is our only way of getting an angle on this problem. You need to milk her for information, anything that could help us. Don't you agree?"

"I guess so, Linda. I'll do it. How should I reach you?"

"Victor, call the cell number I gave you." It was Dieter's voice again. "It's my direct line."

"As soon as I can get my thoughts together, I'll call her back. My guess is that you won't be hearing from me until tomorrow."

Kipling again. "You be careful. Remember that I love you, Victor."

"I love you too, Linda."

Silverstein hung up the phone. He shivered but not from the endearments that had passed between them. Her final comment, *Remember that I love you, Victor*, was one of four variations they had rehearsed at the airport. Loose translation: everything is fine; full speed ahead.

The shiver turned into a shudder, and Silverstein wrapped his arms around himself. The blustery, confident scientist that everyone knew Victor Mark Silverstein to be did not currently exist. His colleague, and recent lover, sat thousands of miles away inside a den of lunatics intent on world domination. Although Silverstein knew the part he would play when the time came, his role was secondary. The very future of Planet Earth rested in the hands of his colleague.

Still, there was an immediate problem at hand, and it rested right here in Monterey, California. The bleak reality was that under no circumstances could he confide in Stigler. The first thing she would do if he told her the truth would be to pass the information higher up the chain of command. And they, in turn, to someone higher. At every step, pressure would build to hatch some form of military operation, with an overwhelming probability that such action would lead to catastrophe. At dinner two nights earlier, the Müllers had made quite clear what form that catastrophe would take.

Silverstein needed to prepare for his conversation with Stigler. He would call her back in the morning. On the way home yesterday, he had worked out the seeds of an explanation that could explain what had happened in San Francisco. He needed to work on the details, correlating time frames with actual events that Stigler might know.

Silverstein stood and stretched his cramped muscles, intending to grab a sandwich from the vending machines down the hallway.

The diminutive ring behind him meant that it was the in-house intercom. "Silverstein here."

He recognized the voice of the receptionist, Peggy, for Building 702 across the street. Normally, he heard from her only when he was expecting a visitor. Silverstein flashed a glance at his desk calendar. *Nothing.*

"Dr. Silverstein, you have two visitors from the . . ." Silverstein could hear voices in the background. "From the Federal Center for Data Examination. A Captain Stigler and a Dr. Peters. Do you mind coming down and escorting them to your office? I'd do it myself, but we're a little shorthanded."

CHAPTER 46

CALCULATED RISK

Naval Research Laboratory, Monterey, California, USA: 36°35'34"N Latitude, 121°51'17"W Longitude
Monday, 2:05 p.m., October 10, 2011

A hundred feet or so separated Building 704 from the parking lot, and Silverstein briefly considered making a dash for it. He hadn't yet returned the rental car. But he couldn't do that. Stigler would know that he had skipped, whereupon she'd speak to Superintendent Kitchen, who would not be pleased. As Dieter Müller had put it less than thirty minutes earlier, Silverstein had to bite the bullet.

As he made his way down the corridor from his office, Silverstein hurriedly reviewed his explanation for the events that had occurred in San Francisco. Any detail that he hadn't fully developed, he'd have to make up on the fly.

* * *

Jane Stigler and Andrew Peters waited in the lobby of Building 702. They had flown from Las Vegas hoping that Silverstein might provide clues to their investigation. Kipling had obviously been the target of Gunter Schnabel. She might be dead, although two facts suggested otherwise. First, there was the witness's testimony that she had walked freely from the building in San Francisco, along with a tall African American, presumably Silverstein. Second, there were the plane reservations for Kipling and Silverstein to return to Monterey. How all of this related to Müller Enterprises and, by association, to Gunter Schnabel was very much of interest.

Stigler's thoughts were interrupted by the entrance of a tall, handsome black man, somewhere in his forties. He looked her in the eye. "Captain Stigler? I'm Victor Silverstein."

Stigler stood and offered her hand. "Dr. Silverstein, I'd like you to meet my associate, Dr. Peters."

They all shook hands, and Silverstein gestured toward the door. "Please follow me. I'm next door."

*   *   *

Silverstein closed the door and took his place behind his desk. Knowing that his every word would be scrutinized, he took a moment to compose himself. "I must say, you've taken me aback. I was going to call you tomorrow. I just got back from a trip, and there's a lot here," he motioned toward the stacks of papers on his desk, "to catch up on." It was time to go on the offensive. "What's so important that made you fly here all the way from Las Vegas?"

Stigler's composure radiated calm and practiced poise. Silverstein would not have expected otherwise. Anyone who had reached the rank of navy captain was intelligent and had their wits about them. "We're hoping that you can give us some insight."

Time to play dumb. "On what, pray tell? I'm a meteorologist. I'm sure you could have located one or two of those in Las Vegas." *Be careful, Silverstein. You know you tend to piss people off.*

Stigler's body language suggested that she wasn't in the mood for frivolity. "We need your help regarding an ongoing investigation."

"I'll do what I can."

"I assume you're aware of the killings back in Washington and the missing scientists in Greenland, all of whom except one were NRL personnel."

Silverstein responded abruptly. "Of course, I am! Everyone at NRL knows about it." He backed off. "But I had no idea your organization tackled street crimes. Still, so much the better. I hope you catch the sons of bitches."

While Peters sat quietly, Stigler asked her first question. "Why were you in San Francisco on Saturday?"

"How did you know that? Are you spying on me?" His was a reasonable response, given on purpose, although Silverstein figured that they already knew everything that had happened there, at least to the extent of the police report. He laughed. "Is this the point in the conversation when I should ask for an attorney?"

"I hope it doesn't come to that."

Silverstein shrugged. "I was there because I was meeting Linda Kipling, my colleague, who had just flown in from South America."

"Dr. Silverstein, I'll cut to the chase. We know that on Sunday morning someone tried to kill her. And we think we know who it is. We'd like to hear her side of the story. But since she's not here, we'll settle for yours."

Okay, Victor. It's showtime. "I have no idea how you know all this, but I've got to tell you, your arithmetic is suspect. You've added two and two and gotten five."

Stigler would have made a good poker player. Silverstein saw no reaction to his cavalier remark. "We know for a fact, Dr. Silverstein, that Linda Kipling was driving your car and was nearly killed by gunfire. I was on the phone with her when the shooting began. We've been in touch with the police since then."

Here goes! Silverstein rolled his eyes toward the ceiling. "Listen to your own words, Captain Stigler. Linda was driving *my* car. Whoever was shooting assumed that *I* was driving because it was *my* car."

"Someone was shooting at *you*? And why would someone do that?" Stigler apparently hadn't even considered this possibility.

"Captain Stigler—"

She cut him off. "Before you answer that, did Dr. Kipling tell you I called?"

Whoa! Think fast, Silverstein. Try not to lie. Answer her question with another question. "You called *her*?"

"Let's get back to my first question. Why would someone be shooting at you?"

"As I was about to say . . ." Silverstein paused because he was pissed off. He didn't like being interrupted. *Be calm, Victor!* "I will tell you what's important, but I will not tell you everything. Some things are personal and embarrassing. And not to be direct, but who is it that you think was trying to kill Linda?"

"We believe his name is Gunter Schnabel."

Silverstein had always wanted to take an acting lesson in college but never found the time. He would make do. With that statement, he stood, backed away from his desk, put his head in his hands, and shook his head. After a moment, he laughed. "I can't believe what I'm hearing. Gunter Schnabel was the man who saved our lives."

*   *   *

Stigler couldn't hide her reaction to this provocative statement. Could she and Peters have been that far off base? She stole a glance at her partner, who seemed equally confused.

"So let me see if I've got this straight. For some mysterious reason that you don't care to share, some unknown men were shooting at *you*, and Gunter Schnabel came to the rescue?"

"That's basically it."

"Pardon me, but do you mind walking us through the details? If I can be blunt, how could anyone mistake you for Kipling?"

"It's obvious, isn't it? The people shooting at her didn't see *her* get into the car. I had driven in the day before, alone, from Monterey. Whoever was after me obviously never figured that someone else would be driving my vehicle. In fact, Linda told me that the shots came only initially. After she had driven a short distance, they stopped. By then, whoever was shooting must have seen that it wasn't me."

What Silverstein was saying was consistent with what she and Peters had heard while on the line with Kipling. "So what happened then?" Stigler knew about the trashed apartment.

"Linda ran back to the condo where I had been writing a thank-you note to my friend who owned the place. That's why I had asked Linda to get the car." Silverstein gestured. "Unfortunately, they followed Linda right back to me."

"And then?"

"Once they had me cornered, they threatened me one more time. It was then that Schnabel and his men came to our rescue. That led to the tussle and the gunshots. Thank God, no one was hit. Mr. Schnabel told them that he would be settling the score for me, and he did. It was a win-win. Everyone knew that the gunshots would attract attention. The bad guys snuck out the back of the place, and we left out the front. That's it."

"And where did you go afterward?"

"Mr. Schnabel flew us back to Cartagena, back to the Müller residence. Mr. Schnabel works for Dieter and Axel Müller, and that's where they live."

Silverstein is admitting that either he or Kipling knows the Müllers! "And why would he do that?"

"That's a good question. In fact, *I* was surprised. After Mr. Schnabel took care of my problem, I think he thought that it would be safest if we lie low for a while."

"Does that mean that Dr. Kipling is still in Cartagena?"

"Yes. The Müllers talked her into staying for a few days. There were some fences that needed mending. As for me, I needed to get back to work. I knew I was no longer in danger. And so," Silverstein drew a circle in the air with his right hand, "here I am."

"Fences that needed mending? Do you mind amplifying on that a bit?"

"In a nutshell, Linda flew to Cartagena last Thursday—without asking me, I might add—to ask for help with my . . . problem. As you've probably surmised, Linda and I are close. When they refused, she left in a huff. She then met me in San Francisco on Friday. After Linda left Cartagena, the Müllers apparently reconsidered her request. That's the way Linda put it to me. The Müllers told Mr. Schnabel to catch up with her. They assumed that she had flown to Monterey, but when they arrived, and she wasn't there, they called her on her cell. That's how they found us in San Francisco. Schnabel saved my life and Linda's."

There was another detail. "Do you know when Schnabel arrived in San Francisco?"

"Mr. Schnabel told us they had flown in the previous night, but it was late. They knew the building we were in but not the unit number. Somehow, during the night, they figured that out. Like I said, things would have turned out differently if they hadn't come when they did."

Silverstein's explanation of when Schnabel arrived in San Francisco jibed with what they knew. Stigler's mind was whirring. Silverstein had spun a fantastic tale that was, remarkably, consistent with the particulars they knew.

The next question was obvious, and Peters took his turn. "Please tell us why the Müller family would do something like this for Dr. Kipling."

Silverstein's reaction was one of surprise. "I thought you knew. Dieter and Axel Müller are Linda's cousins."

* * *

Silverstein had anticipated a reaction to his last statement. It was unlikely they knew of the familial connection, and their physical response confirmed that supposition. Whatever they knew, or thought they knew, obviously had no relation to the theories they had flown here with.

"I'm sorry that you had to come all this way for this. Do you have any more questions?"

Stigler turned toward Peters, who took up the slack. "You're being very casual about a situation that, according to the San Francisco police, was quite dramatic, what with the condition of your car and the apartment."

"I would say that it was less dramatic than you make out." *There was a lie, if ever there was one.* "But all's well that ends well. And no one was hurt, thank God."

"The way you've explained things, would it be unreasonable to assume that the men coming after you wanted money?" Peters gestured randomly. "For whatever reason."

"I'm not going to confirm or deny that. But from what I've told you, I could see where you might come to that conclusion."

"And if that were true, wouldn't something like that be a tad significant . . . in light of your clearances? Someone with gambling debts doesn't exactly make a good security risk."

"You are correct, of course. But that would be assuming that you've interpreted my situation correctly. Would it not?" *If Peters wants to play games, I can play too.*

Peters continued. "How long do you expect your colleague to remain in Colombia?"

Silverstein, still standing, rocked back and forth on his feet. "I don't know. Linda told me to put in an open-ended leave slip for her." He again pointed to his desk. "That's one of the reasons I'm so busy here. She asked me to pick up on some of her work."

Stigler edged to the front of her chair. "One more question, Dr. Silverstein. You obviously know Dr. Kipling very well. Being that the Müllers are her family, could something . . . unusual, shall we say . . . be going on between them that you would not be aware of, that she could be hiding?"

"Anything's possible, but I doubt it. I've worked with Linda for over a decade, and I know her pretty damn well. Do you mind telling me what you think she might be involved in?"

Ignoring the question, Stigler had apparently decided that nothing more could be gained from this conversation. She stood, ready to leave.

Silverstein made a stop gesture with his hand and retook his seat. "Please sit down for a moment, Captain Stigler."

Stigler obliged.

The immediate crisis had passed. However, Silverstein knew that the Müllers were expecting more than a boring account of how he had cleverly explained away their San Francisco shenanigans. He would reframe his earlier question. "I doubt that I've helped you any. Linda and I were stunned by what happened in Washington and in Greenland. Although, for Greenland, I guess we still don't know much." He allowed a moment to pass. "I've answered your questions, and I think you owe me an explanation."

"We don't owe you anything, Dr. Silverstein."

"That's correct." Silverstein nodded. "You don't." He maintained his expectant gaze.

Perhaps thinking that she had been too harsh, Stigler's next words were conciliatory. "We think Gunter Schnabel is a paid killer. We think he may have carried out the DC murders. Whether or not he had anything to do with the missing men in Greenland, we don't know. Until you told us otherwise, we were convinced that Kipling was next on his list."

"That's interesting. Well, I hope I've cleared that up." *Time to lay it on.* "Still, you can imagine how troubling it is to me to hear that Mr. Schnabel may be involved in what happened in Washington." Silverstein stroked his chin. "I'm not a stupid man, Captain Stigler. You didn't come here solely on a murder investigation. If there's something that involves the Müllers, perhaps I can help. You and I *are* on the same team, you know."

* * *

Stigler made an on-the-spot decision, one she hoped she wouldn't regret. As it stood, they would return to Las Vegas with very little. Not as simple as it sounded, Silverstein was either lying or telling the truth. If he was lying, he was one clever son of a bitch. If he was telling the truth, he could be an innocent bystander—and possibly be of assistance. Did Silverstein know about the nuclear submarines they suspected the Müllers had stolen? He had been correct about one thing. The murders were secondary.

She decided it was worth the risk. Except for the requested satellite imagery of Greenland that very well could lead to nothing, they had no leads. *This* pot needed stirring.

"Okay, Dr. Silverstein. I'll tell you what you want to know. What I'll tell you is classified and needs to be treated as such. In 2003, through methods that I can't divulge, we discovered—"

Peters stammered, "Are, are, are you sure you want—"

Stigler reciprocated in cutting off Peters's sentence. She leaned toward him, her glance firm. "I'm sure, Andrew." She returned to Silverstein and continued. "We have reason to believe that in 2003, two Russian nuclear submarines were purchased or stolen by Müller Enterprises. We believe that the NRL employees who were murdered may have stumbled across something they shouldn't have and that they were silenced by Gunter Schnabel. We think, but have no proof, that the two events are related."

* * *

Now, we're getting somewhere! It wasn't hard for Silverstein to maintain the proper composure during Stigler's testimony because her details were fascinating and, at once, consistent with the picture painted by the Müllers Saturday night. Now to try to coax out one more detail. He responded cautiously. "I now understand why you came here. But pardon me for pointing out the obvious: 2003 was eight years ago. If the Müllers were planning something with those submarines, wouldn't it have occurred already?" He made a point of asking his next question slowly. "Have there been any sightings of these submarines in the years since?"

"With regard to your first question, we've been asking ourselves the same thing. With regard to the second, we believe they didn't take the submarines for the craft itself, but for their nuclear reactors. Each of these submarines had two."

Bingo! Silverstein wanted to ask one more question, the one that the Müllers wanted desperately answered, but obviously couldn't: whether Stigler was behind the blackmail.

For now, Silverstein knew most of the pieces to the puzzle.

*   *   *

Stigler and Peters remained silent as they walked to the street outside NRL. A taxicab was on its way to return them to their plane. She correctly predicted the first words out of Peters's mouth. "I sure hope you know what you're doing."

"Me too."

*   *   *

Inside, Silverstein finally made his way to the sandwich machine. He was exhausted as well as famished.

In all the years he had worked for the government, he had never done anything illegal or compromised government information in any way. That was about to change.

CHAPTER 47

POSSUM

Müller Family Compound, Cartagena, Colombia: 10°23'36"N Latitude, 75°32'12"W Longitude
Monday, 4:45 p.m., October 10, 2011

Dieter was curious. He had never witnessed a polygraph test. Axel had insisted that they accept Kipling's offer. He was as convinced that Kipling was lying as Dieter was confident that it was his persuasive arguments that had won her over. Sitting in an adjoining room, he, Axel, and Schnabel listened and watched by way of a television monitor. Their analyst, Dr. Manfred Wagner, had explained that it would be best if only he remained in the room with the subject. Dieter and Axel, with input from Schnabel, had written the questions.

Dr. Wagner had explained the procedure prior to Kipling's arrival. Polygraphs, he said, worked because they made use of unconscious bodily responses to stimuli. Attached sensors measured, among other things, blood pressure, pulse rate, body temperature, and respiration.

Wagner had also detailed his questioning procedure. First, he would pose questions like *What is your name* and *Where do you live?* For these, Kipling would be told to alternately tell the truth and lie, to establish baseline responses that would facilitate later analysis.

The test was about to begin. Schnabel adjusted the sound on the television. Four sets of eyes faced the screen. The fourth pair belonged to one of Manfred Wagner's associates, who had just arrived.

*   *   *

Linda Kipling had been waiting in the adjacent room since their earlier call to Silverstein. Her confession to the Müllers concerning Stigler had prompted that call. She waited, wired from head to foot, tethered to a control box that terminated in a laptop. A small camera mounted on a tripod no doubt provided amusement to her cousins nearby.

The analyst had introduced himself, a short, middle-aged man with premature gray hair. He might remind some people of a favorite uncle. His nature was not menacing and seemed ideally suited for performing such testing, Kipling thought. He had given her a tutorial on the mechanics of the polygraph and emphasized that if she lied, he would catch it. No doubt to make her feel less apprehensive, he asked if he could call her by her first name. He would first ask questions that he called *controls*. For these questions only, he told her to tell the truth or purposely lie based upon whether he held up his right or left hand.

Kipling prepared to do herself justice. She knew that she could remain calm enough to allow no significant physical reactions to appear on Dr. Wagner's machine. In reality, the hardest part was to do the opposite, to stimulate body responses consistent with a lie. To do that, she would generate artificial reactions, by quickening her breath, tensing her body to increase blood pressure and, for good measure, inducing pain by pinching her fingertips with her fingernails. Alternating between the two extremes required for the control questions proved tricky.

*   *   *

"We've completed the control portion of this test," Dr. Wagner explained. Kipling assumed she had done well, figuring that if he had noticed problems, he would have stopped the session or asked more questions. "We'll now move on to the most important part, the real questions. From now on, I want you to tell the truth on every question I ask."

The rest will be easy. "Yes, sir."

For the next twenty minutes, Kipling responded to question after question. Most required yes or no answers. The central questions related to her dedication to the Müller project. Wagner asked whether her returning to the compound yesterday had been a trick. He asked whether she would try to sabotage the project. He also wanted to know if Silverstein could be trusted to toe the line. Her answers were no, no, and yes.

Wagner then spent a few minutes staring at the screen and making notes.

The examination concluded, and Wagner closed his laptop. "Wait here, please. I will return shortly."

*   *   *

Wagner closed the door behind him.

Dieter asked it first. "Well? What do you think?"

Wagner slid his extended left hand under his belt and left it there, reminding Dieter of a college professor he once had. "She passed. When I instructed her to lie on the control questions, her physical responses were off the chart. During the actual test, she never lied once."

Axel, the skeptic, weighed in. "What's important here is whether she's telling the truth. I don't give a damn about your test."

Considering Wagner's initial statement, Dieter was surprised by his response to Axel's question. "To be honest, I don't know. Her responses were textbook perfect. The trouble is I've never seen anyone pass this test with such consistency."

"What do you mean?" Dieter was confused.

"As I explained before we started, her physical responses to my questions are monitored by my laptop where I watch them second by second. Until not that long ago, analysts like me determined truth strictly by studying these tracer movements. I have that expertise, of course, but we now have sophisticated software that performs statistical analyses of the subject's responses. Without this mathematical viewpoint, I would never have questioned what I saw.

"When the test is over, my software provides a single summary number, from one to one hundred, based upon both the control questions and the test questions. For someone unskilled in polygraph analysis, it's simply a matter of checking this number against a table. You could do it yourself. In general, a value below fifty suggests that the subject is lying. Above fifty means they're telling the truth. A number between forty and sixty is equivocal."

Axel again. "What's equivocal mean?"

"What that means is that you can't trust the results. Some people just don't test well. There're nervous going in, and their responses are meaningless. Testing them with a polygraph tells us little."

"So you're saying that Linda's number is in this range?" Dieter was becoming concerned.

Wagner shook his head. "On the contrary! She came in at eighty-nine."

"That's good news, right? She's telling the truth."

"Probably. The problem is that in all my years of testing, I have never seen anyone score above eighty. Linda Kipling is either Mother Teresa—or the devil."

*   *   *

Some time had gone by, and Kipling was worried. Had she failed the test? That was unlikely. From her experience at the Park Service, she knew that she could fool the machine.

Finally, the door opened. Dieter, Axel, and Schnabel followed Wagner. Behind them, a fifth man, unknown to Kipling, entered, carrying a leather satchel and a metal contraption. The satchel was similar to what she'd expect a country physician to carry on house calls.

Kipling addressed her question to Dieter, her arms trying to gesture but held in place by the biological tethers. "Did I fail? I answered as truthfully as I could," she said sincerely.

"No, you didn't fail, but the test wasn't as conclusive as we'd hoped."

Are they playing games with me? "Maybe we should do it again. I've never done anything like this before. I was nervous."

"Linda, as you know, this is very important to us. Unless we can trust you one hundred and ten percent, we have a problem. But we have a suggestion, another testing method that we've used before. We'd like your permission to give it a try."

Interesting! From what Kipling had read in the news, there was a new way that involved MRI imaging that had shown promise, wherein portions of the brain lit up differently when the subject lied. It was unlikely the Müllers had anything that sophisticated. It took only an instant more to realize what they had in mind. The man with the black bag provided the clue.

Kipling did not hesitate. "Anything you want to do is okay with me. Let's get on with it. I've got a ticket to ride, and I don't want to miss the plane." She smiled demurely.

"Linda, I want you to meet Dr. Fiedler. He will explain everything to you." Dieter beckoned to his rear.

Fiedler stepped in front of the others. Kipling had never seen a photograph of Josef Mengele, the Auschwitz physician who had performed unimaginable atrocities on sets of twins. But she imagined that central casting could have chosen this man for the part.

"Hello, Ms. Kipling. I am Leon Fiedler. I'm a physician. I am here because I have been asked to help determine if you are telling the truth."

Kipling played along. "I want to prove that more than anything."

"Have you ever heard of truth serum?" Fiedler opened his case and withdrew a syringe and a vial.

Kipling's eyes darted among the faces in the room. They landed finally on Dieter, and she chuckled nervously. "I'll do whatever you want, but please don't kill me." She addressed Fiedler. "I say this because you need to know that I respond very easily to any kind of drug. If *you* have a headache, and it takes two aspirin to make it go away, for me it'll only take half of *one* aspirin."

Fiedler nodded dramatically. "It's good that you told me that. Don't be afraid." He took the syringe, inserted it into the bottle, and withdrew some liquid.

Again, on purpose, Kipling appeared nervous. *I have to play along.* She watched as Fiedler unfolded the metal contraption. It would hold a saline bag for a drip. "What do you want me to do?"

"The beauty with this method is that *you* don't have to do anything." Fiedler smiled out of the corner of his mouth. "You're still hooked up to our sensors." He pointed to Wagner, who had returned to his laptop, punching keys. "Don't worry. Basically, you're going to go to sleep. Once you're asleep, we'll ask you questions. This won't take long, and you'll be fine. I promise."

Kipling flinched visibly as Fiedler's IV needle pierced a vein in her arm. After making sure that the saline solution flowed properly, Fiedler injected the contents of the syringe into the plastic line.

*   *   *

Fifteen minutes later, the test was complete. Dieter suggested to the others that they wait next door. Fiedler waved them out. "Go ahead. I'll watch her until she comes out of it. Another five to ten minutes, I'd say."

*   *   *

Thank God, they've given me a time frame! The last thing I want is to wake up too soon.

As Kipling's head rested on her chest, saliva drooling from her mouth, she continued her yoga-like altered state of consciousness. She tallied the heartbeats pulsing through her temples and estimated the count at fifty beats per minute. Her breathing was slow as well, not unlike what one might experience during meditation. *Just try not to move for a few more minutes.* That was the hard part. She knew she would have one sore neck tonight.

With Kipling's extreme tolerance to drugs, her telling Fiedler the opposite of the truth had resulted in Kipling barely feeling anything. Whatever this drug was, it did make her feel slightly drowsy, but that was it.

And so, the hardest part of her act was to slur her words sufficiently to make herself appear and sound semiunconscious. The questions were similar to those asked before. Kipling made sure that her responses made everyone in the room feel warm and fuzzy. A second line of questioning dwelled on Silverstein.

I think it's time. Kipling licked her lips and slowly moved her head. She moaned and drooled some more. To add credibility, she briefly considered throwing up as a way of adding a personal touch but decided against it.

*   *   *

Schnabel, Wagner, and the brothers Müller had returned to the adjacent room. Schnabel, who often used this space as his office, offered coffee from his private pot.

The elder of the two Müller brothers felt good about Kipling. In Dieter's eyes, she had passed both tests. Under the influence of the truth serum, no surprises had come from her responses to *any* question. Because Wagner had performed the earlier questioning, he did so again, with hushed coaching by others in the room.

Schnabel faced Wagner. "Dr. Wagner, do you know what drug Dr. Fiedler used?"

"Yes. We use sodium thiopental. Most of us know it as Sodium Pentothal, the same drug anesthesiologists use to sedate patients in the operating room. The only difference is that we use a less concentrated form. We need to keep them on the edge of consciousness. It was actually good that she told us of her drug sensitivity."

Axel, who had been quiet, continued the conversation. "That sounds rather simple to me. I would think that there are fancier drugs."

Wagner nodded. "Both the Russians and the Americans have tried various chemicals. Believe it or not, some swear by simple ethanol, the alcohol in booze. The Russians have claimed successes with that." He straightened himself in his chair. "The idea is to get the person talking. We've all heard of situations where alcohol has loosened lips. That's the whole idea with any of these drugs."

It's time to wrap this up. "I'd say that Linda has proven herself, and there's no reason we shouldn't trust her. I say we let her go to Greenland. Does anyone disagree?" Dieter took his time, glancing in turn at the three faces.

When Axel's turn came, he stood abruptly, walked toward the door, stopped, and turned. "I don't care what your fancy computers and drugs are telling you. I don't know how she did it, but Linda Kipling lied to us. We shouldn't trust her. Mark my word!"

Axel was about to leave when Fiedler emerged from the opposite door, bag and equipment in hand. "Linda's awake. She's fine. I told her to sit quietly for a while." Simultaneously, Dieter felt the buzzing vibration from the cell phone in his pocket. As the others watched, he checked the caller ID, surprised to see a new name on his display. Schnabel had already updated his address book.

Dieter beckoned to Axel, pointed to the phone, and addressed his guests. "I'm sorry, gentlemen. Something's come up." They hurriedly shook hands, and Schnabel led them to the door.

As Wagner and Fiedler left the room, Dieter answered his phone. "I didn't expect to hear from you so soon."

CHAPTER 48

FULL STEAM AHEAD

*Naval Research Laboratory, Monterey, California, USA:
36°35'36"N Latitude, 121°51'18"W Longitude
Monday, 3:45 p.m., October 10, 2011*

Silverstein had waited through eight rings before there was an answer, impressed that the number Dieter had given him actually rang through to the man himself. "I'm as surprised as you. I didn't expect to know something so soon."

Dieter replied, "Dr. Silverstein, I'm here in the room with Axel and Gunter. Linda's next door. Give us a second to retrieve her. In the meantime, I'll put you on speaker."

"No problem."

Silverstein was sitting in his car outside the Naval Research Laboratory. He had decided after Stigler departed that there was no point in waiting to tell the Müllers what he had learned. For Kipling to achieve her goal of entering their inner sanctum, Silverstein's honesty might prove vital.

Dieter again. "Okay, we're all here. Are you by yourself?"

"Yes. I'm sitting in my car outside work. Listen, I think I have some good news."

"Go ahead."

For the next few minutes, Silverstein detailed the surprise visit by Stigler and Peters. He said that he had explained away what had occurred in San Francisco and thought that they had bought his story.

"That's fine, Dr. Silverstein, but how does all that translate into good news for us?"

"It was in our discussion afterward that I learned what I'm about to tell you. They confided in me much more than I expected. Here's the important part. They do, in fact, know a lot about you, including some things that you didn't tell me and Linda."

"Such as?"

"They're convinced that you either bought or stole two nuclear submarines from the Russians in 2003."

"Really?"

"And they've also concluded that you wanted the submarines for their nuclear reactors."

A noticeable pause at the other end. "And tell me why you think this is good news."

"Because I'm convinced that's *all* they know! Here's what I said to them. I said, 'If all this happened way back in 2003, and the Müllers were planning something bad, why hasn't it happened already?' They couldn't answer that. Only you know what's in the e-mail threat you received, but from where I sit, it seems to me there's a good chance your blackmail came from them. I think they were fishing. And if that's the case, I'd say you're in the clear. My recommendation to you is what we say here in the navy: *steady as she goes.*"

Müller Family Compound, Cartagena, Colombia: 10°23'36"N Latitude, 75°32'12"W Longitude

Linda Kipling, still foggy-brained from her experience next door, observed the reactions of the three men in the room. She saw palpable relief on their faces.

Dieter said as much. "I'm impressed with your progress, Victor. So would your recommendation be that we ignore the blackmail?" Kipling noticed that Dieter had suddenly returned to a first-name basis with Silverstein.

"Yes, sir, I would. If they had specifics, they'd have used them against you." A second passed. "Can I talk to Linda, please?"

Kipling leaned in toward the phone. "I'm here, Victor."

"Are you okay?"

"I'm fine. We had a little excitement here this afternoon but nothing to worry about. I'll tell you about it later."

Kipling mouthed a question to Dieter. "Can I tell him I'm leaving tomorrow?"

"Yes," Dieter whispered.

"Victor, things are moving fast. It just so happens that a normal rotation with Greenland starts this week. I'll be on a plane out of here tomorrow."

"You be careful, okay? I worry about you. Can you call me after you get there?"

Kipling looked to Dieter, who nodded. "Yes. Dieter says so."

"Good. Is there anything you want me to do while you're gone?"

"Yes. Let yourself into my apartment, collect my mail, and water my plants. The key to my mailbox is hanging on the nail next to the door."

"Can this wait until tomorrow?"

"No! If my mailbox gets full, the mailman will stop delivery."

"Okay, consider it done."

Kipling backed away from the phone and looked toward Dieter, who picked up the conversation. "Okay, Victor. If you learn anything more, you'll let us know?"

"Of course."

"Good-bye then."

Kipling wondered who would speak first but decided to accept the honor herself. She wanted to make sure her cousins had connected the dots. "You didn't tell Victor and me about the submarines. So if that's the truth, you have proof right there that he's not making this up."

Dieter seemed to think for a moment and then changed the subject. "Since you've earned your trip to Greenland, I suggest that you get yourself something to eat and get some rest. The plane leaves at seven in the morning. Tomorrow's going to be a long day for you."

"That doesn't leave much time. Do you mind if I go for a jog outside the compound?"

Dieter looked at his watch. "If that's what you want, you'd better get going. It'll be dark soon."

*   *   *

The three men sat in silence as Kipling departed. Mindful of Axel's concern over Kipling, Dieter turned to Schnabel. "Is Fred Myer on duty today? He's a runner, isn't he?"

Axel nodded his approval.

Schnabel called the guardhouse and then summarized. "Our timing's good. He's on duty and has his shorts. You heard me. I told him to follow at a distance and to report anything unusual."

With that detail handled, Dieter faced Axel. "Okay, give us your concerns."

Axel made a concession. "It is true that we never told them about the submarines. Silverstein obviously got that information from somebody, and by telling us, he was taking a huge gamble at his end."

"That's what I was thinking, Axel. It makes no sense that if they were plotting against us they'd give us information that would help us. And, I've got to tell you, that e-mail threat scared me more than anything else so far. What Victor just told us has certainly calmed *my* nerves." Dieter jerked, another thought entering his head. "There is something else, Axel. Letting Linda go to Greenland does give us one advantage."

"What's that?"

"Victor obviously cares about her. If she's in Greenland, under our control, we'll have leverage against him in case he has second thoughts about helping us."

Axel seemed unconvinced. "That's a good point, but I still don't like it."

Dieter turned to Schnabel. "Gunter, you haven't said one word about Kipling or Silverstein. Do *you* trust them?"

"You know, sir, it's not my place to question your judgment. Ms. Kipling is your cousin and family." Schnabel was playing the loyal lieutenant.

Axel became visibly upset for the second time in thirty minutes. "Goddamn it, Gunter! Forget the family shit! Everything we've been working on for decades is on the line here. We need your professional opinion!"

Schnabel seemed taken aback by Axel's exclamation. Although Axel had his moments, outbursts like this were rare. Still, from Dieter's perspective, it would be reassuring to have Gunter on his side. Dieter stared at Schnabel expectantly.

Schnabel appeared uncomfortable. "You're asking me to take sides. You two disagree."

Dieter knew that Axel would be disappointed at Schnabel's response. Kipling had passed two different tests. In addition, Silverstein had just revealed information that had to have been gotten from an outside source. To lower the tension in the room, Dieter laughed. "Gunter, we've known each other for decades. Neither of us is going to fire you if you take sides. Axel is correct. We need your professional opinion."

Schnabel took a breath and exhaled noticeably. "Well then, sirs, I will tell you what I think." He shook his head, obvious pain registering on his face. "I believe that your cousin is lying and intends to do you harm. Even if there is a chance that she is telling you the truth, there is too much at stake. I agree completely with Axel. If I had been in charge, both she and Silverstein would have been dead two days ago."

Naval Research Laboratory, Monterey, California, USA: 36°35'34"N Latitude, 121°51'17"W Longitude

Silverstein had returned to his office inside Building 704. He filled out his leave slip, and like the one he had completed for Kipling, left the dates open for his return.

When, on the telephone, he had asked Kipling if she needed him to do anything for her, her reply was a code. What he was asking was whether it was time to proceed with his side of the operation. When Silverstein asked if it could wait until tomorrow, she said no. Her announcement that she was leaving for Greenland corroborated her coded reply that meant he shouldn't wait any longer.

Silverstein turned to his computer, brought up Orbitz, and made the plane reservations. He'd drive to San Francisco tonight and board a red-eye to Washington DC. Knowing the resources that the Müllers commanded, he would take no chances. On the way home, he'd make the call from a pay phone. If the Müllers somehow discovered that he had flown to Washington, he'd explain that it was work related.

From that phone, Silverstein would be making the most important call of his life. He hoped to God that a certain CIA agent would be at the other end to take the call.

CHAPTER 49

A MEMORY PAST

Just east of San Francisco at 22,000 feet
Tuesday, 12:20 a.m., October 11, 2011

The seatbelt sign has been turned off, and you are free to move about the cabin. However, for your own safety while seated, we recommend that you keep your seatbelt secured in the event of unexpected turbulence.

Silverstein had upgraded to first class for his flight to Washington Dulles. He pushed back on his seat, intent on getting some shuteye. The previous night had been short enough, and this one wouldn't have much more to offer. The man dressed in a business suit to his right was already snoring away. Silverstein looked left into the inky void outside the window and closed his eyes. Before a restless sleep took him under its wing, his thoughts took him back to his alma mater, Pennsylvania State University.

*   *   *

Silverstein had many memories from that period in his life, most of them good, a few unpleasant, and several downright devastating. One that included elements from both extremes occurred late one evening while Silverstein and his roommate, also a meteorologist, were returning to their apartment in downtown State College.

Ahead, down the street, walked another student, unknown to Silverstein, but someone whom he had seen often because they frequented the same sidewalks. The young man was Hispanic, another of a small minority at the university in the late 1970s. And *crippled*! It would be a decade or so later when the politically correct term became *disabled*, but back then, people would have called him crippled. One of his legs was misshapen, causing him to walk with a sideways gait. He got around just fine but was awkward and slow. Silverstein felt empathy toward him, knowing that his abnormality would have made him the target of bullies' taunts as a child, not unlike the racial slurs Silverstein had endured while growing up in biracial Atlanta during the 1960s and 1970s.

Suddenly, Silverstein saw two men jump out in front of the student and, as Silverstein learned later, demand money. When the student said he didn't have any, the two punks threw him to the sidewalk, kicking and screaming racial epithets. Silverstein immediately took off running toward him, yelling to scare them away. Silverstein's roommate was of no use, choosing instead to split in the opposite direction. To his dismay, his shouts had no effect. Further, when he arrived, and the attackers saw that he was African American, they offered their opinion that a nigger held a significantly lower position in the human evolutionary chain than even a spic.

When it became clear to them that Silverstein wasn't about to run from their threats, one pulled a knife. What *they* didn't know was that Silverstein's parents had insisted that he take self-defense classes as a teenager. What *Silverstein* soon realized was that the one with the knife was just as tough as Silverstein thought himself to be.

What ensued was a nasty brawl, and Silverstein soon discovered that his attacker had no intention of taking prisoners. What happened next passed in a perceptual blur. The one with the knife lunged toward Silverstein. Silverstein sidestepped his attacker, grabbing the wrist behind the knife and twisting it to the side. The consequence was a heavily bleeding adversary prostrate on the ground. The attacker's accomplice raced away.

About this time, neighbors responded to the ruckus and called the police. Another twenty minutes elapsed before an ambulance took all three men to the hospital. The Hispanic's wounds were minor, consisting mostly of bruises. Silverstein's were slightly more significant, the worst of which required stitches. Unfortunately, his adversary lost so much blood that he died soon after arriving at the hospital.

Although the situation had clearly been one of self-defense, Silverstein took it hard, having just killed a man. His parents flew up immediately from Atlanta and hired an attorney, although it turned out to be unnecessary because the incident blew over quickly. The second assailant never came forward, and the Hispanic testified as to what happened. Further, the university downplayed the incident. The last thing they wanted was bad publicity for one of their prized African American students.

*   *   *

Nearly asleep, Silverstein pried open his eyes to savor the warmth that memory always gave him. He was as proud of that unforeseen moment in his life as he was of any of the numerous awards he had received during his professional career. He had stood up when destiny threw him a curve and had made a good showing, defending a fellow human being who didn't have the wherewithal to do it himself.

In the three decades since that incident, there had been two occasions when fate caused the paths of the attacked and his rescuer to intersect. Tomorrow would be the third.

Back in Monterey, at the pay phone, Silverstein had contacted the only person in the world he knew he could count on in this dire situation, and who had the resources and connections to make things happen. If ever there was a time that Silverstein needed a trusted friend, it was now.

Hector Rodriguez Lopez, senior analyst and operative within the Central Intelligence Agency, the helpless Hispanic from a distant memory, told him not to worry, that he would be waiting when Silverstein arrived in the morning.

CHAPTER 50

PONTIUS PILATE'S LAMENT

Reykjavik Airport, Iceland: 64°7'54"N Latitude, 21°57'04"W Longitude
Wednesday, 12:05 a.m., October 12, 2011

Kipling's eyes flew open as the wheels of the Boeing 737 touched terra firma. They had landed in Iceland, their second stop since leaving Cartagena. Through eyes hazy with sleep, she focused on her watch. It was five minutes past seven in the evening. But that was Cartagena time, five hours behind Iceland. She had been surprised to learn that Iceland shared the same time zone as Greenwich, England, ground zero for UTC (*temps universel coordonné* or, in English, coordinated universal time). Kipling and her fellow travelers had been in the air for twelve hours, with one third of their trip remaining.

Schnabel addressed the sixteen passengers over the plane's intercom. "Most of you know the drill. We change planes here. We'll be on the ground for an hour and a half before we head to Kulusuk. Also, remember that our Dash-8 is a relatively small aircraft. If I were you, I'd use the toilet before we leave. You can grab a bite to eat in the terminal while we transfer cargo."

Prior to their departure from Cartagena, Schnabel had explained their itinerary. He also told Kipling that they had to leave by seven in the morning to guarantee that all flight activity into and out of their inland site on Greenland took place under the cover of darkness. Their first stop out of Cartagena would be Halifax, Nova Scotia, to refuel. Another four and a half hours would put them into Reykjavik, Iceland. Kipling recalled that Müller Pharmaceuticals had its corporate headquarters there.

In Reykjavik, passengers and cargo would transfer into a Dash-8 turboprop aircraft. When she asked why they didn't fly directly to Greenland, Schnabel told her that the airstrip on the eastern side of Greenland could accommodate only small planes—although he confessed that he occasionally cheated with his small jet. From Kulusuk, they would fly inland by helicopter.

Kipling also asked why they had flown up on such a large aircraft. Schnabel explained that the Boeing 737 was the usual corporate aircraft that flew back and forth to their pharmaceutical headquarters. It was important that this flight blend in with the numerous other flights connected with business there.

From Schnabel's occasional snide comments, as well as the reaction of the crew to his presence, Kipling concluded that it was unusual for him to take part in what was, essentially, a ferry job. Her unpleasant deduction was that her cousins had asked him to come along to babysit her.

The purpose of this trip was to swap out personnel on the ice, all males, as Kipling discovered. In addition, their aircraft transported technical parts available only through their Cartagena supply chain. During interim periods, Schnabel had explained, flights direct from Reykjavik supplied the camp with fresh food and other provisions.

Kipling stood and stretched, glancing about the cabin. Because this 737 had only economy seats, with no first class, everyone had scattered about; sixteen men and one woman on a 120-passenger jetliner hardly caused crowding. After Halifax, most aboard had stretched out across the three seats on either side of the aisle. Since they would be arriving on the ice just before sunrise, it made sense to grab some sleep.

Except for Schnabel, no one had spoken to Kipling since they had departed Cartagena. She imagined what he had told the others: *Our female passenger is the Müllers' cousin from America. She's a strange one and prefers to be left alone.* It was of some interest then, during taxi, when Kipling observed Schnabel talking and pointing back in her direction. As the plane rolled to a halt, a slight young man, several inches shorter than Kipling's five foot ten, made his way aft.

"Hello, my name is Daniel Kobler. Mr. Schnabel told me that you are new to our operation and asked that I look out for you." He offered his hand.

At last. Someone I can talk to. "Thank you. I'm Linda Kipling from the United States. I'll try not to be a bother."

"Not at all. Mr. Schnabel tells me you are a meteorologist."

"That's correct. I'm here to learn about your fascinating project."

"As it turns out, I'm sort of your counterpart on the project, although I'm more of a climatologist, with a specialty in glaciology."

"Really? Then you're the person I need to talk to."

Kobler gestured down the aisle. "Do you want to join me for a bite to eat?"

*   *   *

Kipling pushed her unfinished sandwich to the side and noted the time. Only thirty minutes remained before they would depart Reykjavik. Her conversation with Kobler during dinner had skirted around the edges of the project, with nothing substantial yet covered. There'd be plenty of time for that on the ice, she figured he was thinking. But that thought was worrying to Kipling. She needed to get in touch with Silverstein, whose role was to call in the cavalry. When they had spoken back in Cartagena on Monday evening, she had told him, in code, that he needn't wait any longer, that it was time to contact his friend at the CIA.

On Sunday, before Silverstein had departed Cartagena, they had discussed all of this at the airport. The plan was for Kipling to ascertain an optimum time, perhaps in the middle of the night when most were sleeping, for an assault on the Greenland operation. If necessary, she would gain control of the reactor spaces and prevent the Müllers from initiating their doomsday plan.

Timing would be crucial. The idea was for Lopez's assault force to blast its way through the doors and take over. *Easier said than done.* There were two key pieces of information required: *where* and *when.* Unless Kipling could communicate with Silverstein, their plan was useless. That was why she had asked Dieter back in Cartagena whether she could call Silverstein after they arrived onsite.

Kipling had originally intended to make her first surreptitious call to Silverstein during Monday evening's jog outside the Müller compound. The cell phone that Silverstein had purchased waited at the ready in her pants pocket while she ran. Unfortunately, within five minutes after leaving the compound, it became obvious that she was being tailed by another jogger. Her first opportunity to communicate privately with Silverstein had evaporated. That was the bad news. The good news was that, while she stopped to tie her shoes, she had had time to retrieve the Coblank L5000X from the hedge. Later, after washing away the dried blood and skin from the cutting blades, she tested it and found it to be functional.

So here she was at the next to last stop prior to arriving on the ice. Reykjavik might be her last chance to use her cell phone. A tiny town like Kulusuk, on the southeastern side of Greenland, might have no wireless communications. Calling from a pay phone would draw attention.

Kipling needed information, anything that might prove useful. "Tell me, Daniel. I've never been here, obviously, and I have no idea what to expect. Is anything located above ground, or should I say, ice?"

Kobler chuckled. "You're joking."

"Not at all. I know *what* you're doing, but that's about it."

"Then you're in for a big surprise. There's no way we could have kept this operation covert for so long if we weren't completely invisible."

"Invisible?"

"Yes, *everything* is located below the ice." Kobler spoke with obvious pride. "If you flew over with an airplane, you wouldn't see a thing. You'll be amazed by what the Müllers have created here. At the beginning, back in early 2004, teams worked almost twenty-four/seven to get enough built so that by the time the days lengthened, everything was hidden."

"Are you close enough to Kulusuk—is that how you pronounce it?—to get there by land?"

Kobler cocked his head. "That would be impossible, even by snowmobile. We're about ninety miles due west of Kulusuk. The only way in or out is by helicopter, from either Kulusuk or Reykjavik, and that has to happen during nighttime hours only. Remember, we're at sixty-five degrees of latitude. That's good during the winter half of the year when there's plenty of darkness, but in the summer, it's reversed. In June, it gets to the point where it's light almost all the time. That's a tough time on the ice. No supplies in or out for up to a month. You can't go outside to exercise for fear of being spotted by some aircraft flying over. You're stranded, and by the end, you're eating canned pork and beans. No one volunteers for that period."

"So we'll make it to the ice before the sun comes up?"

"We have to. Not only that, but the helicopters—two, they always go in pairs—have to return to Kulusuk before sunrise. One time we had a mechanical problem with one of the choppers, and it had to stay behind during daylight hours. We covered it with a huge white blanket. I can tell you that we were all biting our nails until the other chopper brought back repair parts the following night. Our lives on the ice are controlled by sunrise and sunset tables."

Kipling spurred on the conversation. "Were you there when it was being built?"

"No. I didn't come on the scene until four years ago. I've been rotating in and out since then."

"That must have been a complicated construction job, to get all of the materials in by air, and at night."

"From what I've been told, it was truly amazing and engineeringly complex. Here's an example. Because our facility is located only ten meters below the surface, there's a construction problem that had to be dealt with. It had to do with the firn."

"What's furn?" Kipling had never heard the term.

"It's firn, spelled *F-I-R-N*. When most people think of Greenland, they think that the white they see is all ice. In general, you have to drill down about thirty meters before you run into solid ice. It takes years of compression before the compacted snow turns solid. In terms of building something within the firn, there is a stability issue. We had to drive steel beams down through the firn and into solid ice. For support. Particularly where the reactors sit, there's a lot of weight there."

"The reactors. They must have been the most difficult."

"Yes. There are two of them, you know. For all the big stuff, the Müllers used heavy-lift choppers that flew directly from Reykjavik. And for those big guys, we actually had to create a fuel dump under the ice, to make sure there was always enough fuel for their return to Reykjavik." Kobler was on a roll. "And don't forget the thousands of feet of piping that we had to fly in. What the Müllers did in secret over a two-year period was an unbelievable feat."

"How soon did they get the reactors going? I mean, starting to pump heat down through the ice."

"We had only one reactor operational initially, and that was in the spring of 2005. That was the first time that we actually forced steam down to bedrock. Don't forget, though, that the reactors also generate our electricity. That was important early on so that we could stop using diesel-fired generators."

Two key pieces of information! First, that the site was invisible from the air. Second, importantly, it was located ninety miles west of Kulusuk. An approximate location, but a location nonetheless. Once she determined the exact coordinates, everything hinged on Kipling getting that data to Silverstein.

Kipling made a show of looking at her watch. "Daniel, thank you for filling me in. From what you've told me, I have a thousand more questions. But since our plane's leaving, I better make a pit stop as Mr. Schnabel suggested." She smiled and pointed to the restrooms on the opposite end of the terminal. "I'll catch up with you on the plane. Okay?"

"No problem. See you later."

Kipling stepped away, glancing casually about the eating area where most of her fellow passengers still sat. Schnabel wasn't in sight. With backpack in tow, she headed straight for the women's room. This was one time when she didn't mind being the only female in the group.

After entering the restroom, Kipling moved quickly. She was relieved to find none of the restaurant employees there. She headed to the last stall, entered, closed, and locked the door. She zipped open her backpack and removed her cell. It had been operational and fully charged when they left the store at the Cartagena airport. Importantly, it was quad-band, so that it would connect with any wireless system on the planet.

"Please work," Kipling whispered to herself as she held down the on/off button. Simultaneously, a sharp noise against the wall startled her. The sound had come from the men's room on the other side of the wall. *Probably a dropped toilet seat.* Slowly, the electronic display flickered to life and latched on to a signal. Kipling pressed the preprogrammed automatic dial to Silverstein's cell. He had promised to keep his phone within reach at all times. Kipling subtracted five hours; 1:20 Icelandic time meant that it was 8:20 the previous evening in Washington DC, where Kipling figured he was by now.

Kipling stood, her ears straining for any suspicious sounds. She sat back down and pulled her jacket around her head to muffle her voice. She placed the phone to her ear and heard the ringing. *Thank God!*

"Silverstein here."

"Victor, it's me."

"Is everything okay?"

"Yes. Listen carefully." Kipling kept her voice low. "I have just a few seconds. I'm in Reykjavik, Iceland. We flew here through Halifax. We're changing planes to fly to a place called Kulusuk. From there, we'll take helicopters to the ice site. By the way, Schnabel came along. But listen carefully. That site is ninety miles—repeat, ninety miles—west of Kulusuk. Everything's below ground. There are fifteen—repeat, fifteen—men onsite. Nothing is visible from the air and—"

Unexpectedly, a sharp rapping sound came from the exterior door. Kipling stood, pulling away her jacket from her face. "Mr. Schnabel says we're leaving in five minutes."

"Okay, I'll be right there," she yelled, simultaneously reaching behind her to flush the toilet.

"Victor, I've got to go."

Before she left the restroom, Kipling accomplished three things. First, she removed the SIM card and battery from the phone and flushed them down the toilet. Second, she dumped the phone in the trash. And third, she opened her backpack to make sure that nothing near the top had shifted. Toward the end of their helicopter flight, she planned to sneeze, open the backpack, and root around to find a tissue.

*   *   *

Outside, Kobler approached Schnabel, and they stood together, watching for Kipling to exit the terminal. Schnabel initiated the conversation. "How'd it go?"

"Fine. She asked a lot of questions, mostly about the site and how it worked."

"You did as I told you?"

"Yes, sir. I answered her questions truthfully, just like you said."

"And?"

"And even though she didn't ask, I told her that we were flying to a place ninety miles west of Kulusuk."

Schnabel nodded. In his line of work, he always prepared for the unexpected. And since an unfortunate accident would befall Kipling before Schnabel left the ice station, there was little point in her knowing the exact location of her gravesite, well northeast of the location Kobler had given her.

Back in Cartagena, the decision to end all potential threats from the Kipling/Silverstein combo had been a rough one. Although Dieter firmly believed that his cousin could be trusted, he conceded that he could be wrong. And with that admission, he left the room a dejected man, much as Pontius Pilate had done two millennia earlier, washing his hands of the affair. As a concession to Dieter's distress, Schnabel suggested afterward to Axel that there was no need for anything to happen in Cartagena, that an unfortunate accident on the ice would be preferable all around. He pointed out, not incorrectly, that the ice was a dangerous place.

Schnabel felt proud that his viewpoint had prevailed. And following this assignment, he'd be anxious to head west to California to complete the second half of Axel's order. Doing away with that smart-aleck nigger would be especially gratifying.

CHAPTER 51

SCREEN REFRESH

George Bush Center for Intelligence, McLean, Virginia: 38°57'06"N Latitude, 77°08'40"W Longitude Tuesday, 8:22 p.m., October 11, 2011

Silverstein disconnected the call and took a moment to collect his thoughts. Hector Lopez and his assistant, Marc Miller, looked on expectantly.

Since Silverstein's arrival at Dulles Airport at 8:20 in the morning, the day had been a busy one. Lopez had been waiting, as promised. After hours of paperwork and security checks, Silverstein had finally been permitted to enter the hallowed compound of the Central Intelligence Agency in McLean, Virginia. When, in past years, Silverstein had telephoned Lopez at his office, he imagined his luxurious confines. Now that he was there, he discovered that he had been wrong. Lopez's office was more Spartan than Silverstein's back in Monterey. The only thing special about the room was Lopez's computer monitor, which was bigger than any Silverstein had ever seen, at least three-feet diagonal.

"That was Linda. She's in Reykjavik, Iceland. They flew there by way of Halifax from Cartagena. Their next stop is a place called Kalusek, or something like that, in Greenland. From there they'll helicopter ninety miles to the west. Oh, and one more thing. We know what we're up against. She said that the ice camp is staffed by fifteen men."

Lopez, who had been sitting beside Silverstein in one of his guest chairs, rose and slipped behind his desk, at once punching keys. "I'll bring it up on IWIDS."

Along with Miller, Silverstein followed to watch over his shoulder. "What's Eyewids?" asked Silverstein.

"It's *I-W-D-S*, pronounced I-WIDS, the Integrated World Data System." Lopez stopped typing and turned to stare at Silverstein. "This is secret stuff. Do you understand? If you even mention the *acronym* to anyone outside this office, I will direct Marc to fly to Monterey to assassinate you. Am I making myself clear?" As if to amplify his point, he opened his drawer and removed a handgun, casually placing it on his desk.

Silverstein was about to laugh aloud at what he figured was a typical CIA joke but caught himself. There was no hint of humor in Lopez's face or eyes. Nor in Miller's. Silverstein realized, in time, that a sincere "Yes, sir" was the proper response.

Apparently satisfied with the reply, Lopez continued. "IWIDS came online last year. It's a technological miracle."

Silverstein watched as Lopez moved a cursor about a map of the world.

"You've used Google Earth, right?" Lopez kept manipulating his screen.

"Of course."

"IWIDS is Google Earth on steroids. You know how when you look at an image on Google Earth, you might be looking at something that's weeks or months old, maybe older?"

"Yes."

"What you're seeing here, my friend, is the latest imagery available for any location on the planet. We have banks of computers continually processing new data as it becomes available, both commercial and private. The IT people brag that we can see the imagery within thirty minutes of its capture. But it's more than that. We also have the good stuff, the spy satellite imagery that no one else will ever see, as well as Unmanned Aerial Vehicles, UAVs, and anything else we can get our hands on. As you know, we gained a lot of experience using UAVs back in Iraq and Afghanistan. No matter who asks for the imagery or

288

where it comes from, it gets loaded into IWIDS. In fact, we usually get to see it before whoever ordered it does."

"That *is* impressive."

"Here, let me give you an example." Lopez was obviously proud of their system.

Silverstein watched as Lopez moved his cursor across the Atlantic Ocean, over northern Africa, settling in on Iraq. He then homed in on Baghdad and zoomed in. Silverstein couldn't believe the detail he was seeing at the street level. "Is it true that you can read a license plate?"

"You tell me. This image is one of our better ones, from an upgrade of our KH-13 bird with a five-meter mirror. I'll change the aspect of the image so we're looking in from the side."

Silverstein's eyes widened as the image telescoped downward from city view to street level, and finally to an individual automobile. The letters and numbers on the license tag were legible. "This is incredible. But how much of this high resolution imagery do you really have?"

"That's the downside. Think of the Hubble telescope turned upside down. At our highest resolution, the swatch widths are only a kilometer or two. Everybody thinks that, just because we have all this high-resolution imagery, we can find *anything*. 'Why couldn't we find Osama bin Laden in the mountains of Afghanistan after 9/11?' Congress asked. You've heard the expression 'looking at the earth through a straw'? That said, for locations where we have a continuing interest, we can recover data continuously. But when I say *continuously*, that means only twice a day." Lopez right-clicked and pressed *Date*. "This one's from nine hours ago."

"That's from an orbiter, right?" Silverstein knew a little about meteorological satellites. Orbiting satellites stayed relatively close to the earth, around one thousand miles or less. Geostationary satellites, on the other hand, took their position some twenty-three thousand miles out. Their advantage was that they revolved around the earth at the same rate as the earth's rotation. That meant that they always looked down on the same geographic area, a particularly useful quality for a weather satellite tracking a hurricane, for example.

"That's correct." Lopez shifted in his chair. "We obviously get the best pictures closer to earth, although we do have a couple of geostationaries. Now, where did you say they were flying to in Greenland?"

"It sounded like Kalusek, with a *ka* sound."

Lopez slid his cursor northwest toward Greenland and brought up a city/road map as an overlay. "Here it is, Kulusuk, spelled *K-U-L-U-S-U-K*, on the southeast coast. Let me do a search on the Web." In a new window, Lopez brought up Google and clicked on some links. "Okay, Kulusuk is a tiny town, population around three hundred. It does have an airport but can only handle smaller planes like turboprops." He craned his neck back toward Silverstein. "I bet you Linda's changing aircraft in Reykjavik."

"That's what she said. And from Kulusuk, they'll take a helicopter to the inland site, ninety miles to the west."

Lopez headed west with his cursor. Nothing but white, with no resolution, filled the screen. "We've got nothing up there. There's not much interest in looking at a big piece of ice." He left his seat and walked over to the window. It was starting to rain outside.

Not one to be shy, Silverstein replaced Lopez and began playing with the mouse. "I know. And I'm afraid there's more." He looked up. "She said that the camp is located below the surface and can't be seen from above."

Marc Miller joined the conversation. "You're serious?"

"That's what she said." Silverstein knew that was not the best of news.

Lopez shook his head. "That's a big problem, Victor. How the hell do we mount an attack on a location we can't see? Ninety miles west of Kulusuk? That's hardly precise. From the way you described our threat, we need to move in with absolute precision."

What Lopez said was true, but Silverstein hadn't told him everything. "We have that one covered. As I told you, Linda and I went to the airport together in Cartagena, intending to fly back to Monterey. She didn't tell me until we got there that she planned to stay behind. So before I left, I bought her two things at the airport: a cell phone and a GPS device. She probably used that phone just now. But somewhere near the end of her next flight, she'll activate the GPS.

"By the way, at the airport I checked the manual. If the GPS signal is lost, like when she goes below ground, it will store the last coordinates it receives. And because a GPS only receives, it doesn't transmit, she'll be safe unless they search her."

Lopez nodded and pursed his lips. "You've a clever man, Victor Mark Silverstein."

For the first time today, Silverstein smiled. "I know."

Miller continued the conversation. "Our whole plan then rests with her getting those coordinates to us."

"That's correct. She'll tell us where and when. Either by phone or e-mail."

"And if it's e-mail, where will she send that information?"

"Right here." Silverstein held up his cell phone.

All the while, Silverstein had been playing with IWDS, sliding the cursor across the Greenland ice, west of Kulusuk, trying to discern any details on the ice. There was nothing. Without warning, the computer beeped, and new imagery spread across the screen. The fuzzy white picture was replaced with imagery having astounding clarity, similar to that of a high-definition television picture. He pressed the on-screen control that shifted the viewpoint closer to the surface. He could see details of the glacier itself.

"What the hell are you doing over there?" Lopez had heard the computer's signal.

Silverstein held his hands high, pleading innocence. "I didn't do anything! But all of a sudden, we have these remarkable pictures."

Lopez ran around the desk, shoving Silverstein out of his chair. He ran the cursor across the new imagery. He then right-clicked for additional information concerning the pass. "This *is* from one of our birds. What we have here has one-meter resolution, and the swath width is about eleven kilometers."

Silverstein felt the blood drain from his face. "Is there any way you can find out who ordered this up?"

"Sure. It should be right here." Lopez clicked some more. "It was someone from FCDE, the Federal Center for Data Examination. They're in Las—" Lopez had looked up and stopped midsentence. It would have been hard not to notice Silverstein's reaction. "What?"

"There's something I haven't told you."

Lopez raised both hands in the air, fingers apart. "You've got to be fucking kidding me. There's more to your story?"

291

CHAPTER 52

DECISION POINT

George Bush Center for Intelligence, McLean, Virginia:
38°57'06"N Latitude, 77°08'40"W Longitude
Tuesday, 8:45 p.m., October 11, 2011

"There *is* more. So much has happened this past week."
Silverstein's face flushed. He hadn't meant to hide anything.

Lopez made a face.

Over the next minutes, Silverstein explained their first contact
with Captain Stigler, when she had warned Kipling about Schnabel
back in San Francisco. He then jumped forward to Stigler's
unexpected visit to Monterey and Silverstein's explanation of his
involvement with the Müllers.

"So on top of everything else, you lied through your teeth to a
federal official?" Lopez wasn't amused.

"I wouldn't put it quite that way." Silverstein winced.
"Before you go jumping all over me, you have to understand my
perspective. There's no way I could trust her. If I had told her
what I've told you, and some hotheaded boss decided to send the
military into Greenland, a potential environmental disaster would
have been charged to my ledger. Why do you think you were the
first person I called, Hector? Because you're the only one on this
planet I could trust."

Lopez backed off from his holier than thou attitude. He obviously not only understood Silverstein's dilemma, but also admired the trust his friend had in him, a relationship spawned from an incident that had bonded them together for life. "How much do you think this Stigler knows?"

"For her, I think it started with the disappearance of the two scientists in Greenland and the murder of the three men here in DC. She somehow concluded that Gunter Schnabel was responsible for the Washington murders. And she was right. Stigler then linked Schnabel to Linda—don't ask me how—and called to warn her that Schnabel was in San Francisco and that her life was in danger. In fact, that *was* true—at least until the Müllers changed their mind. However Stigler did all this, it involved some damn clever sleuthing."

"Wait! Back up. They changed their mind?"

"Oh, yeah. That's something else I didn't tell you. The Müllers had received a blackmail threat by e-mail. The blackmailer said that he knew what the Müllers were doing with the nuclear reactors but didn't give specifics. One possibility is that Stigler sent it to try to flush them out. It seemed as if whoever did send it didn't have all the pieces and was bluffing some of the information. So back to your question. The Müllers changed their mind about the hit on Linda when they thought that maybe we were behind the blackmail. In fact, they later told us that they had hoped that was the case."

"This is complicated, Victor." Lopez rolled his eyes and began massaging his temples. "And so, Stigler came to *you* in Monterey because . . ."

"Stigler knew about our little escapade in San Francisco. She also somehow knew that Schnabel flew me and Kipling back to Cartagena, figuring, not unreasonably, that we were in cahoots with the Müllers."

"So that's all she knows, you think?"

Silverstein shook his head. "No, there was one more thing, and it's significant. It surprised the hell out of me that she even told me. Remember that I told you that the Greenland operation is powered by at least one nuclear reactor?"

"I remember."

"Well, catch this. Stigler told me where the Müllers got those reactors. She said that, in 2003, they either bought or stole them from the mothballed Russian fleet. She came right out and said that it wasn't the murders that made her fly to Monterey but the missing submarines and reactors. *But*, and this is a big but, I'm confident that she and this Peters guy are in the dark about Greenland."

"So what do you make of the imagery we just saw?"

Silverstein gave credit where credit was due. "I think Stigler and her cohort are two damned smart people. They're fishing. What they're trying to do is tie everything back to Greenland. As you know, the two NRL scientists vanished after driving their snowmobile away from their camp. I've already told you that the Müllers' henchmen killed them when they stumbled onto their operation. But Stigler doesn't know that. I'll bet you twenty dollars that if you plot the coordinates of the NRL base camp, they'll fall right in the middle of your satellite pass. That's what I would have done. They know that *something* happened to those guys and are trying to find a connection to the Müllers. They figure they'll look in concentric circles until they find something."

The rain had gotten heavier and was pounding against the window. Marc Miller spoke next. "So . . . what's important to us is that they don't arrive on the scene before we do and fuck everything up."

Lopez added, "And the good news there is that Linda says that nothing is visible from the air. These images will do them no good." He waved toward the monitor.

"So what's the resolution of the image that's on your screen right now?" Silverstein wondered if they could see anything on the snow.

"Let's take a look." Lopez clicked his mouse some more. "It's one meter, a little over three feet. You can forget about looking for footprints or anything like that. And," Lopez scanned the numbers some more, "for this one, the swath width is about eleven kilometers."

Silverstein began thinking. "Let's go back to my earlier bet. Could you please plot these coordinates: sixty-six degrees, fifty-three minutes, fifty-four seconds, north latitude; thirty-eight degrees, five minutes, fifty-six seconds, west longitude?" Back in

Monterey, he had memorized the location of the NRL scientists' base camp.

A moment later came Lopez's response. "I've got to hand it to you, Victor. Those coordinates fall in the exact center of this pass."

Silverstein kept thinking. "So what's the distance from the NRL camp to the location Linda gave us?"

"Good point. It looks to me a little over a hundred miles."

Miller interrupted. "One hundred miles? That doesn't make any sense! The NRL scientists snowmobiled away from their camp and disappeared. Right? And you, Victor, said that the Müllers did them in when they stumbled upon their operation?"

"Correct."

Miller shook his head. "Well then, don't you see it? There's no way that they went that far on a snowmobile for a day's outing. I can imagine twenty, maybe thirty miles, but nothing more than that. It's not like they're checking into a motel. You have to double that distance to get back home."

Lopez forced air out through his lips, creating an unintended whistle. "Marc makes a good point. Could you have given me the wrong coordinates, Victor?"

"No, I'm sure they're correct." Silverstein chose not to say what he wanted to say. No one ever questioned his memory.

Miller again. "What that has to mean is that they fed Linda a bogus location."

"That's what happened, Victor. Has to be." Lopez became animated. "For someone they don't trust anyway, why would they give her valid information?"

Silverstein continued that thread. "Okay. I'm with you. So let's go back to my calculation. Let's use your figure of thirty miles, Marc. Thirty miles is forty-eight kilometers. Dividing that by the eleven-kilometer swath means that it would take more than four orbits to arrive there."

"It could be way less than that, Victor." Lopez pointed to the screen. "Take a look at this swath. This satellite is flying from southwest to northeast. If the place we're looking for happens to be southwest of the NRL site, it's already in this image."

Silverstein kicked himself mentally; he *knew* that. But then, suddenly, it hit him. He hadn't asked the critical question. "I can't believe this! I should have asked earlier. Does your satellite only take in visible imagery?"

"No. We have many frequencies, but they're not always active. Let's take a look here." Lopez drew closer to the screen to read the fine print. "Okay, good point, Victor. For this one, FCDE requested both visible and infrared."

Silverstein recognized immediately what Stigler was doing. "Son of a bitch! Of course. This is exactly what I would have done. On the ice, it would be even more important. Stigler's looking for a heat signature. Even if everything is below the surface, it would be impossible to hide any heat escaping into the atmosphere above. And that would show up immediately in the infrared."

The implication of Silverstein's statement came crashing down on him only a millisecond before Lopez saw it too. Lopez started typing feverishly.

"You told me that you would be the first to see this imagery. Has it gone to FCDE yet?" Silverstein put into words what all three men in the room had to be thinking.

Lopez hissed his reply. "I know the question, Victor. I'll tell you in a goddamn second."

The upshot of the question was obvious. If they could intervene before the server automatically transmitted the imagery data to Las Vegas, they could prevent Stigler and Peters from potentially determining one fundamental fact for this case: the exact location of the Müller site on Greenland.

"Damn it to hell!" Lopez buried his head in his hands.

The result was obvious, but Silverstein had to ask. "We're too late?"

Lopez's muffled voice came through his fingers. "Yup. We're too late. It's already gone."

*   *   *

Hector Lopez spent the next ten minutes discussing the situation with the agency's IT department. He had hoped there was some way the process could be reversed. Silverstein understood that was unlikely.

"Okay. All might not be lost." Silverstein tried to be hopeful. "As you said, Hector, it all depends on in what direction the Müller camp is located in relation to the satellite pass. What did you say earlier, that the satellite flies over Greenland from the southwest to the northeast?"

"Yes. And that means if the Müller camp is located southwest of the NRL camp, we're screwed. If it's somewhere else, we have a chance. I'll start the software to analyze the infrared right now."

Silverstein was impressed. "You can generate a false color image using IWIDS?" The term *false color* was a term common to imagery analysis. All it meant was that different colors were assigned to various intensities of the measured radiation. For example, for infrared imagery, where heat was being measured, the idea might be to assign whites and yellows to colder temperatures and progressively redder colors to warmer temperatures. The colors were considered false because the human eye had no capacity to detect differences in temperature.

"I told you that our system was a good one." Lopez was obviously proud of IWDS.

"How long will it take?"

Lopez stood, stretched, and walked to the other side of his office, staring out the window at the continuing rain. "I don't know. A couple of minutes, maybe."

Silverstein glanced at his watch. "Okay, it's six twenty-five in Las Vegas. Unless Stigler's working late into the evening, we'll locate the Müller site before she does, assuming that it's within range of our image." He paused. "Which begs the question, Hector. Just in case, can you make sure that FCDE doesn't receive any more of these satellite passes?"

"I'm way ahead of you, Victor. It's already done."

Miller had been quiet for some time. "I hope you two are thinking ahead. What do we do if we find the Müller camp? If we find it, they find it. Assuming that they've gone home for the night, at best we'll have a twelve-hour jump on them. That means we'll need to kick off our operation sooner—much sooner."

The answer to that question seemed obvious to Silverstein. "That's a no-brainer. Have your boss call Stigler. Tell her that they've stumbled across something that's none of their business, and they need to stand down."

After a long day of serious conversation and worried expressions, Silverstein had no idea that he had just said something funny. Both Lopez and Miller practically rolled onto the floor in hysterical laughter.

A beep from Lopez's computer broke up the fleeting levity.

"There it is." Lopez turned very serious. "In a few minutes, we'll know how soon we're leaving for Greenland."

CHAPTER 53

GRAVE ACCIDENT

*Federal Center for Data Examination, Las Vegas, Nevada, USA:
36°7'51"N Latitude, 115°10'13"W Longitude
Tuesday, 7:15 p.m., October 11, 2011*

Captain Jane Stigler was about to call it a day. She powered down
her computer and leaned back, massaging her shoulders to relieve
the tension.

The past thirty-six hours had been, at best, less than fulfilling
and, at worst, a complete disaster. On Monday's flight home from
Monterey, she and Peters had discussed their conversation with
Silverstein. Peters called Silverstein's story ridiculous. Stigler
couldn't disagree. To augment his point, he charged into her office
this morning with information that supported his point of view.

Peters's first counterargument concerned Silverstein's financial
status. Using information from sources that could get them both
sent to prison if their covert data retrievals became known, he
learned that Silverstein was hardly a pauper. In fact, he was a
multimillionaire. That fact contradicted Silverstein's suggestion,
although he never actually said it, that Gunter Schnabel had saved
their lives in San Francisco by paying off a monetary debt.

As if that weren't enough, Peters discovered another unsettling
fact: within hours of their meeting the previous afternoon,

Silverstein had taken a red-eye from San Francisco to Washington DC—in contradiction to Silverstein emphasizing how much work he needed to catch up on.

Peters had been correct in questioning Stigler's decision to tell Silverstein about the submarines. Knowing that decision might have been a mistake, she imagined scenarios where her lapse in judgment could come back to haunt her. Worst case was one in which Silverstein immediately informed the Müllers. If so, the Müllers' suspicion that FCDE was behind the blackmail would have been confirmed. Stigler could imagine the headlines in *USA Today*: FCDE Blackmails International Company—Navy Captain Jane Stigler hauled before Congress.

Stigler gathered her belongings and opened her office door, arriving face to face with Peters, his hand poised to knock. "I'm in a bad mood, Andrew. Unless it's really important, I suggest we talk tomorrow."

"I'm about to make your day a whole lot brighter." Peters offered a generous smile and pointed to the stack of paper in his hand. "You're going to want to see this *now*."

Stigler motioned him inside.

Peters set the pile of paper on Stigler's desk. The top page looked to her like a satellite image. "You were right, Captain, in ordering the infrared. The visible imagery is useless. But it's a different story here." He motioned to the colored top sheet of a stack of paper about an inch thick."

"What am I looking at, Andrew?"

"As you know, the infrared sensor measures emissions in, roughly, the ten—to twelve—micron wavelength. The infrared is measuring heat."

"Damn it, Andrew." Stigler was in no mood for a tutorial. "You know I know all that."

"Yes, Captain. What you're seeing here are the color-coded temperatures for the first satellite pass that crossed the NRL base camp. This particular satellite moves from the southwest toward the northeast. So this top sheet shows the first image captured as our bird crossed the southwest corner of Greenland. I'm starting here because you can see the shoreline where the Labrador Sea meets the island of Greenland." Peters ran his finger along the coastline.

"Note the warm areas where there's civilization. Also the relatively warmer ocean waters compared to the inland ice."

"When was this image taken?" Stigler bent down to take a closer look.

Peters pointed to some digits on the pages. "About fourteen hours ago. And by the way, we lucked out. There were no clouds to block our view." He opened to the next sheet from the stack of fan-folded paper. "Okay, follow me here. Each progressive page moves continually northeastward toward the NRL camp."

Stigler watched the progression of images. There wasn't much to see once they climbed inland over the ice sheet. "There's hardly any variation here."

Peters kept turning the sheets. "That's correct. Nothing but ice. In general, as we climb inland, the temperature decreases because we're climbing higher into the atmosphere." Peters pointed to a number. "Here, we're about two thousand six hundred meters elevation." He kept turning pages. "We're about halfway across the ice . . . remember, going southwest to northeast. We have about as far to go now to arrive at the NRL camp as we've already moved from the coastline." They had paged through more than half the stack of paper.

Stigler stared in fascination, and Peters kept turning. "Tell me if anything catches your eye."

At once, a patch of color revealed itself. "There!" Stigler pointed.

"Interesting, huh? What you're seeing here, the infrared, has four-meter resolution. When I checked the corresponding visible imagery, which has one-meter resolution, nothing shows up."

"That means that whatever this warm spot is, it's flat on the surface?"

"Probably."

"How far is this from the NRL camp?"

"Around twenty-five miles, give or take."

Stigler concentrated on this information. "A reasonable distance for the NRL folks to have driven by snowmobile?"

"I'd say so."

"So what the hell do you think it is?"

"I have no idea, but if this were over land, the first thing that would come to mind is a pool of water, like where you'd have a geyser or something like that."

"In the middle of an ice sheet?"

Peters shook his head. "It makes no sense to me either. But I suppose it's possible that a geothermal heat source could make its way to the surface."

"But if this were water, wouldn't it show up differently on the visible?"

"You'd think so, but I couldn't see anything. I'm not an imagery interpretation expert. Maybe water and ice look the same under the right conditions. But if this warm spot is a pool of water, I can imagine a snowmobile driving into it and buying the farm."

Stigler knew what she needed to do next. She checked her watch and thought for a moment. "It's seven thirty here, and it's got to be the middle of the night in Greenland. You've done an outstanding job, Andrew. Thanks to you, I'd say we have a pretty good idea where those two researchers are buried."

"So what's our next step?"

"Can you give me the coordinates for that spot, please?" Stigler copied them into a notebook from her desk, gathered her jacket, and headed to the door. "I'll wait a couple of hours until it's morning there and then call the Greenland authorities. I'll ask them to fly up and take a look."

Stigler hung her head. "As pleased as I am that this may provide closure for the families of those men, it doesn't do a goddamn thing to help solve our larger mystery."

CHAPTER 54

UNSTOPPABLE FORCE

Ice Station Helheim: 66°38'00"N Latitude, 38°48'00"W Longitude
Wednesday, 8:30 a.m., October 12, 2011

The alarm on her watch roused her from sleep, an unusual occurrence. Almost without exception, Linda Kipling would awaken prior to the electronic tinkle. She reached over, pressed the button to activate its tiny light, and blinked twice at the electronic display: 8:30. She couldn't remember the last time she had slept for a continuous twelve hours. She peered into the darkness, trying in vain to make visual sense of the blackness of her cubicle. And except for the dull hum of circulating air, there was absolute quiet. But that was what you'd expect thirty feet below the ice surface of Greenland.

Kipling silenced the alarm, flipped on the LED flashlight she kept within reach, and found the light switch by the door.

Most everyone had trailed off to bed about eight the night before. Tuesday had been a full day. Schnabel had ordered her to stay close to Kobler, telling her that Dieter Müller had made it clear that Schnabel was responsible for her safety. She had seen very little of the under-ice compound.

Kipling thanked God that she wasn't claustrophobic. She had her own stateroom, but the accompanying floor space was a mere six feet by eight feet, about the size of a jail cell. Besides the bed, the living area accommodated a small desk and chair. There was more than adequate headroom, which allowed for a surprising amount of built-in wall storage.

Three communal bathrooms, each with bathtub and shower, lay fifty feet down the corridor, sandwiched between a small gym and an entertainment room. The latter came complete with a large-screen TV and hundreds of DVDs. It hadn't occurred to anyone that the presence of a female might require some adjustments by the staff. The cook, a jovial fellow named Arno Maxim, came up with the idea of a sign. He had jokingly asked if Kipling was a high-maintenance type of gal. She told him that she was not and agreed that whenever anyone saw the sign hung on one of the bathroom doors, she would be quick about it.

Concerned that her stateroom might be under video surveillance, her first trip to the bathroom the day before had included a very important job: memorizing the last measurement of the latitude and longitude from her GPS device.

Their arrival by helicopter early on Tuesday had precipitated a military-style change of command. The fifteen onsite personnel had their bags packed and were ready to leave. For a brief period, thirty-one men and one woman (Kipling volunteered to help) worked feverishly to unload supplies and other gear that had been transported by two Sikorsky S-70 medium-lift helicopters. Materials flowed both ways, with large bags of garbage leaving the compound. From the time the choppers set down until they lifted off again was a mere fifty minutes. Having never seen a female onsite, the departing crew reacted with disbelief.

Kipling learned that there had been more than the usual impetus to get the aircraft turned around. A winter storm was expected. In fact, no sooner had the choppers taken off than the weather turned sour, with strong winds and blowing snow.

I've got to get moving! Kipling and Kobler had agreed to meet for breakfast. He had promised to give her a complete tour of the underground compound. She grabbed her things and headed off to the bathroom. All three were unoccupied, and she had her choice. Twenty minutes later, she scurried back to her room and finished dressing.

Kipling headed down the narrow corridor to the dining area, a cramped space that sported three metal tables and accompanying chairs. Against one wall was a self-help eatery not unlike what you'd find at a breakfast-included motel. Cereals, breads, milk, juice, coffee, fruit, and the like sat ready. Always wanting to know where her next meal was coming from, Kipling had accepted an invitation from Maxim the previous day for a tour of the kitchen. Its claim to fame was an industrial-size stove. All food stores were kept in the adjoining cold storage. Maxim had explained that, whatever limitations they had on the ice, there was no limit to their cold storage.

Kobler was already wolfing down a bowl of cereal, staring at a clipboard of paper. "If you like dry cereal, you learn to eat it every day once you arrive. Fresh milk runs out in about four days, and then you're left with powdered milk until the next delivery."

Kipling took a bowl, filled it with something that looked like Cheerios, and grabbed a banana. On the counter were silverware, napkins, toothpicks, soda straws, and the like. "Thanks for the advice." She made her way to the coffee pot before taking a seat opposite Kobler. They were the only ones in the room. "Has everyone else eaten already?"

Between mouthfuls, Kobler filled her in. "Most everyone here works a twelve-hour shift, from six to six. Twelve hours on, twelve hours off. It's sort of like being on a submarine. No weekends, no holidays. About three weeks in, people start getting cabin fever and can't wait to leave. I'm one of them."

Kipling liked her coffee black and took a sip. It was good. "Most everyone?"

"There are three men here, Julius Kantor, Lucas Hoffman, and Paul Koch, who have it a bit easier. They're the ones in charge of the reactors, and, in fact, they're the onsite bosses. I guess, technically, Mr. Schnabel's in charge now, but it's unusual for him to be here. Anyway, to answer your question, to make sure the reactors are always monitored, each of them works eight on and sixteen off. Highly trained men, actually. Two have PhDs in nuclear physics. Since we're so dependent upon those reactors, they need to be kept happy and rested."

Splendid! So much for Kipling's naïve idea of barricading herself inside the reactor room while everyone slept, and Lopez and his team made their assault. "So these guys can handle any complications?"

"I didn't say that. Everyone here has multiple jobs, including me."

"What's your job?" Kipling sliced her banana over her cereal.

"I can repair most of the electronics, but especially the radar and communications gear. If there are issues in that department, they call me. If we need parts, I call Reykjavik."

"But your primary duty is the science of what's going on here, right?"

Kobler leaned across the table and whispered, "Don't tell anyone, but I have the best job in the house. I'm the one everyone comes to, asking how it's going." He pointed to his papers. "I'm the one who monitors the bedrock pool."

"Bedrock pool? What's that?"

"You know that we're trying to accelerate the movement of the Helheim Glacier, right?

So that's where the name Helheim came from! "Sorry. I've been told only generalities."

Kobler nodded. "Where we're sitting right now is just west of a glacier that . . . you know what a glacier is, right?"

"Of course, an ice floe."

"Correct. You have the larger Greenland ice sheet, but on the edges you have places where ice flows down to the sea, the glaciers. They've been here for centuries."

"Why did you choose this one?"

"Excellent question. About 2001, scientists started to notice that this particular one was thinning at the ocean end—which meant that it was retreating."

Retreating? "You lost me. Why would thinning cause the glacier to retreat?"

"You know that the end of the glacier sticks out into the ocean, right? As long as the ocean depth is less than nine-tenths the thickness of the glacier, the glacier won't float. But where the glacier thins where it had previously held fast to the bottom, the front end begins to float, which can lead to its break-up, particularly if heat from the water starts melting the ice from below. So the front of the glacier retreats back toward land. And as you might suspect, the less ice there is touching the ocean floor, the faster it moves." Kobler paused. "Anyway, from 2000 to 2005, the Helheim increased in speed from eight to eleven kilometers per year."

It made sense that the Müllers had linked their project to an area under scientific observation. "I get it. You chose this place because Mother Nature had given you a head start."

"Precisely. Why start from scratch?"

"Do you know why this glacier seems unstable?" Kipling had finished her cereal and was sipping coffee.

"No one knows for sure. Other glaciers are probably doing the same thing. Most figure it's tied to increasing temperatures. Global warming and all that stuff. But we don't really care. We understand what *we're* doing, and that's all that's important."

"That's the part I think I understand. You're melting the ice underneath, reducing friction, so that the glacier moves faster." Kipling smiled, proud of herself. "I get it! The melted water underneath the glacier is what you call the bedrock pool."

Kobler's nodded. "You're a quick study. That's exactly what it is. And a lot of what I do revolves around monitoring that pool."

"And how do you do that? That bedrock must be . . . what . . ."

"To be exact, one thousand sixty meters below where we're sitting. The bedrock at this location is four hundred forty meters above sea level."

As morally bankrupt a project as this was, Kipling couldn't help but admire the ingenuity that had gone into the effort. "This is more sophisticated than I ever imagined. But how can you possibly determine the extent of that melted water?"

"It's a lot easier than you think. We have piping that extends right down to bedrock."

"That's how you channel your steam to the bottom. Getting that in place must have been a major accomplishment in itself."

"Yes and no. As I told you before, the hardest part was to do this in secret, with all of our equipment coming in by helicopter. In terms of the quote/unquote," Kobler's fingers scratched punctuation marks in the air, "drilling, that was pretty easy. Oilmen do this all the time but through rock. For us, it was much simpler. You stand a section of pipe on end and start feeding steam down through it. As the steam melts the ice, the pipe slides down on its own. You can literally do it by hand, adding fifteen-foot sections one at a time. The melted water is forced back to the surface along the walls of the pipe. In fact, four years ago, we added a second reactor and pipe to speed things up. That's how I know so much, because I was here by then."

"Wait! You added a second reactor?"

"Yes. When we started, our engineers weren't sure how many reactors would be necessary to do the job. Because the Müllers aren't ones to do things half-assed, we actually have four reactors total. Two are still in storage back in Brazil. Turns out, two are plenty."

"Back to the pipes. You say that the melted water comes back up?"

"Of course, there's no other place for it to go."

"So you just pumped it outside?"

"That's an astute question, Dr. Kipling. No, that would have been too risky. The water would have frozen immediately, creating a surface feature that would have looked unusual from the air. We couldn't take that chance." Kobler grinned. "I suppose you're wondering where we put that water. As soon as we finish here, I'll give you a tour. And I guarantee that when you see the answer to that question, that will be the highlight of your day."

Kipling tried to put everything into perspective. "Back to my question. So now you have a pipe penetrating all the way through the ice . . . at the bottom of which is a melted pool of water. To keep track of it, you must have some sort of sensor down there."

Kobler beamed. "Bingo. We have a miniature robotic submarine that we control with a tether through the pipe. And when I say miniature, I mean small. Remember, it's got to fit through our six-inch pipe. It's five inches long and only an inch thick. It has a camera and an inertial guidance system. Once a month, we stop the flow of steam in one pipe long enough to send the robot down to measure our pool of water." He flipped through his stack of paper, removed a sheet, and turned it upside down for Kipling to see. "This graph shows our progress."

Kipling finished her coffee and set the cup aside. "And how are we doing?"

"What you see here is a plot of the area of that pool on the vertical, plotted against time on the horizontal." Kobler pointed to the lower left corner. "It starts here in 2005, when we began sending down steam." He hesitated, seemingly to make a point. "By the way, so that you understand, although this pool of water has a good size horizontally, it isn't very deep. It doesn't need to be. On the average, there's about six to eight inches of liquid water."

Kipling was a scientist and could read graphs. The increase in size of the liquid pool was astounding, having grown to twenty square kilometers at their last measurement. Twenty square kilometers meant a square with sides of four and a half kilometers, or nearly three miles. Her discussions with Silverstein after the Müllers had bragged about their operation had been theoretical. Here, action replaced theory, and empirical measurements documented progress.

It was all Kipling could do not to yell out: *don't you realize that you and everybody working here are out of your fucking minds?* But now was not the time to have a philosophical discussion. "You must be very proud of what you've accomplished." She paused to think. "Theoretically, the bigger the pool, the faster the glacier should move, right? Do you have any confirmation that you're getting the job done?"

"Oh, yes. There's no doubt the glacier is moving faster, but I don't have any numbers to show you." Kobler shook his head. "But that result is secondary."

What's he talking about? "What do you mean, secondary? I thought that was the whole idea here."

Kobler pointed again to his graph. "Do you see this horizontal red line?"

In fact, Kipling had noticed it. "Your line intersects the thirty-four square kilometer mark."

"That's correct, and based upon our current rate of progress, we should get there in about twenty-three months."

Kipling was afraid to ask. "What will happen then?"

"Our numerical computations tell us that, at thirty-four square kilometers, we will have achieved the critical size of the bedrock pool necessary to allow the overriding mass of ice to overcome the restraining forces from the front of the glacier." Kobler sat tall in his chair, relishing his explanation. "Once that happens, the momentum will be such that there will be no stopping it, and the entire Helheim Glacier will crash into the sea." He smiled. "I know what you're thinking. When this happens, won't we all slide into the water along with the glacier? Don't worry. Where we're located is west of the glacier itself. Our pipe down to bedrock is angled slightly to the east. Our engineers say that we're perfectly safe here."

"That should be comforting news for whoever happens to be on shift that month."

"That's true, but I haven't gotten to the best part. We're 99.9 percent sure that the Helheim will be history. What we're less sure of—but what our scientists still consider a high probability—is that the energy produced from this massive release of ice will set off earthquakes across the entire eastern seaboard of Greenland. We estimate it's the equivalent of one thousand Hiroshima bombs."

Kobler paused and smiled. "Enough to send a quarter of the Greenland ice sheet splashing down into the North Atlantic. And if that happens, we'll have a rise in the ocean level of nearly a foot." His shit-eating grin was enough to make Kipling want to puke. "Of course, that would follow a tsunami larger than any ever recorded by man."

CHAPTER 55

IF PUSH COMES TO SHOVE

Lear Jet, 550 miles southwest of Keflavik, Iceland
Wednesday, 12:05 p.m. (Greenland time), October 12, 2011

The Lear 60 was cruising at thirty-nine thousand feet. Silverstein could see the southern tip of Greenland as they headed northeast. It looked cold. After a first leg to Newfoundland where they had refueled, their next and final stop would be Keflavik, Iceland, the staging area for their expected assault on the Müller camp in Greenland.

Except for the Lear's two pilots, the passenger manifest included only Silverstein, Hector Lopez, and Marc Miller. Twenty navy SEALs from Norfolk, Virginia, from the Naval Special Warfare (NSW) Command's Group 2, were flying to Keflavik separately on an Air Force-provided C-5 that also carried three SH-60B Seahawk helicopters, complete with a crew of three for each bird.

Back at CIA headquarters, Miller had been the one to coordinate with NSW. Because all men killed by the Müllers, except for one, had been navy scientists, navy brass demanded that it would be *their* SEALs who would make the assault on Greenland. The SEALs' charter that dictated that their operations originate from the sea and return to the sea was waived at the highest level. Further, because one or more nuclear reactors awaited them in Greenland, two of the SEALs had credentials in nuclear propulsion; they knew their way around seafaring nuclear power plants.

When Silverstein had made the mistake of asking whether twenty men would be enough to make the assault, Lopez had asked if he was serious, stating that each SEAL was the equivalent of three ordinary soldiers. They would get the job done, Lopez had assured him.

Lopez explained that they would meet up with the assault team in Keflavik immediately upon landing. Although SEAL and Navy Commander Leopold Wilder would be in charge of the operation, Lopez said, the three of them would participate as well. Before they left Washington, Silverstein had informed Lopez that, when the hammer came down, he wanted to be included in the action. Lopez agreed, asking only that he stay out of the way and avoid getting killed. He complained that the paperwork required for a civilian death would be a total pain in the ass. Accordingly, the SEALs were bringing along body armor, weaponry, and white cold-weather clothing for three additional men.

Silverstein noticed that Lopez's breathing had changed. He had been asleep and was coming around. Miller, in the row behind, had already awoken from his nap. All three had had a short night back in Washington, with a departure time of four in the morning.

Silverstein caught Lopez's attention. "Did you sleep?"

"Yeah, I guess." Lopez unbuckled his seatbelt and went to check with the pilot. He returned. "We'll be there in about an hour. The C-5 has already landed, and they're offloading the Seahawks. We'll be ready to go as soon as we get the word."

The *word* to which Lopez referred was some form of communication from Kipling, telling them where and when they should attack. The *where* part was less necessary now than it had been yesterday. The infrared imagery that had appeared on IWDS pointed to the precise location of the Müller operation. There was no other physical reason why, in the middle of an ice sheet, there would be an area warm enough to appear on a satellite's infrared scan, with nothing simultaneously visible to the eye.

The tricky part would be the *when*. To ensure that Silverstein missed no calls or e-mails from Kipling while they were in the air, Lopez had had his communication section clone Silverstein's cell phone number so that, en route, all calls received at CIA headquarters were routed through to the Lear. Once in Keflavik, it would revert back.

Silverstein chose not to think about the obvious: what would they do if Kipling had no way to communicate? *If I were Schnabel, would I let her talk to the outside world?*

"Tell me again where we're landing, Hector." Lopez had said earlier that they would not be landing at the municipal airport.

Lopez stood again and stretched, steadying himself on Silverstein's seat. "We're landing at what used to be called the Keflavik Naval Air Station. It was Iceland's NATO command center, and it was a hopping place for decades. But back in 2006, we pulled out, and they returned the base to civilian use."

"Then how are we allowed to use it?"

"Not a problem. Although there have been some bumps in the road, we still have reasonably good relations with Iceland, and they'll do us an occasional favor. They're expecting us. We'll have access to refueling and maintenance, and they'll give us accommodations." Lopez added as an afterthought, "By the way, don't confuse Keflavik with Reykjavik. Reykjavik is the capital and largest city in Iceland. Where we're going, Keflavik, is much smaller and lies to the southwest of Reykjavik."

Silverstein shifted in his seat and saw Miller writing on a clipboard. Miller had been handling most of the technical details. "Marc, do we know how far it is between Keflavik and the Müller camp?"

Miller chuckled. "We better. Right around five hundred miles."

That sounded pretty far for a helicopter. "Can the Seahawks fly that far without refueling?"

"The ones we have can. These choppers have the army's ESSS, the External Stores Support System. That means we have enough fuel for nearly fourteen hundred miles, more than enough to get there and back. If we need to, we can always stop in Kulusuk on the return. Going there, though, we'll make a direct shot."

There was one relevant question Silverstein had to ask because it could affect everything. "Have you checked the weather?"

Miller responded, tapping his head with a pencil. "Yesterday was bad. In fact, based on the timing of Linda's call to you last night, I'd guess that they made it to the ice in the nick of time. The weather's better today."

Silverstein turned back to Lopez. "Can I ask you a question? Why did you and Marc laugh when I suggested that you contact Stigler and request her cooperation?"

"Don't be offended," Lopez responded seriously. "We weren't laughing at you. But yours is a typical civilian response. The problem is that what we have here are two significant government fiefdoms, the CIA and the FCDE."

"Wait a minute. The FCDE is new, created just after 9/11. They're tiny compared to you. Right?"

"Doesn't matter. In today's political climate, any organization that has the word terrorism in its mission statement views itself as the cat's meow, having jurisdiction that supersedes everybody else." Lopez shook his head in disgust. "Believe me, we've been through this before. The first thing that would have happened if we'd done like you said—have my boss call Stigler's boss, asking for a favor—would have been for her boss to ask why. He would have demanded to know why what we're doing is more important than what they're doing. Tell us what you know, and we'll talk, they'd say. It turns into a real pissing contest."

"That's sad, Hector. That makes our system of government sound inflexible."

Lopez shook his head. "I don't think the problem's peculiar to us. I've talked to Russians who lived under the old totalitarian state where you'd think that cooperation could be mandated from above. They had the same problem. When you give people power, it's intoxicating. What can I say?"

"I understand what you're saying, but you haven't forgotten what I told you before, about what the Müllers will do if their grandiose scheme becomes compromised? What if Stigler invades Greenland, shows up at their doorstep, and backs them into a corner? We'll be too late. Can't we do anything?"

"Did I say we couldn't do anything? While you were getting your beauty rest last night, I was still on the phone."

"Doing what?"

"Making sure that Greenland was being watched. The CIA monitors all military communications. If there are any operations planned for Greenland, we'll be the first to know."

"What if Stigler doesn't involve the military?"

"What?" Lopez frowned. "You think she and this Peters guy are going to rent a helicopter and go up there by themselves? As much as she'd like to have her own private army, she doesn't." He paused. "But your point is well taken. So another reason I worked late was to coordinate with our folks in SIGINT. That's Signal Intelligence, in case you don't know the lingo. As we speak, they're monitoring every communication from Greenland that they can get their hands on. Believe me, if Stigler is up to something, we'll know about it."

"And what will you do then, if you hear of something?"

Lopez's next statement contradicted what he had said earlier, obviously coming from someone used to getting his way. "When we get to *that* point, *that's* when we'll make it clear to Captain Stigler and the FCDE that no one fucks with the CIA."

CHAPTER 56

COLD STORAGE

Ice Station Helheim: 66°38'00"N Latitude, 38°48'00"W Longitude
Wednesday, 2:35 p.m., October 12, 2011

They were standing by a door opposite the kitchen. This would be the final stop of the tour before seeing the reactors, Kobler said. He reached out to Kipling. "I want you to close your eyes. Here, take my hand. It's dark, and I don't want you to trip."

Kipling did as she was told. She heard the door open and walked cautiously. At once, she sensed a change in the environment. It felt colder, moist. The door closed behind her.

They walked side by side for several feet before Kobler released her hand. "Now don't move and don't open your eyes. I'm going to turn on the lights."

There was a sharp cracking sound, the kind you might hear from a large electrical switch.

"Okay. Now."

Kipling opened her eyes, at once startled by the artificial brightness but then wowed by what lay in front of her: a lake of water about a football field in distance across, with a mist of fog emanating from the surface. It was beautiful. The space in front of her looked circular. On all sides, including where they were standing, was what looked like a beach with white sand, but which was obviously ice. The smooth, low ceiling of ice added to the surreal nature of the scene.

"I bet you weren't expecting this!" Kobler waved across the water as he began a stroll.

"Not at all. What *is* this?"

"Remember when you asked about the water we pumped up as we drilled down to bedrock. I told you we couldn't take the chance of pumping it outside. So for openers, we mined out a tunnel through the ice and began to pump the water here. The ice that we ground up to make this space *is* on the outside. Of course, it's all been covered by snow in the years since."

Wouldn't this water freeze? Kipling tried to think. What she saw was obviously liquid. "But the last time you pumped water here was when you put the last pipe down. Four years ago? Why is the water still . . ." She figured it out before she could complete the sentence.

Kobler seemed happy to oblige. "Come over here and put your hand in the water."

Kipling followed Kobler's lead. The water was noticeably warm. She remembered from her physical meteorology course that the fog she was seeing was called sea smoke, occurring when cold air blew across warm water.

Kobler flicked the water from his hand. "It typically runs around twenty-six, twenty-seven degrees Celsius, about eighty Fahrenheit. When you run any power plant, you generate waste heat. That's why you see those huge cooling towers alongside commercial plants. There are reasons why heat's wasted: entropy, Second Law of Thermodynamics, and all that stuff I've forgotten from physics class." He pointed left. "See those pipes that go down into the water and then come back out? They go down about seventy feet. Over time, our small pool of water has gotten bigger and bigger as the heat melts the ice deeper and deeper."

Unbelievable! But for evil, not for good. "I'm truly amazed, Daniel."

"Okay, Linda, it's time for you to see what makes all of this possible." Kobler pointed toward the door.

Finally! Kipling had been careful not to appear overly inquisitive about the reactors. Most of the details regarding this operation were irrelevant to her ultimate mission: to secure the reactors when Lopez attacked the compound.

Kipling chose to play the vulnerable female. From experience, she knew that such behavior often loosened the tongues of men who imagined themselves the ultimate protectors of the weak female. "I don't know, Daniel. I've been looking forward to this part, but it's sort of scary too. Do you think it's safe?"

"Look at me." Kobler laughed. "Am I glowing? I'll explain everything to you in detail so that you'll be reassured. Don't worry. Okay?"

Everything in detail. Perfect.

Before they exited, Kipling noticed that the front and right side of this cavern-like area housed numerous cabinets of various sizes, some quite large. "What are these?"

"Oh, those. As you've probably noticed, we don't have much extra space around here. As the pond kept getting bigger and bigger, and we had to dig out more ice on the sides, we decided to use the space for storage. For example, all of our backup electronics are here, sealed in plastic to keep out moisture."

Kipling took note of a red phone by the door. They were ubiquitous throughout the compound.

Outside, they continued walking down the corridor. To the right was a solitary door. As they proceeded farther, a set of large double doors faced them ahead. Kobler opened one of the pair and gestured for Kipling to enter. She took note: two deadbolt locks, one for each door. They were keyed on the outside, with turn-knobs inside. Their bolts extended into a hefty metal post in the middle. The locks were obviously designed to keep people out of the room.

Except for the underground lake, this room housing the reactors was the largest in the compound. Her first sensory reaction was one of sound: background humming at various frequencies. Looking across from the double doors, the circular room was divided into two sections, front and back, seemingly for the two reactors. One perpendicular walkway separated the two and culminated at a huge console to Kipling's left; another walkway, complete with railing and three or so feet higher than the interior floor, formed the perimeter around the entire room. Ahead to the right was a second door at the two o'clock position.

If Kipling had been asked to describe the room, her first word would have been *pipes*: pipes that obviously transported liquids or gas, pipes that served as conduit for wiring, etc. The wall to her left looked like a control center that you might see in the movies, with numerous gauges, dials, and buttons. A man in a white coat sat facing the panel.

Kobler led the way to the console. A darkly bearded man who carried a little too much weight around the middle rose to meet them. "Dr. Kipling, I'd like you to meet Dr. Lucas Hoffman." The two shook hands. Kipling smiled warmly, but Hoffman's body language was decidedly negative. He obviously did not approve of their visitor.

"Linda is a meteorologist and is here to look over our little operation and see how we work. Lucas is one of our three nuclear operators. If you don't mind, Lucas, I'll show Linda around."

Without a word, Hoffman returned to his controls.

Kobler led the way toward the door to the right. "These are our electrical generators." He opened the door to let Kipling see. "All that happens in here is that heat from reactor number two spins a turbine that generates electricity. It's very noisy. "I'll show you around if you want, but it is boring stuff."

Boring and irrelevant. "I'll take your word for it. I'd much rather you explain what goes on in this room." She pointed backward.

Kipling grabbed the railing, leaned forward, and scanned the room. Kobler waved to the space in front of them. "Reactor number one's over there. This one here is number two. I guess you know that we got these from the Soviets. They were once the power plants for one of their submarines. We refurbished them and brought them here. Compared to today's technology, they're a little crude but functional. You just have to be a little careful."

"What do you mean?" Kipling appeared concerned.

"All I'm saying is that, fifty years ago, they didn't have the safety backups we have today. You remember Chernobyl. That's why we have people like Lucas running things. He makes sure that procedures are followed."

I need to know the important stuff. "Dieter told me that you have a backup plan, in case this place is ever discovered."

Kobler hesitated for a moment, and Kipling was afraid she had brought up something she shouldn't have. Fortunately, he continued. "If there's anything scary about this place, that's it. The fact that these reactors require such careful attention is also the quality that makes them easy to sabotage. Everyone here knows what will happen if we're ever discovered."

Kipling smiled meekly. "Except me, I guess."

"That's correct, and you deserve to know too." Kobler continued along the circular walkway until they were two-thirds of the way back to the double doors. He pointed down to the side of reactor one. "Do you see that red box?"

Kipling saw a bright red metal enclosure, about a foot square. She scanned across the room and saw an identical one for the second reactor. Each appeared to be held together with a metal chain that included an unusual-looking padlock. "I see it."

"That's what we call our doomsday box. Inside is a timer that will override the control panel and allow the reactor to go supercritical. You know what that means, right? Supercritical?"

Kipling knew damn well what it meant. "Vaguely. Doesn't it mean that the reactor will go out of control?"

"That's correct. The control rods that keep the nuclear fission process contained will be extracted from the reactor core. When that happens, the reactor will overheat and melt down. That's something you don't want to be around to see. It'll probably explode and spew radiation everywhere. The molten core will burn through the floor and melt its way down to bedrock." Kobler waved his hands dramatically. "As bad as that sounds, there is some good news."

Good news? "I hope so. It doesn't sound all that good to me right now."

"The good news is that our bedrock pool has reached the point where that will complete the process of what we're trying to do; the sizzling reactors sitting on bedrock will melt water like crazy. Instead of waiting twenty-three more months to release the Helheim Glacier, it'll be over in hours." Contrary to his earlier enthusiasm, Kobler showed some concern. "There's no one here that hopes it will come to that, though, with all the radiation that would be released into the atmosphere and the ocean. But if we're backed into a corner, that's what will happen."

The terms immoral, corrupt, and maniacal were too mild to describe what Kobler was describing. Kipling had a good poker face but needed every ounce of willpower to control her emotions. "That would be a shame, but I have to agree with you. What can we do if it comes to that?" To understand how the process would work, she asked a critical question. "Why is there a chain around the box?"

Kobler laughed. "Our little joke is that it's to keep any of us who sleepwalk from setting the timer by accident. Can you see the padlock? It's unusual because it takes three different keys to open it. Each of our operators carries one of the three."

"Makes sense to me." Kipling made a visual show of nodding, appreciating the logic. "I guess my only question, then, is that if something like that happens while we're here, is there a plan to get us out of here?"

"Yes. Two helicopters are standing by in Reykjavik at all times. If everything turns to shit, we can be out of here in three hours."

"If I were here when that happened, that would be the longest three hours of my life."

Kobler shook his head. "Not really. Before we leave, there's a lot of final preparation."

"I don't understand. I doubt that you have to worry about the next tenants."

"That's not quite true. We need to make absolutely certain there's nothing left to link this place to the Müllers."

Really? "And how will you do that?"

Kobler gestured toward the door where they came in. "All of our records and documents will be removed and replaced with others that are already here in storage. A lot of thought has gone into this. But for all of this to make sense, there's one more thing. We need someone to blame this on. Follow me."

They returned to the corridor and stopped outside the solitary door that Kipling had noticed earlier. Kobler opened it. It was a foot thick and identical to several others she had seen, meaning that it was insulated. What lay behind this door was obviously cold storage of some sort. As they entered, Kipling could see her breath in the frigid air.

"Stop here." Kobler hadn't yet turned on the light. "You're not squeamish, are you?"

Where was he going with that question? "Of course not. I was the one who liked to dissect animals in high school biology."

"I've been assured that you're as committed to this project as anyone here. Correct?"

"Absolutely! Do you think I'd be here if my cousins weren't convinced of my loyalty?"

"I just wanted to make sure before I show you what's in this room. These guys will get all the credit for what's gone on here." Kobler backed up a few feet to flip the light switch.

Compared to the beauty of the underground lake, what appeared next was shocking at best and utterly reprehensible at worst. Having spent some time in Russia studying the language early in her life, Kipling recognized the uniforms. She counted fifteen.

Kobler elaborated. "Once the glacier starts its slide twenty-three months from now, we—or should I say the Russians?—will blow up this place to try to hide their dastardly deed. We've positioned explosives around the compound to do just that. Unfortunately, for them, the explosives will ignite prematurely and kill them all, leaving behind a lot of incriminating evidence. Alternatively, if we're forced to blow the reactors, they will have died from the resultant explosions and radiation."

Kipling's response was cool, measured, accommodating—and accurate. She stared Kobler straight in the eye, exhibiting no sign of weakness. "The bodies have held up remarkably well."

CHAPTER 57

BEGINNING OF THE END

Ice Station Helheim: 66°38'00"N Latitude, 38°48'00"W Longitude
Wednesday, 3:15 p.m., October 12, 2011

Although mentally shaken, Kipling appeared outwardly unaffected by the sight of the frozen bodies. Her cousins had thought of everything, including how to absolve themselves of their activities under the ice, whether in twenty-three months when the Helheim Glacier was forecast to slide into the sea, or sooner, should they implement their doomsday plan. Either way, the Russians would catch the blame. The alternate documents that Kobler alluded to were obviously written in Russian. After all, the reactors had come from their submarines. To complete the deception, the bodies of the Russian sailors would be positioned about the underground compound.

Kobler suggested that they head back to the kitchen for coffee. As they walked, Kipling let her mind stray from the immediate concern of the reactors. *What about surveillance? What about weapons?* It was important to know the likely sequence of events when Lopez and his team arrived on the scene.

Kipling stopped in the hallway and faced Kobler. "Daniel, were you here when the snowmobilers came along?"

"Yeah, I was here." Kobler exhaled through his mouth. "I've never been so scared in my life. I thought we'd bought the farm."

"I can imagine. What happened? How did you even know they were out there? Or, better yet, how did they find *you*? It must have been just a dumb accident."

"That's what we think, just one of those things. Unfortunately, outside, under calm conditions, I'm told that it's possible to hear the hum from our equipment. I can't hear it, but apparently some people can. I guess they heard something and came over to investigate."

"How did you know that they were there? It's not like you have a lookout tower."

Kobler leaned against the wall and folded his arms. "When we got off the helicopter, did you take a look around?"

"I did but couldn't see much. It was dark. I saw snow and ice."

"The next time you're outside, take a look north. There's what looks like a big mound of snow that's sort of in the shape of a dome. That's our radar. If anything moves on the surface nearby or in the air out to about fifty miles, we'll catch it. And when that happens, you'll know it because a klaxon goes off underground."

Kobler pointed to an industrial-strength speaker near the ceiling. Kipling hadn't noticed it before and counted three others within sight. "Believe you me, you'll hear it. We have monthly tests, and you make it a point to wear earplugs. I'm told that in the six years we've been in operation, that was the only time the klaxon has gone off because of a threat.

"August Wolf? You've see him. Big guy, walks with a limp? He's our radar guy. He's on the job from six to six. Even if he spots something on radar, though, he'll wait to confirm the threat based on visual observation. He has a bunch of TVs that gives him 360 degrees visual. He says that it's too easy to be fooled by the radar. So if the klaxon sounds, we're in trouble for sure. By the way, for the night shift, we rotate the job, babysitting. I hate that job."

"I thought I had seen everything here. You've been holding out on me." Kipling laughed.

"You got me there. Remember where we first entered to go underground?"

Kipling did remember. They had landed, the surrounding area lit only by spots from the helicopters. As they walked down a slight slope, a horizontal door ahead rose out of the snow to reveal what looked to be a large garage. Among various pieces of equipment, several snowmobiles sat at the ready. "Yes, I remember. The big door in the ice. From there, we went down steps to get here."

"Once you walked in, did you notice the other two doors, one to the left and one to the right? The one on the left goes down a hallway, but it's on an incline. No steps. That takes you to the radar room. That's where Wolf hangs out."

Two doors? "What's behind door number two? I hope there's a turbocharged Porsche behind that one." Their relationship had matured enough that Kipling felt comfortable joking with Kobler. In fact, it was possible he considered her comments flirtatious. Back when they had visited the underground lake, his hand had squeezed hers a bit harder than would have seemed normal.

Kobler laughed. "I can't get anything past you, can I? Behind that door is our armory. We have rifles, we have handguns, we have grenades, all Russian-made. They're not Russian, but we even have a dozen Stinger missiles. Barring an attack by a small army, we're prepared."

"I'm impressed. That kind of stuff frightens me. Would *you* get involved?"

Kobler scratched his forehead. "I keep forgetting how little you know about what goes on here. Everyone here has had weapons training. In fact, in the weeks before we come here, everyone reports to a firing range to practice. Even the Stingers, although we don't actually fire them; they're too expensive for practice. If shit hits the fan, everyone's involved. Remember, there are only fifteen of us."

"If push comes to shove, are the reactor guys in charge?" Kobler had told Kipling earlier that they were the bosses.

"You must be kidding." Kobler shook his head. "Those guys are too cerebral. They can shoot, but you wouldn't want them in charge of security. You've met our security team: Fritz Neumann, Fred Huber, and August Mayer. If bullets start to fly, they'll lead the charge."

Kipling remembered to whom Kobler was referring. Compared to everyone else, they looked the part, beefy and macho.

Kipling wondered what else she needed to know. When Lopez arrived, her job would be to delay the setting of the doomsday timer. She imagined how it would play out. The klaxon would go off, preferably in the middle of the night. Everyone would charge off to the weapons armory to defend the compound. Because Gunter Schnabel happened to be here, he would be the obvious leader. In the commotion, everyone would forget about their female visitor. She would rush to the reactor room. Of course, there was the minor detail of dealing with whomever might be manning the reactors at the time. With luck, he would have left his post to assist in the compound's defense. Once there, she would disable the deadbolt locks from the outside by inserting and breaking off toothpicks she planned to pilfer from the dining room. She would then lock the doors from the inside, and wait for the cavalry to arrive. Afterward, she would bask in the glory of having prevented a nuclear catastrophe. *Piece of cake!*

But aside from what can go wrong at every step of my optimistic plan, there's another issue, a big one! How do I get the GPS coordinates back to Victor? The cavalry can't come if they don't know where to go!

As they started to walk again, Kipling chose to be direct. "Daniel, I told my boyfriend, Victor, that I would get back to him after I arrived so that he wouldn't worry. I checked with Dieter before I left, and he said that it would be okay. What's the best way, do you think? Do you have phone, Internet, what?"

Kobler hesitated in his reply, not a good sign from Kipling's point of view. "I'll need to check with Mr. Schnabel."

They had walked only a few more feet when it happened. The obnoxious sound blaring from the overhead speakers was deafening. The look on Kobler's face made clear that this was not a test.

CHAPTER 58

ILLUSORY CAPE

Ice Station Helheim: 66°38'00"N Latitude, 38°48'00"W Longitude
Wednesday, 3:48 p.m., October 12, 2011

A second later, Kipling discovered her own reaction to be identical to Kobler's. His fearful, immediate response to the klaxon meant the worst: something or someone was threatening the compound. *Had Lopez begun his assault?*

Kipling was terrified. Was the situation outside so precarious that Schnabel would initiate the Müller doomsday scenario straight away? *No!* She'd bet her chips on common sense: whatever or whoever had triggered the alarm did not involve Lopez or Silverstein. She would count on the security team to prevail against the intruder.

Following his initial, panicked reaction, Kobler spoke rationally. "We need to find out what's going on. Follow me."

The two charged off down the corridor. At once, Kipling heard huffing and puffing behind them. She turned and saw Hoffman from the reactor room. She noted that he had left his station unguarded.

The three continued past the kitchen, past the staterooms, and up the steps that ascended into the garage. As they climbed, Kipling heard what sounded like gunfire. Not a good sign. But by the time they arrived at the door to the garage, there was silence.

The large overhead door was open. They made their way outside, instinctively holding up their hands to shield their eyes. Compared to the relative darkness of the underground spaces, the reflected light off the snow was blinding.

When they caught up to the others, the drama sprawled in front of them. Fifty yards ahead was a civilian helicopter with its main rotor turning. Halfway between lay two motionless bodies. Crimson stained the snow next to both. If there was any doubt who these men were, the black letters on the white background of their helicopter gave them away: *Police*, written above smaller print, *Municipality of Sermersooq*. Schnabel and his crew had just murdered two police officers. Despite her altruistic intentions in coming here, it wouldn't escape anyone else's notice, Kipling knew, that she had been a party to this debacle. She suddenly felt nauseous.

Kipling looked about to gauge the reaction of the others. One word described the atmosphere: deflation. Everyone understood that what had just occurred meant the end to Operation Helheim. Unlike the incident involving the snowmobile, what had just happened would have repercussions. A situation involving two men out for a joyride on a snowmobile, with no one knowing of their plans, was very different from a visit by authorities in a helicopter. Before long, these men would be declared missing. Dispatch would know where they had flown, and radar records would localize their last position. It wouldn't be long before others came to investigate. It was over.

But how had this happened? Who was behind this? Not Lopez, certainly. He wouldn't have sent a police helicopter.

Schnabel, solemn, addressed the group. "We've all known that this day might come. And now that it has, we need to remember everything we've learned, to revert to our training, and prepare for our departure." He looked up at the sky. "One thing we have going for us is that it will be dark soon. Whoever sent these men wouldn't mount a rescue mission at night. That means that the clock is not an issue."

Schnabel gestured toward the radar man, August Wolf. "Mr. Wolf, when you go back to your station, I want you to call Reykjavik. Tell them what's happened and that they should come get us as soon as possible." Schnabel glanced at his watch. "They should be here by seven thirty. Remember that each of you has a job to do, and we have plenty of time. There's no reason for mistakes. Do you all understand?"

A chorus of "Yes, sirs" warmed the frigid air.

"Are there any questions?" Schnabel glanced about the group.

Fred Huber, one of the security personnel, pointed toward the helicopter. "What should we do with the bodies and the helicopter?"

"Leave the bodies where they are. *We* didn't shoot them. The Russians did. And don't touch the helicopter. It'll stop on its own." He scanned the men, apparently looking for someone. "One more thing. Since I'm here, I'll take charge of the reactor timers. Kantor, Hoffman, Koch! Give me your keys."

Uh-oh! This wasn't good. Would Schnabel set the timers immediately?

Schnabel fielded more questions and dismissed the group, telling them that they should plan to leave the camp by eight thirty. Before Kipling could lose herself among those heading back, he yelled after her. "Dr. Kipling."

Considering the gravity of the situation, the head of Müller security seemed remarkably composed. "Dr. Kipling, do you have any idea how this could have happened?"

Kipling answered honestly. "I'm as shocked as you are. If you're worried about me, I had no idea where we were going until Daniel told me back in Reykjavik. In terms of these guys," she motioned toward the helicopter, "there're obviously locals. Who sent them? Your guess is as good as mine."

After a moment's thought, Kipling realized that what she had just said wasn't quite true.

*   *   *

As Schnabel watched Kipling head back to the garage, he believed that she was telling the truth. Even if she had telephoned

329

someone in Reykjavik, Kobler had purposely given her the wrong location. Schnabel could not pin this incident on her. She was correct. These were locals. If the US government were onto them, they would have sent more than the police.

Concerning Kipling, Schnabel realized that one aspect of his earlier plan required modification. Now that they were closing down the compound, leaving her body behind was not an option. Although the area would be riddled with radiation, at some point in the future, authorities would scrutinize the site, looking for answers. It just wouldn't do to find the body of an American female lying next to a Russian sailor. There was a satisfying alternative. He would push her out the door during the overseas portion of their return to Reykjavik.

Schnabel's thoughts returned to preparing the site for their departure. When they were within an hour of leaving, he would set the timers. With morbid curiosity, he actually hoped to stay airborne long enough to witness the doomed ice camp undergoing self-destruction.

Still, what about Kipling? Could she cause problems? It would be easy enough to lock her in her room until they left. Still, if he turned hostile on her, that could add a complexity that he didn't need just now. From a practical standpoint, the only threat she could pose would be to contact the outside world. To eliminate that possibility, he would notify Wolf that no one be allowed to make calls. That order applied doubly to Kipling, he would tell him. And to make sure that everyone understood the seriousness of that order, Schnabel would permit an exception to the normal rules on the ice. He would provide Wolf with a firearm, as well as himself.

*　　*　　*

As Kipling descended the slope, she recalled her experience in San Francisco. There *was* another group on Schnabel's trail. It was possible that Captain Stigler had arranged for this visit by the authorities. But if so, she obviously had no idea of the gravity of what was going on here.

Kipling held back as she entered the garage, watching the men from the security detail return their weapons to the racks. She briefly considered the value of a handgun. The door was open, but the timing wasn't right. Schnabel wasn't far behind.

Kipling followed the others down the steps. Every man scurried away, each with his job to do. To her relief, Kobler was nowhere in sight. From here on out, it would be to her advantage to remain as inconspicuous as possible. As she made her way down the corridor, Maxim, the cook, rushed by in the opposite direction, pushing a hand truck carrying three stacked cardboard file boxes. They obviously contained documents that would accompany them back to Reykjavik.

Not knowing where else to go, Kipling returned to her stateroom. She needed time to think. Everything she and Silverstein had planned was now meaningless. The inopportune arrival of the police helicopter had not only signaled the end of the Müller operation in Greenland, it had complicated Lopez's plan for an assault. There were only four hours to go.

Kipling could envision only two scenarios leading to a satisfactory ending to this nightmare. One was to somehow contact Silverstein, providing him the coordinates for this location. She smiled at her second thought: to return to the armory, grab a weapon for each hand, and, like Rambo, blast her way through the underground corridors, mowing down anyone foolish enough to take her on. Unfortunately, the odds of a successful conclusion to that scenario were poor.

Unless something drastic happened soon, Schnabel would set his doomsday timers. Tomorrow, or soon after, Planet Earth would awaken to the news of two environmental catastrophes: one, the intentional meltdown of two nuclear reactors with their accompanying release of radiation, and two—if Kobler could be believed—the Helheim Glacier sliding its way into the sea. Even more troubling was Kobler's description of what Müller scientists predicted next: the release of significant portions of the Greenland ice sheet into the Atlantic Ocean.

It was time to do something. Kipling donned the warm, bulky jacket she had been assigned back in Cartagena and scanned her belongings for anything that might prove useful. Only two items came to mind. Realizing that she might have to operate in the dark, her pocket flashlight was an obvious choice.

It was Schnabel who had inadvertently told her where she needed to go. *Mr. Wolf, when you go back to your station, I want you to call Reykjavik.* Likely as not, the radar room was also the communications center for the compound.

This would have been the perfect time for Kipling to don Harry Potter's Cloak of Invisibility. Regretfully, there was no magic to be had here under the ice.

CHAPTER 59

SOONER THAN EXPECTED

Keflavik, Iceland Naval Air Station: 63°58'48"N Latitude, 22°35'01"W Longitude
Wednesday, 4:22 p.m. (Greenland time), October 12, 2011

They had been on the ground for three hours. Their Icelandic hosts had provided excellent facilities, including a humongous hangar for the three Seahawk helicopters. Food had been catered in. To the rear of the hangar was a briefing room sufficiently large for the SEALs, the Seahawk crews, Silverstein, Lopez, and Miller.

Commander Wilder had just completed his portion of the briefing. It included a PowerPoint presentation covering technical details of the route they would take from Keflavik to the Müller site on Greenland. A distance of five hundred miles, coupled with a Seahawk cruising speed of 170 miles per hour, meant three hours in the air, assuming no head winds. Silverstein shivered as he heard Wilder's next statement: except for the last half hour or so, the entire trip would be over water, the Denmark Strait, to be precise. It was one thing to fly over a large body of water in a reliable jet plane, but quite another in a vibrating contraption with no real wings.

Silverstein listened with interest as Wilder reviewed their ditching procedures. When Lopez had told him previously that three helicopters were arriving in the C-5, Silverstein had assumed that the third was a spare in case there was a mechanical problem before takeoff. To his amazement, he learned that there were three crews—each consisting of a pilot, copilot, and a system warfare operator. The third helicopter had been sent as a substitute all right, but as a spare in case something went wrong on the flight over. If something happened to Seahawk One or Seahawk Two, Seahawk Three would rescue everyone and continue on. Additionally, Seahawk Three would provide air support should their convoy come under attack.

Wilder next covered their rules of engagement. Since it was unlikely that they would encounter resistance prior to arriving at the Müller ice camp, what was important was how these rules applied during their assault on the Müller compound. From Silverstein's point of view, it didn't take a rocket scientist to tell you what to do. If someone shot at you, you shot back.

Finally, although everyone there had been briefed prior to leaving the States, Wilder reiterated the seriousness of the mission. Failure was not an option, he said. With all operational aspects covered, he turned the floor over to Lopez.

Lopez climbed onto the stand. "You men don't know me. My name is Hector Lopez, and I work for the CIA. I can imagine that in some of your minds, that is *not* a positive." Subdued chuckling passed among the men. "I've been involved in some hairy situations over the years, several of them with that civilian sitting behind you." He pointed back toward Silverstein. "In fact, during our first meeting, it wouldn't be too much of a stretch to say that he saved my life." Everyone turned to look. "His name is Dr. Victor Mark Silverstein from the Naval Research Laboratory, and we are here because of him. You'll be comforted to know that, although he's a civilian, he *is* navy." With that comment, the SEALs came alive with a rambunctious round of applause.

"I'm offended." Lopez mockingly shook his head. "Why should a stinking navy puke get more respect than me, from the world's foremost intelligence agency?"

Further laughter.

Lopez continued. "Seriously, Dr. Silverstein deserves every bit of your gratitude. As an aside, I'm going to share with you something that only a handful of people know. I can't reveal the details because they're classified. Several years ago, Dr. Silverstein nearly singlehandedly thwarted a terrorist operation that would have done serious damage to our country. Because of the sensitivity of what occurred, everyone involved was sworn to secrecy."

With that grandiloquent statement, all turned quiet, and all of the SEALs turned in unison to take a second look at the individual for whom Lopez could make such a proclamation. They stood and joined in a steady applause that lasted some ten seconds. Silverstein couldn't remember a more embarrassing moment.

The event to which Lopez was referring was the planned attack on the United States in 2005 by Middle Eastern terrorists. With the help of an American genius by the name of Cameron Fitzby, they had targeted Washington DC with a Category 5 hurricane. The details of that attack were never released to the public. Then, in 2009, under the new Obama administration, with a recommendation from Leon Panetta, the director of the CIA, Silverstein had been awarded the Medal of Freedom.

That day, August 12, was memorable. First, Silverstein had been invited to witness the public recognition of fifteen other Medal of Freedom honorees, including the likes of scientist Steven Hawking, Archbishop Desmond Tutu, former Supreme Court Justice Sandra Day O'Connor, and Senator Edward Kennedy. Silverstein recalled sadly that Senator Kennedy could not attend the ceremony and, in fact, had passed away two weeks later.

What no one knew was what had occurred afterward in a private room, with only President Barack Obama, Leon Panetta, and a handful of other dignitaries in attendance. There, President Obama recognized Silverstein for what he had accomplished back in 2005. As bad as it was that Silverstein could never tell anyone about this unique honor—even his colleague, Linda Kipling, who had played a significant role in the event—he left Washington DC *without* the medal. It would be stored in a special, honored place, he was told. Although one of the proudest days of his life, it had also been the loneliest.

Everyone sat down, and Lopez continued. "The reason we are here is that Dr. Silverstein and his colleague, Dr. Kipling, have stumbled onto an international conspiracy that dwarfs anything

I've seen in my two-plus decades of federal service. Before you left the States, you were all briefed on where and why we're going. The bad guys have a nuclear reactor or two that they're threatening to let go. And when I say *let go*, I mean that they plan to allow the reactors to go supercritical. All of you know what that means. That's why two of you," Lopez pointed to the crowd, "are reactor experts. Could you please stand and identify yourselves?"

Lopez acknowledged the two men. "Once you all have the situation under control, it'll be their job to make sure the reactors are defused."

A hand in the back. "Sir, we understand that you have someone on the inside."

"That's correct. Dr. Kipling, Dr. Silverstein's colleague, will be contacting us to let us know the best time to arrive and will be running interference for us. The idea, of course, is for us to get there when they least expect us. At least, that's the plan. If Dr. Kipling *can't* communicate with us, we're going to have to improvise."

The same person raised his hand again, this time looking back toward Silverstein. "With all due respect to Dr. Silverstein, sir, if Dr. Kipling is another civilian scientist, it doesn't sound to me like you have someone who's exactly trained in doing this sort of thing."

Another voice piped in. "Well then, if he has no training, let's just hope that he's a big motherfucker."

The room exploded in laughter.

Silverstein knew that this would be interesting. He watched as Lopez cringed. "Gentlemen, I'm afraid you've made an assumption that isn't quite correct. Dr. Kipling is Dr. Linda Kipling. He's a she."

With that comment, all heads snapped to attention. Silverstein noted that you could have heard the proverbial pin drop to the floor. The second guy, again. "Are you shittin' me? You're counting on a female to back us up?"

Silverstein knew that Lopez remembered Kipling's exploits from previous ventures. First, when Kipling had saved Silverstein's life in Colorado. Later, when she had beaten the shit out of

Cameron Fitzby, the American whose know-how was behind the terrorist operation.

Lopez maintained his cool. "I know that all of you think you're tough guys, and you are. But if I were to put Linda Kipling one on one with any of you, I wouldn't be the one to bet against her. She's smart, she's resourceful, and she's tough. And if that isn't enough to give you jocks wet dreams, I can vouch that she's a babe."

Apparently, all of this was too much for the SEALs to comprehend. They immediately changed the subject and discussed further aspects of the trip. After another few minutes, Silverstein watched as Lopez checked his cell phone, signaling Wilder and stepping down from the platform. He walked to the rear of the room and exited.

Silverstein kept his eye on the door. Lopez had probably received a call from headquarters, maybe with new information. It took several minutes for him to return. When he did, and as he walked back into the room, he caught Silverstein's eye. Silverstein didn't like what he saw.

Lopez jogged back to the front. Wilder stepped aside. Lopez took a moment to compose himself. "Gentlemen, I just received a call from Langley, and it isn't good news. I'm afraid that something has happened that we didn't anticipate." Lopez looked again in Silverstein's direction.

Lopez cleared his throat. "Starting yesterday, we've been monitoring all official communications here in Greenland. Air traffic control, police transmissions, that sort of thing. About twenty minutes ago, Langley began picking up chatter about a missing police helicopter. At that point, my people got involved and made some inquiries. To make a long story short, police from," Lopez checked his notes, "Sermersooq—that's a municipality up here—got an official request from someone besides us in our government. A request to check out something at a specific latitude and longitude." He paused. "Here's the bad news. The coordinates for where they were headed are the same as the ones we have for the Müller camp."

Silverstein couldn't believe it! *Something has happened that we didn't anticipate?* Like hell! What happened was exactly what he had warned Lopez about. Captain Stigler had obviously determined the location of the Müller camp the same way they had. What she had done was to ask the locals to check it out. *Lopez's stupid, foolish, imbecilic CIA pride! If only he had contacted Stigler as I suggested!*

There was no doubt why the helicopter was missing. The police had arrived much like the NRL snowmobilers had the previous week and had met their demise. There was one noteworthy difference this time. Schnabel would understand that, this time, there would be no covering up what had happened.

Lopez, obviously upset, continued. "What this means is that the Müllers' cover has been blown for good. We have to leave *now*. Let's hope to God that we can get there in time."

CHAPTER 60

A MAGICIAN'S ASPIRATION

Ice Station Helheim: 66°38'00"N Latitude, 38°48'00"W Longitude
Wednesday, 4:25 p.m., October 12, 2011

With no small degree of apprehension, Kipling looked in both directions outside her stateroom. She needed to get to the radar room. If she had interpreted Schnabel's order to Wolf correctly, that's where they kept the communications gear.

Kipling was about to make a dash toward the garage when she saw Maxim again, speeding by with his hand truck and stacked boxes. At once, she realized that she would have a good cover if she appeared to be actively involved in the evacuation process. "Arno. Can I help? Are there more boxes?"

Perspiring heavily, Maxim stopped and thought. "Yeah, sure. Go back to the kitchen. Outside in the corridor are lots of boxes. There's another hand truck, too."

There was a certain apprehension in heading in a direction opposite to where she wanted to go. Still, this tack would draw less suspicion. She reconsidered the wisdom of that thought the moment she eyed Kobler ahead. She picked up her pace.

Kobler saw her coming and seemed annoyed. "Where are *you* going?"

"Arno said I could help move boxes to the garage. I'm going to the kitchen for the hand truck." Leaving little time for Kobler to question her actions, Kipling changed the subject. "What's your job? Where are you going?"

Apparently satisfied with her explanation, Kobler continued on. "Schnabel needs help in the reactor room. I'm going to the garage to get some tools."

That's great! That's just great! They were probably already setting the doomsday timers. "Okay, I'll catch you later."

Kipling arrived at the kitchen, located the hand truck, loaded it with three boxes, and made her way back through the corridor toward the stairs to the garage. She passed several others on the staff who paid her no mind. Her strategy to avoid suspicion was working.

I've got to think this through. Because there was no elevator, and she had three boxes, three trips would be necessary. Although people were darting about everywhere, surely on one of those trips, she would find herself alone in the garage.

Kipling's objective was the radar room, to contact Silverstein using whatever communications gear she could find. Abruptly, a second option came to mind. Outside the open garage was a running helicopter, an aircraft with a radio for communications! She pictured the location of the aircraft relative to the view from inside the garage. Because it was out of sight, no one would be able to see her. She could make the call and return. That would eliminate the need to risk a confrontation with Wolf in the radar room.

Kipling arrived at the stairs and grabbed the first of her boxes. As she started up, Kobler was coming back down. She allowed him to pass but, before proceeding, looked past him down the corridor, pleased to see no one else coming in her direction.

Rushing up the two flights of stairs and bursting into the garage, Kipling was disheartened at what she saw. Someone had closed the garage door! If she opened it now, and someone came by, they would be suspicious. Worse, they might close the door, and she'd be stranded outside. There were no other entrances to the underground compound.

Kipling placed her box with the others ready to be transported back to Reykjavik. She glanced about the room. Door number two, the one to the armory, was open! She rushed to the steps, listened, and after hearing nothing, ran quickly into that room.

There were numerous weapons there, many quite large and of obvious high caliber. Most she had never seen before. But from her days as a ranger for the National Park Service, she had come across a variety of handguns. She recognized the Makarov nine-millimeter, a popular Soviet semiautomatic pistol that would be consistent with the Müller plan to blame this operation on the Russians. The rest of the weaponry was probably of Russian origin as well. Nervously looking back toward the door, she grabbed one of the Makarovs and shoved it inside an inner compartment to her jacket. There were magazine clips located on shelves below the weapons. She grabbed two.

Kipling looked for anything else that might prove useful. Although she had never handled a hand grenade before, she recognized one when she saw it. She took two, balancing their surprising weight in pockets on either side of her jacket. Her jacket was getting heavy but was still manageable. It was fortunate that the Müller standard-issue, oversized jacket had so many pockets. She reentered the garage.

So far, so good! Should I leave now for the radar room or carry up more boxes? Kipling had just about made her decision when the door to the radar room opened in front of her, startling both her and the man who came through it. She came eye to eye with Schnabel.

"What are you doing here?" He didn't seem pleased.

"I'm helping Arno move boxes. I have two more at the bottom of the stairs."

As she had done previously with Kobler, Kipling ignored the confrontation and started to move away. This time it didn't work.

Schnabel grabbed Kipling's upper arm. This action frightened her for two reasons. First, she worried that he had found her out. Second, and of immediate concern, she was afraid that his hand might bump against something hard in her jacket. After all, the amount of hardware on her person was enough to give an airport metal detector an electronic aneurism.

Kipling pulled away slightly, allowing her arm to stretch out horizontally, putting some distance between Schnabel's hand and her jacket. She knew she had to play the part, needed to be an advocate. Before he could question her further, she took the lead. "Mr. Schnabel, I'm as anxious as everybody to get out of here. Daniel told me what's going to happen. From what I've been seeing, you need all the help you can get. You said it yourself; we can't make mistakes. Removing these documents is probably more important than anything else you're doing. Besides that, because I've never been here before, I have a different perspective and might be able to spot something that looks wrong. The last thing my cousins want is for this to be traced back to them." She pulled away. "If you don't mind, I have boxes to move."

Schnabel held his grip for a moment and then let go. Kipling descended the steps, surprised that he hadn't followed. She grabbed the second of the remaining boxes and climbed the stairs again. Schnabel was not in sight. Unless he had returned to the radar room, he was in the armory. She headed down for the remaining box. As she entered the garage for the third time, she saw him leaving the armory and locking the door. This time, he followed her down.

With Schnabel behind her, Kipling had no choice but to continue the ruse. Pushing her hand truck, she headed back to the kitchen. As he walked past her, she started loading more boxes. He continued down the corridor leading to the reactor room.

Kipling decided this was a good time to make her visit to the dining area. As she entered, she recognized one of the security personnel who brushed past her. She filled a cup half full of coffee and proceeded toward the condiments. Looking behind her to make sure that she was alone, she opened a pocket and added a handful of toothpicks. For good measure, she took two drinking straws. If what she was planning worked out, they would prove essential.

Kipling downed a mouthful of coffee and disposed of the rest. She returned to her boxes. There were still plenty and no sign of the cook. He had probably taken her at her word and gone off to other duties.

Time was wasting. Kipling added a third box to her hand truck and headed back, grimacing at not having accomplished more than moving boxes. She arrived at the stairs, snatched one, and headed up. At the top, she listened for a moment and heard nothing. She was alone. It was time. She stepped through the door leading to the radar room.

This corridor from the garage was much narrower than the others below and had a downward slope, as Kobler had said. Not only was it constricted, but it was dark, with only a small bulb on the ceiling every so often. She had proceeded a few feet when the grade rose slightly. Not far ahead, she saw a door.

Realizing that a potentially unpleasant confrontation lay ahead, Kipling's mind flashed back to the ethical questions that had plagued her sleep on the flights to Greenland. If it became necessary, could she take a human life? Back in Monterey in her discussions with Silverstein, she had pondered the moralities involved in turning against family. Here, the situation had moved well beyond, to a faction of fanatics intent upon doing irreparable harm to the planet. Kipling had made her bed, and she would lie in it. If and when she appeared before God Almighty himself, she hoped that he would understand.

The door ahead had a window, and Kipling could see light. She opened the inner pocket to her jacket, removed the Makarov, loaded one of the eight-cartridge magazines, and made sure she pushed the safety into the *fire* position. She transferred the weapon to her right outside pocket but with the zipper open.

Kipling arrived at the door and opened it. The room she entered was smaller than she had imagined. A large radarscope straight ahead caught her eye. Along the right wall was a series of television screens displaying images from outside. In the fading light, she saw the dead police officers and the helicopter, with its overhead rotor still turning.

Kipling had startled Wolf, who was leaning over his desk along the far wall. With both hands in her pockets, she had her speech prepared. She would convince him to let her call Silverstein.

"I'm sorry that we haven't formally met." Kipling smiled sweetly. "I'm Linda Kipling. I'm the Müllers' cousin from America. I didn't mean to just barge in on you, but things are a bit hectic back there." She motioned toward the door. "Gunter told me to come see you. He said that it would be okay to call my boyfriend back home."

Wolf's reaction was unexpected. Instead of responding, he looked down to his right. She saw immediately what he was after. There lay a Makarov identical to the one Kipling had in her pocket. This was the first time Kipling had seen anyone with a firearm inside the compound.

Kipling chose to make the first move. There was no point in waiting. She removed the Makarov from her pocket, charged the pistol by pulling back on the slide, stood straight-legged, and, with both hands, aimed at Wolf. She hadn't expected to encounter such a situation so soon.

"Don't do that, August! I don't want to kill you, but I will if you give me no choice."

Kipling's plea had no effect. Wolf's right hand lunged for the gun. Simultaneously, he spun 360 degrees while stepping to his right, perhaps thinking that a moving target would be harder to hit. Unfortunately, for a man his size, this rotation came across more like slow motion.

As he came fully around and faced Kipling squarely, Wolf raised his weapon.

Kipling had no choice. She snapped off two rounds. The resulting explosion of the nine-millimeter within the confined space was deafening. August Wolf was dead before he hit the floor.

* * *

It seemed unlikely that anyone had heard the gunshots in the main compound. There was too much ice and space between them. Still, Kipling had to hurry.

It didn't take long to find what looked to be an ordinary phone. Adding the country code, 001 for the United States, she dialed Silverstein's cell.

He answered on the first ring. "Silverstein."

"Victor, listen. I don't have much time. All hell's broken loose here. We've been discovered, and in less than four hours, we're leaving. The doomsday timers for the reactors will be set. Listen carefully. I'm at sixty-six degrees, thirty-eight minutes, zero seconds, north latitude. Repeat, sixty-six, thirty-eight, zero. For longitude, I'm at thirty-eight degrees, forty-eight minutes, and zero seconds west. Repeat, thirty-eight, forty-eight, zero. Do you copy?"

"Linda, we know where you are, and we also know about the police helicopter. Stigler obviously sent them. We're in Iceland, and we're leaving now. Lopez says it'll take about three hours."

"Victor, it was awful. They killed two men in cold blood."

"Are you okay, Linda? Can you hang on?"

"I'm okay, Victor. Just get here as fast as you can. FYI, our pickups are coming from Reykjavik. Two helicopters. And listen, they have radar here. They'll know you're coming." Kipling was talking faster and faster. "Victor, I have to go."

"Linda?"

"Yes."

"We'll be there soon."

"I know."

Kipling pressed the phone disconnect and looked around. There was little point in trying to hide the body. He'd be found soon enough.

The walls of this tiny claustrophobic corner of the compound seemed to be closing in on Kipling, and she was anxious to leave. She rushed through the door and began to sprint up the grade to the garage when she skidded to a halt on the dusty floor. Silverstein, Lopez, and, with luck, a small army, were on their way. Silverstein had said that it would take three hours; Schnabel said the same. If Schnabel's rescue team left Iceland when he had said, they would arrive ahead of Silverstein.

Kipling understood that Lopez's arrival needed to come as a surprise. She also realized that she was in a position to do something about that. She turned around and raced back to the radar room.

Placing the grenade directly in front of the radar screen, Kipling pulled the pin. On her way out, she made sure that the door was closed to concentrate the blast. With luck, the television screens would meet the same fate as that of the radar.

Running as fast as she could through the tunnel, Kipling had advanced halfway to the garage when the blast went off. The muffled explosion behind her sounded powerful but distant. She held her breath as she entered the garage. The space was empty. All was going well.

It was five o'clock. With three hours to go, there was nothing left to do but wait. Kipling needed somewhere to hide. After considering her limited options, she confirmed in her mind where the best place would be. The danger lay in getting there unseen.

With her two boxes still sitting at the base of the steps, Kipling ran down twice and completed her assignment. Before heading down for the final time, a thought came to mind. If she had to hide, it wouldn't hurt to leave a red herring.

Kipling located the switch that activated the garage door and pressed it. The single-panel door rose slowly. She walked over and glanced outside. Winds were calm, and there were no clouds. Whatever happened in the next few hours, weather would play no detrimental role.

Kipling hurried down the steps, took her hand truck in tow, and headed back to the remaining boxes. She passed three workers on the way. If someone saw her when she arrived at the kitchen, she was prepared to make yet another box run. But fate smiled. She arrived unseen.

Hands on the jambs, Kipling leaned inside the eating area, pleased to see that it was unoccupied. She backed up into the hallway and looked both ways.

Kipling rotated and opened the door opposite. It was dark inside. It was time to disappear.

Chapter 61

Three Wings and a Prayer

Off the eastern coast of Greenland over the Denmark Strait
Wednesday, 6:55 p.m., October 12, 2011

Silverstein's helicopter had been designated Seahawk One, since it carried Navy Commander (CDR) Leopold Wilder, the officer in charge of the SEALs. With a hand-signaled permission from their weapons specialist, the third member of the crew, Silverstein unbuckled his seatbelt, removed his headset, and edged his way forward from his seat near the rear of the helicopter. Excluding the windows surrounding the cockpit, the Seahawk had two forward openings to see out, one on either side.

Crouched on the floor, Silverstein surveyed the ocean from their 4,500-foot flight level. Their Icelandic forecaster had predicted clear skies for the entire operation, and their flight had been ice-smooth thus far. As chance would have it, October 12 featured a full moon. So much for Silverstein's fanciful vision of their swooping down out of the clouds mere seconds before their assault on the Müller ice camp. That said, the SEALs left nothing to chance: before they left Keflavik, every man had been issued night-vision goggles.

Under the full moon, Seahawk Three was clearly visible to starboard. To the port side flew its mirrored twin, Seahawk Two.

Lieutenant Commander (LCDR) Jim Sarver, their pilot and the man in command of all three aircraft, had informed them earlier that he would do two things to lessen their chance of being detected by those at the ice camp. First, none of his aircraft would use exterior lighting. Second, the three aircraft would be flying with their transponders turned off.

A transponder, a device that had its roots in World War II, had been known by a different name back then: IFF, *Identification, Friend or Foe*. All modern aircraft carried such electronic gear. In its present form, when remotely interrogated by a receiver on another aircraft or the ground and asked to *squawk* a specific code, the transponder transmitted back its geographic position and altitude. The transponder code allowed the person viewing that information on a radar screen to identify that aircraft. With its transponder turned off, an aircraft was electronically invisible, except for its reflection on a radar screen.

Silverstein made his way back to his seat next to Lopez and decided it was time to make amends. Silverstein had spent the first minutes of their flight giving Lopez a tongue-lashing. Lopez understood that he had erred in not contacting Stigler, and he regretted that decision. Silverstein patted him on the shoulder and offered up a stick of gum. Lopez nodded, seemingly appreciating the sentiment of his dear old friend.

Silverstein, Lopez, and Miller had received headsets before leaving, both as a courtesy and as a practical matter. Although Wilder was technically in charge of this operation, Lopez's word carried obvious weight. They could listen and contribute to the chatter within their aircraft and among the Seahawks. As far as Silverstein could tell, things were proceeding normally. In fact, Wilder had told them earlier that a tailwind had improved their ground speed by some twenty knots.

When Silverstein had received Kipling's call back in Reykjavik, he could not have been more accurate in telling her that they were on their way. He had just set foot onto the helicopter. Choosing not to trust his memory, he had written down the coordinates she gave him. He then compared them to those Lopez had retrieved back at Langley. They were identical. He hoped that Kipling hadn't taken any unnecessary risks to contact him, since Lopez had already determined the location of the Müller ice camp. Of course, there was no way she could have known that.

Disconcerting to Silverstein had been the tenor of Kipling's voice. What he heard was fear. *Victor, listen. I don't have much time. All hell's broken loose here. We've been discovered . . .* And then, *Victor, it was awful. They killed two men in cold blood.*

LCDR Sarver's southern drawl over the intercom broke into Silverstein's thoughts. "Just to fill y'all in back there, it looks like we have some company up here. About twenty miles ahead, we're picking up two bogies. We've made some discreet inquiries over channels. These two are helicopters that took off from Reykjavik not long before we left Keflavik. Dr. Silverstein, this is consistent with what Dr. Kipling told you. Particularly since they're also running with their transponders off, I'd say these are your boys!"

Very interesting! That begged a question or two. Silverstein keyed his mike. "Silverstein here. Can they see us? Do they know we're back here?"

"Negative. Highly unlikely. Pilots generally don't care what's behind them. And since our transponders are off, they can't see us electronically. The only reason we see them is because we're picking them up on our weapons radar."

Lopez joined the chat. "If this is the first time you've seen them, does that mean that we're going faster than they are?"

"That's affirmative. We're hauling ass, burning fuel like there's no tomorrow."

"Silverstein here. I wonder how this should affect our strategy. Commander, I've met these people, and they're fanatics. Once they know we're coming, they're going to be desperate. You remember that Linda told me they have radar. They just murdered two police officers, and they'll want to do the same to us. I wouldn't doubt they'll try to blow us out of the sky before we even get there."

As you'd expect from a seasoned military officer, Sarver's voice exuded calm and confidence. "That's not a problem, Dr. Silverstein. Their radar won't do them much good because we'll be coming in low, following the terrain at a hundred feet or so. They'll never see us until we're on top of them. Unless they're standing there waiting with SAMs when we appear on the horizon, we'll be okay."

SAM stood for surface-to-air missile, Silverstein knew. He felt compelled to make his point a second time. "Again, Commander, please don't underestimate these people. I wouldn't put it past them, the SAMs." He paused. "But something just occurred to me. If we could catch the two in front of us, would there be an advantage in flying in behind them? Not only would their radar have a rough time picking us out, but we could use them as a shield. They'd be less likely to let their missiles fly if there was the chance they'd destroy their only means of escape."

Silverstein recalled the impact of the SAM missiles supplied by the CIA, American-made Stingers, to the *Mujahideen* in Afghanistan back in the 1980s. That single piece of weaponry had had a significant impact on Russian aircraft, notably helicopters.

"That's a damn good point, Dr. Silverstein. Because it's highly unlikely these civilian choppers carry external weapons, our threats will be coming only from the ground."

Lopez cut in. "Actually, let's hope that's the case. I don't think it would be to our advantage to destroy their only means of escape. If they're backed into a corner, they'll blow the reactors immediately."

The SEAL leader spoke next. "Wilder here. I don't think it'll make any difference, Mr. Lopez. Once we hit the ground, it won't take them long before they'll know they're doomed. We have enough explosives to blast our way into Fort Knox, but we have to be fast. Ultimately, our chances of stopping them are going to hinge on your man—excuse me, your woman—inside. It's going to come down to whether she can delay them the minutes or seconds that we'll need."

CDR Wilder couldn't have stated it better. Silverstein closed his eyes, tuned out the noise and vibration of the helicopter, and said a short prayer. *Please, God, help Linda. Help her stop the goddamn sons of bitches out to destroy our planet!*

CHAPTER 62

UNDERWATER

Ice Station Helheim: 66°38'00"N Latitude, 38°48'00"W Longitude
Wednesday, 7:35 p.m., October 12, 2011

Gunter Schnabel set the second of the two reactor timers. It would activate within seconds of the first. When the time came, each would signal the reactor mechanisms to withdraw the control rods. He examined both again, secured the lids to the metal boxes, ran the chains through the metal clasps on the boxes, and attached each chain to itself using its lock. He wouldn't need the three keys to open them anymore but put them in his pocket in case their rescue helicopters were delayed. He wanted to be well clear of this place before the witching hour of 8:45.

Schnabel looked about the room and did a final check. Three frozen Russian bodies were sitting strategically: one slumped over the console and two lying on the floor by the reactors. Others had been placed at various locations about the compound. Operation manuals written in Russian had replaced those used by the staff. The German versions had been carried up to the garage, awaiting transport.

Schnabel tried the phone again. He had failed to reach August Wolf some twenty minutes earlier. He wanted to check the progress of their helicopters. Considering the controlled pandemonium going on within the compound, Schnabel wasn't concerned. But for the second time, there was no answer. Because he had finished his task in the reactor room, he decided it was time to make his final rounds.

"I'm going to the radar room if anybody needs me!" Schnabel shouted to no one in particular. Kantor, Hoffman, and Koch were monitoring their various dials and gauges while several underlings stood around nervously. Hoffman had explained that by bringing both reactors up to full power, they would be primed for meltdown when the timers activated.

Schnabel walked down the corridor toward the kitchen and arrived as Maxim was loading the last of the boxes. "Maxim, why isn't this done already? I thought Kipling was helping you."

Maxim shook his head. "I thought so too, but she disappeared. I figured you had given her other orders. That's her hand truck right there." He pointed.

"When was the last you saw her?" Schnabel didn't like what he was hearing.

"More than an hour ago, I'd say."

As Schnabel started to jog away, Maxim yelled after him. "Who opened the garage door? It's freezing up there."

Was zum Teufel? What the hell? Schnabel took off at a run. He arrived at the stairs and rushed up. The garage door stood open. *Where's Kipling? Is she trying to escape?* As he recalled his order that they leave the helicopter running, he felt suddenly sick. If she knew how to fly a helicopter, she could be long gone, a disaster in the making.

Schnabel grabbed a flashlight and raced outside. His light proved unnecessary. A full moon provided ample illumination to see the police helicopter in the distance, with its overhead rotor still turning. *How stupid not to have incapacitated the aircraft!*

As if that thought hadn't been enough to cause cardiac arrest, Schnabel considered another reason Kipling might have gone outside: the radio in the helicopter! He sprinted to the helicopter and looked around. There was nothing to indicate that she had been there. After stomping around in all directions from the compound entrance, Schnabel convinced himself that she was not hiding outside. *Surely, she couldn't have been stupid enough to run away into this frozen hell. That would be suicide.*

On his return to the garage, Schnabel commanded himself to calm down. He considered the logic. If Kipling had left the compound to make a call from the helicopter, why hadn't she closed the door when she returned to hide her tracks? Finally, he decided that none of his mental machinations mattered. Once he found Kipling, she'd tell him the truth, one way or another.

Schnabel triggered the motor for the garage door and headed toward the radar room. He checked his watch. He had spent valuable minutes fretting over this niggling, irritating bitch. He cursed himself for not locking her in her room earlier.

As Schnabel ascended the slope to the radar room, his pace slowed. *Something's wrong!* There was no light visible through the glass window in the door. Still carrying his flashlight, he snapped it on and shined it ahead. With his right hand, he reached for his handgun.

Schnabel pushed the door open with his foot and suspected what had happened even before his flashlight illuminated the scene. There was a strange odor in the air. It wasn't long before he saw direct evidence of his suspicion. The radar screen as well as the television monitors had been shattered. What he was seeing were the effects of an explosion.

A second later, the beam of his flashlight found the body of August Wolf. *Did the blast kill him?* Wolf lay on his stomach, his Makarov a few feet away. Schnabel saw effects to the body consistent with an explosion. But when he knelt down, he noticed something more: blood, a lot of it. After rolling Wolf's body onto its back, the reason became obvious. Wolf had been shot to death.

Abruptly, everything Schnabel had seen and learned in the past minutes congealed in his mind. Kipling!

Schnabel searched frantically about the room for the switch to the klaxon. He found it, pressed it, and went charging out the door. As he approached the entrance to the garage, he could hear the obnoxious sound in the distance. Whatever blast had gone off in that room hadn't affected all of their electronics.

*   *   *

353

From her hiding place, Kipling could hear the klaxon. She checked her watch. It was too early for either Schnabel's rescue party or Lopez to have arrived. She figured there was a good chance that the alarm had been set off in her honor, particularly since its activation switch was likely located in the radar room. Someone had discovered Wolf.

With the lights off, Kipling lay back and waited in the darkness. For now, there was nothing to do.

*   *   *

By the time Schnabel made his way down the stairs, he met the others moving in the opposite direction, heading to the garage, fearing the worst. He held up his hand. "We're not being attacked." He put his hands to his ears. "Does anyone know how to turn that damned thing off?"

After more painful seconds, auditory peace returned to the hallway. By then, everyone had arrived and crowded around Schnabel. "What's going on?" one asked.

Schnabel responded with a question instead. "Has anyone seen Kipling?"

Maxim raised his hand and repeated what he had said earlier.

"Anybody else?" Schnabel began to seethe, looking for scapegoats other than himself. But in the end, the blame was his. "Kobler! I thought I told you to keep an eye on her."

Kobler, head lowered, responded, "Mr. Schnabel, what did she do?"

Schnabel inhaled a chest-full of air before replying. "She killed August Wolf and blew up the radar room." He watched as all eyes in front of him grew large. When the realization hit that an outsider had murdered one of their number, surprise changed to rage. He could see a lynch mob forming.

"Gentlemen, I'm as angry as you are, but we can't lose focus." Schnabel checked the time. "We don't have much time to get out of here. The timers are set for eight forty-five."

With that remark, fourteen sets of eyes checked their wrist watches.

Maxim interrupted. "Mr. Schnabel, do you remember my telling you that the garage door was open. Did you check outside?"

Maxim was asking a reasonable question, but Schnabel reacted angrily. "Yes, goddamn it! I checked outside. She's not there!"

Schnabel realized that he was doing exactly what he had told the others not to do, allowing himself to lose focus in this critical last hour on the ice. He spoke in a softer voice. "Listen, we've got to keep our heads. Here's what I think. I think there's a chance that Kipling called someone on the outside. I think that's why she went to the radar room. I also think she blew the place up to disable the radar so that we couldn't detect any incoming aircraft."

Several of the group became noticeably agitated and began talking among themselves. Schnabel held up his hand. "Gentlemen! Even if Kipling managed to call out, there's no way that anyone could arrive before our people do."

Schnabel pointed to Fritz Neumann, the most senior of the security team. "Fritz, is everything buttoned down?"

"Sir, I'd say we're ninety-nine percent there. All documents have been substituted. All of our personal effects have been removed. The Russians are in place. And since the exploding reactors will kill them, there'll be no need to set off the explosives."

"Okay, that's good." Schnabel had almost forgotten that they had planned for an alternate method for the Russians to die in twenty-three months.

Schnabel continued. "As I've already said, even if Kipling managed to call someone, we'll be long gone before anyone gets here. By then, the place will be self-destructing." He pointed. "But because we have so much at stake, there's no point in taking chances. Kobler! You're our backup radar man, right? I want you to get our replacement radar screen out of storage and back online. From what I saw back there, there's a good chance the explosion didn't damage the electronics."

Schnabel gestured to the group. "I need two of you who are finished with your tasks." Two hands rose. "I want you to help Kobler. I want that radar up and running in fifteen minutes." He bit his lip. "Get moving!"

Schnabel addressed his security team next. "Okay, again, we're just being cautious. I want you three to get all the weaponry outside, especially the Stinger missiles." He would have preferred using a Russian-made SAM but knew from the *Mujahideen*'s experience in Afghanistan that the American-made Stinger was superior to the Russian SA-7. "Power them up and be ready to go. If someone *is* coming, we need to be ready." He reached in his pocket, removed the key to the armory, and tossed it over.

As his security personnel rushed up the steps behind him, Schnabel assessed the remaining, anxious group of men. "Two more volunteers." Hands rose, and he chose two.

To those remaining, Schnabel stated the obvious. "Okay, get done what's left to be done, and get yourselves upstairs and ready to leave."

Schnabel turned toward the other two. "The three of us are going to find Kipling. It shouldn't be hard. Start looking."

As the two rushed away, Schnabel called after them. "If either of you find her first, I don't want you to lay a hand on her. Call me, and I'll take it from there."

*   *   *

With only her head out of the water, Kipling heard the sharp crack of the electrical switch. The lights that illuminated the underground lake blinded her, but not before she could make out three men entering the room. One was Kobler.

Kipling blew residual water from the two straws in her mouth and eased herself below the surface of the warm water.

CHAPTER 63

PREMONITION

Seventy-five miles east of Müller Ice Camp on Greenland
Wednesday, 7:45 p.m., October 12, 2011

LCDR Jim Sarver came on the intercom, this time on overhead speakers for everyone to hear. "Okay, listen up, everybody. I'm now talking to Seahawks One, Two, and Three. In about thirty minutes, we'll be arriving at the Müller ice camp. Right now, we're a mile back from two helicopters that we're sure have been called in to evacuate the bad guys. Rather than go in low to avoid radar, our normal MO in a situation like this, Seahawks One and Two will use a different approach. We can thank Dr. Silverstein for this bit of strategy.

"Because there's no reason to suspect that the rescue helicopters are armed, Seahawks One and Two will fly in tight behind them, just in case the bad guys have SAMs ready. They'd think twice before firing if they thought they'd take out their only means of escape. Our job is to get you on the ground, hopefully somewhat near each other. Seahawk Three will separate from us and provide suppression fire as needed. Once y'all are on the ground, Commander Wilder is the boss. Commander Wilder, do you have some final words?"

"Men, this is Wilder. I have little to add. All I can say is that speed is of the essence. You SEALs, your job is to take this place as quickly as possible. We've all been briefed on what will happen if we fail. You nuclear men need to be ready to move when we've gained control. And as we all know, it won't be hard to recognize the friendly here. He's a she, and there's only one of her. Seahawk Three, stand by for suppression fire. Seahawk Three, do you copy?"

A new voice over the intercom: "Seahawk Three standing by. We'll be there."

Ice Station Helheim: 66°38'00"N Latitude, 38°48'00"W Longitude
Wednesday, 8:01 p.m., October 12, 2011

"What do you mean you can't find her?" Gunter Schnabel was furious.

One of the two volunteers stood with Schnabel outside the kitchen. "Sir, I've checked the living quarters and the bathrooms."

The second volunteer approached. "Sir, I looked in the kitchen, the dining room, the gym, the TV room, and all of Maxim's food-store locations."

"What's left?"

The first volunteer again. "There's the radar room, the garage, and the armory."

Schnabel was becoming increasingly irritated. "I've been to the radar room; she's not there. She's obviously not in the garage because everyone else is there. As far as the armory, there's literally no place there to hide. Where else?"

The second volunteer. "Sir, the only other places are the reactor room, the cold storage room where we kept the Russians, and the cooling pond room."

Schnabel took the lead back toward the reactor room, volunteers in tow. He blasted through the double doors and yelled out. "Is there anywhere in this room or there," he pointed toward the electrical generators, "where Kipling could hide?" Every man shook his head. Schnabel turned back to his volunteers. "Go check anyway."

Schnabel could sense his blood pressure rising. *If only I had taken her out before we arrived! If only I had locked her in her room! If only . . . !*

Both volunteers returned, shrugging their shoulders. Schnabel stormed through the double doors on his way to the cold storage room. He entered and switched on the light. The room seemed larger now that their frozen guests had departed. He walked the perimeter. There were no storage cabinets, no holes in the ice, nowhere for anyone to hide. He headed next to the area containing the cooling pond. *She has to be there, goddamn it! There's nowhere else she could be.*

Wednesday, 8:08 p.m., October 12, 2011

To the rear of the ice cavern, farthest from the door, Kipling floated on her back. The warm temperature of the water was not at all unpleasant. Since ten minutes earlier, when she had watched Kobler and his helpers unpack what looked to be a new radar screen, no one had entered the room. They had left the lights on, and her eyes had acclimated to the brightness. Visibility was not at all consistent. There were times when she could not see the door because of the fog. Kipling realized that, for most of the time, there was no need to hide below the surface of the water. It would be hard for anyone across the way to see her.

What Kipling had thought earlier to be a circular room wasn't. It had been an illusion fostered by the fact that it was the lake in which she floated that was round. Her estimate of the diameter of the lake had been accurate, however, about the length of a football field, residing in a square room of ice that came within ten feet of the water at its closest point, allowing plenty of space for the storage cabinetry. All cabinets sat to the right as you entered the room.

Diagonally opposite the cabinets, a series of eight-inch pipes protruded through the wall. These pipes angled downward into the water to release their heat by conduction to the cooler water. They then returned parallel to the incoming pipes back to the reactors.

When Kipling had entered the room to hide, she hadn't dared turn on the lights. She had used her LED flashlight to make her way, moving as fast as possible because this had been when she was most vulnerable. She had had to make a significant decision: how much clothing to remove before entering the water? Her bulky jacket, with its sensitive hardware, had to stay dry. She decided that was all she would remove. As unpleasant as it would be to exit the room in drenched clothing and shoes, there might be no time to dress. Rummaging inside the cabinets, she had found an empty five-gallon paint container with a plastic lid in which she hid the jacket.

Kipling checked her watch. It was eleven minutes after eight. It wouldn't be long before Schnabel's helicopters would arrive. She had a tricky decision to make. When should she leave the water? No one had been here since Kobler, but that didn't make any sense. She knew that Schnabel would look everywhere for her, and the cabinets were an obvious hiding place.

As if her thoughts were synchronized with Schnabel's actions, Kipling heard the door open. Rather than descend below the surface to use her straws, she lowered her head so that just her eyes and ears broke the surface. She could make out Schnabel, along with two of his lackeys. They headed immediately to the cabinets.

Schnabel's voice carried well across the water. "I want the two of you to think. Is this the only place left that we haven't searched?"

"Yes, sir, Mr. Schnabel."

"I want you to open every cabinet here. I'm going to walk the perimeter." Schnabel headed counterclockwise around the pond, retracing the steps Kipling had taken earlier.

Kipling ducked below the water with her straws in place and paddled gently away from the perimeter. Away from the sloping edge of the ice, she treaded water to stay in place.

Wednesday, 8:13 p.m., October 12, 2011

Schnabel was at his wit's end. He couldn't remember another time when he had become so paralyzed from not being in control. Maintaining control had always been his strength and ally. In an occupation that often involved dangerous and unfamiliar situations, he had bested his opponents by maintaining discipline, by outthinking his opposition. Now, here he was, brought down to an unusual level of incompetence by a woman. If Kipling wasn't outside the compound, she *had* to be inside. But if she was, where *was* she? His men had looked everywhere. But if she wasn't here, she must be outside. But that made no sense either. *Damn it all to hell!*

Making his way along the icy shoreline, Schnabel let his eyes gaze across the water. He had seen this subsurface marvel on several occasions over the years. Each time it had gotten larger. It was quite beautiful, with its wisps of fog radiating off the surface. He wondered why no one had ever considered swimming here. The water was as pure as it gets, he was told.

Schnabel had walked about halfway to the rear when the phone by the door rang. "Will one of you get that?" He headed back.

Across the water, volunteer one yelled, "It's Kobler, in the radar room."

Schnabel jogged over to the phone. "Schnabel."

"You were right. There was no damage to our electronics. As soon as we hooked up the replacement screen, we were back in business. But that's not why I'm calling. Our choppers just radioed in, and they're about ten minutes out."

"Good work, Kobler. That *is* good news." He checked his watch: 8:16. This would be cutting it close. "Okay, Kobler. Call the reactor room and tell them to abandon ship. Get everyone else into the garage and ready to go. But I want you to stay by the screen until I tell you to leave. Call me immediately if you see anything unusual. Do you understand?"

Schnabel hung up the phone and saw that his men had finished searching the cabinets, one of them nervously checking his watch. Volunteer two provided the summary. "There were only a couple of bins large enough for her to hide in, sir. I'm sorry, but she's not here."

"Kobler says our helicopters will be here soon. Get yourselves up to the garage. Get going—now!" There was no need to repeat the order.

Schnabel paced to the door and looked back nostalgically. They had achieved so much over the past decade. It was a damned shame that it had to end like this. *Should I turn the lights off?* When the radiation had died down sufficiently, forensic authorities would comb the site for clues. Would it matter if they found the light switch in the on or off position?

Before heading upstairs, he wanted to make one final check of the reactor room. After all, their crowning accomplishment would be the destruction of the Greenland ice sheet, accelerated by two boiling reactors melting their way through millennia of built-up ice.

Before he closed the door to the cooling pond behind him, a thought occurred. Schnabel switched off the lights.

Wednesday, 8:17 p.m., October 12, 2011

After Kipling's eyes had adjusted to the brightness of the lights, her world turned to absolute blackness. Should she leave the water now? No! The feeble light from her flashlight would prove useless until the rods in her eyes had regained their vision.

From out of nowhere, a second thought added weight to the first. A voice suggested that there might be another reason to wait a little while longer.

Wednesday, 8:19 p.m., October 12, 2011

Schnabel made his final check of the reactor room. Everyone had gone. He briefly considered closing and locking the double doors. He had the master key and could do that. He decided otherwise. Although there was a good chance that much of this room would soon lie at the bottom of an ice shaft created by the melting reactors, he couldn't count on that. In contrast to whether forensic personnel might question whether a light switch had been left on, they might wonder why someone would have locked the doors to the reactor room.

As if someone might be listening for his footsteps, Schnabel walked on the balls of his feet as he approached the entry to the pond. It had occurred to him that there was one additional place where Kipling could have hidden. Unlikely but possible.

Schnabel's childhood had not been one of means or privilege. He recalled turning out the kitchen lights at night to draw out the cockroaches that infested their wretched apartment. He reached out slowly to the doorknob and gave it a quick jerk. He ran in quickly, turned on the lights, and scanned the area. *Nothing. A silly thought indeed.*

Schnabel checked his watch. Less than twenty-five minutes to go. As he bounded off down the hallway toward the garage, he could hear wall phones ringing behind him.

CHAPTER 64

FINALE

Ice Station Helheim: 66°38'00"N Latitude, 38°48'00"W Longitude
Wednesday, 8:22 p.m., October 12, 2011

As Schnabel charged through the door into the garage, Neumann of security was waiting, phone in hand. "You need to talk to Kobler."

What now! Schnabel grabbed the phone. "What is it?"

"Sir, there's something going on here I don't understand. Our choppers just radioed that they're on their way and that we should be ready to leave."

They're right on schedule. "So?"

"Here's what's strange, sir. From what I'm seeing on the radar, it looks to me like there's more than two aircraft coming in."

Schnabel understood aircraft and radar, having been a pilot once himself. "Are their transponders switched on?"

"No, sir. What I'm looking at is strictly their paint on the screen."

"Radio back and tell them to activate their transponders."

"Hold on, sir."

Schnabel could hear Kobler in the background radioing transponder squawk codes.

Kobler came back on the line. "They're squawking, sir." A moment passed. "I see ours, but I'm telling you, there are definitely other aircraft in their vicinity. Three, to be exact."

How could Kipling's call have triggered so quick a response?

Years of involvement in thorny situations where quick decisions were necessary had prepared Schnabel for this moment. Putting aside the dilemma posed by the missing Müller cousin, he reverted to the resourceful person the Müllers had always counted on, barking orders, the first into the phone. "Kobler! Stay on the line."

The remainder of Schnabel's staff stood waiting for directions. Hands on hips, he told them what no one wanted to hear. "Okay, the news isn't good. Kobler is reporting that three other aircraft are following ours. We have no idea who they are, but they shouldn't be there. Except for Kobler manning the radar, I want everyone else outside." He pointed. "Neumann, are all of the heavy weapons in position? Are the SAMs powered up?"

"Yes, sir, on both counts. We have a dozen Stingers ready to go. But we can't go firing them off anywhere near our own helicopters."

Schnabel needed to invent tactics on the fly. "Okay, here's what we're going to do. Do we have night-vision goggles?"

"No goggles, sir, but we do have three pairs of night-vision binoculars."

"That's even better. Neumann, Huber, Mayer! You're the most experienced. I want you outside with the SAMs. You're the ones who'll need the binoculars. Kobler says there are five aircraft total. I want the three that aren't ours eliminated. Don't hesitate to use every last one of our Stingers." He gestured to the others. "I want the rest of you ready with the fifty-calibers. They're probably helicopters. If any of them do land, it'll be your job to take them out."

Neumann again. "About my question, sir. How do we not hit our own aircraft?"

Schnabel brought the phone back to his ear. "Did you catch all of that, Kobler?"

"Yes, sir."

"I want you to stay on the line and wait for my signal. When I give the order, I want you to radio our men. Tell them they're being followed and that they need to take immediate evasive action. The one on the port side needs to peel off severely to his left. The one to the starboard should do the same to the right. Tell them that their very survival is at stake, because we're going to fire SAMs at the aircraft behind them. It's their job to get out of the way."

Schnabel handed the phone to Maxim. "Stand here and wait for my signal."

"Let's go." Schnabel led the others out the door and up the slope. Outside, everyone stood quiet, waiting for some auditory or visual indication of the incoming aircraft. The police helicopter had finally run out of gas, returning to this desolate, godforsaken location—with no vegetation, wildlife, or, presently, wind—its distinction as one of the quietest spots on the planet.

The three security men scanned the night sky with their binoculars. The others remained motionless with their eyes to the sky.

This strategy was risky, Schnabel knew. They might end up losing their own aircraft. He hoped for the best. One loss was acceptable. Each helicopter had enough capacity to get everyone out.

As everyone's eyes acclimated to the outdoors, their night vision improved. Still, there was nothing to see on the eastern horizon.

Schnabel checked his watch: 8:27. Only eighteen minutes until doomsday. *This is cutting it too damn close!* He'd have to return to the reactor room to reset the timers.

Not many more seconds had gone by when Neumann was the first to see them. "Here they come. I can see them now." Huber soon added his confirmation. "I see them . . . I can make out two . . . No, I see four."

And finally, Mayer verified the total. "I see five, but one of them has broken formation and is flying at a lower altitude. He can't be ours."

Schnabel spoke to the three. "Now, of the four that are in formation, remember that ours are going to veer off to either side. Your job is to take out the ones in the middle as well as the one coming in low. Tell me how long before you want Kobler to radio our choppers."

Neumann's voice was professional. "It's time. Call him now."

Schnabel sprinted back to the garage to relay the message to Maxim. It was 8:31. The timing was bad indeed. He'd have to leave his men, but he had no choice.

Three miles east of the Müller Ice Camp on Greenland
Wednesday, 8:31 p.m., October 12, 2011

Although the inside of the helicopter was chilly, Silverstein's palms were wet with sweat. Those in the back, he, Lopez, Miller, and the ten SEALs, could do nothing but sit tight. The gap had narrowed between them and the two helicopters in front. Decisions had been made: Seahawk Two would trail the one to the port side. Seahawk One would follow the other to starboard. Seahawk Three had already dropped out of formation and was flying in low. At the first sign of aggression from the ground, Seahawk Three would ride in with guns blazing.

For the past minute or so, there had been no chatter among the three Seahawks. At once, that all changed. "Uh-oh!" was the rather calm exclamation from Sarver in Seahawk One. "Something's going on. Bogey One's breaking away."

Seahawk Two's retort was calm. "Ditto with Bogey Two."

Concurrently with those outbursts came a sensation in Silverstein's body more severe than any he had ever experienced in an amusement park ride. Instantly, the chopper turned what seemed like ninety degrees sideways and pulled a G-force that Silverstein had experienced only once before. He recalled flying along in the backseat of a two-seat Citabria aerobatic airplane during college. His friend had demonstrated flying a *loop,* in which Silverstein remembered pulling three Gs. What had just occurred felt stronger.

Once that sensation had made its way through Silverstein's body came the opposite, a feeling of weightlessness. Then, they headed upward with what he could swear was a seventy-five degree angle. Sarver was obviously trying to stay behind the helicopter he was tailing.

Sarver gave some voice to what those in the back were experiencing. "Hang on back there, men. Our bogies finally realize they have company. The sons of bitches are trying to lose us. And my guess is they're doing that because something's happening on the ground. But they're going to have to do a little more fancy flying than this if they think they're going to lose me. How are you doing over there, Seahawk Two?"

After a moment, "I'm right behind mine, sir. These guys don't know who they're up against."

And then a voice that Silverstein had heard only once before, the voice of Lieutenant Steve Framley, their weapons officer and the third member of the crew. "They've got SAMs, all right. Two of them just lit off. I'm picking up the heat signatures. Seahawk Three, they're coming in your direction! Take evasive action! Release flares! Release flares!"

The roller coaster ride continued. On the turns when the Seahawk raked sharply sideways enough that Silverstein could actually get a glimpse of the ground, he guessed they were perhaps a thousand feet above the surface. Movements were coming fast and frequent. Silverstein figured it was the adrenaline streaming through his body that kept him from throwing up. His mind was clear.

And then words that Silverstein had feared to hear.

Sarver again. "Seahawk Three, do you copy? Seahawk Three, over?"

After a stomach-churning moment, Sarver came back online. "Seahawk Three's down. I saw the blast myself."

Framley's voice again. "Oh, shit! I count three hotties coming *our* way. Releasing flares now."

Sarver again. "How many SAMs do these motherfuckers have? We need to get the fuck on the ground."

Ice Station Helheim: 66°38'00"N Latitude, 38°48'00"W Longitude

Although Schnabel felt an obligation to monitor the air war behind him, he had no choice but to proceed to the reactor room. There were less than fourteen minutes left before his digital timers would broadcast their death knell. The events now unfolding would require more time to resolve, and he needed to reset the timers. He vaulted down the steps two at a time, sprinted down the hall past the kitchen and down the corridor toward the double doors of the reactor room. He was just about there when he hit the brakes.

Ahead of him, the double doors stood closed. *I left them open! I know I did!*

A reflection on the floor caught his eye. *Water! Fuck! I should have trusted my instincts!* He withdrew his Makarov, pulled the slide back to arm the weapon, and approached the doors warily, his weapon trained ahead. When he arrived and looked through one of the windows into the room, he couldn't believe what he was seeing.

* * *

Kipling had been watching the door, knowing that she would soon experience one of the most satisfying moments in her lifetime. Sitting atop the red box of reactor number one, legs folded, she dangled the chains from both reactors, at the ends of which were the locks. When she caught sight of Schnabel, she smiled sweetly and swayed them back and forth, in unison.

Everything couldn't have gone more according to plan. Kipling had crawled from the cooling pond, retrieved her jacket, checked the corridor to find that all was clear, and made an uneventful entry into the reactor room. Knowing that she had no idea how much time was remaining on the reactor timers, she had worked frantically.

First, she rammed toothpicks into each of the two outside deadbolt locks and broke them off, preventing anyone from entering with a key. She then closed and locked the doors from the inside. From Kobler's description, Kipling understood that the only thing preventing her from getting to the timers were the two chains and locks. She removed from her jacket the trusty Coblank L5000X that had saved her bacon back in Cartagena.

Kipling examined the crude locking arrangement for reactor one. At first glance, she was worried. Both the chain and the lock were substantial, more than a match for the L5000X's cutting blade. It was doubtful that it could sever the hardened metal. However, whoever had designed this makeshift locking system hadn't considered the weakest link in the proverbial chain. Although the lock and chain were sturdy enough, the metal hasp through which the chain passed was not. The L5000X cut through it easily. Once that was done, she removed the chain, followed by the red lid that exposed the timer. She repeated the process for reactor two.

Kipling exhaled demonstratively when she read the clocks. Both had more than sixteen minutes remaining. Trying to make sense of the seemingly crude combination of digital clock and wires and deciding there would have been no reason to install a booby trap, she counted to three and turned off one of the timers. Seconds passed, and nothing happened. Kipling repeated the process with the second timer. Considering the worst, that Schnabel might return and overpower her, Kipling briefly considered trying to destroy either the timers or the control panel in an attempt to permanently prevent a nuclear meltdown. She promptly nixed that idea, realizing that she had no idea what to do and that anything she did might make things worse. Besides, it would be only minutes before her rescuers arrived, she figured.

As Kipling watched Schnabel's reaction through the window, the sound of muffled explosions began competing with the reactor room noises; this was music to Kipling's ears. In case Schnabel's hearing wasn't up to snuff, when he next looked in, she cupped one hand to her ear as if trying to make out the sounds, pursed her lips, and nodded.

Kipling jumped from her perch and ran to the door, caution taking a backseat to the smugness she felt from her success. She wanted to enjoy Schnabel's frantic efforts in closer detail. As she arrived, he began jerking the doors in and out. He also tried to insert his key into the locks. With only inches separating their faces, Kipling stared through the glass. She removed an extra toothpick from her pocket and held it up for him to see.

Enraged, Schnabel backed away from the door, raised his weapon to the glass, and released a flurry of six shots. Although the wire-meshed glass suffered damage, it withstood the fusillade.

*   *   *

Schnabel was livid. Whatever it took, he would get his hands on this bitch and make her regret ever having taken on the Müllers. He was acting irrationally, he knew, but now was the time for such behavior. Again, he backed away from the door and, this time, took two shots at the locks. He stepped over to check the results. The upshot of his effort were two minor dents. These were good German locks.

Schnabel eyed the window. Kipling stood there watching, making him look the fool, shaming his masculinity. Well, he'd show her! If she wanted to play with fire, so be it.

In fact, Schnabel had heard the explosions from outside. But what was happening there was secondary now. He raced down the corridor, up the stairs, and into the garage. No one was there. They were all outside fighting off their intruders. They didn't need him. Besides, whether they did or not, he had timers to reset, reactors to blow. At this stage, it was the mission that mattered. Neither his life, nor the lives of any of those fighting outside, meant a goddamn thing.

From inside the armory, Schnabel grabbed enough C-4 explosive to do the job, about eight pounds worth. From experience, he figured that would be sufficient to blow the metal doors. He added a coil of wire, a detonator, and an electrical timer. He headed back down, anxious to make his point to his nemesis inside the reactor room.

*　*　*

After an eternity of gut-wrenching aerial maneuvers and missile attacks, Seahawk One was finally on the ground. Thanks to the daredevil piloting of Sarver and their various countermeasures, they had survived the SAMs. Amazingly, in the heat of battle, their adversaries on the ground had shot down one of their own helicopters.

Sarver had landed about a hundred yards from the source of the fire, to the rear of a snow embankment that provided them protection. But once they cleared the crest on foot, they began taking heavy incoming. The cascade of firepower churning up the ice was terrifying.

The SEALs had spread out and were now giving as good as they were getting. Silverstein was heartened by the comforting sight of Seahawk Two, also on the ground and with its SEALs moving around in a flanking movement. The ice camp defenders were getting it from both sides. This part of their assault would soon be over, Silverstein knew, but that was only half the battle. *What's going on under the ice? That's the $64,000 question!*

*　　*　　*

Kipling trained her eyes through the windows in the door but saw nothing. Schnabel had left. Had he conceded defeat, leaving to help his men outside? The sounds of gunfire were becoming more frequent. It wouldn't be long now. Just a few more minutes, probably. Whatever force Lopez had brought with him was surely a match for the sixteen who resided here. Scratch that! Fifteen. Kipling had personally reduced their number by one.

Once Schnabel was out of sight, Kipling used her time wisely. Although he might not return, she couldn't be sure. And if he did somehow manage to enter the room to reset the timers, she needed to slow him down. With that in mind, she replaced the chain and locks, running them through their broken hasps, but prying their metal back into place so that, at first sight, everything appeared to be intact. Schnabel's first impulse would be to use his keys to open the locks. Those extra seconds might prove crucial. *Where are you, Victor?*

Kipling returned to the window to keep her vigil. To her dismay, Schnabel came back into view. It was his turn at show and tell. He held up to the window a block of something. *Uh-oh! Explosives?* She watched as he labored outside the door, starting at the floor between the double doors and moving upward. He then uncoiled a string of wire down the corridor. *Shit!*

Kipling removed her Makarov from her jacket and briefly considered opening the door. But there was risk in doing that. Besides, based on the activity outside, she'd surely need only a minute more before the cavalry arrived.

Choosing to avoid direct confrontation, Kipling needed to protect herself. Fortunately, there was a good hiding place, the adjacent room that housed the electrical generators. A stout metal door separated the two spaces. She would be safe there. What had earlier seemed to be a slam-dunk operation was now less so. She hurried to her sanctuary, closed the door, ran to the rear of the generators, lay flat on the floor behind one of the massive, whirring pieces of metal, and waited.

But not for long. The sound of the blast was terrifying, something that she never wanted to experience again.

*   *   *

Schnabel had retreated to the eating area by the kitchen after setting a thirty-second delay for the detonator. He shut the door behind him. He had experienced the effect of C-4 on several occasions and wanted to keep his hearing intact.

In the few seconds remaining before the explosion, he searched the floor by the entry for what he figured he would need next. If he had thought this through properly, he knew exactly where Kipling would be. But just in case she wanted to cause trouble, he released the spent clip from the Makarov and jammed in another eight-rounder.

Following the detonation, Schnabel raced back down the hall. The C-4 had done the job, blasting open the double doors into the reactor room and splaying them horizontally on the floor. Their lower hinges had held, keeping them attached to their jambs.

As the returning, conquering hero, Schnabel jumped onto the doors, pistol fanning back and forth. As he expected, Kipling had retreated to the generator room for protection. His suspicion was confirmed in the next second when the door to that room swung open, and he saw the Makarov leveled in his direction. He ran and dived to the floor behind reactor number one—in the process, stumbling over one of the thawing Russians—as the first of two shots came flying in his direction. Schnabel fired once, forcing Kipling to retreat behind her door.

Schnabel knew that he couldn't just hide while Kipling kept him pinned down. As much as he wanted to believe that his men outside were decimating the enemy, he had to assume the worst. He raised himself to his haunches. Kipling was still hiding behind the metal door, an excellent shield. For him to reset the timers, he needed to confine her to that back room. Straight away, he was on his feet and scurrying for the walkway to the left side of the room. As he moved, he fired two shots, preventing her from returning fire. Because the door to the generator room had its hinges on his side, Kipling's only option to shoot involved exposing herself around the edge. He had her now. She would soon be rendered powerless.

* * *

After jumping behind the door to avoid Schnabel's fire, Kipling had watched through the small window. She hadn't expected him to react so quickly. He jumped the rail on the walkway to her right and dropped out of sight. Her position was secure, however, and she wasn't worried. In the same way that she had jammed the locks on the double doors, she had done the same here.

* * *

Schnabel approached the door carefully. It was too late for Kipling to open it and take him on. If she did, he would slam the door back in her face. Arriving at the hinges, he reached into his pocket and removed the two rubber doorstops he had taken from the eating area. From his knees, he shoved them into place. Now that he was safe, he could take his time. He stood and gave each a swift kick to ram them firmly into position. Looking through the glass, he again faced Kipling eye to eye. This time, it was his turn to smile.

* * *

Kipling knew she was in trouble when she saw Schnabel walk casually away, continuing along the circular walkway. She turned open the deadbolt lock and pushed. Nothing. *Son of a bitch!* He had jammed the door shut. That was something she had not counted on. *How stupid could I be!* She ripped off her jacket, dropped to the floor, and stared underneath. There she could see two obstructions, undoubtedly wedges of some sort. She slid her fingers underneath, trying to dislodge them, but they were stuck.

Kipling leaped to her feet and stared out the window. Schnabel was walking toward the timer box for reactor one. She scanned the room for something strong and thin that she could use to push the wedges outward. There was nothing obvious, and no time to look. She inserted her second remaining magazine into her Makarov and knew what had to be done.

From her jacket, Kipling removed her sole remaining weapon and looked to see where it would be most effective. As luck would have it, the grenade was large enough to lodge between the doorjamb and the doorknob. She yanked out the pin and retreated once more to her hiding place. She inserted her index fingers deeply into her ears. When the grenade went off, she wondered if she had done so, the explosion was so loud.

Even before the echoes had abated, Kipling was on her feet sprinting toward the door, the Makarov in her right hand at the ready.

Kipling gave an audible *Thank you, God* when she saw the effects of her grenade. The door was still there, but the top half had bent outward far enough for her to escape.

*   *   *

Schnabel couldn't have been more surprised when the blast occurred. He had just finished using his three keys to open the lock securing the chain for reactor one. Instinctively, he faced away from the blast and hit the floor. *Grenade?*

No sooner had Schnabel come to his senses, jumping to his feet and turning around, than he saw Kipling climbing through the opening, firing three shots as she did so. Schnabel ducked behind the timer box, escaping her line of fire. When he looked next, he watched her walking doggedly along the circular walkway toward the double doors, exposed to the world, firing two more shots, her eyes lasered in his direction. Because his position would become more exposed as she completed her arc around the side room, Schnabel crawled frantically to the backside of reactor two. As he did so, he squeezed off two shots, more for self-defense than actually aiming. Concurrently, Kipling let loose two more in his direction.

Schnabel knew that his luck had run its course when he felt a searing pain in the calf of his left leg. Damn it! It was time to strike back. Here he was, the one shot and hiding on the floor while his adversary was walking tall, fully exposed. He crawled rapidly to his left and, from there, stood without hesitation and began firing. Not knowing initially where to aim, his first shot went wide, his second caught Kipling in the shoulder, and the third apparently missed high. By then, Kipling had ducked down and hidden behind the timer for reactor one.

*　*　*

Kipling was hurt, and bad. Her left hand impulsively made its way to her right shoulder and came away red. As serious as that wound might have been, it wasn't the shoulder that worried her. She sensed warm liquid running down the right side of her face. She reached for her scalp and realized that the last of Schnabel's bullets had caught the side of her skull just above the right temple. The burning blistering sensation from that wound amplified the stabbing pain from her shoulder.

One . . . concentrate! Without warning, she felt herself going faint, catching herself with her left hand as she fell backward to the floor. From the medical training Kipling had received as a ranger, she knew that it wouldn't be long before loss of blood would send her into shock.

Kipling needed to think. *Two, three . . .* She looked down. The top of her pants were now soaked. She had never seen so much blood. She forced her breathing to slow. *Stay conscious! Keep your brain clear! Help is on the way! Think! Four, five . . .*

Schnabel's voice interrupted Kipling's self-diagnosis. "Linda, are you still alive! I think I got you once."

As the neurons in Kipling's brain streamed back into action, her combative nature took hold. "Just a scratch, Gunter. I would have thought you'd have better aim, being the professional you are."

Kipling's head listed to the side, her mind woozy again. *Think, Kipling! Concentrate! Six, seven, eight!* With her brain screaming for oxygen, Kipling decided there was no more time. She had to roll the dice. She would be unconscious soon.

As if each action required a day's worth of effort, Kipling began. First, using her left arm on the side of her body not yet incapacitated, she slid her Makarov onto the top of the timing box in front of her.

Kipling then raised both hands into the air for Schnabel to see. But it was only the one connected to her uninjured left shoulder that made it very high. "I lied, Gunter. You got me bad, not once but twice. I give up."

Another wave of fog blew across Kipling's consciousness. Summoning her last ounce of willpower, she staggered to her feet and faced the timer box for reactor number two, behind which Schnabel was hiding. She could no longer keep her hands in the air. She fell forward, catching herself on top of the timer box.

Seeing that she was no longer a threat, Schnabel rose to his feet and stepped out in the open. "I guess I did get you. You look a fright." He shook his head in dismay. "I wish I could say that I won't enjoy this, but I can't."

Schnabel raised his Makarov and pulled the trigger. *Nothing!* He pulled the slide on his weapon and tried a second time, again without effect. Kipling had counted correctly! He had fired all eight rounds from his Makarov. She had taken a calculated gamble. If Schnabel had had time to insert a fresh clip, she would be dead.

Kipling ordered herself to action. *It's not over until the fat lady sings, Linda!* She used her good arm to grab the Makarov lying below. Through mind-altering pain from her right shoulder, the right hand met the other, and the two raised the heavy pistol in Schnabel's direction. "How many shots do you think *I* have left, Gunter?"

Schnabel's reaction, first to the lack of response from his own weapon, followed by Kipling's retort, left him paralyzed. Like Lot's wife who made the fatal mistake of taking one final glance back at Sodom and Gomorrah, he seemed incapable of moving.

With blood streaming directly into her right eye, Kipling had only her left to aim with. With consciousness waning, she squeezed the trigger, the explosion echoing throughout the room.

Kipling had nothing left to give. As her ravaged body collapsed in upon itself, she imagined her name being called somewhere off in the distance.

EPILOGUE

LOOSE ENDS

Naval Research Laboratory, Monterey, California, USA: 36°35'34"N Latitude, 121°51'17"W Longitude Monday, 7:55 a.m., November 7, 2011

Because Kipling knew that Silverstein would be upset if she returned to work too soon, she tried to sneak into her office. She had parked to the rear of Building 704 and entered through the back door.

The past three-plus weeks had been a blur but considerably less so than the twenty-four hours following her standoff with Schnabel. After passing out next to reactor one, she remembered coming to inside a helicopter on its way to the hospital in Nuuk, on the western side of Greenland. The SEAL medics had decided that one less hour of flying time might prove crucial to Kipling's survival, she had lost so much blood.

Later, in the hospital, Silverstein provided details of their operation. She was impressed to learn that the attack on the compound had been accomplished with only twenty navy SEALs. Although Schnabel's men had succeeded in shooting down one of the navy's three helicopters—in addition to one of their own—the crew escaped with minor injuries. The second Müller helicopter hightailed it out of the area. Of the twenty SEALs, there had been four casualties, sadly including two deaths. The two wounded SEALs, whose injuries were less severe than Kipling's, had made the same flight to the hospital with her.

The loss of suppression fire from Seahawk Three had made the assault more difficult. Two advantages, however, one simple and the other technologically sophisticated, had swayed the battle in the SEALs' direction. First, their polar-white outfits made them nearly invisible against the ice. Second, although the full moon provided some illumination, their night-vision goggles gave them the edge. It was noted afterward that none of the enemy wore them.

Once inside the compound, it didn't take long to locate the reactor room. According to Silverstein, everyone had stood in awe of the devastation left in the wake of the Kipling/Schnabel battle. He complimented Kipling on her aim. She had killed Schnabel with one shot to the chest.

After Kipling was on the mend at Nuuk, Silverstein admitted the stark truth: had it not been for the SEAL medics and their expertise, she would have died. Thanks to technology developed during the Iraq and Afghanistan wars, when injuries involving huge losses of blood were common, she had survived. Most important were the hemostatic dressings, special bandages impregnated with compounds that not only stopped the bleeding, but also sealed and protected the wound. Those, together with considerable saline and oxygen, had allowed her to survive the long flight to the hospital. There, surgeons had operated on her shoulder and scalp.

As Kipling had suspected, the wound to her skull, three inches above the right ear, had been the more serious. The surgeon told her afterward that the bullet had sliced to within a whisker's distance of the temporal artery, a major artery in the skull. If that artery had been severed, she wouldn't have made it. In fact, he remarked that he found it astonishing that she had remained conscious from the concussion she had suffered.

Silverstein had insisted on staying by Kipling's side through those first critical hours. Once the crisis was over, she spent another four days in the hospital. Because the surgeon would not allow her to fly, she spent ten more days in a rented apartment. After three days of recuperation there, by which time Kipling could function on her own, she insisted that Silverstein return home to take care of business and make sure that their boss hadn't given away their jobs. They had gone shopping, and Kipling had enough clothing and essentials for the rest of her stay.

Seven days later, Kipling left the apartment on her own and departed Greenland on a CIA-provided jet, courtesy of Hector Lopez.

Part of the reason for Lopez's generosity was his request that Kipling stop by Langley for a debriefing. That had taken the better part of two days, but separated by a weekend. With that accomplished, she had arrived back in Monterey a day later, on Tuesday, November 1. After five boring days at home, she decided that work would heal her mind and body quicker than sitting around in an apartment.

Kipling had climbed the stairs and had just entered the hallway leading to her office. It had been too much to hope that she could arrive unnoticed by Silverstein. "Why are you here? You know what the doctor said." And then he couldn't help but rub it in. "Thought you'd sneak in without me seeing you, didn't you?"

"How did you know?"

Silverstein smiled naughtily. "I have spies." Then he hesitated as he took a closer look at her as she approached. "Your hair *is* growing out. It's too bad you weren't here last week for Halloween. With a little fake blood, you would have given the trick-or-treaters a fright."

"Ha, ha." They had shaved the whole right side of Kipling's head in the hospital.

Kipling had her key ready. "You know that I don't want any special attention." As much as she had hoped to arrive unnoticed, it was not at all an unpleasant surprise to have Silverstein waiting. It had taken a lot of willpower to kick him out of her apartment over recent nights.

Kipling unlocked the door, with Silverstein close behind. She joked, "Come on in, why don't you?"

"I was hoping to get some work done, but if you insist."

Kipling's eyes took in the office she hadn't seen in weeks, and they grew wide at the huge flower arrangement waiting on her desk. *Didn't he just criticize me for coming in early? The stinker.* "Why did you do this, Victor?"

"You'd better read the card. You'll see that this is from the entire staff. Word has gotten around, you know. You're a goddamn hero."

Kipling took her seat and read the humongous card that accompanied the flowers. It was covered with signatures from her colleagues. "Am I the hero, Victor? I sure don't feel like one. I know that I did what I had to do, but all that's left of Mom's family now are Dieter's kids. They'll never want to see me; that's for sure." Knowing what had happened in the past weeks made her eyes well up.

While Kipling was recuperating in Nuuk and after Silverstein had returned to Monterey, they had talked daily. He had reported on the raid by Colombian authorities on the Müller compound in Cartagena. She was not surprised to learn that they found no one there. No gardeners, no housekeepers, no one. Kipling had figured that, with the resources available to her cousins, they would have little trouble disappearing—exactly as they did after the war.

But Kipling was wrong. Within a week, an international force instigated by Germany and led by the United States spewed out justice faster than anyone could have imagined. After chasing the Müllers literally around the world, it all came to a close not that far from where they started, on the eastern coast of Brazil. The end came quickly when two Hellfire missiles from a Predator drone took out a nondescript house on the outskirts of the coastal city of Salvador.

Dental records and DNA confirmed the demise of both Dieter and Axel, Dieter's wife, Amelia, as well as the Müller elder parents, Friedrich and Gertrude. Afterward, a commission was formed to delve into the Müller family financial holdings, its purpose to root out all remaining Nazi sympathizers.

The public found it interesting that, except for Dieter's children, the family had chosen not to split up in its final days and hours. A few newspaper editorials questioned the decision of not taking the Müllers alive, likening the hit to the killing of Osama bin Laden the previous spring. The prevailing opinion, however, was that the world community had no desire for a trial that would have resurrected memories from one of the twentieth century's darkest periods.

Silverstein cupped his face in his hands and slowly drew his fingers down across his eyes. "I can only imagine what you're going through. But you did what you had to. *You* stood up to evil. *You* made a difference." He wiped his eyes. "That's enough of all that. Okay? Suffice it to say, I'm proud as hell of you for what you did."

It was time to change the subject. "Any word from Captain Stigler? How long do you think you'll be in jail for lying to a government official?"

"Funny you should mention that." Silverstein laughed. "She called last week, and we had a good talk. As hard as it was for me to say, I said that perhaps I should have trusted her. But between you and me, if I had to do it all over again? I still would have lied to her. There was no way I could trust her with that information." He pointed his finger to make a point. "Just like you, I made a rational decision based upon the facts as I knew them. My decision to lie isn't going to keep me awake at night. And neither should yours concerning your family." He grinned widely. "Thus spake the prophet, Victor Mark Silverstein."

Silverstein snapped his fingers. "I almost forgot. Important new information! Everything's going to be okay in Greenland."

In the hospital, after regaining consciousness following surgery, Kipling had become frantic, telling Silverstein that she had to talk to someone, to explain the bedrock pool, that it was going to release the Helheim Glacier. Silverstein told her to calm down, that they knew everything.

He explained what had happened back in Greenland. Following the SEALs' attack, all of the defenders lay dead—except for one, Kobler, who had hidden in the radar room. Compared to his comrades, he capitulated quickly and seemed eager to cooperate. With that break, progress was swift. Within two hours, the two reactor experts from the SEAL team had stopped the flow of heat into the bedrock pool.

Within twenty-four hours of that action, a team flew to the ice from Denmark, the country responsible for Greenland's security. Two days later, several of the world's leading glaciologists arrived to assess the situation.

Silverstein continued. "The really good news is that the bedrock pool is freezing again. It started to mend itself not long after the reactor stopped sending heat down the pipes. According to the glaciologists, though, we didn't arrive any too soon."

"That *is* wonderful news, Victor." It was time, indeed, to bask in their accomplishment. "You know, Victor, you and I did it."

Silverstein shook his head. "You were the one who did it, Linda. I was just along for the ride."

Kipling rose, walked around the desk, and settled into Silverstein's arms. "Remember not to squeeze, please. It doesn't take much. Every time I laugh, I'm reminded of my shoulder." His embrace felt good, but the ring of the phone spoiled the moment.

The voice on the line was familiar, and Kipling answered appreciatively. It was Lopez's initiative and wherewithal that had saved the day. "Hector, it's good to hear your voice."

"I tried your home number first and decided to call your office. How are you?"

"I'm fine. I was so bored at home that I thought I'd come to work for a few hours. As a matter of fact, Victor's here in the room with me right now."

"Oh, he is, is he? Can you put me on speakerphone? I'd like to talk to both of you."

Silverstein leaned forward. "I'm here, Hector. What's up?"

"After a month or so, after Linda's recovered, I'd like to invite the two of you back here."

Kipling had zero desire to undergo yet more debriefings three thousand miles away. It was time to stay home. "If you need more information from me, you can call me anytime; you know that."

"That isn't it." A pause. "What the two of you did has not gone unnoticed by my bosses."

Kipling figured it out. "You want to give us an award?"

"Not exactly. We have something a little different in mind. I can't say anything right now, but we'd like to make a proposition to the two of you."

Kipling looked across at Silverstein. She could imagine his mind turning over the same thought she had. *Now that would be interesting, wouldn't it?*

CAST OF MAJOR CHARACTERS

Armstrong, Peter: one of two Naval Research Laboratory researchers who inadvertently stumble upon Ice Station Helheim in Greenland

Bragley, James: friend of Rick Uphouse at the Naval Research Laboratory in Washington DC, who Rick asks to decipher recorded phone message from Greenland

Brody, Samuel: FBI agent credited with inventing the *Brody Trap* in the early 1950s

Fiedler, Dr. Leon: Müller physician who administers the truth serum to Linda Kipling in Cartagena, Colombia

Gudrinko, Captain Alexseyev: Russian naval officer responsible for the sale of the nuclear submarines to Axel Müller

Kipling, Inge: mother to Linda Kipling, sibling to Heinrich Müller, and husband to Winston Kipling

Kipling, Dr. Linda: principal protagonist and colleague of Victor Silverstein

Kipling, Winston: father to Linda Kipling, husband to Inge Kipling

Kitchen, Dr. Harry: superintendent of NRL's Marine Meteorology Division in Monterey, California; Victor Silverstein's boss

Kobler, Daniel: scientist at Ice Station Helheim who shows Linda Kipling around the compound

Lopez, Hector Rodriguez, Jr.: CIA senior investigative officer in counterintelligence

Marshall, Dr. Richard: Silverstein's friend from Penn State, an expert on reactors and nuclear physics

Miller, Marc: CIA agent, Hector Lopez's colleague

Müller, Axel: along with his brother, Dieter, the principal antagonists, the brains and funding behind Operation Helheim

Müller, Dieter: along with his brother, Axel, the principal antagonists

Müller, Hans and Helga: grandparents to Axel and Dieter; Hans was responsible for the Müller family's escape from Germany in 1945

Müller, Friedrich and Gertrude: parents to Axel and Dieter; aunt and uncle to Linda Kipling

Peters, Dr. Andrew: technical director at the Federal Center for Data Examination in Las Vegas, Nevada; reports to Captain Jane Stigler

Ringwald, Mike: Silverstein's friend who works in NRL's Chemistry Division in DC

Sarver, Jim, Navy Lieutenant Commander: pilot in command of three helicopters for assault on Ice Station Helheim in Greenland

Schnabel, Gunter: chief of security for Müller Industries

Silverstein, Dr. Victor Mark: colleague of Linda Kipling at the Naval Research Laboratory in Monterey, California

Smithkline, Henry: one of two Naval Research Laboratory researchers who inadvertently stumble upon Ice Station Helheim in Greenland

Stigler, Jane, Navy Captain: director (successor to Tom Uphouse) of the Federal Center for Data Examination in Las Vegas, Nevada

Uphouse, Tom: first director of the Federal Center for Data Examination in Las Vegas, Nevada

Uphouse, Rick: boss of Peter Armstrong and Henry Smithkline at the Naval Research Laboratory in Washington DC; brother to Tom Uphouse

Wagner, Dr. Manfred: Müller employee who administers the lie detector test on Linda Kipling in Cartagena, Colombia

Wiener, Kurt: Müller guard who attacks Linda Kipling outside the Müller compound in Cartagena, Colombia

Wilder, Leopold: navy SEAL commander in charge of the assault on Ice Station Helheim

Wolf, August: employee in charge of the radar and communications at Ice Station Helheim

GLOSSARY

Bedrock pool: the layer of melted water created by the flow of heat to the base of the glacier at Ice Station Helheim

Brody Trap: invention credited to FBI agent Samuel Brody in the early 1950s; an undetectable and irreversible booby trap that alerts the user to a sabotage

CIA: Central Intelligence Agency

Enhanced 911: a cellular telephone system that locates callers for emergency dispatchers

FCDE: Federal Center for Data Examination, in Las Vegas, Nevada; commissioned one year after September 11, 2001

Geostationary satellite: a satellite that follows a geosynchronous orbit, an orbit above the equator (approximately 22,300 miles) in which the satellite's rotation rate around the earth matches the earth's speed of rotation, such that the satellite always sits above the same geographic location

GISP: the Greenland Ice Sheet Project (GISP), a decade-long project to drill ice cores in Greenland that involved scientists and funding agencies from Denmark, Switzerland, and the United States

Google Earth: a Google computerized software system that allows the user to view satellite images of the earth's surface from around the globe

GPS: global positioning system; GPS is a series of satellites positioned in earth orbit; developed by the US Department of Defense, this system allows users to determine their position on the earth

Helheim Glacier: one of Greenland's largest outlet glaciers, located in the southeast quadrant of the island; it received increased scientific scrutiny as its movement accelerated from eight to eleven kilometers per year between 2000 and 2005

IWDS: Integrated World Data System; CIA software system for displaying near real-time worldwide imagery—satellite, UAV (Unmanned Aerial Vehicles), etc.

IR: infrared

Morton's Fork: a choice between two equally unpleasant alternatives

NCAR: The National Center for Atmospheric Research; a federally funded research and development center devoted to service, research and education in the atmospheric and related sciences. NCAR's mission is to understand the behavior of the atmosphere and related physical, biological and social systems; to support, enhance and extend the capabilities of the university community and the broader scientific community – nationally and internationally; and to foster transfer of knowledge and technology for the betterment of life on Earth

NRL: Naval Research Laboratory; NRL operates as the Navy's full-spectrum corporate laboratory, conducting a broadly based multidisciplinary program of scientific research and advanced technological development directed toward maritime applications of new and improved materials, techniques, equipment, systems and ocean, atmospheric, and space sciences and related technologies

NRL Monterey: Marine Meteorology Division of NRL, located in Monterey, California; conducts a research and development program designed to improve the basic understanding of atmospheric processes and the atmosphere's interaction with the ocean, land and cryosphere; to develop and implement automated analysis, prediction, and weather interpretation systems for Department of Defense users; and to study the effect of the atmosphere on Naval weapons systems

SAM: surface-to-air missile

SEAL: US Navy SEAL, member of a Naval Special Warfare unit trained for unconventional warfare; SEAL is an acronym for Sea, Air, Land

SIGINT: signal intelligence; the gathering of military or other intelligence by the interception of electronic signals

SOSUS: Sound Surveillance System; a navy system originally intended to track Soviet submarines as they passed between Greenland, Iceland, and the United Kingdom (the GIUK Gap), SOSUS represented a series of sensitive microphones, called hydrophones, that rested on the ocean floor

UTC: universal time coordinated, also known as Greenwich mean time (GMT), refers to time kept on the Greenwich meridian (longitude zero); times given as UTC are invariably given in terms of a twenty-four-hour clock. UTC is five hours ahead of eastern standard time in the United States

CPSIA information can be obtained at www.ICGtesting.com
Printed in the USA
LVOW05s1627041113

359952LV00003B/758/P